A SON OF THE SHADOWS

The Earthborn Saga Vol. I

Steven Bissett

Copyright © 2023 Steven Bissett

All rights reserved.

No portion of this book may be reproduced in any form without permission from the publisher, except as permitted by U.S. copyright law.

This is a work of fiction. Names, characters, places, and incidents either are the products of the author's imagination or are used fictitiously. Any resemblance to actual persons, living or dead, businesses, companies, events, or locales is entirely coincidental.

CONTENTS

Title Page
Copyright
Chapter 1 — 1
Chapter 2 — 29
Chapter 3 — 48
Chapter 4 — 70
Chapter 5 — 89
Chapter 6 — 113
Chapter 7 — 137
Chapter 8 — 154
Chapter 9 — 178
Chapter 10 — 202
Chapter 11 — 224
Chapter 12 — 248
Chapter 13 — 276
Chapter 14 — 294
Chapter 15 — 330
Chapter 16 — 366
Chapter 17 — 382
Chapter 18 — 448
Chapter 19 — 461

CHAPTER 1

A man tore breathlessly through a frozen forest as a terrifying roar filled the air.

"Pick up your feet, Rex, or we're goners!" shouted a voice only he could hear.

Rex Hunt moved as quickly as he dared across the hard, icy snow. One slip and he'd tumble to the ground, instantly becoming dinner for the massive bear that chased him. In his left hand he clutched an artifact, a small glowing medallion that possessed mild healing powers. He'd found it near the den of a mother bear and her two small cubs, and she had resented his intrusion.

"I told you to leave it alone," chided the voice in his ear. "But you had to go after it anyway!"

"How about you save the lecture until *after* we survive this?!" shouted Hunt, tearing through icy branches that stabbed at him through his environment suit.

"It's gaining on us," said the voice with alarm. "Double-time it to the hideout, or we're dead meat!"

"I'm nearly there," Hunt said, bursting out of the forest and scaling a shallow, rocky hill. A moment later the bear rushed into the open and paused, bellowing from deep inside her belly and looking for Hunt. She saw him clambering up the hill and took off after him.

"She sees us, Rex," the voice said. "I hope you've made

your final arrangements."

"Don't worry," Hunt said, smiling in spite of his breathless condition. "We're there."

He moved around a boulder, momentarily losing the bear. He approached a wall of solid rock and walked through it. On the other side stood a small mirage generator of alien manufacture. The space it hid was small, only five feet high by two feet deep. But it was enough to conceal him if he twisted to the side and leaned his hand on one knee.

The bear thundered up to where she had seen him last, roared her confusion at his disappearance, and sniffed the air.

"If that thing pokes its head through the mirage, we're finished."

Hunt couldn't respond. The slightest sound would alert the bear. He stood absolutely still while the creature smelled the tracks he'd left on the ground. She roared half-heartedly, hoping to scare him out of wherever he was hiding. A minute passed anxiously, Hunt's body beginning to tremble as his muscles tired from holding such an awkward stance after his desperate run. Finally the bear lowered her head and ambled slowly back down the hill and into the forest.

"We can't afford any more stunts like that," the voice said, as Hunt sighed his relief and sat down on the snowy ground behind the mirage.

"Come on, Wellesley, you know how it is," Hunt replied, slipping off the helmet he wore and letting the frigid air cool his hot nerves. "All the good stuff close to town has been taken. We've got to head further out if we're gonna find anything worth selling. People don't go for trinkets anymore."

"You can't make a profit if you're *dead*, Rex," Wellesley said. "I wish you humans weren't so money conscious all the time."

"If we weren't I never would have dug you up out of the snow, old friend," Hunt said with a smile, knowing he held the trump card. "It was the human spirit of enterprise that rescued you from that drift you were in."

"What a blessing, indeed," replied the AI sarcastically. "Drawn from the snow so I could end up in a bear's stomach. Oh well, perhaps I could have given her indigestion in the process. Then my sad life would have meant something."

Hunt shook his head but said nothing. Wellesley was in one of his dark moods and nothing would shake him from it. He had been built for a nobler purpose than that of assistant to a poor greenhouse worker and part-time scavenger of artifacts. A relic from an extinct alien race known as the *Kol-Prockians*, Wellesley was on par with the most advanced AIs of the time. Such AIs, because of their potent intelligence, were strictly controlled by the empire, at least out in the fringe where Hunt lived. The risk that they would be used to plan and coordinate anti-government activities was too great a threat to be tolerated. Private ownership was very nearly an act of treason.

And the fact that Wellesley, previously named *Allokanah*, was an advanced *alien* AI doubled the nature of Hunt's offense. The wealth of information he possessed on an extinct race made him one of the greatest finds of the decade. Keeping all that data for himself violated numerous laws which, again, specifically governed the outskirts of the empire. Numerous measures were tightly in place to keep the dwellers of the fringe from gathering any more steam than they already had towards revolution. Alien intelligence, culture, and history only served to strengthen their sense of separation from the rest of the empire, building their momentum. To say Hunt was walking a narrow, dangerous path was an understatement. Violations such as his would have earned him a life sentence in the prison that stood just a few miles above the little rundown town that he called home.

Assuming that he was convicted of one of the lighter forms of treason, of course.

But that required someone to find out about Wellesley. And Hunt was too careful for that to happen. At least so far.

"I think the bear is a good way off by now," Hunt said,

peeking around the boulder. "She's got better things to do than chase us." He collapsed the mirage and picked up the little round artifact that had generated the effect, slipping it into a pocket on his hip. He put the helmet back on his head, his face quickly growing cold in the elements.

"It's going to be dark in three hours, Rex," Wellesley observed. "We need to head back to the city. Barring the unforeseen, it'll take us a little over two hours. And I know how you like to ramble about, exploring side paths."

"I've found a lot of valuable tech that way," countered Hunt, climbing down the hill backwards, using the snow covered rocks as handholds. He could see the wide groove in the snow that the bear had carved with her rump, sliding down the hill to level ground. Her pawprints led back into the trees.

Taking his general direction from the sun, Hunt started walking towards the west. Since the authorities didn't allow weapons because of the prison, Hunt strode unarmed through the snow, pausing every little while to listen to the wind. But after an interval his intuition told him that there was no danger nearby, and he began to relax. Soon he was crunching loudly through the snow, paying very little attention to his surroundings.

"Haven't you learned anything in the last hour?" the AI asked in exasperation. "Do you have to be actually *eaten* by a bear before you'll be more careful?"

"Aw, we're alright," replied Hunt.

"And how do you know that?"

"I can just feel it," he replied. Then, tapping the back of his head, "Back here."

"It's a wonder you humans ever got off Earth with an attitude like that. You fancy yourselves to be rationalists. But you're dominated by innumerable mysticisms."

"We seem to be doing a lot better than your lot," replied Hunt, plunging his feet deeply into the snow, his breath becoming labored. "At least we're still knocking around."

"My people were a lot older than you humans," replied the AI. "A race, like an individual organism, has a lifespan. Theirs just ran out. Someday yours will, too."

"Don't bet on that," replied Hunt. "We humans are pretty crafty about surviving. I reckon we'll hold on longer than anyone else."

"Yes, I'm sure."

"What's got you in such a bad mood?" asked Hunt. "You've been riding me ever since we left this morning. I've got half a mind to leave you at home next time."

"I don't like the risks we're running," said Wellesley, glad to finally have the chance to get it off his chest. "The government is clamping down harder than ever on black market trading. If they catch us out here you'll be in big trouble. They'd lock you up just like your father."

"Don't talk about him," flared Hunt. "Don't ever talk about him. I can't stand to think of what they did to him. It makes my blood boil."

"Alright, fine. But you can't keep flaunting the government this way. Sooner or later they're going to nail you. They'll say the apple didn't fall far from the tree and throw the book at you. And for what? You don't make a lot of money doing this."

"That's because of the stuff they're hauling out of Quarlac," groused Hunt. "I offer them good, quality artifacts. It's just the market is glutted."

"That, and having to pay the Underground's fees to have them smuggled off world," added Wellesley. "Whatever the cause, the result is the same: we're getting less and less for our troubles. We should really pack it in while we've got the chance.

"I'd die of boredom if I did that," groaned Hunt.

"I had a feeling this was about more than just the money."

"Well, wouldn't you get stir crazy if you worked in a greenhouse all day, six days per week?" asked Hunt. "I practically grew up in that sweatshop. It's all I can do to keep from screaming while I'm in there, just to break the monotony. If I didn't come out here," he said, spreading his arms to indicate his surroundings, "I'd go nuts. Playing the role of 'good citizen,' going about my tasks and never doing *anything* exciting would snap my twig. I just couldn't take it."

"I suspect there's another reason you play it dangerously like you do," mused the AI.

"Spare me the mumbo jumbo, Wells," Hunt said. "I'm in no mood for it."

"Fine. But all the same, you won't have any freedom at all if they catch you. They'd put you in solitary for a good year as a start. Then you'd be wishing for the grand old days when you could amble around the city without restraint."

"Heh, some city," retorted Hunt. "It's a slum, nothing more. Nothing ever happens there. The people are too scared to do anything."

"Well, there *is* Wanda. She raises your pulse a little."

"Just enough to keep me from dying," replied Hunt, thinking of the chunky little barmaid at an Underground tavern he sometimes visited. Some of the workers gathered there from time to time and talked idly about overthrowing the empire's forces on Delta-13. Most of its customers were old laborers who couldn't work anymore. They'd barter or beg for a drink of low quality moonshine and then crawl back to their shacks before curfew.

"I'm just saying that things could be worse. A lot worse. If you keep looking to the horizon to find something better than what you've got you'll just end up tripping over your own feet."

"I don't think so," replied Hunt. "I've outsmarted them so far. I don't plan to let 'em beat me."

"*Neither did your old man,*" the AI thought, as his companion trudged onward. "*And look where he ended up.*"

◆ ◆ ◆

"Not much to look at, is it?" asked Sadie Roy, looking out the window of the *Emerald Glow*, a transport ship bound for the frozen world of Delta-13. Floating far out on the fringe of human controlled space, the power of the empire was scarcely felt. Smugglers, pirates, and all forms of desperadoes filled the area. They acted as they pleased, and lived according to laws that were agreeable to themselves alone. Without hesitation they plundered and pillaged the ships that traversed the region. Only the largest convoys, which could afford to pay for their own private protection, were left alone. Smaller operators took their chances and frequently lost. The only other exception to this rule were the very occasional government convoys that passed through the area. These were also left in peace, the pirates not wishing to offend the imperial government and risk them sending a larger garrison force to secure the region. The *Emerald Glow* had just broken away from such a convoy, and was slowly limping toward the mysterious iceworld. It was an older vessel, and more than once during the journey from Earth it had occasioned the halt of the entire group with which it traveled in order to undertake repairs. The other ships, most of which had business with the modest spaceport that floated above the planet, were glad to see it go.

Delta-13, though intrinsically almost worthless, served a single function that more than made up for its lack of innate value: it was the final stop point before outgoing ships would begin the jump to the Quarlac galaxy. Quarlac contained a vast trove of alien technologies, many of which had enriched human life, advancing everything from space travel to recreation by decades. Outposts had been established in Quarlac years before. But the hostile environments of the planets it held, to say nothing of the numerous races which called the galaxy home, made it difficult for humanity to secure much more than a toehold. This necessitated a constant influx of personnel and supplies, all of which required a jumping off point to coordinate their efforts.

    Delta-13 had possessed many names throughout the countless millennia of its use as a spaceport. Ancient races which had preceded mankind had also seen its utility as a halfway point between Quarlac and the Milky Way. They had found it, fought over it, and abandoned it in their turns, no people ever quite managing to maintain a steady hold on it. Something about the planet made it difficult to control. Machines broke, people went mad. Cults would rise and fall, preaching esoteric doctrines that felt natural to a world that seemed almost to have a mind of its own. Some, in fact, asserted that it *did* have a mind of its own, and that it occasionally communicated with them. Such people were usually written off as victims of an environment that proved too harsh for them to handle. It was said that the isolation and monotony of perpetual winter had pressed on their minds until it fractured their sanity, causing them to seek a strange companionship with the world that had broken them. However, even the most rationally minded, after a short stay, invariably admitted that there was something strange about the place.

    But it was the last suitable position for a base this side of Quarlac, and thus the imperial government stuck its flag in the frozen ground and built a base. A cold, inhospitable world, its inhabitants spent the majority of their lives indoors. A hot day saw temperatures reach ten degrees fahrenheit. The nights plummeted until only people in special suits, or animals adapted to the cold, could spend more than a few minutes without the heat being drained from their bodies. The planet was pure, forbidding, and covered in snow from one pole to the other, with great frozen lakes hidden beneath its white surface. Deep scans performed by the imperial government revealed that it had once been a lush world, teeming with life. But some cataclysmic event had changed that forever, with only the toughest plants and animals managing to survive.

    Mankind, a late arrival to the game, would have to see if

he was one of them.

"Don't be too rough on it, Sadie," Lily Tselitel said, joining her assistant at the window and putting a hand on her shoulder. "It'll be a good place to get away from all the strife and hustle of the inner worlds. Out here you can hear yourself think. It's so primitive and empty, like something sliced out of man's early colonial history, when the stars were new and empty and we were as afraid of space as we were fascinated by it. That was the time to live, when you could feel the rawness of a new planet under your feet. Now everything is so settled and stable that there's nothing to tie us to our own primitive past. The empire is just one giant, rolling city, spread out across the stars."

"I would have preferred a vacation resort if you wanted a little peace and quiet. At least something warmer than that!" Roy said, pointing out the window at the slowly growing orb. She was a short woman, twenty-five, with long brown hair that poured like a waterfall down her slender back. "Doctor Tselitel, why did we have to come here? Nothing good can possibly happen this far from civilized space. The region is filled with pirates from one end to the other. If this wasn't a government vessel we'd probably have been boarded already."

"I don't doubt it," the doctor replied, taking a seat on a bench that ran along the reinforced window. In her early forties, Lily Tselitel was a prominent, if unorthodox, psychiatrist with connections high in the government. Through much wrangling, particularly on the part of a maternal uncle who had more than a little pull, she managed to get assigned to Delta-13. Long considered a loose cannon by the psychiatric community, she was surprised at the resistance she experienced in getting the Delta-13 post, for she had anticipated that many high-placed figures would be more than willing to banish her to the edge of space.

Roy regarded the doctor for a moment, and then sat beside her. Her gray eyes contained an odd mixture of sympathy and intellectual reserve, as though a warm, vibrant heart beat passionately behind a wall of rational self-control. Her thin, refined features, high cheekbones, and frail white hair gave her an ethereal aspect that belied a core of strength and conviction. Nature, it seemed, had robbed her body to build her mind and spirit. Roy respected her inner fortitude, and the stamina it gave her to follow her own lights, though she feared that the more unorthodox opinions of the doctor would be attached to her and damage her budding career. She had tried at times to tone her down, but to little effect. Tselitel followed where her intuition led, in spite of the consequences. Often it led to brilliant insights that helped even the most intractable of her patients to recover their equilibrium and live a normal life. But occasionally it resulted in courses of treatment that, to Roy, looked more like an arcane ritual than anything based in science. With a partially throbbing conscience she pushed these concerns aside, aware that an apprenticeship with such an illustrious mentor couldn't fail to get her an excellent position when it was over, despite the reserve with which many viewed her.

It was Tselitel's intuition, combined with a number of very detailed rumors, that told her something momentous was happening on Delta-13.

The government had established a prison on the barren world almost a century before. There they housed those deemed to be the greatest threat to the inner stability of the empire. It was an admirably efficient place to keep them. They couldn't possibly try to escape into the countryside: the climate saw to that. And strict control over the spaceport kept them from leaving the planet.

No prisoner had ever escaped Delta-13.

Often the families of the prisoners were exiled along with them, the government feeling that they were at heightened risk of following in the prisoner's footsteps. This harsh policy was generally kept out of the news, and most had the sense to avoid questioning it openly, especially given the ever increasing difficulties with the fringe. The last thing an ambitious soul with eyes on a government post would wish was to be tied to revolutionary sentiment.

The families of prisoners often worked in government industries that supported the base. Greenhouses, factories, and other productive enterprises were established to support Delta-13's population. This was done in part to ease the logistical burden of bringing supplies out from the inner worlds. Shipping was expensive, and the government saw no reason why the inhabitants of the world shouldn't support themselves as much as possible.

For several years reports had been growing about prisoners going mad for no apparent reason. Many chalked it up to the peculiar nature of the planet and the conditions under which its residents lived. But the imperial government had been too eager to clamp down on the reports, and that told more cynical observers that something else was going on. A handful of powerful self-styled humanitarians got ahold of the reports and began making noise with them, eventually forcing the government to act. There it agreed to an informal probe of sorts: a prominent psychiatrist would be allowed to analyze the prisoners in question. It wasn't much: the probe would have no power to interview anyone who worked at the prison, or indeed to conduct any act independent of the authorities on Delta-13. It would be an entirely guided tour. But it was an opportunity to dig around for a scandal, which is what the so-called humanitarians wanted most of all. Many of them shared the sentiments of the fringe, and they hoped to find a plethora of abuses with which to attack the government. For this reason it was necessary to send someone whose high profile and record of integrity would give them enough authority to challenge the government. Many names were floated, but Tselitel's finally bobbed to the top.

"Doctor, I know you feel sympathy for anyone who's hurting," Roy said after a few moments. "But these are some of the worst criminals in the empire. They've been sent here because of actions they've committed against public safety.

Many of them are terrorists, or worse! Frankly I don't feel safe living among them. Who knows what could happen to us down there."

"Nothing, I'm sure," replied Tselitel with a faint smile. "The security standards at the prison are absolute."

"I've heard rumors of assaults on the staff," replied Roy darkly, her spirit shrinking back as the frigid sphere grew, filling most of the window.

"If you'd prefer not to be present when I interview the prisoners, you don't have to be," replied Tselitel. "I can handle the hands-on work on my own. You can take care of the administrative end."

"No, I'll go where you do," replied Roy, ashamed at her lack of courage. "But I don't promise that my teeth won't be clattering the first few times!"

Tselitel chuckled.

"That's okay. Just don't let the prisoners hear you," she said. "We must at all times retain our air of authority. It's the only way to get them to work with us. Most of these people only understand the coercive power of force. For them, the authority of the prison is both their enemy and their god. They rise in the morning and lay down at night according to its dictates. They've been separated for too long from any other kind of motive to be moved by anything else. We'll only be relevant for them as long as we're identified with the prison and its unblinking, unhesitating authority. The moment that is lost, our hold on them will be, too."

"But you said that the prison is their enemy, too," countered Roy. "Won't that set us up for defeat from the start? Who would work with their enemy?"

"It's a strange dualism, to be sure," replied Tselitel. "By coercing them, the prison becomes a foe, something to be overcome. But this desire to rebel is quickly stamped out by the efficiency of modern techniques. The prisoners rapidly realize they haven't got a chance, and so they sullenly succumb to a power greater than they. Their rebellion is pushed into the unconscious, and there it festers like an infestation of roaches, receding into the walls and waiting for an outlet. That is why unblinking confidence on our part is crucial: if the mystique of the all-powerful prison is broken, the unconscious will to rebel will have found the weakness it needs to strike. It will lash out in an instant and seek to overcome us."

"Not really making me feel more confident, Doctor," Roy said.

"Don't worry. You can watch the first few interviews from behind one-way glass, just to get the feel for how I'll handle it. Then you'll be fine."

"Yes, Doctor," Roy said, looking from Tselitel back to the planet. "Still, this is a strange assignment. It's said that shadows can be seen moving in the forests at night. You wouldn't believe the stories that come out of this place."

"I don't. Not most of them, anyway," replied the doctor, turning to the planet as well. "But something is going on down there, Sadie, and I'm going to find out what it is."

"It's so barren and empty," observed Roy, the icy world sending a chill down her spine. "It looks like a place someone would go to die."

"Yes," replied Tselitel. "Or to start over and live anew."

Hours later the transport descended to a small concrete pad just outside the prison complex. A tall wall, with razor sharp spikes on the top, surrounded the prison. Guard towers were stationed every one hundred feet, ensuring absolute coverage of every inch of the compound. Guards with rifles stood at the ready to fire at the slightest provocation.

"Can't imagine anyone ever getting out of there," Roy said, watching from a small window as the ground rushed towards them. She and the doctor were strapped into their seats for the final approach.

"No one has. Not for a long time," Tselitel said, holding her seat tightly.

Takeoff and landing was always the worst for her. A near fatal crash in her early twenties scarred her for life, though she admitted that fact to no one. Space travel was a part of her everyday life, and it didn't help any to dwell on it. She would just dash up a little prayer and close her eyes until it was over. Her seat shook as the transport touched down, sending a little involuntary jolt through her system. Then she sighed her relief at having survived yet another landing, opened her eyes, and unbuckled her belt.

They gathered up their bags, put on heavy hooded coats and gloves, and walked to the back of the transport. A ramp situated between the ship's two engines lowered and touched the ground. The two women walked down it, their lungs instantly shocked by the startlingly cold air.

"Never...expected...this," gasped Roy into the harsh wind that greeted them, trying to force her lungs to suck in the frozen air. Her previous two posts had both been on warmer worlds. Indeed, most of her life had been spent at temperatures of at least seventy degrees.

"Breathe through your glove," Tselitel advised, pressing her wool mitten to her own lips as her lungs likewise recoiled from the cold and wind. She concentrated on her breathing and forced an even tempo, ironing out the jerking gasps of her diaphragm. She had just managed this when she saw a man in warm, thick clothing striding towards the pad with a pair of guards at his heels. He was tall, in his late thirties, with thick brown eyebrows and a touch of a potbelly.

"*Too much indoor living*," Roy thought, as he ambled awkwardly towards them across the slippery ground.

"Doctor Tselitel?" the man asked, approaching the two women and talking loudly over the dying noise of the transport's engines.

"Yes, that's right," replied the doctor, extending the mitten she'd been breathing through.

"I'm Warden Kelbauskas," he said, taking her hand warmly in both of his. "And who is this?" he asked, looking at Roy.

"This is my assistant, Sadie Roy."

"How do you do?" he asked, greeting her with equal warmth.

"I think I'm half frozen already," she said bluntly, the cold environment making her forget her manners.

"Yes, I'm afraid our climate must come as a terrible surprise to you both," he replied with feeling. "Nobody is ever truly prepared for it in advance. Even we natives are regularly shocked by it."

"You grew up here?" asked Roy with surprise. "I thought only prisoners and their families truly 'lived' here."

"Figure of speech," he said with a smile. "I've been on this snowball for almost ten years now. It makes me feel like a native. But come, here I am talking and you're both freezing! Let's get inside and warm you two up."

"Don't have to ask me twice," replied Roy, quickly trotting alongside the warden.

Doctor Tselitel moved with long, willowy strides that caused her to slowly fall behind as she strove to keep her balance on the snow. Kelbauskas noticed this and dropped back.

"Are you alright, Doctor?" he asked with concern.

"Oh, yes," she replied with a slightly embarrassed smile. "It's just this wind and cold is shocking my system. I'm afraid I'm not used to roughing it."

"Please, take my arm," the warden said politely, offering his left to her. Roy decided to take it as an open invitation and seized his right with both her mittens. He turned his head and laughed delightedly at her forwardness, pulling the two ladies along to a small building outside the wall.

"Let me take your coats," he said once they were inside and the door had been shut tight behind them. The warm air caressed their faces, beginning to defrost their already numb cheeks. "You'll warm up quicker without those extra layers. I hope you both like tea. I took the liberty of ordering some when I saw your transport land. We live on a steady stream of it. That, and coffee. I'm sure if you drew our blood, you'd find it consisted of them in almost equal parts."

"Yes, that will be fine," Tselitel said politely, as she and Roy settled into a pair of chairs that stood before his desk.

"I can't tell you how glad we are to have you here, Doctor," Kelbauskas said, taking his own seat behind the desk. "To have a specialist of your talent and experience examine the patients is a rare pleasure. I hope you'll be able to uncover something that our people have missed. Our team has applied every possible technique they can think of without result. The cases seem incurable."

"In my experience, no case is beyond help," Tselitel said, putting one thin leg over the other and lacing her fingers together over her stomach. "It's simply a matter of finding the right approach to take."

"Yes, of course," he replied.

At this moment his attendant entered from another room, bearing a tray of tea things. The warden poured out servings for his guests and handed them off before continuing.

"We'll give you all the help we can, Doctor. But I'm afraid there's precious little that we know. The cases seemed to develop spontaneously. Each of the inmates in question lived the same routine as the rest. We haven't been able to find a link between the cases."

"I assume they were all subject to regular medical examinations?"

"Naturally. We keep excellent track of the health of our inmates. They may be reprobates, Doctor Tselitel," he said with pride, "but we consider it our duty to take the best care of them possible. The prison is the only life they'll ever know."

"Of course," replied Tselitel, sipping her tea and taking a moment to reflect on his words. She felt they indicated a genuine desire to look after those under his care. But the mixture of moral superiority was an interesting twist, to say the least. "Before I can interview them I'll need all the background information you have. Everything related to their past life, their time in prison, and the circumstances in which their first symptoms were manifested."

"I'll have my people get on it at once," the warden said obligingly. "We should have the first reports ready for you tomorrow. There are twenty-three cases in total, so it will take a few days to get all the data together."

"That's fine. I'll only need a few to start with," replied Tselitel, struck that it should take the imperial machine so long to grind through such a simple request. Finishing her tea and setting her cup on a small table beside her chair, she changed topics. "I saw a town downhill from the prison as we landed. Is that where we'll be staying?"

"Oh, of course not," replied Kelbauskas emphatically. "Conditions in Midway are neither sanitary nor are they safe. There are renegades down there that would attack you just for being associated with the government. And that's saying nothing of what the so-called Underground movement might attempt. No, you'll stay in official housing here, near the prison."

"Midway?" inquired Tselitel. "I wasn't aware the town had a name."

"Officially it doesn't," replied the warden. "It doesn't warrant one. But that's what the residents call it."

"Why is that?" asked Roy.

"Well, it's a cynical expression, really. They call it Midway because it's the place they'll pass the time between birth and death. It's a midpoint for them. They refuse to think of it as a home since they don't have a future there. It's just a place to fill time before the grave."

"They sound terribly depressed," the doctor commented.

"It's a depressing circumstance to be in," replied the warden. "But they brought it on themselves, more or less, and will have to make the best of it. All we in the government can do is keep them orderly and leave them to their business. But even that's tough. There's a robust black market at work, and somehow they manage to manufacture liquor of a terribly inferior quality. More like poison than anything, to be honest. Sometimes they drink too much and get into fights. But for the most part it eases their burdens a little, and helps them get past the boredom."

"I'd *die* of boredom if I had to live in a place like this," said Roy, quickly growing comfortable with the warden. "All the monotony. Just snow everywhere! It's very drab. I'm used to living in places with a little…variety."

"Fortunately government employees have more options for entertainment than the people down there do," he said, tossing his head toward the town. "We're a pretty tight knit community. We regularly organize events to socialize and have some fun. We have to, or we'd all go nuts in a snow globe like this."

"That's good to hear," replied Roy with relief. "I had visions of being cooped up in my room bent over work papers."

"I don't think you'll have any trouble getting on with the other residents," replied the warden with a smile, gently indicating the young woman's attractiveness. "We're always glad to see fresh faces around here."

"Excellent," the doctor said, uncrossing her leg and rising, wishing to break the bonhomie for reasons she could only vaguely feel. "I'm glad that we'll be well taken care of. But now I'd like to see our quarters. The trip has been very tiring, and I'd like to lay down before dinner."

"Yes, of course," Kelbauskas said solicitously, grabbing the ladies' jackets and helping them put them on. Throwing on his own, he made for the door ahead of them and put his hand on the knob. "Don't try to breathe until you've been out in it for a few seconds. It lessens the shock." With this he pushed the door open against the harsh wind and let them go out ahead of him. He mutely pointed to a large structure a short distance away and slowly padded towards it through the snow.

The two ladies followed closely. Roy walked directly behind the large warden, letting him cut the wind for her. Tselitel was a little off to his left, covering her face with her hand and trying to see through the snow that was being driven into her eyes. She became aware of a dull pressure inside her head but ignored it, focusing on the building ahead.

Kelbauskas looked behind him every few seconds to make sure his guests were keeping up. The fourth time he did this he looked at Tselitel in time to see her eyes widen and her face go blank. She fell headfirst into the snow and didn't move.

"Doctor!" exclaimed Roy, her voice almost drowned out by the wind. She dropped to her knees and, with the warden's help, turned the unconscious woman over. Her eyes were closed and her mouth hung open.

"We've got to get her out of the cold!" Kelbauskas shouted into Roy's ear. "She'll freeze in minutes out here!"

The warden was not a particularly strong man. But with Roy's help he managed to carry Tselitel back to the building they'd just left to await a medical team from the prison.

◆ ◆ ◆

Hunt stood under the broken awning of an old shop on the edge of town, watching the flashlights of the police move up and down the streets. They were looking for people, like himself, who had violated the curfew.

"Looks like we're in a bit of a mess," Hunt said under his breath. Suddenly he ducked back into a shadow as a flashlight's beam darted across the front of the shop. "Only missed it by forty minutes."

"I told you that cave wasn't worth it," said Wellesley.

"Yeah, but we didn't *know* that until we'd actually gone inside," countered Hunt.

"Probability was against it from the start," replied the AI factually. "It was too close to town, so any artifacts were likely found ages ago."

"Whatever," replied Hunt, aware his friend was right but unwilling to admit it. "The fact remains we didn't know what was there until we looked. I had a good feeling about that cave, too. Somehow it just seemed right."

"It would seem that your feelings aren't infallible."

"I guess we're about to find out," Hunt said, getting just such a feeling at that moment. He perceived a gap between a pair of police patrols and bolted from the shop. He slipped between the two groups and climbed over a low brick wall just as they doubled back on each other and bathed the path he'd taken in light. "That 'feeling' of mine seems to be holding up alright so far," Hunt said quietly in his helmet, as the sound of boots crunching on hard snow came slowly closer.

"I'm going to die of fright if you keep pulling stunts like that," Wellesley said, trying to keep his grip. He valued a level head above all else. But Hunt's antics had pushed him to the brink of losing control on many occasions. The fact that he possessed no body of his own heightened his sensitivity. Wherever Hunt went, he went. He was contained in a large medallion that dangled around Hunt's neck. Through contact with his skin electrical impulses enabled communication.

Hunt glanced over the wall and saw the patrols striding away from him again. He rose into a crouch and moved quietly from the wall, sticking to the shadows. The snow beneath him had long since been trodden into ice, making it treacherously slippery. Twice he nearly lost his balance.

"Slow down, will you? They'll catch us for sure if you go tumbling to the ground."

Hunt stopped for a moment and centered himself. He was rushing because he was keyed up by the patrols and the risk of getting caught. Though he didn't admit it to Wellesley, he was concerned about his chances of getting back. The curfew was famously hard to beat. The police seemed to know just where to pop up to nail the few who tried to violate it.

He moved a few steps further and ducked into an alley. It was packed with garbage from the buildings that ran along either side of it. The stench snuck into his helmet and half choked him. Pushing past the refuse, he trudged through the dirty snow and emerged at the opposite end. He could see the buildings loom up in the darkness, the visor of his helmet shielding his eyes from the driving snow. Like mournful ghosts the structures rose sadly around him, offering only modest protection from the wind and the cold.

"Coffins for the dead," he muttered, contemplating the buildings and their relation to the people who lived in them.

"What was that, Rex?" Wellesley asked.

"Nothing," he replied, shaking his head. It was unusual for Hunt to wax poetic about the world around him. Every once in a while the mood just seemed to take him for a moment. Then it would pass, and he'd be embarrassed for having gone through it, feeling it smacked of melodrama.

He walked for several minutes along the south end of the city, trying to work his way farther inside to where most of the population lived. The town had been laid out with the residential section in the middle. It formed a nucleus around which was wrapped the various buildings in which the residents worked during the day. This was meant to break some of the wind and snow that seemed to blow almost perpetually through Midway, the workers preferring to be cold at work rather than at home. Or at least less cold. Only a handful had homes that were actually warm, the rest living in ramshackle affairs with scanty insulation.

Aware that curfew breakers would be trying to get home, the police concentrated their attention in the residential section after nightfall. Hunt moved halfway through one of the outlying neighborhoods before a loud crunching sound told him he wasn't alone.

"I think we're surrounded," Wellesley said with concern in his voice. "We just picked up a patrol behind us."

Hunt looked over his shoulder and saw a pair of lights moving towards him, no more than a hundred feet back. A light shone down the street ahead of him, and another pair was visible to his left. With so much snow in the air visibility was low. But the police were sure to catch him in a few more moments if he did nothing.

Seeing a low balcony above him, he climbed on top of a thin wooden handrail and grabbed it with his hands. Pulling himself upward, he slid his body onto the balcony and inched away from its edge just as the patrols converged on his location.

He could hear them talking to each other in low tones. But they were too far away to understand with the wind whistling through the buildings. They chatted for several minutes before they broke up and went their separate ways.

His nerves tighter than a bowstring, Hunt watched the lights grow dimmer in the blustery darkness. With a sigh of relief he saw the last patrol disappear into the night.

"That was too close," Wellesley said. "We need to get under cover fast."

"I know just the place," Hunt replied, dropping from the balcony and moving in a half-crouch through the snow.

Several minutes later he knocked a particular rhythm at a non-descript door. An unseen woman looked at him through a peephole off to his left, and then nodded to a man behind the door. He opened it and Hunt slipped in.

It was an Underground tavern, one of several throughout the city that Hunt used as hiding places whenever he needed to get away from the authorities for a little while. The locations changed every few weeks to keep the police off their scent, and an elaborate initiation process meant only a handful ever knew where the taverns were located. Hunt had donated more than a few artifacts to the Underground movement, the proceeds from which helped to keep them intact despite the lock the government kept on the city. Mainly the money was used to purchase communications and tracking equipment from the black market. These could be smuggled in small quantities by independent traders and the occasional guard from one of the larger convoys. But weapons remained out of their reach, no one daring to run the risks associated with illegally possessing one and bringing it to a prison planet.

Hunt was refreshed to step into the warm building after spending so many hours in the cold. Despite his environment suit the elements still affected him, particularly after nightfall. He took off his helmet and breathed in the comforting, humid air.

Wellesley, who through linking with Hunt saw, heard, and felt all that he did, was reminded of why he didn't like the Underground. The people were mostly outcasts, ruffians who, in his view, couldn't accept the way things were. They'd been dealt a bad hand by life, and he thought they should make the best of it, not commit petty acts of treason by whispering about rebellion in the darkest corners of the city. He felt their plots for overthrowing the government on Delta-13 were just fruitless fantasies.

But not Hunt, who like many other young people on the planet felt their lives had been stolen from them by a senseless policy that punished them for crimes they didn't commit. They were angry, bitter, and willing to take risks to try and get something better for themselves. For them, rebellion carried with it a real chance for success.

"*Having never truly experienced defeat,*" Wellesley thought, "*they have no fear of the consequences.*"

The ancient AI, having tasted more of victory and defeat than any human ever would, was weary of emotionally charged ideas like freedom and revolution. As he saw it, one lived or died, and the important thing was to live as well as possible with what came to hand. Dreaming about a better tomorrow, even if it was technically possible, was reckless and insensible. It just didn't pay to put one's faith in things unseen.

Hunt looked the modest room over. A handful of regulars recognized him and nodded, nursing their moonshine and whispering to each other. Silence was the absolute rule in the taverns. They couldn't afford a laugh, a cough, or even a loud sneeze to give away their position to a cop who chanced to be nearby.

"I hope you don't plan to drink," Wellesley communicated to Hunt. "We need your wits to be as sharp as possible."

"I don't," replied Hunt seriously, his near encounter with the police several minutes before restraining his usual flippancy about danger. "I just want to warm up for a little while and get off my feet."

"Okay."

Hunt quietly stomped the snow off his boots and moved to a dark corner where a table and two chairs stood. He dropped into one of them and rubbed his eyes with his left hand, holding his helmet against his thigh with his right. Searching for artifacts, running from the bear, sneaking around the city: all these activities now weighed him down. He felt very tired, the warm air making him drowsy. Without opening his eyes after rubbing them he lowered his head to the table and sighed.

"Hey, don't go to sleep just yet," said a voice across the small table.

"Hello, Antonin," Hunt said without looking up, easily recognizing the charming smuggler and leader of the Underground movement by his voice. Antonin Gromyko was also an important figure within the black market, helping to connect rich buyers and poor sellers, such as Hunt. His sly, fox-like intelligence and intuitive grasp of how to evade the authorities had already made him a legend to many of Midway's residents. This he cultivated, presenting himself as a dashing, romantic figure upon whom they could place their hopes for a better tomorrow. His slick black hair and angular features enhanced his appeal, particularly with the women of the city who found in him an appealing image they could weave their fantasies around.

"You sound beat," observed Gromyko. "Hard time evading the cops?"

"They're crawling up and down the streets like fleas on a dog," replied Hunt. "Twice they nearly nailed me. I'm not sure I can get back to my place without being spotted. You know how the patrols are the closer you get to the city center."

"Indeed I do," replied the smuggler softly, nodding slowly. "Perhaps I can help you with that," he said brightly. "But first, I must ask you something important."

"Fire away," Hunt said, raising his head and looking at him through weary eyes.

"There are rumors about an artifact that permits the user to see hidden places," Gromyko began, lowering his voice until he was barely audible. "You can imagine why such a device would concern me. Should it fall into their hands, the government could easily sniff us out and destroy us. We wouldn't have a chance."

"I'm not aware of any such device," Hunt said, shaking his head. "It sounds more like fantasy than science. All of the artifacts are just leftover technology from an extinct race, not magic items that can grant special powers. I think what you heard was just idle talk from people who had drunk too much."

"Then you don't consider such a device even remotely feasible?" persisted Gromyko.

"No, not even remotely," replied Hunt. "Why, do *you* think it's feasible?"

"Normally I wouldn't," said the smuggler. "But recently two of our taverns have been broken into without warning and all their occupants seized. We've kept it quiet for the time being, not wanting to scare the populace. They need to feel that we're always one step ahead of the government in order to keep their hopes up. But I've been over the details of each incident a dozen times and I just can't see how they figured it out. There was nothing to give them away."

"Maybe a traitor, someone working on the inside?" offered Hunt.

"No, I don't think so. Everyone caught was immediately taken to the prison and locked up. Only two other people and myself knew their locations, and I know the other two are absolutely loyal."

"Well, I don't think the answer is gonna be found in magic artifacts, or whatever this device is supposed to be," replied Hunt, stretching his legs alongside the table and yawning. "But I admit it is troubling."

"But you'll keep your ears open for rumors about such a device?"

"Yes, I will," replied Hunt.

"Excellent, that's all I ask," replied Gromyko with a smile. "And now, to help you sneak back to the center of the city." The smuggler arose and beckoned Hunt to follow. Slowly rising to his feet, he put his helmet back on and joined him by the door.

"Is it clear?" Gromyko asked one of the lookouts, who nodded in the affirmative. "Come on," he said, slipping out into the cold in a light jacket and gloves.

"That nut is going to freeze in five minutes," Wellesley said, as the smuggler led Hunt into the night. "It's got to be thirty below out here."

"Probably forty," replied Hunt quietly, his eyes fixed on the gray coat that floated in the darkness a few feet ahead. "But he knows what he's doing."

Gromyko led Hunt up and down the streets, indirectly working towards the center of the city. Every little while he ducked into a tavern, or a little smuggler's nook that broke the wind and allowed him to warm up. His knowledge of Midway's hiding places was vast. They never spent more than a few minutes at a time in the open.

"In here," he said, sliding open the window of an abandoned house. Hunt climbed over the sill and into the darkness inside. Gromyko had just joined him and slid the window down when a pair of flashlights came around the corner of a house half a block away.

"That was a close one," Gromyko said with relish, squatting beside the window with Hunt. "But that's what keeps us alive, eh?"

"He's as bad as you are," Wellesley said.

"I don't understand how it is you haven't gone numb yet," Hunt said, noting the casual ease with which the smuggler sat in the frigid room.

"Long underwear," he joked.

"Come on, Antonin," chided Hunt.

"Well, a few months ago a medallion appeared on the black market that has the power to regulate my body temperature. It evens out the highs and lows." He lifted it from inside his shirt and held its dimly glowing form up for Hunt to see. "It's not a miracle device. I couldn't run around out there in just a pair of shorts. But it keeps me from needing to wear a heavy piece of kit like you've got."

"Pretty neat," Hunt replied, handling the device. It was the size of his palm and surprisingly heavy. "Most have cost you plenty."

"Oh, it did," replied the smuggler, slipping it back inside his shirt and pausing to listen for the police outside. "They're getting close. Don't move, the floor is very creaky."

Hunt strained his ears for half a minute before he could hear their footsteps. Finally the sharp crunching of boots on bitterly cold snow and ice filtered in through the dirty panes of the window and made his pulse quicken. He realized they should have moved away from it, just in case they decided to lift it and take a peek. But it was too late for that. He sat perfectly still, his jaw tightly clenched. The sentries stopped and spoke quietly to each other for a few seconds. One of them stepped up to the window, and Hunt knew his time had come. Silently he shifted onto the balls of his feet, ready to leap up and attack should they open it. But he felt the restraining hand of Gromyko on his shoulder as he did so, the smuggler invisibly shaking his head back and forth in the darkness. The seconds passed with painful slowness, until finally, with relief, he heard the patrol walk unsuspectingly away from their hiding place.

Gromyko gave them two minutes to leave the area, and then breathed on one of the panes and wiped away a little of the dirt that had accumulated. Peering around and seeing no one, he raised the window and climbed out, motioning for Hunt to follow.

"Come on, we'll head back the way they came," he whispered, patting him on the shoulder and walking gingerly to the south.

After nearly an hour of dashing like cats in and out of unseen sanctuaries, the pair finally reached Hunt's rundown little shack.

"And here you are," said Gromyko triumphantly, as though pulling a rabbit out of a hat. "Safe and sound."

"I owe you one, Antonin," said Hunt with relief, certain he wouldn't have made it on his own.

"Nah, we're even," replied the smuggler with a firm handshake. "You've done plenty for the Underground over the years. We can't let our best scavenger of artifacts end up in prison, can we? Although," he continued humorously, "if you ever feel like parting with that mirage generator, I'll be glad to take it off your hands."

"Good night, Antonin," Hunt said.

"Good night, my friend," he replied with a smile, disappearing into the blackness.

CHAPTER 2

Doctor Tselitel came to consciousness without opening her eyes. Slowly, hazily, the world around her began to push away the dream land she'd lived in for days. First she noticed the warmth of the room, how it surrounded and comforted her. Then she heard the beeping of the machines that monitored her vital signs.

Suddenly the room was too real, an invasive force she sought to keep out. She gripped the thin blanket that covered her and wanted to hide under it. A moment later the mood passed.

"I've never wanted to hide like that before," she thought, thoroughly confused. The dim sense that something was pressing in on her remained, though only in the background of her mind. It had been present ever since her meeting with Kelbauskas, and it made her wonder about the tea she had drunk. She instantly dismissed the idea of being poisoned, though a vague sense of suspicion toward the warden remained.

"Are you awake, Doctor?" she heard Roy ask from her bedside, interrupting her thoughts. She opened her eyes and saw her young assistant peering into her face. "I hope I didn't wake you. But you looked like you weren't sleeping anymore."

"No, I wasn't asleep," replied Tselitel groggily, surprised at the husky lack of clarity in her voice. "Where am I?"

"The hospital wing of the prison," Roy replied. "They moved you here after you passed out."

"Passed out?" she repeated, trying to remember what happened. "All I can recall is sitting in the warden's office." She stared at the wall for several seconds, racking her brain. "Did we go outside after that?"

"Uh huh. He was showing us to our quarters when you collapsed in the snow. We had to carry you back inside and phone the hospital for help. You've been here ever since."

"How long?" asked the doctor, closing her eyes and swallowing to lubricate her dry throat.

"About a week."

"A week!" she exclaimed. "How is that even possible? Did I have a stroke or something?"

"That's just it," replied Roy uneasily. "The doctors don't know what happened. All of your vitals have been normal. Although you *have* been showing a high degree of brain activity ever since they brought you here. But there's been nothing concerning in your condition."

"Wouldn't you consider a week-long coma concerning?" asked Tselitel. "That's not normal."

"Of course, Doctor," replied Roy soothingly. "I just meant there's nothing medically wrong with you. All your organs are functioning normally."

"I've never enjoyed robust health," mused Tselitel, more to herself than to Roy. "Maybe the tension of the trip, followed by the nasty weather, pushed me over the edge." She thought for a moment. "No, nobody blacks out for a week because of a little traveler's fatigue. There's got to be another answer."

"Well, don't worry about it right now," Roy said, patting her thin arm. "Just rest. You need to get your strength back."

"Have you examined the paperwork for the madness cases?" asked Tselitel, turning to familiar ground in order to get some sense of control.

"Yes, Doctor," replied Roy quietly, wishing her boss would simply relax but knowing she wouldn't. "As the warden said, the cases are perplexing. I've been over each one several times but can't find any cause for their condition. Like he said, they seemed to occur spontaneously."

"Every effect has its cause," replied Tselitel logically.

"Of course. But the medical data gives us no clues."

"Then we'll have to start interviewing the patients and see what they can tell us."

"That might not be so easy," replied Roy. "Many of them have gone mute, apparently dead to the outside world. Others are climbing the walls and screaming hours on end. Only one of them seems to have any control over himself, and he's a real tough case. I doubt you could be in a room with him without a pair of armed guards to protect you."

"What is he, a serial killer?" joked Tselitel.

"As a matter of fact, he is," replied her assistant soberly.

"Alright, we'll save him for later," the doctor said seriously. "I'll examine some of the mute patients first, see if I can get a spark out of any of them. They'll be easier to work with than the screamers. They'll probably need sedation just as a starting point, unless I can reach them somehow."

"The warden has promised every assistance he's capable of as soon as you're ready to start," Roy said brightly. "I'm sure he'll accommodate whatever you need."

"That's good," replied Tselitel, laying back on her pillow and closing her eyes. "Because I think we're going to be here for a while."

Forty-eight hours later Tselitel was released from the hospital. Despite her protests the warden insisted on escorting her personally to her quarters. Roy hovered close to her as they walked, fearing another blackout.

"I'm not an invalid," Tselitel said in a voice that mixed irritation with humor. "I think I can walk a few hundred feet on my own."

"Yes, Doctor," replied Roy obligingly, sticking as close as ever.

The government's employees were housed in two large apartment buildings, the one situated behind the other. Theirs stood closer to the prison, and was clearly the older of the two structures.

"Here we are," Kelbauskas said, showing his ID to the guard. "We have very tight security protocols here," the warden said with a smile. "In the event of a breakout the apartments will be locked down instantly, preventing anyone from getting in."

"Good to know," Tselitel said without enthusiasm, her thin hands shoved deep inside the pockets of her jacket.

Inside a modest lobby was decorated with a massive rug and several potted plants that stood along the walls. Paintings of sunnier climates hung from the walls, adding a little cheer to the setting.

"Just a moment while I get your key," Kelbauskas said, leaving the ladies in the middle of the lobby while he strode to the desk to speak with the clerk.

"Quite a gentleman, isn't he?" Roy enthused. "He insisted on escorting me to my room once we knew you were safe and sound in the hospital, though I'm sure he had a lot to do. And he's been nothing but kind to me and solicitous about you ever since the accident."

"He seems bound and determined to take care of us," Tselitel replied, curious if it was an act. The cases of madness had no known cause. But she felt the warden could still be afraid that some blame might fall onto him once the cause *was* discovered.

A number of people passed through the lobby as they waited for Kelbauskas to return. They looked at the women with polite interest but didn't talk with them. By that time the news both of their arrival and of Tselitel's accident in the snow had spread across the entire complex, producing an avalanche of gossip. Many speculated that Tselitel had had an epilepsy, or even a mild stroke. Those who saw her carefully watched for any signs of lingering damage as she moved about. She knew that for at least another week they would be observing her minutely, trying to figure out why such a famous psychiatrist had collapsed in the snow twenty minutes after arrival. It was an inauspicious start to her stay, and she was certain it would cast a shadow over her subsequent activities.

"Here you are," the warden said, handing the doctor her key and guiding her further into the building. "Your apartment is on the ground floor, towards the back. I'm sorry, but the only rooms we had available face the prison."

"I prefer it that way," replied the doctor. "It will help me to keep my mind on the task at hand."

"Of course," replied Kelbauskas. "But we find it useful to break our thoughts away from the prison on a regular basis. Otherwise it dominates our lives, and we become inmates ourselves, unconsciously timing our lives around its happenings."

He stopped before a pair of doors on the eastern side of the building.

"This is yours, Doctor," he said, indicating apartment 138. "I thought you'd want to be near Miss Roy to facilitate your work, so she's in 137."

"Thank you," replied Tselitel, forcing a smile.

"Please don't hesitate to contact me if you need anything," he said kindly, shaking their hands warmly.

"We won't," replied Roy with a smile.

Once he'd turned and walked some distance down the hall, Tselitel opened her door and went inside, Roy close at her heels.

"Hadn't you better get back to work on those patient reports, Sadie?" she asked pointedly, her patience wearing thin.

"Oh, I can take care of them later," replied her assistant, unwilling to leave her alone.

"Sadie," Tselitel said significantly, turning and looking her in the eye.

"Well, perhaps you're right," Roy said, taking the hint and closing the door behind her. A moment later her key jingled in the lock next door.

Tselitel shook her head and wondered how much longer

her assistant would feel the need to mother her.

Her apartment featured a tiny lobby that led into a guest bedroom to the right, a small bathroom to the left, and a living room straight ahead. A small kitchen adjoined the living room, separated by a beige counter. A master bedroom, bathroom, and a tiny laundry room finished out the apartment.

"Two bedrooms for just one me," she mused. "I wonder how much room they think I need."

Walking to her living room window and opening the curtains she could see the prison. She ruminated about the many people who would spend their lives there, never having any hope of seeing the outside world again. In spite of their crimes it made her gloomy to think about it. She felt sorry for them.

Closing the curtains and walking to the kitchen, she opened the fridge and saw that a few staples had been provided for. Finding a glass pitcher that had been filled with water, she drew it out and poured herself a glass.

"Who would refrigerate water on a snowball like this?" she laughed. Then her face grew serious again, the brief spike of levity crushed by the low mood she'd had ever since her coma. Walking to the master bathroom and looking at herself in the mirror, her mouth was drawn tightly closed, and her eyes were narrow and skeptical. "This isn't like you, Lily," she said quietly, disturbed by the change that had come over her. Her demeanor had always been open and accepting. Now she wanted to hold the world, and everyone in it, at a distance. Roy's solicitous mothering, for example, would have amused her before. But now it annoyed her.

She bent over the sink and splashed cool water in her face, drying it off with a nearby towel. She looked in the mirror again, but the same face looked back, a little redder this time as blood rushed to the surface of her thin skin.

"There's something wrong with me," she said in a low voice. "Ever since that collapse in the snow I haven't been the same." She raised her hands in front of her, irrationally expecting some change to be evident. But they were just the same two hands as always. "No, whatever has come over me is in here," she said, tapping her temple. She put her hands on the counter and gazed into the mirror. Her eyes were tired, but otherwise normal.

Walking to the master bedroom, she found all her luggage had been piled against the bed. She dug through her bags and found a small tablet on which she liked to write her thoughts. She turned on the screen and sat down on the soft mattress.

"Two days ago I awoke from a week-long coma. I have no idea what caused it. The medical staff of the prison are baffled. I feel fine now, physically at least. But I'm moody and short-tempered. I fear some subtle form of damage has been done to my brain that the doctors can't find. I did take a pretty good tumble into the snow when I lost consciousness. Heh, maybe I shook some of my marbles loose. I guess time will tell.

"I got a good look at the prison when I left the hospital. It's a steel-and-concrete affair that boasts the best security money can buy. Security doors with armed guards divide the structure into a million little airtight segments, all of which are locked instantly should so much as a hair be out of place. I doubt a small army could take it.

"Sadie is making eyes at the warden and getting swept off her feet. She thinks she's being subtle, but I know her too well. He's a charmer, to be sure. But I've been a psychiatrist too long to miss the signs. He's trying to butter our toast. But I guess he could genuinely like Sadie as well. She is a looker. And she has a warm vulnerability that makes her appealing to many, though, ironically enough, she never forgets (or forgives) a slight. If Kelbauskas is just pushing her buttons, he'll definitely end up in her little book of scratched-through names."

Tselitel looked up from her tablet and thought for a moment.

"I'm concerned about the civilian population on this planet. The nights are bitterly cold, and even in my government-

furnished apartment I can feel the wind beating against the walls, sending a subtle breeze past me as I write. The hospital was warm because it's part of the prison, and thus surrounded by massive walls that break the wind. But those poor people down there must be half frozen each night.

"My work begins in earnest tomorrow. I'll finish getting settled in, and then go over some of the paperwork tonight. I doubt I'll be able to see more than a handful of patients anyway, so not much preparatory work needs to be done. It sounds like the reports the prison has filed aren't very useful anyway. According to Sadie they provide no clues as to the cause of their condition."

Setting aside her tablet, she leaned back on the mattress and gazed at the ceiling. She tried to focus on the perplexing task that stood before her. But she couldn't help getting sidetracked again and again by the strange way she was feeling after her collapse. Annoyed at her own self-absorption, she shook her head to clear her thoughts. But just then she was interrupted by a knock at the door. Putting her tablet back into her bag, she slid off the bed and went to see who it was.

"Oh, Sadie," she said. "You don't have to knock. Just come in whenever you feel like it."

"I didn't want to intrude if you wanted to be alone," replied her assistant a little warily, feeling chastened by Tselitel's earlier sendoff. "I was just wondering if you'd like to get some lunch. Joris was telling me that our building features an excellent cafeteria."

"Joris?" asked the doctor, following her assistant into the hall and locking her door.

"Warden Kelbauskas," Roy said. "His first name is Joris. In fact he told me that he put us in this building because the food is better here than in the other one. He thought we'd get used to the planet more easily that way."

"Thoughtful," Tselitel commented dryly, shoving her hands into the pockets of her slacks and walking slowly.

"Isn't he?" Roy asked. "He's just about the nicest man I've ever met. He's put so much consideration into our stay here."

"I expect that's largely for his own sake," replied the doctor.

"Oh, I'm sure he's laying it on a little thick for his job's sake. But so would anyone else in his position. I know I would," she laughed.

Tselitel nodded but said nothing more. One advantage of her situation, she realized, was that she could drop out of conversation whenever she wanted to, and Roy would just consider it part of the healing process and give her space.

The cafeteria was a simple, almost homely affair, clearly designed to put the residents at ease. Wooden tables and chairs were placed tastefully around the room, giving it an aura of almost rustic relaxation. A buffet line ran along the western wall.

"Grab a plate and load it down," Roy said brightly, following her own advice. "Government employees eat for free."

"Really?"

"Uh huh. Joris said being stationed here has to have *some* benefits. Food used to be deducted from the employee's salaries, but he abolished that practice six years ago and juggled a few expenses to make it budget neutral. He said Earth couldn't care less as long as the workers don't get fat. He also had this whole space redesigned," she said, waving her free hand around to indicate the cafeteria. "It used to be sterile, like an operating room. But he brought in a designer at his own expense and had her spruce up the place."

"Sounds like he really cares about the people who serve under him," Tselitel commented, curious if she'd judged him too harshly at first as she put a few light items on her plate. "I'm going to grab a table. Meet me when you're finished loading up," she said with a quiet chuckle, as Roy continued to pile things on a plate that clearly wasn't as big as her appetite.

Walking from the buffet line towards an empty table, she heard a buzzing in her ears. Slowing her pace as the room began to spin, she gripped her plate tightly and sat down in the nearest chair. She glanced around the room but clearly no one had noticed her condition. Closing her eyes and taking a deep breath, she resolved not to mention it to Roy, or anyone else. They'd just fuss over her without knowing what was wrong.

"Think I about emptied them out," Roy said cheerfully, sitting down across from the doctor with a plate piled high with delicious fare. She looked at the modest salad and handful of vegetables on her chief's plate and shook her head. "Are you sure you don't want some of this?" she asked, spearing a piece of roast beef and lifting it up.

"No, I'm alright," Tselitel said in as buoyant a voice as she could muster. "I don't want to weigh myself down. I need a clear head to go over those reports. I know you said that they don't provide much detail after the onset of symptoms. But maybe if I comb over their lives before that something will come up."

"I hope so, because otherwise we'll have no leads at all," Roy said frankly, taking a bite of roast beef and chewing it before continuing. *"Patient X went nuts. We don't know why. All vitals normal. Patient Y went nuts. We don't know why. All vitals normal. Patient Z...*It goes on like that page after page. I'd almost think they're trying to hide something, because their lives after the onset of symptoms have almost no unique details. Presumably that's due to their condition. After all, people who either sit mute or climb the walls all day aren't gonna show much variety. But I still would have thought that there's be *some* differences between each case. The reports read almost like they were, well," she said, pausing and looking around.

"Go ahead," her boss urged her quietly, aware what she was thinking already but wishing her to actually say it out loud.

"Well, like they were written out in *advance*," she said in a guilty tone. "Oh, I'm not suggesting a coverup," she backpedaled quickly. "I have the utmost faith in the empire's choice of staff on Delta-13."

"As do I," Tselitel replied with an imperceptible shake of her head, disappointed at her assistant's lack of courage and willingness to accept the official line. "Still, doesn't it strike you odd that only the prisoners have been affected?"

"What do you mean?" she asked cautiously, breaking a piece off a slice of cherry pie and raising it on her fork as though to hide behind it. Many times her mentor had tried to maneuver her into making critical observations about the government, and each time she had managed to avoid the bait. She knew already that this was another such occasion. But the doctor's low mood and touchiness of late made her worry how she'd take another dodge.

"Well, why haven't there been any cases with the guards? Or any of the other employees for that matter? To say nothing of the people in Midway?"

"I can't imagine," replied Roy carefully. "Only the worst of the worst are sent to Delta-13. Maybe they were unstable to begin with. Add the nearly solitary conditions they're kept under, and that might be enough to snap some of them, especially if they're wracked with guilt. I was talking to–"

"Joris," inserted Tselitel with annoyance.

"Yes, Joris," Roy said with hesitation, unsure why he bothered the doctor so much. "He was wondering the same thing, why only the prisoners were affected. He ordered a check of everything from their water supply to their medical histories, reaching back to their earliest known moments. Absolutely nothing came of it. It seems to be just as he said, totally spontaneous."

They ate quietly for a few minutes, Roy stealing glances at Tselitel to gauge her mood while the latter mostly poked her food and thought.

The silence was becoming intolerable for Roy when a tall man of about thirty-five approached their table. Squarely built, with a dark beard that he kept closely trimmed, his eyes were round and kind, but with a certain air of experience about them. A subtle note of watchfulness was evident in his manner, as though nothing passed his eyes without his being aware of it.

"Excuse me, ladies, but are you the new arrivals? I don't think I've had the pleasure of seeing you before."

"That's us," said the younger woman happily, glad to drop the former subject. "I'm Sadie Roy. And this is Doctor Lily Tselitel."

"Charlie Palmer," he smiled. "May I?" he asked, indicating their table.

"Please," Roy said, scooting over so he could sit in the chair next to her.

"I was sorry to hear about your accident, Doctor," Palmer said with feeling as he took his seat. "I work in the hospital and was one of the first to know. How are you feeling now?"

"Much better, thank you," Tselitel said, half-honestly. Her ears were still buzzing, and she was glad to be off her feet at that moment. "You say you work in the hospital?"

"That's right," he replied. "Let me tell you, we're all very glad to have you here. The so-called 'mad' patients have us at our wit's end. Everything we've tried to do for them has failed."

"Then you've had contact with them personally?" she asked.

"Oh, yes," he laughed. "A great deal of contact." He rolled up his cuff and showed them an ugly scar on his forearm. Roy gasped and then gingerly touched it with her finger.

"What happened to you?" she asked, her eyes wide.

"Some of them got violent," Palmer said, putting his sleeve back. "The first few cases were mutes. Then we had a rash of loud ones. They'd scream their heads off, babbling all sorts of nonsense. And they'd do *anything* to escape the room they were in. Truth be told, we'd gotten a little careless. We thought all of them would be mutes after the first half dozen were. This one," he said, tapping his forearm, "proved us wrong."

"Well, how did you know they were affected *before* they took to screaming?" Tselitel asked. "I thought some went mute and some screamed from the very outset."

"Oh, I should have explained," Palmer said. "You see, in each case the patient would suddenly lose all interest in the world around them. They'd just pull into themselves and stop eating and drinking. Blankly staring into space, they'd sit for days on end, not moving an inch. For some reason it works that way both with the mutes and the screamers. Eventually the latter pull out of it and just explode onto their surroundings."

"And that's how you got the scar?" the doctor asked.

"Uh huh," he nodded with a laugh. "This was lucky number seven. The first six were inert. We could load them on stretchers and move them about without difficulty. We'd cart them out of their rooms, nourish them, and bring them back. It was seven who suddenly snapped out of it. He stabbed me with a pencil when I tried to feed him intravenously. Then he jumped on me and started beating my skull against the floor. I guess he thought I was trying to attack him with the needle. I'm only talking to you now because a pair of guards outside the room heard us struggling and clubbed him off of me."

"How awful!" exclaimed Roy.

"You're telling me," Palmer said emphatically. "I've never been more shocked in my life. After that we took a lot more precautions with the inmates, even the mute ones. We always have armed guards nearby whenever we interact with them now. We can never know when they might snap out of it and go after us like seven did."

"Tell me, seven didn't show *any* abnormal signs until the moment he attacked you?" probed Tselitel.

"No, none at all," said Palmer slowly, thinking over his case history. "He was like all the others until that moment. But he's been a violent screamer ever since. It's like he's trying to get out of his body through sheer force."

"What makes you say that?" the doctor asked.

"Well, the expression 'climbing the walls' is both

literal and figurative in his case. He circles his room like a caged animal, hands on the walls, always looking upwards. Screaming and babbling, it's like he's constantly looking for some hole in the ceiling that will allow him to escape. His eyes are wide and unfocused, but he's always looking. He can't tolerate where he is, no matter where that happens to be. He tries to escape both his cell and the hospital room we feed him in with the same wild abandon. I think he'd act the same way even if he was outdoors. It's the most bizarre thing I've ever seen."

"Bizarre is certainly the word for it," Tselitel said quietly, pondering Palmer's words. "And he never stops?"

"Only when he sleeps," replied Palmer. "And most of the time he only does that because we give him a powerful sedative. I think he'd just exert himself to death if we didn't."

"Do you have any idea what caused it?" Roy asked.

"None whatsoever," he replied, shaking his head. "It's got the entire hospital stumped. We've been kicking around theories ever since it started. But even the doctors who have been on Delta-13 the longest don't have a clue." He looked at Tselitel and smiled. "That's why we were so excited when we heard a psychiatrist of your stature was coming all the way out here, Doctor. We hoped you'd be able to find out what's been going on."

"So do I," she replied with a faint smile, the buzzing in her head growing worse during the conversation. She pushed her plate away from her, having barely touched its contents. "I don't really feel like eating," she said, pulling her chair back and standing up as steadily as she could.

"Heading back to your apartment?" Roy asked. "I'll go with you."

"No, I'm alright," Tselitel lied. "Stay here and chat for a while. I'm just going to look over a few of those case histories."

"Well, if you're sure, Doctor," Roy said, glad to stay and talk with the handsome Palmer.

Tselitel forced the best smile she could, and then walked

slowly back to her apartment. Upon reaching it she rested her head on the door and sighed, squeezing her eyes shut and gathering strength for the last few feet. She dug her key from her pocket and fought to get it inside the lock. The world was hazy and wobbly, as though she'd been drugged. Opening the door and forgetting the key in the lock, she slammed it behind her and stumbled to her bed, dropping onto it.

She looked up at the ceiling and saw little shapes form on its white surface. Spheres and squares drifted in and out of view, making her recall geometry class from years before. She blinked her eyes but they remained.

"*Am* I *going nuts?*" she thought, panic growing in her stomach and reaching up to seize her heart. It began to beat loudly in her ears, and she ruminated darkly on the irony of a psychiatrist going mad. She rolled onto her side and closed her eyes, still seeing the shapes against her eyelids.

Soon the world melted away around her, and she found herself floating in an expanse of darkness. She no longer saw the shapes, and the darkness was so thick she could scarcely see her own extremities. She drew her hands and feet close to verify they were still there.

As soon as she had done this the darkness evaporated and she was descending from the sky down to a thick forest of pines. Reaching the snowy ground below, her bare feet not at all shocked by the cold, she walked among the trees in a thin white dress. A wreath of bright flowers was in her hair, and everywhere her foot fell the snow disappeared and was replaced by green grass. Birds started to sing in the trees, and small, timid creatures began to peer at her from under the branches. She knelt on the ground and beckoned them to her. They were sickly and morose, moving slowly and with great hesitation. A beautiful song spontaneously came to her lips, and she began to sing. Hearing this the ailing animals found their courage, and came to her in droves. She knew at once that her purpose there was to heal them, and she reached out her hands and stroked their rough and tangled fur. Each creature she touched was revitalized, and they began to hop and dance through the trees.

But one stayed away, a little rabbit with dark eyes. She beckoned to it, but it averted its gaze, sniffing the east wind and watching for danger. Directing her song to the rabbit alone, she tried to draw near to it. But each step she took was matched by the rabbit, who soon disappeared.

A terror suddenly seized her, and all the other animals broke away in fear. The sky clouded over, and a terrible wind began to blow. The grass she had caused to sprout died and was covered with snow once more.

Despairing, she ran into the trees to search for the rabbit. Eventually the trees gave way to hedges of thorn bushes which surrounded her on every side. Looking around her every which way she found herself in a labyrinth of them. She walked down the first path she saw, and was soon terribly lost. For hours she walked but found no way out. Finally she sat down in a heap and began to cry.

Something stirred in the bushes behind her, but she was too distraught to bother looking. Tears ran down her face and dropped into the snow. Her body grew deathly cold, and she felt that she would soon freeze to death.

Suddenly a warm little nose brushed against her leg. She looked and saw the rabbit from before. He moved swiftly about her body, warming each place he touched until she had completely recovered from the cold. She took it up in her arms, but he fought her embrace until she put him down. He stood up on his hind legs proudly before her, and suddenly took on the shape of a man, though his face was impossible to make out. Offering her his hand, he led her to the thorn bushes and caused them to open before him. The snow had gone, and all around her was grass and flowers and living things. But just as joy filled her heart at the sight of these things, the man released her hand and collapsed into the grass. She rushed to his side and placed her hands on his chest. But he was dead, his body already cold.

Tselitel awoke in terror, her body soaked in sweat. The images of the dream vividly passed before her eyes. She fished around in the darkness for her tablet and wrote down every detail, and then followed with this commentary:

"I have no idea what any of this means. It seems I am supposed to bring health to the planet, but I can't do it by myself. There is a man here who I need to find, for according to the dream I cannot do my work alone. I will start – but something will turn it all to ash. Only by pushing myself to the very limit of life itself will I find him. It seems I will nearly die in the attempt. Nearly.

"But who could this man be? I mustn't have met him yet, or his face wouldn't have been blurry. No, he's a stranger to me.

"And why did he first appear as a rabbit? That's not a very impressive figure, especially for one who is apparently able to save my life. The rabbit must symbolize something about him.

"There is something oddly compelling about this dream. It feels real, like a message from the outside, and not just some fantasy cooked up in my own head."

She put away her tablet and turned on the light, its brightness hurting her eyes. Wandering into the kitchen, she washed her face in the sink to rinse away her grogginess.

At that moment the front door opened.

"Doctor, are you alright?" called Roy with alarm from the doorway.

"Of course," she replied, beginning to feel better than she had in days. She rounded the corner from the kitchen and looked into the lobby. "Why wouldn't I be?"

"You left your key in the lock," her assistant said, holding it up for her to see. When she saw the clear, calm look on her face her fears faded. "You look much better, Doctor. Did you rest for a while?"

"As a matter of fact, I did," replied Tselitel in a light mood. "I feel like a weight has been lifted off of me. But I had the strangest dream."

Over the next quarter of an hour Tselitel related everything she'd experienced, starting with the shapes she saw before losing consciousness and ending with the mysterious man's death.

"I wonder what it means," Tselitel mused afterwards.

"It doesn't mean anything," replied Roy simply. "You're just getting over your stay in the hospital. It makes sense you'd be out of sorts for a few days. It's normal for our waking experience to be reflected in our sleep. Life has been strange for you lately, and so you had a weird dream."

"Normally I'd agree with you," Tselitel said. "But this was so compelling, so visceral. Typically I can tell when I'm dreaming. But this felt more like a vision, though it was represented in an almost fairytale form. It really felt like someone was trying to communicate with me."

"Err, who would that be?" asked Roy with discomfort. Despite her general rationality, Tselitel had a streak of mysticism running through her personality that made the younger woman uneasy. It was one of the facets of her personality that Roy tried to keep from the public eye as much as possible. This statement, on top of her already rocky start on the planet, made her fear that coming to Delta-13 had been a mistake.

"Oh, I don't know," replied Tselitel, perceiving the strange look in her assistant's eye. "I'm sorry, I'm just running along at the mouth," she said, trying to backpedal.

"No, no I want you to say what's on your mind," replied Roy in a soothing, almost motherly tone. "I'm here to help you, Doctor, no matter what you're going through."

"Just forget what I said about the dream," Tselitel said with a chuckle, making light of it. "I only awoke a little while ago. I guess I'm still a little dreamy."

"I'm sure that's it," Roy said, nodding her head a little too vigorously. "Do you want to get some dinner now? I think they're closing the cafeteria in another hour."

"Sure, that sounds great," Tselitel said, happy to deflect attention from the dream. Following Roy into the hallway and locking her door, she wished she'd kept her mouth shut. *"Now she'll think* I'm *nuts!*" she thought, chiding herself.

CHAPTER 3

"You need to quit hanging around with loose cannons like Gromyko," Wellesley said to Hunt as they entered his shack over a week before Tselitel's dream. "He's gonna get you locked away if you keep this up. It's a wonder he hasn't been already."

"The man is an artist, Wellesley," replied Hunt, sliding the deadbolt shut on his flimsy door and taking off his helmet. He sat on the corner of a little wooden table and scratched his head. "The authorities will never catch him. He's got the instincts to survive."

"So do animals," replied Wellesley. "But a determined intellect can always hunt them down and kill them. It'll be the same with Gromyko."

"You sound almost like you *want* him to get caught," replied Hunt a little uneasily.

"I'm not *eager* for his demise," he replied. "But his way of life is so imbecilic that I can't help but scorn it. He lives on the edge purely for the thrill of it. I think he's part of the Underground just for the rush it gives him."

"Plenty of the things I do are for the thrills," Hunt observed, unzipping his environment suit and stepping out of it. "Does that mean you scorn me?"

The AI was silent.

"Wellesley?" he prodded, putting away his suit and dropping into a chair.

"It's different with you," he replied. "You do it for a

different reason."

"That being?"

"You're running from the past," replied Wellesley. "You're not a true thrill junky. You use it as therapy."

"That's absurd," replied Hunt, the AI hitting a little too close to the mark for comfort.

"I can detect it when you put yourself in danger," Wellesley continued, ignoring Hunt's reply. "There's a subtle hesitation right before you jump in, like you're wondering if it's really a good idea or not. Gromyko doesn't hesitate because he *needs* risk in order to feel alive. You do it to escape your life, to feel something greater than yourself for a few brief moments. The powerful impulse to live connects you to the innumerable humans who have gone before you and passed those impulses on to you. You're participating in an instinctual community in order to escape your troubles."

"I haven't got any more trouble than the next guy in Midway," countered Hunt. "Why don't they do it, then?"

"Because there's something different about you," replied the AI. "Truth be told, you remind me of my last master, *Kalak-Beyn*. He was a great warrior, but impulsive like you. He needlessly fell in single combat towards the end of the *Kol-Prockian* civil war."

"And you think I'm gonna follow in his footsteps?"

"I think you're heading in the right direction for that," said Wellesley. "Gromyko is a mercenary, plain and simple. He organized the Underground because it facilitates his smuggling and gives him contacts that he couldn't otherwise get. He'll use you, or anyone else, to further himself. And if it ever comes to a choice between him and you, he'll toss you out like a rotten piece of meat."

"Then how do you explain him sticking his neck out for me tonight?" Hunt countered. "He ran the same risks I did. He could have gotten caught right along with me."

"Oh, he had to look after his best supplier of artifacts," the AI said dismissively. "It was just business."

"Maybe so," replied Hunt, growing too tired to argue anymore. "But it saved our skins all the same."

Slipping the medallion off his neck, he laid it on the table and stretched out on his bed. For hours he'd felt an oppressive weight inside his head. Too much time in the cold sometimes did that to him, and he regretted the headache he'd have in the morning.

Soon he was asleep.

Day followed day with very little to differentiate them. He worked mechanically in the greenhouse, grinding through his tasks without enthusiasm. The other workers did the same, lacking the motivation to do more than the minimum required in order to survive.

Hunt looked at the gray, lackluster faces that labored around him, and he began to understand more fully the appeal that Gromyko held. With his dashing manner and larger than life personality he gave them something to hope for, even if they felt deep down it was just a fantasy. Most of them believed it was their lot in life to suffer, and they saw no reason to try and overcome fate. Some people were born to success, and some to failure, and there was no point, in their estimation, in trying to beat their destiny.

Hunt reflected on Wellesley's words of several days before, when he said there was something different about him. He'd always felt it instinctively, but tended to write it off as youthful egotism, the desire to see himself as uniquely special. He felt it was just a fantasy of his own, a soothing tale he could tell himself whenever life got to be overwhelming. But there *was* something different about him, a subtle subcurrent in his temperament that kept him from being broken like all the rest.

They could accept a bleak, pointless existence – one that had been chosen without their consent.

But something reared up within Hunt at the thought, and he wanted to lash out, to strike those who had taken his life from him and consigned him to Delta-13. But he had learned to conceal such thoughts, to keep them well hidden behind an outward mask of dull acceptance like the others. Even his supervisor, a sympathetic man in the government's employ, hadn't the slightest idea what violent emotions agitated his heart and disturbed his sleep at night.

"Someday I'll make them pay," he mumbled, pulling ripe vegetables out of the soil and dropping them a little too sharply into a nearby bucket.

"Hey, easy with those, Rex," said Sergo Perkons, the man who oversaw the massive greenhouse in which Hunt worked. "We don't want them bruised."

"Of course, sir," replied Hunt in a bland voice. "I'm sorry, Mr. Perkons."

"How many times have I said you could call me Sergo, Rex?" asked the friendly manager, leaning against the raised plant bed and smiling at him. He was about twenty years older than Hunt, and married to a nurse in the prison hospital. Perkons always tried to build rapport with the younger workers in the greenhouse, seeing them as his children and treating them with as much indulgence as his position afforded, which wasn't much. "I wish we could be friends, Rex. You're a good worker. You never give me any trouble at all."

"Yes, Mr. Perkons," Hunt said.

"Is there something troubling you?" he asked, lowering his voice confidentially, trying to open a channel for Hunt to speak. "If you need to get off a little early today I can swing it. We've got a few more hands than we really need."

"No, that's alright, Mr. Perkons," Hunt replied, keeping the same air of formal distance as ever. "I thank you anyway."

"Well, alright," the manager said, unsatisfied but certain he couldn't make any more headway. He patted him on the shoulder and strode away.

"He's a good man," Wellesley communicated through his skin. "Too bad he's on the other side."

"We often end up in situations that don't suit us," replied Hunt, continuing to pull up vegetables. "It's one of the facts of life."

Wellesley thought about this but didn't reply. Ever since that day dodging the curfew Hunt had been moody and depressed, and it worried the AI. Something was working on him, but even his enormous experience couldn't reveal what it was. He resolved to watch Hunt very carefully for any other signs that might shed light on his condition.

"Want to head to a tavern this evening?" Wellesley asked uncharacteristically, trying to brighten his mood. "Maybe have a few quiet laughs and a drink?"

"I don't think so," Hunt replied almost inaudibly, as several other workers moved closer in the course of their duties and prevented further discussion.

A blizzard that had been threatening the area since early morning finally rolled in an hour before dark, blasting freezing winds down the streets and dropping an enormous amount of snow. People could scarcely see ten feet in front of their faces, and had to wade slowly along, groping buildings as they went. Children were strictly kept off the streets to prevent them being lost and frozen in minutes.

"Alright, people," Perkons said as the blizzard grew worse. "I'm cutting the work day short. Get home while it's still light. Be as quick as you can, and stick together for as long as possible. We don't want to lose anyone out there. Good night."

With this the workers put down their tools and made for the lockers that held their outdoor clothes. Patched jackets, gloves with missing fingers, and boots that were too large were common. Hunt's side income allowed him to purchase black market goods a cut above what the rest could afford, and he always felt ashamed at his relative prosperity compared to the others.

Slowly they all filed towards the door, none of them leaving until the entire group was ready. Then, as a mass, they proceeded down the street, losing a few people every block as people reached their homes and got out of the cold. This would continue until the group disintegrated with the last worker reaching his door.

The worker in question was an old man named Ugo Udris, a quiet fellow who kept to himself. None of the others really knew him, and many spun theories about what he was really like. Hunt liked him for some indefinable reason, and decided to stick with him until he made it home, bypassing his own house.

"You don't need to come along," he shouted over the wind, pausing momentarily. "I'll get home alright."

"I'd prefer it this way, if you don't mind," Hunt said deferentially, careful not to wound the man's pride.

"I'm alright, you go on home. It's too cold for charity."

Udris started walking again, and Hunt trailed along behind him. He glanced over his shoulder, saw him following, and shrugged his acquiescence.

The wind stung Hunt's skin, numbing his cheeks and making it hard to breathe. Drawing a tubular cloth mask up from his neck and around his face and the back of his head, he fixed his eyes on the old man's jacket and strode determinedly through the mounting drifts.

"Come on in for a minute," Udris said once they'd reached his place. "You must be half frozen by now."

Hunt was pressed for time, the dim light fading fast. He calculated that he could just make it home if he left that very second. But, chilled to the bone, and unwilling to offend the old man's hospitality, he mutely followed him into his dark abode, a modest house which smelled sweetly of flowers.

"Take your things off and relax a while," Udris said, pulling off his stocking cap and sitting down with a sigh in a beaten up old wooden chair near the door. Hunt watched as he pulled off his boots and stood up, shaking off the snow that still clung to his jacket and pants.

"I really should get back, Mr. Udris," Hunt said. "It'll be dark soon, and I need to get home before the snow gets any worse."

"This blizzard is gonna be a nasty one, son," Udris said, fixing his cool blue eyes on him. "I wouldn't want to set foot out in it again, not until it passes in the morning. No, you'd better stay here for the night. "

"What makes you think it'll pass by morning?" Hunt asked, as he reluctantly slipped off his boots and jacket.

"Call it an old man's intuition," replied the old man with a wink. "I've seen enough of Delta's weather to feel its ebb and flow in my bones. Now, come on. My granddaughter will fix you something hot to drink."

"Granddaughter?" Wellesley asked, echoing Hunt's thoughts. Everyone at the greenhouse *knew* the old hermit lived alone. He'd made no friends there, and most of the workers thought he didn't even like people. Always eating his lunch alone, he'd sit in a corner and unobtrusively watch the others chat about their lives, never joining in.

Hunt followed Udris deeper inside, savoring the warm, homey atmosphere after being in the cold. A distinct feminine touch was visible in the decor.

"Brought company with me, honey," Udris said, walking into the kitchen and hugging a plump female. She held him tight for a moment, and then looked around him to see who the guest was who stood in the doorway.

"Wanda?" Hunt exclaimed at the same time as Wellesley. The last person he expected to see was the fleshy tapster. Her black hair tumbled down her back in a long, unruly flow. A bright smile formed on her lips, revealing a gap between her two front teeth.

"Hi, Rex," she said happily, striding quickly towards him and giving him a hug.

"I didn't know you two were related," Hunt said awkwardly as she released him.

"Most people don't. And I try to keep it that way," said the old man, his lanky form sauntering into the back of the kitchen.

"He likes his privacy," Wanda said confidentially.

"Yes, I do," Udris said loudly to show he'd heard her. "It's a precious thing. You can never get it back once you lose it. And *everyone* is trying to take it from you."

Wanda made a face to Hunt, indicating that it wasn't the first time the old man had held forth on the virtues of privacy.

"I'm sorry if I've intruded," Hunt said hesitantly. "I didn't mean to–"

"Oh, I didn't mean to include you in that remark, son," replied Udris, returning to the doorway for a moment, holding a teapot. "I was just commenting generally. Go into the den and sit down. There's something I want to talk to you about, once I set the tea to boiling."

"Right in there," Wanda mouthed, pointing to the next room and patting his shoulder.

Hunt ambled into the next room and sat in the first chair he saw. A long, ratty couch ran along one wall, and a fireplace stood in front of the other. The back of the room had a window that had been shuttered against the storm.

"Wonder what the old codger's got to say," Wellesley said.

Before Hunt could respond Udris entered the room and sat on the couch.

"Young man, I get to the point when I've got something on my mind," Udris said.

"Yes, sir," replied Hunt, unsure what else to say.

"You don't need to be so formal," Udris said. "Just call me Ugo. I'll call you Rex."

"Yes, sir–. I mean Ugo," Hunt stumbled.

"He isn't going to eat you," Wellesley chided. "Just take it easy."

"We've had our eye on you for a long time," Ugo began, leaning forward and resting his elbows on his knees. "But you've hesitated an awfully long time."

"Sir?" asked Hunt.

"There are some of us who feel that things need to change on Delta-13. Change in a big way," replied Ugo. "We're well aware of your activities in service of the Underground.

But you've been half-hearted in your actions against the government. We want you to commit, to really get behind it."

"You're a part of the Underground?" asked Hunt, surprised at the thought.

"Heh, no," replied the old man, shaking his head as though the idea was ridiculous. "The Underground is too...immature for us. Our organization is much older, and much better run. We don't content ourselves with talking about rebellion in taverns."

"Doesn't Wanda work with the Underground?" Hunt asked, sensing an incongruity.

"Yes, but just to keep tabs on them," she replied, walking into the room and taking a seat beside her grandfather. "We need to know if they're planning anything that might double back on us. They're reckless and impulsive – when they act at all. They're a constant risk for us. At any time they could drive the government to clamp down hard on Midway."

"The aim of our organization is to bring to light the activities of the government on Delta-13, and force a change in how things are done on Earth. We seek nothing short of a power change at home."

"On Earth?" repeated Hunt, incredulous. "But that's–"

"Ridiculous?" anticipated Ugo. "Not at all. Support for the government is at an all-time low. Its draconian policies are costing it supporters every day. Sure, the central worlds are doing fine. But the middle planets are growing uncomfortable with its one-sided use of power. And the fringe is worse off now than it has ever been. The latter of these two segments is ripe for rebellion. And we're confident that the middle worlds will start to waver when they see that even rustics such as ourselves are capable of standing up and telling the government no."

"He's nuts," commented Wellesley, his attitude conservative as always. "You can't push over the government because of the mistreatment of a few prisoners on an ice cube nobody cares about."

"Isn't that going to be tough?" asked Hunt, translating the AI's words into a more polite form. "Most people don't care about what happens this far out."

"They do if the authorities are experimenting with mind control to shore up their support," Ugo said.

The room was dead silent for several moments.

"That's what we're up against, Rex," Wanda said in a tone of appeal. "That's why we need your help."

"If we can get proof of this off of Delta-13, spread it around the fringe and the middle worlds, they'll ignite like a pile of matches," Ugo continued. "But the proof has to be ironclad. There can't be the *slightest* doubt of its legitimacy, or the whole thing will fall flat."

"Even the *Kol-Prockians* couldn't get mind control to work," Wellesley said. "And their insights into the nature of the psyche were much greater than anything humanity has yet achieved. I don't think there's anything to worry about on that score."

"Would you stop listening to *Allokanah* for a few minutes and pay attention to what I'm saying?" asked Ugo with annoyance, seeing the far away look in Hunt's eyes as he listened to the AI – a look that was suddenly replaced with one of shock and alarm.

"Yes, I know about your AI," the old man continued. "We've known for quite some time. We don't contact someone without spending a *lot* of time monitoring him first. If the authorities were as effective as we are, you'd already be serving time for a half dozen different violations."

"But how did you know his name?" asked Hunt, slowly recovering from the shock.

"You may not know this, but he's actually a very famous AI, servant to the warlord *Kalak-Beyn*. He led the *Boe* faction in their civil war."

"Yes, I know," replied Hunt, nodding his head. "He was put into hibernation after the battle of *Prossoc*, where *Kalak-Beyn* was killed."

"Is that what he told you?" Ugo asked significantly.

"Yes," replied Hunt, his tone uncertain.

"There's a little more to the story than that," replied the old man. "You see, he didn't always serve the *Boe* faction. He started out as a very effective member of the *Rhee* half of their war. To oversimplify enormously, the *Rhee* faction favored a centralized system of government, rather like we have now. The *Kol-Prockians* had been governed by a loose confederation since time out of mind. They valued the autonomy of their worlds almost to the point of anarchy. It served them pretty well while they were more or less alone among the stars. But contact with other races soon put pressure on them that their system couldn't grapple with. Their fringe worlds began suffering raids from these other races, and the system as a whole didn't respond."

"Why?" asked Hunt.

"Oh, politics and local envy," replied Ugo with a wave of his hand. "You see, each world in their confederation had an equal vote in their *Rheauum*, or senate. And each world maintained its own local defense forces. To combat the raiders and help the fringe worlds would have required the planets farther in to surrender some of their military might to a centralized command structure that would conduct the war. This would have weakened their standing while simultaneously giving an enormous amount of power to a combined fleet that none of them alone could control. It seemed like a recipe for a military dictatorship and they put it off for years. This was easy, since only the fringe worlds were suffering. The older, more prosperous inner planets of their confederation were strong enough to repel any incursion, and so few were made.

"I don't understand," replied Hunt, shaking his head. "How did this lead to the civil war?"

"I'm getting to that," replied the old man with an impatient frown. "A movement began to grow among the outer worlds for a different form of government, one that would rule over all the planets of the confederation, drawing their military forces into a single command for the defense of all. An empire was what they sought, with a single ruler who would feel the insults to any part of his realm equally. The movement spread quickly through the fringe, where attacks, and casualties, were mounting daily. Some in the inner worlds were alarmed. But most felt it was just hot air from a bunch of backwater rubes, and so did nothing. It wasn't until the fever began to spread to the middle planets that they were moved to act."

"Assembling two great fleets, they paraded through the middle worlds to scare them back into line. They succeeded in this, and the middle worlds that had favored an empire reverted to support for the confederation."

"But the fringe was outraged by this act. The inner worlds had shown themselves willing to submit to the necessity of combining their forces, but only in defense of their own prerogatives. Many also felt that the fleets assembled would soon be turned against them, as the breeding ground of empire. Thus they met in secret, and formed the *E-Poh-Annah*, or Imperium of the Fringe. Governed by a single leader, a reckless warlord named *Koln*, they assembled their fleet, a ragtag assemblage of older vessels and converted merchantmen."

"Naturally the worlds of the confederation sent a fleet out to crush *Koln*. But they were defeated in a surprise attack, many of their vessels surrendering with scarcely a struggle. You see, the navies of the confederation worlds were strong, but inexperienced, having fought very little. Essentially they were ceremonial forces, with most of their sailors, and many of their officers, almost completely green. Meanwhile the fringe planets had been battling pirates and raiders for years, and consequently had an enormous amount of combat experience. They were outgunned by the inner worlds, but their understanding of space warfare was nothing short of masterful."

"*Koln*, and his subordinates, drove the confederation forces far into the middle worlds, building a base of support that soon encompassed nearly half of *Kol-Prockian* space. During this time, *Allokanah* was the able assistant that made all of *Koln's* plans possible. He was a master of logistics and management, doing all the behind-the-scenes work necessary to keep the impulsive *Koln* winning battle after battle. Without *Allokanah* to lean on, there is no doubt *Koln* would have failed long before he drove the confederation fleets out of the fringe."

"To shorten this story a bit," Ugo said, "the civil war raged for decades. The confederation finally found an effective leader in *Kalak-Beyn*, and began to stem the tide. The industrial might of the central worlds began to tell, and the improving skill of their warriors finally equaled that of their brethren from the fringe. Slowly the latter were driven back, but with massive losses. It was at this time that *Allokanah* defected from the imperium to the confederation for reasons that the historical record does not make clear. He provided *Kalak-Beyn* with a masterful plan to break the imperium in pieces. Pinning down *Koln's* forces in a series of complex battles, he had his most trusted commander slip behind enemy lines with a modest fleet and conduct a scorched-earth campaign that savaged the shipyards that supported *Koln's* forces. Any loss on that score would be devastating, since the fringe had so little capacity to replace the damage done. This broke the back of the imperium, and *Koln* saw his support collapse around him. It's an open question who would have won the war had things continued as they began. But the treachery of *Allokanah* sealed the imperium's fate."

"Delta-13 had long been a holy world to the *Kol-Prockians*, and *Koln*, seeing the writing on the wall, decided to fight his final battle there. Instead of waging a one-sided battle in space, *Koln* appealed to an ancient *Kol-Prockian* custom, whereby an outgunned commander could ask for a battle between a fixed number of combatants. The two sides would then agree to terms to be carried out in the event of one or the other's victory, and select their forces for the engagement. The armies would fight with ancient, ceremonial weapons."

"*Koln* requested permission to flee *Kol-Prockian* space with the rest of his fleet in the event of his victory. *Kalak-Beyn* agreed to this, provided the former would peaceably disband his forces and surrender himself should he lose."

"They met on the frozen surface of Delta-13 and fought a fierce battle, both sides having brought the cream of their forces. The sun went down on their conflict, and arose the next day without a winner. Bodies were strewn across the snow, their blood discoloring it. Finally *Koln* asked for a brief ceasefire, and proposed that the two commanders meet in single combat to spare their brave followers any more suffering. This the noble *Kalak-Beyn* agreed to immediately, unwilling that any more should die."

"The two commanders fought, but *Koln* was the superior warrior and killed his opponent after a brief struggle. Seeing the medallion of *Allokanah* around his neck, he lifted it from the corpse of his fallen foe and held it for a moment. His anger rose within him as he thought of the AI's betrayal, and he considered destroying it then and there. But then he remembered how the imperium had only risen with the AI's help, and how it could never have made a stand without it. In recognition of this service, he spared the traitor's life, but consigned him to a tomb buried deep in the snow of Delta-13. We know this, for he explained it to some of *Kalak-Beyn's* surviving warriors, though he hid the medallion only after they'd departed. Centuries passed before he was dug up by a pair of human treasure seekers, who ended up fighting over him and killing each other, leaving him in the snow for you to eventually find, Rex."

This revelation stunned Hunt, who sat mute for several moments as it sank in. The old man could see the conflict written on his face as he processed what he'd heard and weighed it against what the AI had already told him.

Wanda gazed into his face with sympathy, feeling sorry

for the ordeal he was going through. She longed to reach out and touch his hand, offering any support she could. But she knew her grandfather would never tolerate that and restrained herself. His was a harsh school of thought, where the best lessons hit hard and fast.

"Well, what do you think?" Ugo asked after a couple of minutes had passed in silence.

"I want to talk with Wellesley for a moment," Hunt said, rising from his seat and leaving the room without looking at his hosts. He reached the lobby where his snowy boots were leaving a puddle on the floor and stopped, gazing through a window into the blizzard that still raged outside.

"Why did you turn traitor?" asked Hunt somberly. "Why did you betray the people who depended on you most?"

"Because they couldn't win," replied the AI matter-of-factly. "They had a chance, up until *Kalak-Beyn* finally got the confederation's forces whipped into shape. From the beginning of the war until that point, they could have attacked the inner worlds and broken the confederation for good. They should have struck hard and without mercy, waging the kind of scorched-earth campaign that I later advised their enemies to carry out. Had they done so, had they shattered the industrial base of the inner planets before it could be organized against them, they couldn't have helped winning. But *Koln* was as archaic in his thinking as he was reckless as a commander. He couldn't accept what needed to be done and insisted on keeping the fighting away from the civilian population. This allowed the inner worlds to fall back on their factories to make good the losses their incompetent leaders forced upon them. Eventually *Kalak-Beyn* was elected to the supreme command, and when that happened the war was over. The most merciful thing for the *Kol-Prockian* people was to end it swiftly, which I helped them do."

"And this doesn't bother you at all?" demanded Hunt, finding his pragmatic tone offensive.

"Of course it bothers me," retorted Wellesley. "It's

tortured me every moment of my life since then. But what else was I to do? Spare my conscience while untold millions died from the war? Would that have truly been the right course? How could I, who was built to serve the *Kol-Prockian* people to the best of my ability, let them rip themselves apart needlessly to spare myself guilt? I only had one option before me and I took it. I would take it again, even if it destroyed me to do so. By the time I switched sides the fringe had lost its chance to establish an empire, and further loss of blood was pointless. The imperium was the last chance for unity they had, and I desperately wanted it to succeed. The *Kol-Prockian* people were surrounded by races that were rapidly maturing, in both technology and ambition, and they needed a central government that could protect all of their planets equally, not playing favorites with the inner worlds. But *Koln* was a romantic warrior. Noble, indeed. But a dreamer, altogether lacking the practical hard-headedness needed to win. He considered himself a kind of knight-errant – a warrior seizing opportunities to demonstrate his honor. He lacked the ruthlessness needed to break his foes, and shrank back from what needed to be done. And in that he doomed the *Kol-Prockians* to suffer endlessly the depredations of their neighbors. It was these very neighbors who finally broke them, shattering the confederation navy several centuries later, and carrying away the population into slavery. That was the end of the *Kol-Prockians* as a major race in the galaxy."

"You've suffered a great deal from this," Hunt replied thoughtfully, his tone softer than before.

"More than I can express," said the AI. "It would have been kinder of *Koln* to have destroyed me after he defeated *Kalak-Beyn*, instead of leaving me to be haunted by ancient memories."

"It takes courage to do wrong for the right reasons," Hunt said.

"Indeed it does."

Hunt thought about this for a moment, and then

returned to the den where his hosts were waiting.

"I've heard his explanation," he said, taking his seat once more. "And I'm satisfied with it."

"Alright," replied Ugo, nodding slowly. "And what do you think of my proposal? Are you ready to join us?"

"No, not yet," replied Hunt, shaking his head. "My head is spinning and I need time to think."

"There *is* no time to think!" barked Ugo. "We're up against a brick wall with no way around it. We can't afford to have you dragging your feet a moment longer."

"Then I bid you both goodnight," Hunt said formally, ignoring the old man's outburst and making for the door. He had just grasped his jacket when he heard Wanda quickly approach him from behind and put a gentle hand on his arm, slowly turning him around.

"I'm sorry about that," she said sincerely. "He gets overwrought these days. He barely sleeps anymore. His work keeps him up all night. And then he has his shift in the greenhouse, too. It's an awful lot for an old man."

"It's an awful lot for anyone to endure," replied Hunt knowingly, sliding his arms into his jacket and bending over for his boots. "I don't hold it against him."

"Then please stay," she pleaded, grasping his jacket and pulling him upright. "The blizzard is too fierce to be chanced tonight. And your jacket and boots are wet from your last walk in it. It would be dangerous to head out now."

"She's right, Rex," Ugo said, rounding the corner from the den and walking slowly towards them. "I-I'm sorry for what I said," he added reluctantly, his pride too large to be easily swallowed. "Of course you need time to mull things over. I've given you a lot to think about."

"You have," agreed Hunt, looking at the older man. "But I'll not be pushed on. Not here or anywhere else. Either I'm free to make up my own mind, or I walk."

"You're free. Absolutely free," replied Ugo, nodding as he spoke. "You'll get no more pressure from me."

"Then I'll stay," he said, a smile slowly crossing his face.

"Oh, good!" Wanda said emphatically, clasping her hands happily. "I think it's time for dinner. I'll have it whipped up in a flash," she said, bustling off to the kitchen while Hunt slid out of his jacket.

"You really would have gone out there, wouldn't you?" Ugo asked as Hunt hung his jacket on a nail near the door.

"Absolutely," he replied stoutly to remove any lingering doubts the old man might have had.

"You've got principle, nobody can gainsay that," said the old man. "We could really use a man like you."

"Remember what I just said," Hunt cautioned him.

"Oh, I'm not putting the heat on you," replied Ugo. "I'm just commenting. Come into the den. I want to show you something."

Hunt followed the lanky man back into the den and sat where he indicated on the couch. He drew a small object from a jar on the fireplace and sat next to him.

"I was given this by my father," he said, turning the small gold disc over in his hand several times. "He was one of the first human residents of Delta-13."

"A prisoner?" Hunt asked.

"No, I mean a resident, like we are. His wife was implicated in a plot against the government and they sent her here. The family policy wasn't as harsh then as it is now. But he elected to come so he could be near her. He was a scrounger like you, digging up artifacts whenever he could. That's where this came from."

"What does it do?"

"Hold it and find out," the old man said mysteriously, a grin forming on his lips.

Accepting the challenge, Hunt grasped the disc. He felt his mind broaden in some indefinable way, like his awareness was expanding. Suddenly the house didn't seem to contain him anymore, and he felt as though the whole planet was speaking to him, relaying what was going on at every point on its surface. He said as much to Ugo.

"You're very perceptive," Ugo said approvingly, taking the disc back and setting it on a small table in front of the couch. "Most people don't notice anything when they hold it. It's an ancient relic from the *Kol-Prockian* priests who used to practice here. Like I said before, Delta-13 was a holy world for them, the only one they recognized."

"I don't understand," replied Hunt, confused by his experience. "Does the object enhance your perception?"

"No, dear boy," laughed Ugo. "It connects you to the planet."

"But a planet is just rock and plants. There's nothing to connect with."

"You're absolutely right," agreed Ugo. "In most cases, that is. But some worlds are different. Some are *intelligent!* They can think and communicate, Rex. They're ancient, of course. Incomparably ancient. The things they've seen and heard," he uttered wistfully, savoring the thought of getting ahold of all that knowledge. "But they often keep quiet. Only rarely do they reveal themselves, even to the pure-hearted. It seems to be a principle of theirs not to interfere with the normal workings of our lives. But occasionally someone sniffs one out, and manages to open a dialogue. I'm not aware of anyone ever learning *how* a planet can live. Maybe there's a kind of nerve center deep beneath the surface. But one way or another, it sometimes communicates with those sensitive enough to listen." He pointed at the disc. "Your experience just now proves that you're one of them. I'm certain it's been working on you for quite some time, though in the background. It tends to approach people through their unconscious minds."

"Is it good or bad?" asked Hunt, alarmed at the idea of such an invasive presence in his psyche.

"Neither. The planet is a healer, and tries to help those who live upon it achieve balance," replied Ugo. "It helps the conscious and the unconscious relate to each other. You see, they tend to exist semi-autonomously in most people. The planet has a great capacity to heal those who are hurting, if they approach it correctly. That's why the *Kol-Prockian* priests thought it was a holy world: it helped them achieve wholeness."

At this moment Wanda broke up their discussion by calling them to dinner.

Hours later, climbing into the bed his hosts had provided for him, Hunt pulled the covers over his body and looked up at the ceiling.

"You've been quiet all night," he said to Wellesley.

"Haven't had anything to say," the AI replied. "Where do we stand?"

"Same as always," he said with a grin. "You did right as you saw it, at tremendous personal cost. I don't see any reason to change things now."

"Good," replied Wellesley, a subtle note of relief in his voice.

"Why, would you miss me if we parted ways?" asked Hunt with a chuckle.

"Well, I've gotten used to you," said the AI grudgingly. "You're kind of fun when you're not being moody."

"I'll try to be sunnier from now on."

"That reminds me," said the AI. "What *has* come over you the last few days? You've never been this blue."

"Oh, I don't know," replied Hunt, running a hand through his hair. "Ever since that night with Antonin I haven't felt the same. It's as though I'm sinking into some kind of dark pool. I just feel depressed and heavy, like there's a lot of responsibility suddenly on my shoulders."

"Responsibility for what?" asked Wellesley.

"I haven't the slightest idea!" exclaimed Hunt, exasperated at his own ignorance. "It's just a feeling I have. Who knows, maybe it's the planet, based on what Ugo has been saying."

"Could be," mused the AI quietly. "And this sense of

responsibility, it bothers you?"

"It does," admitted Hunt. "It really does. I don't know how to get out from under it."

"Maybe that's not the answer," replied Wellesley. "Maybe you just have to accept it."

"I think it would kill me to do that," replied Hunt. "I don't think there's anything so crushing as the burden of responsibility without any kind of reward in sight. I mean, what possible reason would there be for me to take up that kind of load?"

"Everybody's got to find their own reason in a case like that," said Wellesley. "There's no one answer that suits everyone."

"Well, I don't think there's any answer that will suit me," replied Hunt, rolling onto his side. "I'm not the responsible type."

Soon he was asleep, leaving the AI to his thoughts. He'd noted the change in his friend first with concern, and then with ever growing curiosity. A change *had* come over him, a significant one. But it seemed to be taking time for it to fight its way to consciousness. Like a shadow standing behind him and whispering in his ear, it was influencing him without being seen. It would take time for it to manifest itself, to become a visible, palpable part of his life. For now it would guide him like fate, leading him to places he'd never been before.

Wellesley had seen it before, in the early days when *Koln* was undecided about the rebellion. He had consciously vacillated for a long time, trying to balance the pros and cons while fate was guiding him helplessly towards the cause he eventually espoused. It was the unconscious mind, that semi-autonomous element that Ugo had mentioned earlier. As it had seized control of *Koln's* life, so now it was making itself felt in Hunt's life, directing him towards a cause that would add meaning to his gray existence. For a long time the AI had feared his impulsive companion would succumb to his surroundings as his fellows had done, eventually ground down by the hopelessness around him. Once the sprightliness of youth had left him, he felt sure Hunt would lose his spirit. He feared it was starting to happen when Hunt fell into his present funk.

But the words of Ugo reminded him of *Koln's* experience, and he kicked himself for not thinking of it sooner. The young man was not *sinking*, he was undergoing a transformation. An old attitude was dying in him, and a period of mourning for it was appropriate. That was the cause of his depression. Soon a better version would emerge, Wellesley felt sure. One that had finally cast off the reckless naivete of youth and replaced it with the certainty and purposefulness of a mature man.

"It was the war that finally matured Koln," the AI thought with satisfaction. *"Soon another war, a war of the mind, will do the same for Rex."*

CHAPTER 4

"I've been interviewing the mutes for days. But I can't get even a spark of recognition out of them. I've tried every technique I can think of. Absolutely nothing works."

Tselitel put down her tablet and exhaled with exasperation. She sat at the counter that divided her kitchen and living room, a beige wooden stool beneath her. Getting up and walking to the large window that faced the prison she mused on her experience.

"Everything, absolutely everything," she repeated in a whisper, letting her mind drift over the inmates.

"Almost everything," she suddenly heard within her head.

She shook her head and clasped her hands behind her back.

"No, that's not the answer," she replied.

Tselitel had the peculiar ability to occasionally hold a dialogue within her head, as though another personality had taken up residence beside hers. This, she recognized, was just another part of her own mind, a segment that often took up the opposing view to that which she consciously held. It had an annoying tendency to cut through her rationalistic excuses with simple, elegant intuitions.

"Everything else has failed," it said. "You owe it to your patients to try it."

Tselitel frowned. She'd hoped it wouldn't make the one

argument she couldn't resist. But knowing her as well as she did herself, it couldn't possibly miss the bullseye.

"Try it," the voice persisted.

"You know I can't do that!" she exclaimed helplessly. "They'll never understand the reason for it. They'll say I've lost my *own* mind, and I've taken to scribbling on the walls. I'll be the laughingstock of the entire prison!"

"Er, who are you talking to, Doctor?" asked Roy from the kitchen. Tselitel had been so absorbed that she hadn't heard her enter. The young assistant stood doubtfully looking at her chief. Her concern for her hadn't slackened as the days passed. She noticed little changes that the doctor tried in vain to hide, and they were building into a very dark picture in her mind. In the cafeteria she often withdrew into her own head, ignoring Roy's attempts at conversation and mumbling things under her breath. Twice she'd absentmindedly gone into her assistant's apartment instead of her own, so absorbed was she in her work.

And now she was holding full-fledged conversations with herself in her living room, pleading with unseen people.

"Oh, Sadie," Tselitel said, her face flushing. "I was just trying a...new therapeutic technique that I thought might help with the mutes."

"I don't think anything can help them," replied Roy, unconvinced by her dodge but willing to play along for the time being. "They're like stone, Doctor. Nothing can reach them anymore.

"They're human beings, Sadie," countered Tselitel. "They have senses just like you and I. They *can* be reached. We just have to figure out how. I think they must be overwhelmed by some inner experience that is drowning out every other sensation, like holding a radio against your ear while someone is talking. They don't look *vacant*, just impossibly distracted. I don't know...It's just an intuition I have."

"Intuition has very little to do with science, Doctor," replied Roy, plunking down on a stool. "As scientists we have to deal with what can be rationally understood. Otherwise psychiatry degenerates into subjective mysticism, and the psychiatrist who practices it becomes nothing more than a witch doctor."

"No, Sadie, as scientists we must grapple with *what exists*, whether or not it conforms to rational laws as we conceive them," corrected Tselitel, taking the stool next to her. "It's not enough to fill our minds with intellectual laws. We must always be willing to grow and change."

"But the mind is such a fluid, uncertain thing," countered Roy. "We'll get lost if we go venturing into dark paths. There's probably nothing so difficult to plumb as the human psyche."

"The moment we're too afraid to explore is the very same moment we need to give up calling ourselves 'scientists' and undertake another profession," replied Tselitel, her emotions rising. "Something more suitable to a timid spirit."

"Yes, Doctor," replied Roy submissively, trying to calm her. Inwardly she was alarmed, but did her best not to show it. Brightening her demeanor and changing the subject, she asked, "Have you had anything to eat yet?"

"No, nothing," replied Tselitel, shaking her head and looking distracted. "I'm too busy to think of that right now. I-I need to get back to work."

"Yes, Doctor," Roy said again, nodding slowly and leaving her alone in the apartment. She closed the door and looked at it for a moment, and then mumbled, "I hope it's nothing serious."

"Hope what isn't serious?" asked a voice from behind her. She jumped and turned to see Warden Kelbauskas standing behind her with a concerned look on his face.

"Oh, Joris," she said, placing a hand on her heart. "You scared me."

"I'm sorry," he replied solicitously. "I was just coming to see if you two ladies would join me for dinner tonight. I was thinking about a small dinner party in my apartment, with just the three of us. It would give us a chance to get to know each other a little better, and discuss your recent work more closely. I'm eager to hear first hand what progress you've made."

"I'd love to, Joris," Roy said with a warm smile. "But I'm afraid Doctor Tselitel isn't feeling like it this evening." Concern unconsciously flashed across her face as she glanced back at the doctor's door for a moment. Then, brightening, "She's much too preoccupied with her work right now to take any time off."

"Perhaps the two of us, then?" offered Kelbauskas.

"That sounds perfect," replied Roy, her heartbeat increasing.

"Great! I'm in apartment 233. Will an hour from now be alright?"

"That'll be perfect."

"Then I'll see you there," he replied happily, smiling at her a moment longer than strictly necessary before turning away.

She watched him walk back towards the lobby and disappear around a corner. Her first urge was to tell Tselitel, who had always been her confidant. Her hand touched the knob, and then she withdrew it.

"No, better not," she thought. *"Who knows what that might do to her. She doesn't like Joris."* Instead she went into her apartment next door and prepared for her evening alone with the warden.

An hour later she clacked the little knocker that hung from the center of his door, just above the peephole. She was dressed in a pleasant light pink dress and heels, her hair tied back in a ponytail. He opened the door and brightened visibly.

"Sadie, you look marvelous," he said with enthusiasm. He wore a dark blue polo, with black slacks and dress shoes.

"So do you," she said approvingly.

For the next two hours they ate and chatted casually, enjoying each other's company immensely. Neither wanted to get to the subject of the inmates, though that was the ostensible reason for the meeting. Eventually Kelbauskas brought it up, and the light, joyful attitude on Roy's face vanished in an instant.

"I'm sorry, I didn't mean to bring you down," he said with concern.

"Oh, it's not you," replied Roy quickly. "I'm just, well, I'm concerned about Doctor Tselitel."

"What's the matter?" he asked. "Is she still suffering from her fall in the snow?"

"Perhaps I shouldn't say," Roy said. "I don't want to betray her confidence."

"If you've noticed anything serious, I strongly urge you to tell me," he said. "Some people take very badly to Delta-13 and can't stay long term. We don't know why, it just seems to happen. Why, my predecessor only lasted four months before requesting a transfer to another post. I think she reported having visions, but that was over ten years ago, so I may be wrong. I think the severity of the weather has something to do with it. Some people just can't stand being cooped up all the time."

"I don't think it's the weather," Roy said hesitantly. She looked into the warden's wide, warm eyes and decided to trust him. "She's been acting strangely. Just a few hours ago I heard her talking to herself."

"A lot of people do that," said Kelbauskas. "Especially on a world as confining as Delta."

"Yes, but she was holding an argument with herself," elaborated Roy. "She said 'You know I can't do that! They'll think I'm crazy!' out loud, like someone else in the room was trying to convince her of something she didn't want to do. I've been with her for years now, and I've *never* heard her talk that way. She's always been so self-contained and put together."

"That *is* concerning," the warden replied, putting his elbows on the table and leaning closer, knitting his fingers together. "What else has she done?"

"She told me about this strange dream she had. Well, it was more of a *fairytale* than a dream, complete with rabbits. But she thought it said something about reality, like it was a premonition. I honestly can't believe I'm saying this," Roy laughed mirthlessly. "She has *always* been so objective, so scientific with phenomena of this kind. Everyone knows that dreams are just the product of the mind, a mishmash of our waking thoughts jumbled around and rendered into nonsense. The fact that she put weight on it scares me. I can't help but wonder if that fall in the snow did something to her. She's been acting strangely ever since leaving the hospital."

"Is that why she couldn't come tonight?" Kelbauskas asked gently.

"Uh huh," she said, nodding her head. "I tried to get her to come out and grab a bite with me, but she said she had too much work to do. In fact, she hasn't eaten anything all day. She was withdrawn and preoccupied when I left, like something had taken total possession of her attention and I just didn't matter anymore. She's *never* done that before we came to Delta-13 – become so absorbed in her work that she lost sight of the present moment. It's like she's in some kind of fantasy."

"Maybe I should ask her to check into the hospital," Kelbauskas said. "They can look her over and see if anything is wrong."

"She won't go," Roy said firmly, shaking her head and crossing her arms defeatedly, resting them on the table. "She's stubborn when she thinks she's right. You'd have to force her to go, and that's too drastic of a step. Besides, the hospital didn't find anything wrong with her before. What could they hope to find now?"

"I guess you're right," he said. "But I'm concerned about her. Delta-13 isn't to be taken lightly."

"I'll pay special attention to her from now on," Roy said. "I'll leave her alone just as little as possible."

"Good. Let me know if anything else strange happens. If push comes to shove I'll order the hospital staff to evaluate her for her own good. We can't have anything happen to her, not now."

The next day Tselitel was in a secure room at the prison, examining one of the inmates.

Sixty, with close cut silver hair and a clean shaven face, he looked like a kindly grandfather. His record indicated that thirty-seven years before he had been responsible for the killing of two government officials in connection with an unsuccessful insurrection on Earth. Banished for his crimes, he lived quietly in the prison, until one day he was found sitting stiffly on his bed staring into space. He had become totally inert.

"Mr. Vilks," Tselitel said softly, glancing at the clock as her time with the man began to dwindle, "I want to try something new ."

Roy sat outside the room per the doctor's instructions. Two guards sat with her, watching for any sign of trouble from the patient.

Tselitel drew a piece of white chalk from her pocket and walked to the far wall, where Vilks was staring. She drew a circle on the wall and stepped back so he could see it. Something within her urged her to do it again, and she did, drawing another little circle and then stepping aside. She did this over and over, until the wall was filled with them.

Roy's face flushed. She wanted to run away and hide as the guards squinted through the one-way glass, trying to understand what the doctor was doing. They glanced at each other doubtfully and leaned back in their chairs, wondering what else their illustrious guest would pull out of her hat.

"Nothing, Mr. Vilks?" Tselitel asked, looking at the vacant face. But he betrayed not the slightest sign of recognition.

"We'll try again tomorrow," she said soothingly, putting a hand on his shoulder and leaving the room. "Alright, you can call the hospital staff in and have them take him away," she said to the guards in the next room. "I'm done for today."

The guards arose from their chairs, darting glances at her as they squeezed past her in the small space. One of them went into the other room to wait with Vilks, while the other picked up a phone on the wall and rang up the hospital. Normally the medical staff would have been on hand when she finished. But Tselitel had called it quits nearly twenty minutes earlier than usual, and they hadn't arrived yet.

Roy watched with concern as Tselitel dropped into one of the guard's chairs with an exhausted sigh and rubbed her red eyes with her fingers. Covering her face with her hands momentarily, she drew in a long, slow breath.

"Did you sleep last night?" Roy asked gently.

"No, not at all," she said, releasing the breath she held and moving her hands off to her cheeks so she could see. "What I've tried today is the last thing I can think of. If *this* doesn't show any results, then I'm stumped."

"Drawing on the wall?" Roy asked insinuatingly, trying to show the doctor how far off the beaten track she was.

"Oh, it's more than that," Tselitel said wearily, grasping the implication but too tired to get angry about it. "It's symbolism. The sphere symbolizes wholeness within the unconscious world – a complete human being. The conscious mind has been overloaded by some kind of strain. That, or the severe conditions of the planet have caused them to surrender the burden of conscious thought, and retreat into a fantasy world composed of unconscious ideas and images. A sort of personal vacation resort, as it were. For that reason I'm trying to 'speak' in a language the unconscious will recognize. If I can communicate with it, maybe I can produce enough of a stimulus to bring Vilks and the others back to the surface."

"But how can you say that, Doctor?" Roy asked. "They're clearly beyond us. They're catatonic, and nothing is going to bring them out of it. The hospital staff have tried every kind of medication and therapy available to help them, but nothing works. The most we can do is make them comfortable."

"Call it an intuition," replied Tselitel, aware of just how

little weight such things carried with Roy, but unwilling to trim her sails. "I just feel a connection to these poor souls. I know I can help them."

For the next week Tselitel persisted in her symbolism, working exclusively with Vilks. Word spread through the prison of her 'doodles,' and the rumor soon grew that she was as nutty as the patients she was trying to treat. Walking down the halls of the hospital to her work each day, bedraggled and unkempt, she could hear the medical staff talking in low tones as she passed by. More than once Kelbauskas 'accidentally' ran into her and would strike up a conversation, trying to feel out her condition. Each time she held him firmly at arms length, usually muttering something about being too busy to stop and talk.

"Doctor, I'm begging you: please stop with the drawings," Roy pleaded as they walked from their lodgings to the prison one morning. "People think you've cracked. You can't do the inmates any good by destroying your reputation this way. Just leave them in the hands of the prison staff. Enough of this personal crusade."

"Let them think what they want," she said harshly, striding shakily through the snow. Her already lean frame had lost nearly fifteen pounds since beginning her work. Her cheeks were hollow, the skin hanging loosely from her high cheekbones. Hair rumpled and clothes wrinkled through sleeping in them, she looked increasingly like a patient herself.

Reaching the entrance to the prison, they flashed their IDs to a guard who couldn't help but stare at the deteriorating condition of their celebrated guest.

"Doctor, I was just coming to see you," the warden said kindly. "I wanted to have a chat about how you're feeling."

"I'm feeling just fine," she said in a distracted voice, walking past Kelbauskas.

"We're concerned about you, Doctor," Roy said, seizing her arm and pulling her to a stop just short of the elevator that would take her down to the hospital and her appointment with Vilks. "We need to talk *now*."

"*We?*" snapped Tselitel, looking between Roy and Kelbauskas. "Oh, I see," she said with narrowed eyes. "You've been spying on me! Reporting my activities to the warden!"

"She hasn't been spying, Doctor Tselitel," the warden said. "She's been worried about you. And so have I. Now, we need to get you to the hospital for a thorough examination," he said, nodding to a pair of nurses who stood mutely watching several feet away. "These nice ladies are going to take you downstairs and give you something to help you sleep. Once you've had some rest we'll see how you're doing."

"I'm not brain damaged, you imbecile!" shouted Tselitel. "I can understand perfectly well what you're doing! But I have to finish my work." she said, stamping her foot. Pointing down through the floor in the direction of the hospital, she said, "That poor man Vilks needs my help!"

"You can't be any help to him in this condition," Kelbauskas said, more firmly than before. "I'm afraid this isn't open for discussion any longer." He looked at the nurses. "Ladies, if you would."

They came and took the doctor's arms in their experienced hands and guided her towards the elevator. Before entering, Tselitel looked sharply over her shoulder at Roy, betrayal written on her face.

The pair watched as the nurses took her into the elevator, the doors shutting slowly on her.

"I hope I've done the right thing," Roy said, wringing her hands anxiously. "I feel like I've just had my own mother committed to an asylum. I don't think she'll ever forgive me for doing this to her."

"It was the only option available, Sadie," Kelbauskas said, putting a hand on her back for support. "Something's come over her, and we need to understand just what it is. Letting her embarrass herself with her patients wasn't the answer."

"She'll never forgive me," Roy repeated, shaking her

head. "Not in a million years."

That evening, Kelbauskas was working in his office when the doctor examining Tselitel, Mantague Prisk, came in.

"What have you got for me, Prisk?" the warden asked, leaning back in his seat as the older man approached.

"I don't know what to tell you," he said, dropping into a chair in front of the warden's desk. "Medically there's nothing wrong with her. But she's driving herself like one possessed. I've never seen someone beat themselves to pieces like this before."

"There's got to be *some* cause, something you can cite," Kelbauskas replied.

"Maybe *you'd* like to look her over for yourself, Joris" snapped Prisk.

Kelbauskas flinched at the use of his first name. He'd never liked the withdrawn, brooding doctor, and he disliked the air of patronizing informality with which he invariably addressed him.

"Don't call me that," he replied sternly.

"This is no time to be putting on airs, Joris," Prisk said, making it clear he wouldn't back down. "We have a job here that's greater than both of us. It's greater than Tselitel, too. Honestly, I can't see why you sent her to me at all. She was doing a perfectly good job of unraveling herself until you intervened." Here the doctor paused and eyed the warden for a moment. "Maybe her little assistant has something to do with it?"

"You leave her out of this!" Kelbauskas flashed, the doctor hitting too close to the mark.

"So she *is* part of this," Prisk laughed. "Just don't forget this, Joris: Earth wants her gone *immediately*. She's threatening everything we're trying to accomplish here. Now, you've been a good teamplayer until now, and you've only got to put in a few more good months to pick any assignment you want. Don't jeopardize that by taking your eye off the ball."

"You think I'm doing this for *my* sake?" he asked hotly.

"I'm here because humanity stands on the brink. I couldn't care less about my professional advancement at this point. You know as well as I do what we're up against. Petty personal ambition is the last thing on my mind."

"Have it your way," replied Prisk. "But don't forget this: our superiors expect *results*. Get rid of Tselitel as soon as you can."

"That's why I sent her to you!" Kelbauskas flashed. "She's clearly crumbling into dust. I expected you to issue a diagnosis of some disease that had befallen her, and then we could ship her back to Earth. What am I supposed to do if there's nothing medically wrong with her? It's not like I can have her killed, you know!"

"Oh, calm down and stop talking like an idiot," Prisk said. "I couldn't issue a false diagnosis – only a handful of the staff in the hospital are on our side. The Order has enough snoops working there that the truth would be spread across the empire almost as soon as our little bogus report got off world. Besides, if we send her back prematurely she'll just get some other doctor to check her out, and they'll issue a clean bill of health. That'll give the busybodies just the excuse they need to launch the kind of investigation they've always wanted. They'll ask why we're so hot to get rid of her, and the pressure on us will triple. No, she's got to legitimately crack, or it's no good."

"So what are we supposed to do?"

"Just let her go back to work," Prisk said sagely. "She's her own worst enemy at this point. Her reputation is already on the rocks; she's fighting with her friends; she's not taking any kind of care of herself at all. And everyone knows about the spat she had with you and Roy in the hospital. If you let her carry on like she has been, she'll have a breakdown in a week."

"It's a bad way for a great psychiatrist to end her career," Kelbauskas said with regret. "She won't be able to practice after this. Nobody is going to want a head doctor who came apart herself."

"It's the situation we find ourselves in," Prisk said without feeling. "Don't let that soft heart of yours baby her. And don't let your little girlfriend twist your arm, either. Tselitel has got to go, and the sooner, the better."

"I'll do what's necessary," Kelbauskas said quietly, his anger growing.

"See that you do," Prisk replied, rising from his chair and leaving the warden's office.

Kelbauskas watched the door through which he'd left for several moments and then slammed his fist down on his desk. He had hoped that Tselitel would examine the patients, find them impossible to treat, and then head home. He'd never wanted to be a party to breaking her down or watching her destroy herself. In truth he had been genuinely excited when such a famous psychiatrist had been assigned to his prison, and it was with real pleasure that he had greeted her at the landing pad the day she arrived. It tore at his heart to see her deteriorate.

Arising from his chair and walking to a window that faced the prison, he eyed it for several minutes absentmindedly, his thoughts rolling back over his career, and what had led him to that moment. He remembered his elation, and fear, when he was first assigned to Delta-13 after his predecessor's rapid exit. The years of slow, steady progress in improving the conditions in the prison made him swell with pride despite his low mood. And then, that fateful day when an agent from Earth recruited him for his present task – a task he considered both necessary and inexcusable. He sighed and shook his head.

"I hope someday I'll be forgiven for what I've been forced to do," he said, reflecting on the harm he'd already done to those under his care. He knew a great deal more suffering was to follow, if he was to succeed in his task.

The next morning Tselitel was released from the hospital with a clean bill of health.

"You can start seeing patients again tomorrow, if you

feel up to it," Kelbauskas said, walking alongside her out of the hospital wing of the prison.

"I'm certain that I will," she said sourly, resentful of his interference and determined to pick up where she'd left off.

"I'm sorry that it was necessary to have you examined yesterday," the warden said with feeling as they approached the outer door. "But you must understand that we're all just concerned about your wellbeing. I'm glad that nothing was wrong."

"I'll be back here by eight am," Tselitel said coldly, ignoring his overture and walking out of the building alone.

Shoving her hands into her pockets, she strode across the snowy ground that separated the prison from the massive wall that surrounded it. Showing her ID to the guard, she passed through the gatehouse and headed for her apartment.

"Good morning, Doctor Tselitel," the guard at the apartment said when he saw her. "I hope you're feeling–" An angry glance from the doctor stopped his words, and he watched mutely as she walked down the long corridor to her apartment. Jamming the key into her lock, she pushed the door open and slammed it behind her.

"*First they want my help. Then they shut me up in the hospital. Now they let me go and tell me I'm doing just fine?*" she wrote in her diary, trying to make sense of it. "*There's something going on behind the scenes. I wish I knew what it was. I'm so angry I could scream!*"

She stopped and thought for a moment.

"*The imperial government was never too hot about me coming out here. Maybe Kelbauskas had orders to interfere with my work.*"

Dimly seeing her reflection on the tablet's screen, she switched it off momentarily to get a better look.

"*Although I must admit, I'm* not *looking great. Maybe they don't want someone with my high profile croaking on their hands. But if that's the case, then why tell me I'm doing fine? Why not keep me in the hospital? I'm so confused.*"

The bright screen hurt her eyes, and she slid it back into her bag beside her bed. The buzzing in her ears was back, growing louder with each passing hour. She took a painkiller and laid down for a nap.

Soon she was standing in a dreamland, a lush meadow filled with flowers. A beautiful doe walked along a tall growth of grass, in which a barely concealed wolf sat. It was perfectly still, waiting as she came ever closer. Suddenly a voice called out, and Tselitel turned her head to see a man beckoning to the doe, trying to get it away from the wolf. The doe saw him, but kept moving along the tall grass. Suddenly the wolf jumped out and seized her, snapping her neck in an instant.

The shock of the dream woke Tselitel at once. Fear filled her heart, and she sat up in bed panting for several minutes. Many hours had passed, and the buzzing in her ears had dropped considerably.

"That's got to be a vision," she said at last, surprised at her words but unable to say anything else. "I can just *feel* it."

"*I think I must be the doe,*" she wrote quickly, while the dream was still fresh in her mind. "*When the wolf seized her, I just had the most horrible feeling, like I was about to die. I instinctively identified with her. But what is the dream trying to warn me about? And how can I even be writing this, anyway? Dreams can't tell the future!*"

More confused than ever, she slapped her tablet down on the bed and walked to her living room window. Opening the blinds she saw night had fallen. She was about to walk away when she saw a dark figure standing in the snow several feet from her building. He seemed to be looking at her.

A powerful urge seized her, and she opened the window and stuck her head out.

"Hello? Who are you?" she asked. "Please come closer. I want to talk to you."

But the man turned and fled down the hill towards Midway.

Pulling her head back inside and closing the window,

she pondered what had just happened. A knock at the door disturbed her thoughts.

"Doctor, did you call out?" Roy asked from the other side. "Are you alright?" She tried the knob, but the door was locked.

"Go away, Sadie," Tselitel said harshly. "I don't want to see you."

"Please don't shut me out, Doctor," Roy pleaded. "I was trying to help you. So was Joris."

"Next time, don't," Tselitel retorted coldly, going into the bedroom and closing the door so she couldn't hear any more from Roy.

For days she worked in the prison, continuing her symbolic approach with Vilks and completely ignoring her young assistant. The latter had ceased to exist for her, so terribly had she hurt her by going behind her back. The one thing she couldn't abide above all else was the betrayal of her trust. It rattled and humiliated her, and necessitated the total rejection of whoever perpetrated it. Eventually Roy stopped accompanying her to the sessions, finding it too painful to be rebuffed by her mentor.

Nearly two weeks after her release from the hospital, a ragged and dejected Tselitel entered the room where Vilks waited as always. She walked to the wall and drew the chalk from her pocket. But as she raised it to write, a hand awkwardly seized hers. Startled, she turned and saw Vilks standing next to her.

The guards burst into the room and were about to grab him when she signaled for them to stop where they were. Pausing skeptically, they watched the prisoner for any sign of violence against the doctor.

He stood there for a moment holding her hand. Then he drew a rough circle on the concrete and released it.

Astonished, she looked at him for any sign of cognizance but saw none.

Raising the chalk she drew a circle of her own.

His hand reached over and took hers again, making another crude circle with the chalk. Then his hand fell to his side and he stood there like a statue.

"Incredible," she said, looking between the circles and Vilks. "Absolutely incredible."

"Ma'am?" asked one of the guards.

"Oh, it's alright," she said. "Please, go back into the other room. I don't want him unsettled by too many people."

"Ma'am, our orders are to ensure your safety," replied the other guard.

"So that I may pursue my work," she replied testily. "And I can't do that with you here. Now will you please go? Or will I have to call the warden?"

Without another word the guards withdrew, closing the door behind them.

"Can you understand me?" she asked Vilks when they'd gone. But he gave no sign or reply, just standing there mutely.

"That's much too advanced," she thought. She drew another circle, and so did he. For hours they drew circles, her constant hope being that this would stimulate something within him. Each time he reached for her hand he did so without focusing his attention in the slightest. His eyes perfectly open, staring blankly at the wall, he would reach over and grasp it, seeing it in his peripheral vision. Guiding it in front of him he would trace a crude circle and then open his fingers and drop his hand. This went on until the hospital staff came for him. She pleaded for more time, but they were adamant and took him away.

"I *knew* he could be reached," she said to herself once they'd gone. "I just *knew* it wasn't hopeless."

Gathering her things from the next room, she put on her jacket and gloves and stepped into the elevator that would take her to the surface. When the doors opened she saw Kelbauskas standing before her, and her mood immediately soured.

"Doctor, I heard the good news about Vilks," he said

enthusiastically, falling in beside her as she walked past. "Congratulations!"

"Thank you," she said coldly, not looking at him.

"Do you think he'll be able to speak soon?" he asked. "We're anxious to learn whatever we can from him about his condition. Perhaps we'll discover something that will help us to prevent other inmates from succumbing."

"I can't predict what progress we'll have," she said clinically. "We can only take things one step at a time. It took weeks to get this far. I can't imagine it will be anything less than months before he's capable of even basic communication."

"Yes, of course," replied the warden. "Tell me," he began. But she pushed open the outer door and stepped into the frigid night before he could finish.

"He's got some nerve," she said, pulling her thick winter hat down around her ears and hunching her shoulders against the cold. She was most of the way back to her apartment when a stick snapped near some trees a short distance away. She turned her head and saw the same figure from before standing there, watching.

"Wait! Please wait!" she pleaded, jogging in his direction across the loudly crunching snow. She'd only covered thirty feet when he stepped into the trees and disappeared from sight.

"Oh, no you don't!" she said decisively, determined that he not elude her a second time. A desperate yearning to meet him had welled up inside of her, as though he were somehow connected to her destiny. Reaching the trees and plunging into them, she looked for tracks in the snow that she could follow. But the night was already so dark that she couldn't find any. She hesitated momentarily, glancing towards the apartments and wondering if she should turn back before she went any further. As if in answer to this question a powerful intuition seized her, and she bolted deeper into the forest.

Working her way farther into the trees, the canopy

above her gradually thickened until it obscured the faint glow of the stars. The masses of trees around her concealed the lights of both Midway and the government facilities, robbing her sense of direction. She turned around and around, trying to figure out where she'd come from, but it was hopeless.

Fear began to grow within her as she realized how cold she had already become, the frigid night pressing its icy fingers into her flesh. It suddenly dawned on her that she was in danger of freezing out there, all alone. Holding her numb hands under her arms, she bent low over the snow, trying to find her tracks in order to retrace them. But the darkness made this impossible. Hearing something behind her, she turned sharply but saw only more darkness. The subtle sound of feet brushing through the snow sent her into a panic and she turned and ran head first into a low hanging branch. Falling onto her back in a daze, she could just make out a dark figure approaching as she lost consciousness.

CHAPTER 5

Hunt awoke after a long, tempestuous night sleep. The blizzard outside was still blowing, lasting longer than anyone had expected but losing much of its force by dawn. Soon it would pass off towards the west, leaving the town buried in snow but able to function once again.

"Sleep well?" asked Wellesley, having spent the entire night around Hunt's neck, which was unusual for him. Instead of being separated and left to his own thoughts, he was constantly stimulated by Rex's unconscious wanderings. He couldn't see what was happening within Hunt's dreamworld. But the rises and falls in his companion's brain activity, plus the occasional sentence fragment spoken in a tone of alarm, whetted his curiosity.

"I don't think I've had a worse night," Hunt said, sitting up and staring blankly into space for a moment, scratching his head. "It's like I was having an argument all night with some unseen figure. If I didn't know better I'd think I was possessed!"

"Maybe you were," Wellesley teased. "Plenty of people have gone nuts on this rock, you know."

"Oh be still," Hunt said, slipping his feet onto the cold floor and pulling his shirt on. "You don't believe in that nonsense."

"There were a lot of things I didn't believe until we ran into that old man," the AI said. "I've got to admit, he's expanded my understanding. That bit with the medallion kind of threw me."

"Yeah, me too," agreed Hunt, pausing for a moment and thinking. "You think he was telling it straight? That the planet was communicating with me?"

"Don't see any reason to doubt it," replied Wellesley. "It's the strangest thing I've ever heard. But I've lived too long, seen too many things to be prudish about what *can* and *can't* be. Can't hurt to humor him a while longer. If he's just an old kook we'll know soon enough. You can't make that kind of stuff up and keep it plausible for more than a little while."

"Guess you're right," replied Hunt, sitting down on the bed to pull on his socks. He sat there when he was done, still unable to shake the sense of having spent the night in the presence of another personality. It couldn't have been Wellesley, he thought. More than once he'd fallen asleep still in contact with him and hadn't felt that way. It was something else, something ethereal that he couldn't quite touch.

"You alright?" Wellesley asked.

"Yeah, just fine," replied Hunt, shaken from his reverie. "Let's see what they've got for breakfast."

Ambling down the creaky stairs to the ground floor, he saw Wanda and Ugo talking quietly near the door. Ugo was dressed in his outdoor clothes, leaning against the door that led outside. He saw Hunt and straightened up, his face brightening.

"Started to wonder if you'd ever wake up," he said with satisfaction, seemingly pleased by his guest's long rest.

"I must have overslept," Hunt said. "What time is it?"

"Time for our shift at the greenhouse to start," replied Ugo.

"What! That late?" Hunt exclaimed, rushing to his boots and jacket.

"Take it easy, son," Ugo said. "You've got a lot of work to do today."

"You bet I do," agreed Hunt. "What, with a short shift yesterday I'll have extra to make up today."

Ugo chuckled.

"No, I mean up *here*," he said, tapping his own temple. "You've got a lot of *inner* work to do, and not a lot of time to do it."

"But I can't! The greenhouse–"

"Will do without you for a day," Ugo said with certainty. "We'll manage to muddle through on our own."

"But I can't be absent! I-I'll be penalized! You know workers can't just give themselves day's off!'

"I'll talk with Perkons," Ugo said. "He'll give you the day off."

"But what if he doesn't?"

"Oh, he will. Believe me," the old man said with a sly look on his face.

Confused, Hunt looked to Wanda who nodded her agreement.

"I won't be back until after nightfall," he said to his granddaughter, kissing her on the forehead. "Make the most of the time you've got. We need to make all the progress we can." He smiled at Rex, and then stepped out into the frigid morning.

Hunt watched him go, feeling guilty to see such an old man struggling against the cold while he stood inside in his socks, warm as a fresh loaf of bread. But he knew argument would be of no use, and simply watched him disappear into the white sheets of snow that the wind drove against the buildings that flanked the street. Watching the place where he'd lost sight of Ugo, he felt Wanda draw closer.

"Don't worry about him," she said soothingly. "He's an old man. But he's tougher than an iron rod, and just as stubborn. I should know," she laughed prettily. "There's nothing you could have done to stop him. And he really is right about your inner work. You must begin at once."

"I don't understand," Hunt said, still looking into the desolate snow. "What am I supposed to do? I don't even know what 'inner work' is."

"I'll show you," Wanda said, taking his hand and pulling

him from the door. "But first I'll give you breakfast. You must be starving. Dinner was over twelve hours ago."

Hunt was distracted throughout breakfast, unable to shake the feeling that some unseen hand had seized him and was carrying him along a path not of his own choosing. Always fancying himself the master of his own fate, the idea that outside forces had taken an interest in him disturbed him greatly. Even the benign influence of Wanda began to feel like the pressure of some dark force. Above all he wanted to get out of the house and return to his normal, if cloistered, life.

And yet he didn't. Something deep within him refused to stir and follow his conscious will. He was unable to flee. Another element within his mind told him he had to stay, to submit himself to these odd people that he barely understood. Their world was so different from his. They took for granted things that until a day before he had considered the sheerest nonsense. But now, to his surprise, he found himself half-believing in such things as well. He didn't want to admit it, but the idea of a living planet resonated with him. It satisfied a deep, if unformed, mystical streak he'd long denied in himself. It made him feel more connected to his environment than he'd ever felt before. Such a connection both fascinated and scared him.

He was half nibbling a biscuit as he thought on this. Suddenly aware that Wanda was staring at him, he put it down and looked at her with a question in his eyes.

"Oh, I'm sorry," she said with a nervous chuckle. "You just looked so far away. I was wondering what you were thinking."

"Why didn't you ask?" he asked.

"Because I don't think you *know* where you were," she replied kindly. "Not yet."

"Is everything around this place a mystery?" he asked in exasperation. "Isn't anything straightforward? I feel like I've tumbled into some kind of dream ever since coming here last night."

"I can understand how it would be strange for you," she said reassuringly. "But we're normal folks, like anyone else in Midway. We just happen to know a great deal more about the planet, and its workings, than pretty much anyone. Well, I mean grandfather does. I just do the best I can with what he's already taught me."

"But to hear the planet is *psychic*! And that the government is working on *mind control*! That's a lot to swallow all at once. And now you guys want me to work with you? I'm afraid my head is spinning," he said, growing agitated. His familiar world was coming apart. The more he thought about it, the more he realized that the clear, crisp materialism that he'd always lived by was being shattered like a mirror.

"It will all make sense in time," she said, putting her hand on his wrist and patting it. "And the first step towards understanding is for us to get underway."

"Underway with what?" he asked doubtfully. "I made it clear to Ugo last night that I wasn't going to rush into anything."

"Of course," she replied. "And we wouldn't dream of trying to force you. But even if you never join up with us, you'll still benefit immensely from inner work. It will help you resolve long-standing problems and give you a new perspective on your life. Now, are you ready?"

"As much as I'll ever be," he replied.

She chuckled lightly and rose from her chair.

"Come on, the den is the best place for what we have to do."

He followed her there, standing in the doorway as she closed the blinds, shutting out the scant sunlight that managed to make it through the blizzard. Once it was dark she lit several candles along the edges of the room.

"Is that really necessary?" he asked uncomfortably, the aura of a seance filling the space.

"We find it helps the uninitiated," she said.

"So there have been others?"

"Of course. How do you think our organization has grown?" she asked. Then, taking his hands and leading him to the center of the room, she sat down on the floor, drawing him down as well.

"Do I have to cross my legs?" he asked in a sarcastic tone, trying to retain some control over the situation.

"Don't be a jackass," Wellesley said. "The girl's just trying to help you."

"That's alright, *Allokanah*," Wanda said simply. "Resistance is common. It's actually a good thing. If he simply surrendered his conscious position and was like putty in our hands he wouldn't be any use to us. He's got to keep his own thoughts during this process, even those that are *opposed* to the process."

"How did she–" Wellesley began.

"Hear what you said?" Wanda asked with a playful smile. "We all have our gifts, *Allokanah*. In fact there are many human psychics. But the faculty is buried so deeply in their unconscious that they can never meaningfully access it. It manifests only sporadically, as unexplained insights into other people's thoughts that come up like bubbles out of a pool of water. The planet helped me navigate the dark space between the two sides of my mind, so that I could build paths into the unconscious and bring this incredible talent to the fore. Now I can use it at will."

"Do I have a power, too?" asked Hunt, his resistance temporarily quieted by the stimulation of the idea.

"Grandfather thinks so," Wanda said without committing herself. "He's the chief recruiter for the Order on Delta-13, and he wouldn't be if he wasn't right most of the time."

"Then only people with a gift can join?" asked Hunt.

"Not exactly," she said slowly. "Anyone who is sympathetic to our aims can join. But naturally we prioritize those with gifts, since they can be of the most use to us. The vetting process is slow and thorough, and we have to use our resources as effectively as possible by recruiting strategically. And it just so happens that you have what we need, according to grandfather, anyway."

"And what gift does he think I have?" Hunt asked.

"We'll get into that later," Wanda said, shaking her head as though she didn't want to talk about it. "We don't have time now." She closed her eyes and drew a deep breath, releasing it slowly. Then she reopened them. "Now, I'm going to take your hands and help you get started."

"How?" he asked, his resistance instantly returning.

"By guiding you towards the unconscious," she said quietly. "That is why grandfather left us alone today. I need peace and quiet to enter your mind and help you."

"Enter my mind?" he asked with alarm.

"I would never do you harm," she said tenderly. "I only use my talent for insight and to heal. Now," she said, stretching out her hands and holding them palms upwards, "are you ready to begin?"

Hunt looked at her for a moment without moving.

"What have you got to lose, Rex?" Wellesley asked.

"It has to be his own decision, *Allokanah*," Wanda said. "No one can make it for him."

Another moment passed, and then Hunt reached out his hands and took hers.

"Be calm," she said, closing her eyes and concentrating.

Suddenly the room began to swirl away from him. He tried to pull his hands from hers, but she held on firmly.

"Be calm," she repeated, as the den disappeared.

In an instant they were in a fantasy world, still sitting and holding each other's hands. Everything was dark around them. Wanda opened her eyes, released his hands, and stood up.

"It's okay, you don't need to sit anymore," she said.

He got to his feet and looked around him, still seeing only darkness.

"Where are we?" he asked.

"Sort of a waiting room," she said. "It's easier for me to put us here while I search for the best place to start. It lessens the load."

"How long will we be here?" he asked.

"Just a moment longer," she said, closing her eyes and concentrating. "Okay, that's where we'll start," she said, nodding towards a narrow stony path. "I'll have to take your hand," she said, holding up her right. "It would be bad if we got separated. I'd have to find you and valuable time would be lost."

"How can we lose each other? We're standing right next to each other."

"You'd be surprised," she said with a cryptic smile. "Please."

Shrugging, he took her hand in his left and walked down the path with her. He could only see a dozen feet ahead, everything beyond being shrouded in darkness.

"Where are we going?" he asked after a few minutes of walking.

"I'm trying to carry you into the unconscious mind very slowly," she explained, squinting into the shroud ahead. "You've repressed it far more than I realized, and too sudden an exposure to it could be disastrous. We need to take things slow."

"Why?" he asked cockily. "I think I can take whatever it can dish out."

She stopped suddenly and looked sternly at him.

"Don't *ever* underestimate the unconscious," she said seriously. "You need it. It balances out your conscious attitude towards the world by taking up opposite positions and stances. It helps you develop a well-rounded approach to life. But it can get twisted and nasty when neglected, which yours has been for a long time. A sudden flood of its contents could overwhelm your conscious mind and make you psychotic. You'd almost become a different person, which would be bad for you, and for us."

"I see what you mean," he replied, thoroughly chastened. "Sorry."

"Don't be," she replied, her sweet demeanor instantly returning. "You've got to approach this naturally, which you just did. Anything less would be an act of repression on your part, which would be dangerous. You need to address the unconscious honestly. Just be open to correction, and you'll be fine."

They walked for several more minutes, and then Hunt spoke again.

"You say I'm more repressed than you expected."

"Your unconscious is," she said, gently correcting him. "I've never come across someone who had so totally buried it beneath the floor of his conscious mind. It's like you never wanted to hear from it again. Yet it pops up here and there, giving you insights."

"Psychic insights?" he asked.

"Not exactly," she replied, tipping her head. "I can't say precisely what kind just yet. But I don't think your talent lies in seeing the thoughts of others. I'll know more the deeper we go. Right now I'm just getting whiffs of what your unconscious is sending up. Or trying to."

"But why am I repressing it so much?" Hunt asked, puzzled.

"I don't know that either," she said simply. "We'll have to get deeper to find out."

They walked slowly on, careful not to overtake the darkness that slowly receded before them as they penetrated his mind. The path became more jagged the deeper they went. Soon the stones were placed haphazardly, scarcely forming a path at all. Suddenly it stopped altogether, and nothing but darkness lay before them.

"What does this mean?" he asked, looking around and continuing to hold her hand.

"It means we've reached a dead end," she replied. "That happens sometimes. I'll have to find another way inside," she said uneasily.

"What's wrong?"

"Well, that was the gentlest path I could find," she replied, looking up into his eyes. "You have very few paths into your unconscious. And the ones you *do* have are charged with a great deal of emotion, angst, and insecurity. The unconscious contents come rushing down them when they pile up and require release. Thus it's inherently risky to use them."

"Can't you find another path like the one we were on?" he asked.

"No, that was the only one," she replied. "It was some old conduit you used to have. But it has long since been severed. Maybe it was an artistic outlet, something through which you could release yourself. The stony path suggests it was something in the natural world. The fact it was a path implies it was something you would build."

"I used to make little buildings out of snow when I was a child," said Hunt, after a moment's reflection. "It would relax me whenever I felt agitated."

"That was probably it," Wanda said. "Humanity has a deep need to shape and build the world around us, and you satisfied that need through building little snow structures. Once you let that go an outlet was lost, and the channel to the unconscious eventually atrophied. Why did you stop?"

"Just didn't seem important after a while," he replied evasively.

"I see," she said, unsatisfied but willing to let it rest for the time being. "In any event we need another way in. But it won't be comfortable."

"I'm ready," he said firmly.

"Alright, give me a minute." Closing her eyes and concentrating, the stony path disappeared and they were left standing in darkness once again. He found himself wishing that Wellesley could have come along. But the psychic plunge they had both taken hadn't included the AI.

"Okay, I'm getting something," she said. "It's an

emotional connection you have with certain archetypal ideas."

"Archetypal ideas?" he repeated.

"Yes," she replied, digging for the right words. "Uh, they're notions common to all mankind, like heroism or a sentimental attachment to your home. This emotional connection links one of your conscious ideas to one that is archetypal. It's your sense of loneliness."

"And what is it linked to?" he asked uncomfortably, uneasy that she had hit upon one of his major anxieties.

"I don't know, we'll have to find out together," she said. Before them a smooth, reddish-purple stretch of ground appeared. "Ready?"

Without replying he stepped onto the ground and began to follow it into the darkness. As the minutes passed and they walked ever deeper he found himself sinking into depression, overwhelmed by the feeling that he would never have anyone to accompany him through life. His stomach hollowed, his heart began to ache, and the most dreadful sense of abandonment filled him.

"Try to remember this isn't real, Rex," Wanda said, feeling what he was going through.

"It feels terribly real," replied Hunt. "I know I'll never be anything but alone, like I am now. I live by myself in a shack, Wanda. There isn't a soul in the world who would–"

"Stop it, Rex," she said stoutly. "You're being carried away by the *emotions* of loneliness, not the fact thereof. Try to keep that in mind. You're going to experience a great many more nasty things before we're done here, and you can't be swallowed up by them, either. You've got to keep your head."

They walked for ten minutes more. In spite of himself Hunt began to hunch over, the negativity of their approach finally growing too strong.

"Let's take a break," she said, once it was clear he couldn't go on any farther.

"What, and end our session?" he asked.

"No, I mean we'll just pause for a little while." She found

a brief memory off to the side that they could dwell in for a few minutes, something happy. It was a pleasant little scene, with Hunt as a young boy sitting in a kitchen on a cool spring morning, warm sunlight streaming through the windows.

"I remember this," he said, looking the scene over as they stood within it as spectral observers. The little boy sat on a small stool, his feet dangling over the side, a look of happy expectation on his smiling face. His mother then entered the room and returned his smile. She headed to the counter and began whipping up breakfast.

Unconsciously tears began running down his face. Wanda saw this and squeezed his hand a little tighter.

"What can you tell me about this memory?" she asked quietly, trying to get him to delve deeper.

"It was before coming to Delta-13," he said slowly, absorbed in the vivid image of his mother seemingly come back to life before his eyes. "I was three or four years old. We had a nice life then. Mom took care of me while dad worked for the government. It was a happy time."

"What happened?" Wanda probed.

At that instant thunder crashed through the scene and the happy memory faded. A vicious thunderstorm broke above them and began to pour rain.

"Stop thinking about that!" she shouted, taking his other hand and pulling him close, the wind blowing so hard they could barely stand. "It's too soon for such a terrible memory. Think of something nice. Reassert control over your emotions."

He closed his eyes and tried to think of something pleasant, but couldn't. The storm grew worse, and the wind gusted so strongly it knocked them over, Wanda falling on top of him.

"Can't get it out of my head," he yelled, squeezing his eyes shut and trying desperately to separate himself from the moment and overcome it. The rain began to gather in puddles on the dark ground, soaking them as they lay in it.

Seeing that this approach wasn't working, Wanda did the only thing a resourceful girl could do: she wrapped her arms around his neck and kissed him.

Suddenly the storm lost its ferocity and vanished as if it had never been, the tempest ending with the emotion that had brought it on. She held on for a long moment, their lips not parting until she was certain the strength of the memory had been temporarily effaced.

"That *can't* be in the official manual," Hunt said with a smile as Wanda pulled back, her cheeks turning red.

"It's not," she said in a worried tone. "Don't ever tell my grandfather that I did that. I could get in a lot of trouble," she said, getting to her feet.

"What for? I don't mind," he said jocularly. "In fact, I've never felt so good."

"That's *exactly* why," she said, lowering her voice confidentially despite the fact no one else could hear them. "You're excessively vulnerable in this condition. Remember how your emotions keep overwhelming you? That would never happen in your normal, wakeful state. Everything you think about right now gets center stage – it isn't suffering from the usual fraying of attention that we experience in our conscious lives."

"So you're saying you could seduce me in this state?" he asked, his jovial attitude replaced by one of unease.

"Without any effort at all," she replied. "That's why psychics in the Order are bound to a very strict code of conduct whenever we plunge into an initiate's mind. You're just as vulnerable now as you would be strapped to a surgical table while I held a razor sharp knife."

"There's a cheery thought," he replied.

"So you can see why I'd get in a ton of trouble if you said anything about it," she continued anxiously. "Please promise me you won't."

"I won't," he said with a smile. "You have my promise."

"Good," she replied, relieved beyond words. "We'd better

get going while you're still feeling good. We've got a long way to go yet."

"Back to the purple path?" he asked, as she took his hand.

"Uh huh. It's our best shot."

They stepped across a short space of darkness and set feet back on the path, Hunt's mood immediately sinking as they did so.

"Ready?" she asked.

Before she knew what happened he bent over and kissed her quickly a second time.

"For medicine purposes," he said lightly. "Let's go."

Chuckling and shaking her head, she walked alongside him towards the receding darkness.

After nearly thirty minutes of progress Hunt began to slow down and breathe in short, quick breaths.

"Something's wrong," he said, finding it hard to stand. "I-I feel…" he trailed, trying to find the words.

"Like what?" she asked.

"I don't know. Like I'm in a very bad place." He looked up and saw dim shapes around him. "Do you see those?"

"What?" she asked, following his eyes but seeing nothing.

"I don't know. I can't make them out," he said, squinting. "Wait, yes I can. They look like me. Gray, transparent visions of me. What sense does that make?"

"They're images of dead ideas that are related to you," Wanda explained. "Old hopes and dreams that have been shattered through the disappointments of life. You're still holding onto them."

"I never knew," Hunt said quietly, astonished to see how many of them there were. "I thought I'd moved beyond them."

"You didn't move beyond them, you just buried them," Wanda said. "It's one of the chief ways we undermine ourselves. Most of us don't let go of the impossible, we just stop admitting to ourselves that we still want those things. We let our hopes live on in the unconscious, where they cause untold mischief. They pile up and make us hate our lives because of all we think we're missing out on. We become resentful and feel sorry for ourselves."

"Incredible," Hunt said, still watching the ghostly figures as they moved around him.

"Come on," she said, pulling on his hand and continuing down the reddish-purple path. "We can't stay here. There isn't time to process this old stuff now. Our top priority is getting you in touch with the unconscious in a reliable, healthy way."

"But isn't this the unconscious?" Hunt asked, waving his hand to indicate the spectral images.

"Yes it is," she agreed. "But not the part that we can interact with, not now. The unconscious contains both positive and negative content. You've neglected yours for so long that it is piled high with the negative. But we can't try to form a link with it because it would just overwhelm you. A connection has to be formed with something positive, something you can reach for over and over in order to build a bridge into the other part of your mind."

"I'm not sure there *is* anything positive to find," Hunt said. "You know what life in Midway is like."

"There's *always* something positive," she said decisively. "Even if it's just a memory or a dream for the future. There's *always* a productive channel that can be established. But it might take a while to find it."

"What about that memory from earlier?" he asked. "The one in the kitchen?"

"Not deep enough," she shook her head. "It's got to be something buried way in the back. At any other time I would be more than happy to start there and work our way in as you developed your connection. But we have to move quickly. The mind control experiments have been temporarily halted at the prison. But they can start up again any day now. We fear they're getting close to achieving their aims, so there's no time to lose. We need you functional immediately."

"Isn't there a risk that I'll be overpowered by the unconscious by proceeding this way?" Hunt asked.

"I'm glad you asked that," Wanda said with approval. "You're getting a feel for the contours of your mind already. Yes, there's plenty of risk. The channel we open could be co-opted by the storehouse of negativity you hold within."

"But it's better than having my mind dominated by the scum running the prison," he said.

"You took the words right out of my mouth."

They strode in silence for several minutes, and then she pulled him to a stop. "How are you feeling now?"

"Like nothing," he said. "I don't feel anything."

"We're between spaces," she said. "But we're close to something powerful. In fact, we're about to step right into it."

"Bad?" he asked,

"I don't know. It's loaded with energy, though. You see, notions are charged with different levels of energy. If one gets a high enough charge–"

"It bursts into consciousness," he finished for her, not sure where the idea came from.

"Exactly!" she said happily. "You're progressing very rapidly."

"I don't know how I knew that," he said. "The words just seemed to form on the tip of my tongue."

"You're beginning to get a connection with the automatic processes of the psyche. Instead of thinking everything through in the front of your mind, you're beginning to make use of the faculties at the back. These faculties already know how they work, so you have an instinctive grasp of the things I'm telling you. You just have to get in touch with them, is all."

"You mean I could do all this myself?" he asked. "But this world seems so bizarre, so unlike anything I've ever seen before."

"You *could* do this yourself, but only with many years of reflection. It'd be like reinventing language or mathematics:

you could, but it would take an incredible amount of effort. The main value of your instinctive grasp of these processes is that you get inner confirmation of what I'm telling you. You don't have to take my word for it. Instead you can feel the truth of my words, provided you continue to stay connected with the unconscious. That makes things move a lot quicker."

Hunt looked ahead and saw that the path narrowed as it progressed. He pointed at it carelessly.

"What's happening to our walkway?" he asked.

"The line we're following is being pressed in on by other mental contents."

"That big idea that's floating to the top."

She nodded.

"This is where it gets tricky."

"Why?" he asked.

"Because this idea could flatten you and overwhelm your conscious mind, as represented by yourself here," she said, tugging his hand to indicate his body. "Whether the idea is positive or negative, a charge that strong could dominate you."

"Could you pull me out of it in that case?" he asked, a subtle strain of determination growing in his voice.

"Yes...I believe I could," she replied slowly. "But it would happen in a flash. Stepping into that idea could flood you so totally that even ending our session wouldn't break its hold on you if you had more than a moment's exposure. It might possess you for weeks."

"So it's a gamble," he summarized.

"Yes, a high stakes one," she said. "Oh, I wish I could ask grandfather about this! He'd know what to do."

He squeezed her hand and looked into her eyes.

"It's the risks we take that help us grow," he said. "Now, I'm ready if you are."

Doubtfully she returned his gaze for a moment. Then she nodded.

"Alright, let's go," she said, walking with him as the path

grew ever narrower.

"I can feel something," he said just a few seconds later. "It's like a charge building within me."

"I can feel it too. We're just on the threshold now," she replied, looking down to where the purple terminated. "This is it."

Without another word Hunt stepped into the darkness beyond.

Suddenly he saw a powerful warrior-magician terrorizing an entire army through the use of his magic. As a mass they ran headlong into a river and were drowned in their attempt to escape the horrors he cast into their minds.

"Rex?" Wanda asked.

"I'm alright," he replied, fascinated.

"It's very powerful, Rex," she said dubiously. "Are you sure?"

"Yes, completely," he said, nodding his head vigorously. "Now leave me alone." He released her hand and began to float upward in the darkness.

"Rex!" she called, kicking off the ground and flying up towards him. "Come back!"

But he was too powerfully attracted by the vision to hear her words. Instinctively he knew the magician represented himself, and that he would have great power. It was all so exhilarating that he began to lose his head, and every other consideration fell by the wayside. Army after army arose, and the powerful wizard decimated them all through the use of his arts. No one could stand before him.

Just at that moment, when his spirit soared to its highest point, Wanda grabbed hold of his legs and pulled him out of the unconscious. The session was over.

"Why did you do that?" he barked the instant his mind had returned to the dimly lit den. "Don't you realize what I had found? I was powerful! I could destroy all our enemies with a wave of my hand! For once I had the capacity to *do* something meaningful!"

"In a fantasy," Wanda said quietly. "The unconscious doesn't predict the future, Rex. It's just another part of your mind."

"That's not true," replied Hunt. "What I felt was real. Why did you take it away from me?"

"Because it was swallowing you up," she explained. "It had hold of you and was about to smash you to pieces."

"What, a mighty wizard smashed?" he said incredulously.

"Yes, like a glass mirror."

"How can you say that?"

"Because I could see ahead of the vision," she said. "My gift allowed me to tap a little farther into it than you. In another moment the wizard would have fallen, killed by one close to him. The force of the realization would have shattered you. Remember the kiss."

Hearing this he stopped and looked at her.

"Are you certain?"

"Dead certain," she said, nodding her head vigorously. "That's why exploring the unconscious this way is so dangerous: everything hits you full force. There's no holding back. If your ego had identified with the wizard and then saw him fall, you would have been unable to separate yourself from it. You'd be helplessly convinced on the deepest possible level that your fate was to die. You'd grow despondent and helpless. Only weeks of the most strident effort on my part would have a chance of breaking its hold on you, because in your mind you would have *become* the wizard. His fate would be yours, to your thinking."

"Then we failed?" Hunt asked.

"Not by any means," Wanda said, standing up and opening the blinds to let in more light. "We've made excellent progress towards linking you to the unconscious. And by connecting with that powerful idea, that of the hero-magician, we were able to transfer some of its energy into your conscious mind. The fantasy is now both useful and less dangerous. It will begin to give you guidance and courage, helping you to become what you were born to be."

"Which is?" he asked, standing up as well and rubbing his aching legs.

She was blowing out a candle, facing away from him as he asked this. Turning slowly and significantly, she looked him in the eye and said, "Why, a hero, of course. It's in your blood."

"There's nothing but shame in my blood," Hunt said heavily. "My father was a criminal who used illegal procedures on his patients. I hate the government for sending him here, for destroying his life and mine. But he ultimately brought it upon himself, and on me."

Wanda drew close and put a hand on his shoulder.

"Your father was a *hero*, Rex," she said. "He was never a criminal."

"The court that found him guilty disagrees with you," he replied.

"A court which is a part of the same government that is laboring in secret to develop mind control technology," Wanda said. "This isn't something new on their part, Rex. They've been working on it for decades. Their test subjects were severely damaged by the crudity of their early experiments, and your father tried to treat them any way he could. He had the support of both the patients and of their families. Only radical treatments were open to them, and he made sure they understood the risks. He was trying to save them, Rex, not hurt them."

"Then why did he end up in prison?" Hunt demanded, unsettled to have decades of certainty uprooted in a moment. "Why did the families testify that he'd deceived them with false promises?"

"Because they were under pressure to do so," Wanda replied. "The imperial government threatened them. They made sure the trial went against him, and then specifically placed him out here to get him as far away from prying eyes as possible. They had to silence him because he knew too much about their research. He could have blown the lid off of everything because of his prominent position in the medical community. A man of his stature had to be destroyed."

"And how do you know all this?" Hunt asked.

"Because he was one of our best agents," Ugo said from behind him. Hunt jerked around to see the old man standing in the doorway, a light dusting of snow on his shoulders. "I just stopped by for a minute. I have to get back to the greenhouse." He looked at Wanda. "Honey, I left without my lunch this morning. Could you throw something together quickly?"

"Of course," she said, bustling past them both into the kitchen.

Hunt, overwhelmed by the news he'd just received, sat down on the couch, his head spinning. Ugo stalked to the couch and joined him, his joints stiff from the cold.

"I know it's hard to learn something like that," Ugo said. "Even good news is disturbing when it unsettles our most fundamental understanding of things."

"But why?" Hunt asked, feeling ridiculous. "Why should I be so thrown off by this? I ought to be glad!"

"Because your whole identity is built around being the child of a criminal, an outcast," replied the old man. "Now you have to rebuild your understanding of your place in the universe."

"This is too much for one day," Hunt said, leaning back on the couch and exhaling slowly. "First Wanda and I go spelunking in my brain, and now this."

"You're being fast tracked, that's for sure," Ugo said sympathetically. "But I'm afraid our hands are tied. You're gonna have to hold together as well as you can." He turned to Hunt and lowered his voice. "Your father was a good man, Rex. One of the best I've ever known. He recruited me back in the day, and I'll never be able to repay him for that. He opened my eyes to a whole new world."

Wanda returned to the den with a bag in her hand.

"I've got to go," Ugo said, grunting as he rose to his feet.

"They need me at the greenhouse today since we haven't got you." He locked eyes with Hunt for a moment, who looked at him doubtfully. "Be proud of him, Rex." Then he took the bag from his granddaughter, kissed her on the cheek, and left.

Wanda walked slowly to the couch and sat down beside him. Still as a stone, he stared into space and tried to process the load on his mind.

"Is there anything I can do to help?" she asked.

"No, I just need time alone to think," he replied, rising and going upstairs to his room.

"A hero? One of the best agents they had?" Hunt said, trying to come to terms with what he'd heard.

"Better than being a criminal," Wellesley chimed in.

"Quiet, I need time to think," Hunt said, turning it over and over again in his mind. He felt the back of his mind slowly wrapping around the new data, beginning to form a stance. Ugo had been right: his whole identity was built around being an outcast, a perpetual loner who had the cards stacked against him from the start. To learn that his entire life on Delta-13 was caused by a government cover up made him feel that all the suffering, loneliness and loss he'd experienced was nothing but a sham. At least there had been a certain legitimacy in the old story. But to be shunted aside, along with his father, so that shadowy figures could continue their dark work infuriated him. Anger welled up within him until he beat his fists against the wall.

"Calm down, Rex," Wellesley said. "This isn't the way."

"It's *my* way," he retorted, furiously kicking at the wall, his face growing red with rage. "How could they do this?" he demanded at the top of his voice, his body trembling.

He felt that at any moment he must burst. Bolting down the stairs and running out into the icy cold, he dropped to his knees and screamed up at the sky. He beat the ground with his fists and writhed furiously, disgorging a powerful mental charge that had built up in the back of his mind. It reached its climax and then passed, the unconscious fury finally forcing itself into conscious acceptance. Suddenly he was calm. He stood up in his socked feet, and looked around him at the silent street.

Snow fell thickly as far as he could see, but the wind had lost its force and the worst of the blizzard was over. He felt it was an apt metaphor for his inner condition. A shift had taken place, and he could accept his position. Somehow he'd always known that the official story was false, that he and his father had been wrongly sent to the frigid world. But he had clung to what he was told because it offered some little shred of stability in a world gone awry. But he didn't need that kind of stability any longer. A powerful pillar of strength was rising within him, and external supports became superfluous. The reassuring certainty of the government's story wasn't necessary.

"Are you done?" Wellesley asked quietly. "Any longer and we'll start to attract attention."

"Let them look," Hunt said calmly, a new confidence in his voice. "They'll be hearing more from me very soon." With this he strode back inside the house. Wanda was waiting for him near the door.

"I heard you outside," she said.

"I think everyone did," Wellesley commented.

"Yes, that's probably true," she chuckled. "But the path of individual growth sometimes requires us to do strange things, at least in the eyes of others. I can feel an inner calm has filled you."

"Yes, it has," Hunt said, his voice sounding fuller, almost older. The previous high-pitched tension was gone, replaced by a settled sense of certainty. "I have accepted the world," he said cryptically.

"Meaning?" Wellesley asked. "Remember, I'm just a brilliant military AI. I'm not up to speed on all this mumbo jumbo."

"All his life Rex has run from his world, from the pain and suffering it brought him," explained Wanda. "Until this point he has always pulled into himself, shying away from the truth that we only have one life and must accept the lot we are given, good or bad. He sees that now. The shock brought on by the truth of his father's fate has shaken loose his old attitude and cast it away forever. Now he can begin in earnest to fight back against those who have brought this upon them both."

"Then the training is complete?" the AI asked.

"Oh, no," replied Wanda, shaking her head. "It has only barely begun. But his frame is now correctly oriented. He's got the right attitude to progress."

"What do we do now?" Hunt asked.

"Now we eat lunch," she said with a smile. "I'm starving."

CHAPTER 6

"You've made good headway, Rex," Ugo said, lighting up his pipe on the third evening of Hunt's stay with them. He sat down in a rocking chair he'd brought down from the attic and placed in the den. "Wanda has never seen a pupil advance so quickly. Why do you think that is?"

"Probably just the talent of my teacher," Hunt said modestly. "I've never had any familiarity with this kind of thing before. But it all comes so easily to me. I reckon she's just guiding me to all the right places."

"I don't agree with you," Ugo said, puffing on his pipe. "I think there's more to it than that."

"Like what?"

"Like the planet has made a special effort to help you," he said slowly, dropping his tone for emphasis.

"What, it can do that?"

"My boy, there's all sorts of things it can do," Ugo laughed. "The little I've told you doesn't even scratch the surface. Now, I said before that it helps people find wholeness. That's entirely true, and the majority of its activity is directed towards this end. But there's more. At times it perceives a crisis and intervenes to resolve it. I believe that is what it's doing with you. I think it is guiding you along, speeding up the process dramatically."

"But why me?" asked Hunt. "What makes me so special? Whatever my gift is, there have got to be people with more powerful ones on Delta-13."

"That's true," agreed Ugo, nodding his mostly bald head. "But who said the planet had to select you because you were the most *powerful*. I feel another reason motivated it."

"That being?"

"That you had suffered more than anyone else," he said quietly, his blue eyes shimmering under his thick eyebrows.

At this moment Wanda entered with a tea tray and set it before them on the little table that stood in front of the couch. She looked to her grandfather, but he shook his head and took another puff on his pipe. Pouring some for Hunt and herself, she plopped down beside him on the couch and sipped from her steaming cup.

"Honey, what gift do you believe young Rex here has?" Ugo asked. "I know there's something unusual knocking around inside that skull of his. But for the life of me I can't feel out what it is. All I know for sure is that it wants to break forth and spill itself onto others. It has an offensive quality, like a handgun. It's angry and repressed, and wants *terribly* to affect his environment."

"I can't say with certainty," she hedged, looking down at the floor for a moment and taking another sip to buy time. "But two things seem significant to me."

"Those being?" the old man prodded.

"First, the total degree to which he has repressed the unconscious. Until now he's treated it as an enemy, and that has produced a severe one-sidedness that has allowed it both to fester, and has held him back in terms of normal maturation. Simply put, he's walking around with half a personality. His normal mode of living is pointed outward toward the world. He's denied the inner world because, on a deep, instinctive level, he finds it abhorrent."

"You're avoiding the question, my dear," Ugo chided. "Please, come to the point."

"Second," she continued, "I was struck by the immense number of negative images and ideas that were to be found in his unconscious. As I just said, it has been festering, and that always leads to an excessive buildup. But it's more than that: his unconscious is like an engine for negative, frightening ideas."

"That's not very flattering," opined Wellesley.

Wanda looked at the large medallion that hung around Hunt's neck but said nothing since her grandfather couldn't hear the AI's comment.

"Rex had a vision that he was a great magician, and that through the manipulation of his enemies he could destroy entire armies. Now, the vision was a mixture of fact and wishful thinking. Its grandiosity was a compensation for his sense of inferiority brought on by his captivity on Delta-13. And the poverty and turpitude that has accompanied him ever since coming here. It was a grand picture of what his unconscious felt was possible if he only surrendered totally to his gift and became its instrument. It's not unusual for the unconscious to try and override the conscious mind with such seductive ideas."

"I don't understand what you're driving at," Hunt said.

"Just this: that your gift has some connection to powerful, negative imagery. Your unconscious seems to think it will give you the power to decimate your enemies."

"That's quite a stretch, my dear," Ugo said. "I don't think there's enough information to justify that kind of conclusion."

"It's where my intuition leads me," she replied. "It feels pretty solid to me."

"Well, how can we know for sure?" asked Hunt. "Is there a way I can test it out?"

"No, not yet," replied Wanda. "We've made great strides with the unconscious. But your connection still isn't strong enough to direct your gift at will. Even if you could contact it, the power would still be too great, and it would overwhelm you like the vision of the magician did the first time. Your ego needs strengthening."

"I think his ego is strong enough at present," Wellesley said.

"You're thinking of his *pride, Allokanah*," Wanda said, saying his name so her grandfather would understand whom she was addressing. "When I say ego, I mean that portion of the mind we are aware of, the conscious center of our thoughts. He favors it by default, as we all do in our waking lives. But when faced with the insistent certainty of an unconscious impulse we tend to cast it aside, as he did when the vision of the magician carried him, literally, off his feet. This weakness of the ego was also present when the emotions of loneliness started grinding him down."

"What do I have to do?" Hunt asked. "How do I strengthen the ego?"

"By recognizing its equal legitimacy alongside the unconscious," Wanda explained. "Both sides of your mind are valid, even when they oppose each other. As long as you insist on making one 'true' and the other 'false' you're going to oscillate between the two of them, tipping back and forth unsteadily. You have to accept that both are part of the same system, and thus not truly at odds with each other. They are constituents of the whole. But yet, and believe me, I know this sounds like a contradiction, you must assert the ego *over* the impulses of the unconscious when you know them to be destructive. The ego must be the first among equals in order to give your psychic life direction."

"I don't know if I can do that," Hunt said.

"Most people can't," commented Ugo. "My granddaughter has described the ideal case, which most of us never attain. A form of oscillation is the typical result, even among our best operatives. But oscillating in the *right way* is what makes all the difference. You must learn the proper points at which to yield to your unconscious in order to both bring out your gift and achieve enough balance to make your life healthy and normal."

"Then we're not looking for a complete, total solution?" Hunt asked.

"Anyone who ever does that is misguided," opined Ugo.

"All we can manage is a succession of provisional answers that serve for the present moment. Nothing ever stays the same, especially our own psyches. We need constant adjustment."

"So what, practically speaking, are we looking to accomplish here?" Wellesley asked. Wanda relayed his question to Ugo, who drew his pipe from his mouth.

"We are attempting to make young Rex here into a weapon," Ugo said. "Not that this will entail any harm to him. But we are attempting to develop his powers only to the point that he can be useful to the Order, and through the Order save mankind from slavery. We have no time for anything else."

"And why does it rest exclusively on his shoulders to perform this task? Surely there are others who can help carry the load." said the AI, Wanda once more relaying his words.

"Because he is unique," Ugo explained. "An aura surrounds him that I noticed from a mile away. He's marked, in a sense. Most everyone who bears a powerful gift has a kind of glow about them, whether good or bad. But Rex's is different. His capacity to hurt people is immense."

"Excuse me?" Hunt asked.

"Don't get me wrong, Rex," Ugo said quickly, leaning forward earnestly in his rocker. "You're a good man. And as a matter of fact, we need a man like you. Most of the Order's other members on Delta-13 have powers that enable them to heal, or to learn. I have a profound capacity to intuit the nature of others, for example. And Wanda here can communicate and delve into the secrets of the mind. But what we need is someone who can take the battle to the enemy."

"And you think that's me?" asked Hunt.

"I *know* it's you," said the old man firmly. "I've never been more sure about an initiate in my life. That's why I was about to contact you when you saved me the trouble and walked home with me that day. Something spoke in your ear and directed you to stick with me. It was time."

"I just wanted to make sure you got home alright," Hunt said.

"That was the *conscious* reason given. But you've let me walk home during blizzards before. *This* time you were motivated to act, because a hidden impulse was brought to the fore, probably through the intervention of Delta-13."

"But what makes you think I can hurt others with my power?" asked Hunt. "You admitted earlier that you didn't know what my gift was."

"I don't know what it *is*, but I can feel its *nature*," said Ugo. "Your gift flows *outwards*, applying itself to things around it. Often that's the sign of a healer, and we have many of them in the Order. But this outward flow can also be accompanied by an inner darkness that sends not health, but woe into another human being. I haven't seen too many cases firsthand. But I can pick them out every time. Their nature is too distinct to be missed."

"You're certain of this?" Hunt asked, feeling rather chagrined at what he was hearing.

"Dead certain," the old man said, fixing his eyes on Hunt's. "You may rest assured on that score."

"It's a rare gift, Rex," Wanda said, seeing the uncertainty in his face. "You're just what the Order needs right now."

"But isn't there a risk that this power could turn to evil?" Hunt asked. "The 'ability to hurt others' sounds dangerous."

"It is," replied Ugo. "And it's a good sign that you're aware of that fact. You're right: it could turn to evil if abused. Should it possess you, you'd become a monster and use your power to crush those around you. But that's why we need you, Rex: properly controlled, your gift will give us what we need to take the fight to the enemy. On Delta-13, if not always elsewhere, our organization is one committed to healing the minds and nurturing the spirits of those in trouble. For that reason, we truly can't do without someone of your talents."

"A dark element," said Hunt.

"If you like, yes," replied Ugo. "But sometimes we need darkness to sweep away the shame and wrong that surrounds us. At times the rules must be broken in order to preserve their spirit. Correctives are often bitter pills to swallow."

"But the fact remains that I could turn to evil," Hunt said.

"Technically, yes," Ugo admitted. "If the unconscious gift overpowers you, and uses you as the instrument of its expression, then you will affect everyone around you for the sheer pleasure it gives the unconscious urge to manifest itself. You see, such gifts are always trying to fight their way to the conscious realm to find validity. That is why you must keep their power in check by regularly, and intelligently, using them. Letting it pile up within runs the risk it will eventually boil over on its own. And simply surrendering to them runs the same risk. You must *never* surrender the position of the ego when confronting the unconscious. You must let the gift speak, but not dominate you."

"A symbiotic relationship," Hunt said.

"Just so," nodded Ugo.

Hunt rose from the couch and walked to the window, looking out into the flurries that fell gently from the sky. Despite being able to use it for good, the risk of being dominated by his gift disturbed him greatly. It shook his sense of stability to hear that his psyche was not a flat, solid object that could be depended on without thought, but rather a delicate balance that had to be maintained at all times to avoid disaster. It was like walking around with a bomb implanted in his chest, ready to go off at any time. It was an enormous responsibility, and required a degree of self-awareness that he had never practiced before. From then on, especially since they had begun the process of integrating the gift into his conscious mind, he would have to carefully monitor himself to ensure it didn't get out of hand and hurt those around him.

He stood by the window for several minutes, running these heavy thoughts over and over again in his mind.

Ugo glanced at him periodically through the smoke of his pipe, and eventually determined that a woman's touch was needed. He nodded Hunt's way once he'd caught his granddaughter's attention, and then rose silently and went up to bed.

Absorbed in his thoughts, Hunt didn't notice Wanda draw near until he felt the warmth of her body by his side. She took his hand, but he held it so limply that she eventually let go and stood there.

"I know it's hard, Rex," she said after a long spell of silence.

"But you don't really know that, do you?" he said somberly. "You hardly know anyone with a 'dark' gift, do you?"

"Not many," she admitted. "But there have been a few. And they've all been very useful to our organization, Rex. They've done a lot of good."

"But they haven't been 'marked,' have they? It wasn't their destiny to be an out-and-out destroyer, was it?" he asked in frustration. "You and your grandfather can build and help things grow. You can guide and teach and support." He nodded out the window towards Midway generally. "You know as well as I do how important that is in a hopeless town like this. Why should it be my lot to just make things worse? Even if I justify it by using it against bad people, it's still a nasty kind of destiny. I find it a hard fact to accept."

"Others have," she said quietly. "So will you."

"Heh, like who?" he countered.

"Like your father," she confided in a whisper.

"What?" he asked, turning sharply to face her. "He had the same gift I do?"

"I can't say," she replied, shaking her head. "I don't know for sure what your gift is yet. But he had the power to cloud the minds of others, leaving them confused. He could drive people insane if he pushed it hard enough. When he was younger he did just that, dragging up such a mass of unconscious material in his victims that they were flooded beyond help. They spent the rest of their days staring into space. It was a terrible way for their stories to end."

"And what happened then?" he asked, gazing out the

window once more.

"Your father was so horrified by what he'd done that he vowed never to use the power again. He studied medicine and practiced in all the worst parts of the empire, trying to make up for what he'd done. Naturally he couldn't keep his vow: to reject the gift would have forced it to well up within him until it burst, doing more harm than he'd ever done before. Luckily the Order found him and trained him to use it moderately, keeping it in check."

"There's nothing to keep me from following in his footsteps," Hunt said. "I might lash out and do the same thing."

"No, the planet clearly thinks you're to be trusted with this power," Wanda said. "Otherwise it wouldn't have given you so much help in developing your connection with the unconscious. Besides, you know too much of suffering to inflict it needlessly on others. You'd only use your power as a last resort."

"You've got a lot of faith in me," he replied.

She grasped his chin and turned it towards her.

"Yes, I do. A great deal. So does grandfather."

"And so do I," chimed in Wellesley.

"See, even the 'brilliant war AI' thinks you can handle this," she chuckled, a sweet smile on her lips. "And he ought to know: he's lived longer than any of us have." Her smile faded and she grew serious. "Believe in your own goodness, Rex. Your heart is too true to falter."

Leaning close, she kissed him on the cheek.

"Now get some sleep. It's been a long day, and we have a lot of work to do tomorrow."

He turned back towards the window as she shuffled wearily through the den. Her feet could be heard on the stairs a moment later, creaking their way up to bed.

"I like that girl," Wellesley said. "Good head on her shoulders. Little plump, but warm hearted. She'd make a good wife."

"Sounds like you'll be very happy together," Hunt said

lightly, some of his old good humor finally starting to shine through.

"Oh, I never date humans," Wellesley said. "Too...organic. Now, let's follow the young lady's suggestion and go to bed. I need my sleep."

"You don't sleep," Hunt said, flicking off the light in the corner and going upstairs.

"No, I was just being tactful," replied the AI. "*You* need your sleep. Too many more late nights and early mornings and you'll burn out."

"Don't think Ugo's gonna give me much choice on that score. Like he keeps saying, I've got to be ready as soon as possible. After all," he finished, laying his hand on the doorknob of his room, "they need to sharpen their weapon."

The force of this statement didn't hit him until after he'd said it. The cynical idea that he was being used forced its way into his mind with full force and turned his previous good humor to bitterness. Wellesley knew him well enough to anticipate this would happen at some point and was prepared for it.

"They aren't just using you, Rex," he said. "Sure, you're useful to them. But they genuinely care about you."

"People often put on a show of interest when they want something from you," Hunt said. "I've seen it before. They're just sweetening the deal until their 'dark element' can explode all over the enemy. Then I'll just be an inconvenient memory."

"That's your background talking," the AI said firmly. "You've lived on the edge for so long that you can't tell when someone *isn't* trying to take food out of your mouth, or the coat off your back. These people are kind, Rex. They aren't trying to hurt you. I wouldn't sit silently by if I thought that was going to happen."

"Wanda can be very charming," Hunt countered, sitting on the bed and pulling off his socks. "You said yourself you liked her."

"Oh, tut tut," the AI said. "*Kol-Prockian* AIs aren't

susceptible to female wiles. We see things just as they are. Now stop being dense and get some sleep. You always get suspicious when you're tired."

"I guess you're right," Hunt said, climbing into bed and pulling the covers over himself, too tired to argue anymore. "I'm just jabbering nonsense."

"I'm glad you see that."

Hunt turned off the little lamp that stood next to his bed and looked up at the dark ceiling for a few moments.

"Wellesley?"

"Uh huh?"

"You really think I can handle this gift, whatever it is?"

"Without question."

Hunt smiled in the darkness.

"Goodnight, old friend."

"Goodnight, Rex."

Day after day Hunt and Wanda worked on establishing a solid bridge to his unconscious, filling out that first tenuous connection they had formed during their initial excursion into his mind. Somehow Ugo managed to get Hunt out of working at the greenhouse over and over again. But each time he asked how he did it, the old man just smiled and ignored the question.

One crisp morning Wanda and Rex went into the den as always. Ugo had gone to work, and they had the place to themselves. They sat on the floor as before. But instead of extending her hands to him, Wanda kept them folded in her lap.

"It's time, Rex," she said significantly. "We have to revisit the vision of the magician and learn what your power is."

"I had a feeling we were going to," Hunt said with a smile slowly crossing his lips. "You've been acting funny all morning."

"Have I?" she laughed, her cheeks growing red. "I didn't mean to. I guess I'm just a little nervous. I only barely saved you last time. But grandfather thinks it best if we do this on our own, as at the first. He said we have to trust our own abilities."

Hunt reached his hand out and took hers.

"You'll do great," he said. "I don't have any doubt."

She smiled her cute, plump little smile and took his other hand.

"Ready?"

Hunt nodded.

Just like the first time the den swirled away from them and they were deposited in darkness. Having established a broader connection to his unconscious in the meantime, they found a wide path waiting for them, leading straight into the deepest recesses of his mind. She took his hand and they began to walk, the darkness receding far from them.

"Do you ever get bored with this?" Hunt asked after a short time walking.

"Bored with what?"

"Oh, this," he said, waving his free hand to indicate the shrouded world around them. "Does it ever get monotonous jumping into other people's thoughts? You must see a lot of the same themes over and over again."

"Oh, absolutely not," she said emphatically. "Everyone is different, even if it's just a little bit. Every mind has a take on the world wholly its own. There are no duplicates in nature."

"I like that statement," he said, turning it over in his mind. "Is that a Wanda original?"

"No, I read it someplace," she said mildly. "A book grandfather got me when I was a child. I can't remember the name of it now. But it helped clarify a lot of my ideas, even at that age. It showed me that we have to take each person on their own terms, as unique individuals. It's really helped me with my work. Otherwise I'd be spending too much time plotting the similarities between my pupils to really notice what makes them special."

"And what makes me special?" he asked lightly.

Reluctantly she turned to him, a serious look on her

face.

"Your pain," she said.

His smile melted away, and they walked the rest of the way in silence.

"We're just on the threshold of the vision now," Wanda said. "I can feel the charge. It's a little lower than the first time. The contact you made with it before helped to moderate it. But it will still hit like a ton of bricks."

"I can feel it," he said, extending his free hand ahead of him and sensing the energy it contained. "Any advice before going in?'

"Keep your head," she replied. "It's all a battle between the ego and the unconscious impulse. Just when you feel yourself getting swept away remember that the ego *must* have predominance over the vision. The ego is the caretaker of your psychological garden: without the garden he loses purpose, but he must always maintain his position of authority over it. They are symbiotic, yet the ego rules. Understand?"

"Yes, I've got it," he said firmly.

"Alright," she replied, releasing his hand. "We have to go in separately. The vision must be tackled by you alone. But I'll be on hand in case things go wrong." She stepped slightly to the side and gestured forwards. "Enter whenever you're ready."

Rex drew a deep breath and exhaled slowly. Then he stepped through the shroud that separated him from the vision.

Instantly he felt himself exhilarated, his spirit effervescent. He could see the magician as before. But this time he wielded a long, dark staff. He was surrounded on each side by armies numbering in the tens of thousands. A shadow emanated from the staff and struck the armies. They began fighting each other, perceiving their comrades to be the darkest, most horrific creatures imaginable.

Hunt's spirit swelled at this sight, and he started to float off of the ground. The power of the impulse was almost irresistible, and he felt a delicious sense of strength and freedom flowing through him. All his past struggles seemed inconsequential before the power that bore him up. The message was clear to him: he needed only to surrender to the impulse to enjoy might, ease, and perfect clarity of mind and purpose. No more internal friction need trouble his thoughts. Just succumb to the power of the impulse, and all other considerations would fall by the wayside, leaving only the satisfying expression of itself to be thought of.

Just short of the point of no return he recalled Wanda's words and reasserted the control of his ego. The impulse strove against this, offering all the inducement it could muster. It drew from his memory one painful moment of weakness and suffering after another, using them as examples of what it could prevent in the future. But he slowly lowered until he was back on solid ground once more. The struggle was over. He had achieved mastery over the vision.

At this moment a massive red dragon flew up into the sky, screeching evilly. It did a somersault over the wizard, descending towards him at the bottom of the movement. It released a terrible stream of darkness which struck the wizard and sent him tumbling over backward. He regained his footing just as the dragon flew past, knocking him over with the wind produced by its wings. Desperately he cast bolts of thick darkness at the beast, but without effect. They fought for nearly an hour, with Hunt anxiously watching the entire contest. Somehow neither party ever showed any sign of harm from the blows they received, and with no diminution of stamina they carried on.

"It's a strange vision," Wanda said, drawing near at last.

"It's like it's stuck in some kind of loop," Hunt said with frustration, eager to know how it would end. "I feel like my fate is bound up in this somehow."

"This isn't a premonition, Rex," Wanda said. "It's some construction of your unconscious mind."

"No," replied Hunt, shaking his head. "This is real. Terribly real. I can feel it."

They observed a moment longer, and then she took his hand.

"Come on, Rex. It's time to go."

"But the vision," he said, his voice trailing as he continued to watch.

"If it's nonsense it won't matter how long we watch it," she said. "And if it's real–"

"It is," he cut in.

"And if it's real," she repeated, "you won't be able to get away from it. It'll pursue you, especially now that you've mastered the scene that preceded it. It'll have an easy time accessing your conscious mind. You'll probably dream about it soon."

He watched the wizard fall twice more. Then he turned from the scene and looked at Wanda.

"Alright, I'm ready," he said, taking her hands and shutting his eyes.

The screeching of the dragon, and the shouts of the wizard, faded until they were barely audible. Soon the crackling of the den's fireplace could be heard, and he knew they were back.

"We did it!" she cheered, throwing her arms around his neck and hugging him. "And we did it all on our own! Well, you did. I just had to get you inside."

"I couldn't have done it without you," he smiled.

"Yes, you could have," she said firmly. "You bested the vision by yourself. That was the hard part. Any second rate psychic could have gotten you inside. But it is a true triumph of self-control to overcome a power fantasy like that, especially with so little training. You should be very proud of yourself."

"Thank you," he said, rising to his feet and offering her his hand. She took it and stood up. Then his face grew heavy. "Now we know what my gift is," he said in a low voice, looking off into space as she peered up into his eyes. "Much like my father I can unleash the unconscious in my victims."

"Yes, but with a twist," she added. "He flooded the

conscious mind with data, confusing his victims, or driving them mad if he pushed it far enough. But you specifically target their darkest fantasies, playing upon them until your targets are beside themselves with terror. You are an agent of fear."

"A nice thought," he said with a grimly ironic smile.

That night he slept deeply, all that he'd experienced in recent weeks flooding through him in a succession of images. His mind was consolidating its memories, preparing him for the next step in his life. He felt a sense of completeness filling him even as he slept. The old life was being put away, packaged in tight bundles and ushered off into the deepest recesses of his psyche. Space was being cleared for what lay ahead, and the dangers that needed to be overcome.

This done, he descended into a dream. A dark gloom surrounded him. The only color he saw was that of green grass beneath his feet.

Then he saw a thin, ethereal woman standing a great distance off on her own little island of grass. She possessed a reality that made him feel she was not a mere figment, but an actual person. He could feel a force pulling them together, but they drew no closer than they already were. She began reaching her hands over her head, as though trying to grab something unseen. This continued for some minutes, until she began to tire and sat down on the ground, looking dejected.

Two figures stepped from the shroud behind her. Nasty creatures, they looked like men combined with bats. Dark, spindly wings sprung from their backs and flapped noiselessly, autonomously, as they approached the unsuspecting woman. They drew back their hairy cheeks and revealed fangs that dripped yellow saliva. Their hands raised in anticipation of seizing their prey, they bent down to grab her.

"No!" shouted Hunt in a booming voice that filled the dark space. Stretching forth his hand toward the creatures, a stream of black mist shot from his fingers and struck them both. They fell to the ground in fear, writhing and tearing at the air. They tumbled against each other and began to fight, chewing each other's wings and scratching at the other's eyes.

The woman, completely unaware of the fight behind her, saw Rex in the distance and stood up, a hopeful expression on her face. She walked gingerly forwards, covering half the distance between them before fear replaced her hope and she shrunk away from him, like an uncertain doe retreating before a strange sound. Slowly she walked backwards.

"Wait! Don't go back!" he pleaded, trying to follow her but unable to move. "I need you!" he said spontaneously.

The woman hastened away, disappearing into the darkness.

Suddenly Hunt awoke. The light streaming through the small window of his bedroom told him it was dawn.

Going down to breakfast and seeing only Ugo at the table, he slid into a chair and scratched his ruffled hair, trying to work some alertness into his groggy mind.

"Busy night?" Ugo asked knowingly, his pipe hanging from his mouth as he looked over the top of a thick book he'd been reading.

"And how," Hunt replied emphatically. "Where's Wanda?"

"Off to pick up a few items we need. She'll be back soon enough," he said casually, still reading his book. "Left your breakfast on the counter over there," he added, nodding behind the younger man, who arose and brought it back to the table.

Hunt ate slowly, deeply troubled by the dream he'd had. The woman's face wouldn't leave his mind. The sense of hope, of deliverance, followed by such a terrible expression of fear and anxiety made him feel low. He couldn't escape the feeling that something within him had driven her away, that sudden awareness of some hidden evil had frightened her once she was close enough to perceive it.

"You'd better tell me about it," Ugo said with a reluctant sigh, slapping his book shut and laying it on the table beside a steaming cup of tea.

Briefly Hunt recounted the dream.

"There's something about that woman," he said distractedly when he'd finished. "She was so real. I'm certain she would have felt like a real person if I could have only touched her."

"Describe her to me," Ugo said.

"Well, she was very thin. Her face was like some delicate sculpture that someone had made out of the finest materials possible. I got the distinct impression that goodness radiated from her, as though some healing aura was emanating from her body. It was like she glowed. I don't think–"

"Enough of the spiritual description," Ugo cut in. "Just finish telling me what she looked like."

"Like I said, thin, almost ethereal," Hunt said rather flatly, his blood warming from being cut off. "Her hair was white like snow. She was very lightly built, like an academic who under ate and never once felt the sun against her skin if she could help it. Frankly I think a good strong wind would blow her over."

"Very interesting," Ugo said, holding his pipe as he puffed away at it. "And you say you couldn't approach her, yet you felt a force drawing you two together?"

"That's right," nodded Hunt. "It was like gravity."

"A felicitous metaphor if there ever was one," Ugo laughed.

"Meaning?"

"And she recoiled once she got close enough to you?" the old man asked, ignoring Hunt's question.

"Yeah, I think I've covered that already," Hunt said shortly, growing irritated with Ugo's mysterious manner.

"No need to get tart, son," Ugo said light heartedly. "I heard you the first time you explained it. I just need to let the details circulate in my mind a little more before giving an answer. It's just how my intuition works. Now, let's see: beast men; a vulnerable healer who recoils from you when she gets too close to you; an invisible force pulling you two together. And grass...Why on earth was there grass..." his voice trailed. "Oh! I see," he said, his eyes lighting up. "I'm glad to see your gift in evidence within the dream. The fact you reached for it automatically means you've integrated it very well."

"There's one more thing," Hunt said after a moment. "I didn't mention it because it seemed silly."

"There's nothing silly in a dream of this nature," Ugo said firmly, almost critically.

"When the woman drew back," he said, hesitating a moment. "Well, I begged her not to. I shouted that I needed her."

"And why did you do that?" Ugo asked, puffing once again.

"I have no idea. It just came to me."

"Nothing just 'comes' to us, dear boy," he said. "There's always a reason for the things we do, though it might not be the reason we're most comfortable with. Something about this woman appealed to you."

"That's true enough," admitted Hunt. "She had a quality, a spirit that I can't define. But it was marvelous. I knew I couldn't let her go once I'd seen it. When she drew back I felt like a dagger had been plunged into my heart, that she had rejected me in the most painful way possible. I tried to follow her, to keep her within sight. But I couldn't move. Then she disappeared into the gloom."

"Fascinating," Ugo said. "You should never leave any detail out, Rex. This makes it clear at once what the dream was about. I nearly headed down a wrong path until you added this 'silly' bit of information."

"Well. what does it mean?" Hunt asked, too intrigued to be annoyed with Ugo's didactic manner.

"Well, to start with," he said, leaning back in his chair, "the woman *is* a real woman. There's no doubt about that. Her name is Lily Tselitel. And you're right, there *is* something special about her. She has a special gift for healing, though she doesn't know it yet. Her own awareness of the unconscious is terribly academic. She *knows* it exists, even interacts with it effectively with her patients. But her personal experience with it is limited by fear."

"Of what?"

"Of the darkness that lies within," Ugo said sagely, warming to his topic. A small, satisfied smile crossed his lips as he settled comfortably into his element. "Light and dark exist in all of us, you see. It finds palpable expression in your gift, Rex. But for most of us it is more like a shadow that flits around the edges, making us uneasy in moments when we're alone and undistracted. It raises those little doubts about whether we're such decent people after all, once the guests have gone home and the rest of the house is empty. A girl like Tselitel has dedicated her whole life to healing others. She's repressed the darkness just as much as she possibly can. This makes her doubly averse to any expression of it. She fears it will link up with the bit of it she carries within and cause it to explode outwards, dominating her."

"Then why did she draw towards me at first?" Hunt asked. "I must have had some appeal for her to do that. I saw the hope on her face, the sense of deliverance."

"You're right, you *did* offer her deliverance," Ugo said. "You see, despite her repression she *wants* to integrate the darkness. But she's so terrified by it that she doesn't even let herself think about it. Unconsciously you offered her another option. *You* could carry out that dark role, thereby lifting the need to integrate her other side from her shoulders. At least that was the dream she had, the fantasy."

"But then she recoiled," Hunt said.

"Yes, the darkness got too real for her and she wanted out. The cure wasn't worth the risk once she had it in front of her, so she took to her heels."

"But what about me?" Rex asked. "I was attracted to her as well. She spoke to my heart like the fulfillment of my deepest dream. I would have done anything to keep her near me. I was obsessed the moment I saw her."

"It's the same story for you, but in reverse," Ugo said. "In her you find a counterpoise for the darkness you carry. You feel, deep down, that as long as you have her bright, healing example to reinforce the little spark of light within, that you can never go very far astray. She would keep you well, in other words. Just as you would do the necessary destroying work to keep her way of life safe from those who would harm it. To use a gardening metaphor, she plants the flowers but you pull the weeds. It's a symbiotic relationship."

"Those seem to be cropping up everywhere," Hunt said with annoyance, his sense of independence violated. "Can't anything just stand on its own? Does everything need a counterpart?"

"Pretty much everything," replied Ugo calmly. "It's the way life works, for some reason or other. I don't bother to ask why anymore. You see opposites everywhere. It's just a fact."

"A tiresome fact," Hunt said.

"Most are!" Ugo laughed enthusiastically. "But we must accept them all the same, or we'll get trampled by life's circus."

"You still haven't explained the beast men, or the gravity pulling us together," Hunt said.

"I'm coming to those," Ugo replied, tossing a leg over the other and sipping his tea slowly before continuing. He knew these actions exasperated Rex, who rolled his eyes impatiently. But he savored the status that his role as interpreter gave him, and he wanted it to last as long as possible.

"To begin with the beast men, they represent a composite image. Their obvious vileness symbolizes their purpose, their intent. They want to do all sorts of nasty things, and this is, as it were, written in their bodies. The cruel, spindly wings show their lack of common humanity. They can soar above the rest of the race and avoid the burdens we have to deal with on a regular basis. They drop in out of the sky like bats, snatching their prey and returning to their safe havens. Fangs are used to inflict harm, and the yellow saliva dripping from them indicates that they will bring sickness or disease of some kind. The fact that these two elements are linked together shows that the one will follow the other. Their desire to inflict harm on others will lead to great illness. They must represent the scoundrels in the prison and the work they're prosecuting to the detriment of mankind."

"And what of the sense of gravity?" he asked.

"Again, I must say that that is a felicitous turn of phrase you've chosen," Ugo said approvingly. "The 'gravity' you describe is being generated by Delta-13. It is trying to draw the two of you together. But it can't *force* you together because it never works that way. It only helps those find what is within themselves. The problem is neither of you wanted to reach the other."

"What are you talking about?" Hunt nearly exploded. "I never wanted anything more in my life!"

"On one level that is true. But on another level it is false."

"Stop talking in riddles," Rex snapped.

"I'm not," replied Ugo slowly, looking through his bushy white eyebrows as he took another sip. "Part of you wants her with you more than anything else because she represents legitimacy for you. You feel she will keep you from descending into wrong. But another powerful part of your personality fears that you will soil her if she gets too close. You don't want to handle her, as it were, because you're afraid of polluting her and removing her purifying force. Not that you could, of course. But that is your fear all the same."

"I don't believe that," Hunt said stoutly. "I didn't move because the dream wouldn't let me."

"Dear boy, the dream *is* you," explained Ugo. "It's all a construction from within your mind. Things don't just *happen* in a dream. Especially not one as prophetic as that. There are no accidents in such a fantasy."

"So that's it then," Hunt said glumly. "I don't want her near me, and she doesn't want that either."

"We'd better hope not, or we're all in big trouble," Ugo said.

"What do you mean?"

"Hasn't it occurred to you that Delta-13 is trying to bring you two together for a reason? It thinks you need each other. You have to cooperate in order to complete your work. That's why there was grass where either of you were standing. It represents growth, new life, a counterpoise to the terrible fate we shall be consigned to if you fail."

"I'd say we have a tough road ahead of us, if we're repelled by each other," Hunt said moodily.

"Well, just because opposites attract, it doesn't mean there isn't friction," Ugo smiled.

"Then what do I do?" Hunt asked.

"That's a question you're going to have to ask yourself," Ugo said. "My time as your teacher is drawing to a close. Soon you'll have to step out on your own and follow your own lights. It's the only way you'll grow strong enough to complete the task set before you."

"But I can't do that!" Rex said, suddenly feeling very alone at the thought of losing one of his only supports. "I'm only an initiate! I haven't plumbed the mind for decades like you have!"

"But you have Delta-13 on your side," the old man said. "That's as much help as any man needs. It will help you understand all that you need to. Just be careful to listen when it speaks, for it *will* speak to you. Not in words, but in meaningful dreams, ideas, and associations. You'll find yourself simply *knowing* what to do. It will be the planet guiding your inner processes, helping you find the answer already within you."

Ugo glanced at an old clock that hung quietly ticking away behind Rex's head.

"And now I've got to get down to the greenhouse and start my shift," Ugo said, downing the rest of his tea and standing up.

"Just one question," Hunt said, looking up from the table at the lanky old man before him. "How have you gotten me off work for so many days?"

"Simple," the old man replied. "I told them you'd gone missing in the blizzard, and that your body must be buried until three feet of snow."

"What!" exclaimed Hunt, leaping out of his chair. "You told them I froze to death? What's going to happen when they see me again, magically returned from the dead? I can't hide out here forever."

"They won't see you again," Ugo said. "Not until your work is finished. If you succeed and the lid is blown off the travesty they're trying to commit here, then nobody will care if you suddenly revive. And if you fail, nobody will have the independence of thought to care."

CHAPTER 7

Two nights later Hunt stood in a nook formed by the awkward joining of two buildings. Twice the patrols had walked past, barely missing him with their flashlights as they worked their beat, enforcing the curfew. The numbing cold was gradually working through his clothes, causing Wellesley to doubt the wisdom of being there. In his environment suit he could have waited almost indefinitely, out of the wind as he was. But that, along with his helmet and the rest of his gear, was locked away in his little shack, beyond his reach. Ugo had thought it best to leave the house completely untouched, since any sign of disturbance might tip off the authorities. They often monitored the haunts of those reported missing for weeks, even months at a time, to ensure the story was really true. More than a few people had tried to get out of work by 'disappearing' in one of Delta-13's periodic blizzards, typically by hiding out with friends. But they always needed to touch base with home eventually, and it was then that the police usually nailed them.

Hunt was waiting to meet Gromyko. The crackdown on the Underground taverns had redoubled since the blizzard, the government hoping to knock out the resistance while everyone was still reeling from the storm. The frozen streets, piled high with snow, had made it impossible for the organization to move their wares – the cheap alcohol that supported so much of their operating costs. The police seized this opportunity to thrash them as harshly as possible, and Gromyko had subsequently taken to the streets, hiding where he could. Through sheer luck Hunt had managed to slip him a message through an old contact, and had received word to wait in the nook.

"If Gromyko wanted to sell you out, this would be a fine way to do it," Wellesley said sourly. "Put you out here so that you can freeze half to death, then have the cops jump you when you least expect it. It'd be a pretty good way to keep his neck out of the noose."

"He wouldn't do that," Hunt said quietly, the cloth mask over his face muffling his voice.

"I think he might," persisted the AI. "Look, the Underground is being beaten into hash. It's only a matter of time before the police break it. With the organization gone, Gromyko will need some kind of friends if he wants to keep trading on this planet. The pirates won't work with a solo operator, no matter how famous he *once* was, so he'll have to turn to the government and beg a little indulgence to continue his work. With the list of black market operators he's got up his sleeve, he can trickle out information and keep them off his back for months, maybe years. They'll gladly let him carry on in exchange for such information. But first he'll have to prove himself. And what better way could he do that than to turn over a powerful adversary?"

"Your logic is sound," replied Hunt with a smile. "But you've made a fatal error."

"That being?"

"Nobody knows I'm a powerful adversary – yet. As far as the government is concerned, I'm just a dead gardener."

Before Wellesley could respond a shadow darted between two buildings across the street. Hunt saw it and pulled as far back into the nook as he could. Moments later a head shot around the corner.

"Rex?"

It was Gromyko.

"Right here," Hunt replied, extending a hand that was gratefully received. "Do we talk here?"

"No, too many patrols," Gromyko said tensely. "Come with me."

Without another word the smuggler slipped around the corner of the nook into the street. He was half a building away by the time Hunt had pushed off of where he'd been leaning and emerged. He bolted after him, crunching loudly in the snow. Gromyko sharply gestured for him to keep it down, and then moved quickly down the street.

Gromyko led him along every bypath he could think of, taking the most indirect route he could to a little hideaway halfway across the city. He constantly looked over his shoulder, pausing every couple dozen feet to listen. The mere sight of a patrol would almost make him jump out of his skin.

"He's gone paranoid," Wellesley commented.

Inwardly Hunt agreed with him. He could see the equilibrium of the resistance leader had been badly shaken, and that he doubted everything, and everyone, around him. The old cockiness that had always characterized him was gone, though Hunt hoped not for good. He'd always drawn strength from Gromyko's airy sense of invincibility. The last thing he wanted to see was the shattering of yet another spirit by the oppressions of the authorities.

"In here," Gromyko said at last, ushering Hunt through a small wooden panel that he pulled away from the side of an abandoned house. Slipping in after him, Gromyko guided him to an interior room. Quietly he slid the room's door shut, its movement impeded by what sounded like foam packed around the frame. Then Gromyko flicked on a small light he carried with him.

"Don't worry, there aren't any cracks in here. They can't see it from outside," he said.

Hunt looked around him and saw they were standing in a small square room, freshly painted white. He shot a confused look at his companion.

"Painted it myself," the latter grinned. "That's how I know there aren't any cracks. They haven't bothered with this old house for years, so I figured it was the perfect place to set up camp for the time being. Keeps out the wind pretty good, too."

They sat down on a pair of upside down buckets and looked at each other silently for a moment.

"It's good to see you, Rex," the smuggler said. "They've been hounding us from morning till night. I'm afraid this is the end of the resistance on Delta-13. It'll take years to rebuild our network, if anyone even wants to bother trying. The fact is we've been running on dregs for years now. Ever since Quarlac started sending more and better artifacts back here, the margins for ours have collapsed. We managed to hold on with moonshine, but just barely. We've had to chop our operating budget by over sixty percent in the last five years. You just can't mount a successful resistance on starvation rations."

Hunt looked but said nothing. After all he'd learned about the Order from Ugo and Wanda it was hard to take the petty efforts of the Underground seriously anymore. But Gromyko was his friend, and he tried to show as much concern as he could muster.

"Ah, but you must be hungry, spending all that time in the cold," the smuggler said, concluding that that was the reason for his friend's silence. "Here, I've got an old police ration that I snatched last week. I'll split it with you," he said eagerly, peeling open the wrapper and snapping the dry bar in half with his gloved fingers.

"No, I'm alright," Hunt said, bothered by the idea of taking food from his obviously starving friend. The smuggler had lost at least ten pounds since the last time he'd seen him. His cheeks were growing gaunt, and a haunted hollowness showed in his eyes. His hands fidgeting nervously, his feet shifting every few seconds, he appeared a mere shadow of his former, jaunty self. Devouring the ration without hesitation, it was clear a great deal more would be needed to fill his belly for the evening.

"So, what can I do for you?" he asked, trying to put some of his old zest back into his voice.

"I need help finding someone," Hunt said, dropping his voice despite the security of the location. "Lily Tselitel. She's a psychiatrist working for the government."

"I know of Tselitel," Gromyko said, the zest fading from his voice as he contemplated her. "The government was tied up in knots when it heard she was coming out. She's been critical of them for years. Well, as critical as you can be, in times like these. Rumor has it she comes from a long line of anti-imperial types. Supposedly some of her ancestors fought against the establishment of the empire a couple of centuries ago, and their opinions haven't really changed in the meantime. Who knows, maybe it's genetic! She could be a powerful asset, if we could establish a link. But I'm afraid it would be impossible to meet her."

"All I need to know is where she is," Hunt said. "I can take care of the rest."

"No, you can't," replied the smuggler with a weak laugh. "First of all, she spends every waking minute she can inside the prison. Word is she's pulling herself apart trying to help some comatose guy. She only goes home when they close down the psychiatric wing of the hospital for the day. And then she spends all of her time in her apartment."

"What floor is it on?"

"First."

"At least that's in my favor," Hunt said to himself.

"Rex, you can't be serious," Gromyko said with an incredulous shake of his head. "The apartments are guarded constantly. Patrols work the grounds twenty-four hours per day. You're asking for a stint in solitary if you so much as *approach* that area without a pass..."

"I need to see her, Antonin," Hunt said. "Just tell me what apartment she's in."

"I don't know if I should," he replied, eyeing his friend. "I don't want you to get captured."

"One way or another I'm heading up that hill to see her," Hunt said determinedly. "I'll waylay her on the path between her place and the prison, or I'll get her when she's home. But I've got to see her."

"What, are you suddenly in love with this woman?" the smuggler laughed. "What is so important about her that you *must* see her?"

"That's my business," Hunt said.

"Ooh, going to be mysterious, eh?"

"I can't imagine you tell *me* everything that you do," Hunt replied gamely.

"Ha! That's true enough. I suppose every man is entitled to a few secrets. But first you must answer a few questions."

"If I can," replied Hunt guardedly.

"First, what is this business about you being dead?" Gromyko asked. "I was shattered when I heard it, so you can imagine my surprise when I got your note asking for a meeting. At first I suspected a trap. But our heavy-handed police wouldn't bother with such a ploy if they already knew how to contact me. They'd just beat down my door and drag me away."

"Let's say I've carried my campaign against the government to the next level," Hunt said cryptically. "I needed to disappear for a while, and the blizzard provided the perfect excuse."

"That's true," nodded Gromyko. "More than a few people have frozen to death in recent years. Why, I remember a police patrol that went missing for *three months* before they were finally found in a snow drift near the edge of town. And the storm that did them in wasn't half as bad as the one that's supposed to have carried you off."

"Alright, *now* will you tell me her apartment number?" Hunt asked.

"Soon, very soon," Gromyko said, holding up his hand for patience.

"Jackass," Wellesley muttered.

"This Tselitel, is she important to you personally, or as part of your campaign against the government."

"Both, if you can believe it," replied Hunt.

"But you've never met her before?"

"That's not exactly true," he replied. "I've...seen her from a distance."

"And that was enough for you?" asked Gromyko with a chuckle. "You must be desperate for a woman if that's all it takes for you to fall in love."

"I'm not *in love*, Antonin," Hunt said testily. "Now, are you going to tell me, or shall I just find out for myself?" he asked, standing up.

"Easy, my friend, easy," Gromyko said, putting a hand on his arm and pulling him back down to his bucket. "Very well, she is in apartment 138. But it would be suicide to try and reach her there. The only chance is the path between her place and the prison. And even that chance is too slim to consider. No, you had best give up the idea now. You'll never manage to pull it off."

"I might surprise you," Rex replied with a grin, an inward reference to his growing powers.

"That I doubt very highly," replied the smuggler. "I've got a good sense of what people are capable of, Rex. You're a great scavenger. You've got a real nose for the business. But you've always been second best at evading patrols. So I'd better go with you to make sure you make it."

"No dice, Antonin. I'm not gonna drag you into this. You've got enough trouble on your hands already."

"And how can this make things worse? I'm already on the run, as is the rest of the Underground. At least out there I'm *doing* something by helping you in your fight. It's that or sit in here for the rest of the evening while my teeth clatter from the cold."

"I don't think he can make it out there," Wellesley said. "He's lost so much weight and strength."

"You don't believe I can handle it?" Gromyko asked, seeming to hear Wellesley, though that was impossible. "I made it here tonight, didn't I? And the path we had to take coming here was long, with many pauses along the way that kept us in the elements. But our course to the apartments will be straight as an arrow once we're a little way from this house. Naturally you understand that I must be careful near here to avoid attracting attention, so we shall have to be a little indirect at first."

"Of course," replied Hunt, his tone indicating that he was still undecided.

"Please, Rex, do this as a favor to me," Gromyko said earnestly, his hungry eyes pleading. "I've felt so powerless lately that it has almost destroyed me. Give me this small opportunity to hit back at them for all they've taken from me."

"Just do it," Wellesley said after a further moment of hesitation on Hunt's part. "You're going to say yes anyhow, so let's get a move on."

"Alright," he said at last, to the immense relief of Gromyko.

"Oh, thank you, my friend!" he said happily, jumping to his feet. "We shall leave at once. I know the perfect path through the forest. We'll have to go out of town towards the west and cross a large expanse of open ground first. But then we shall be under cover almost until we hit the apartments."

"Let's get going before we think about it too much," Wellesley said gloomily. "This has got enough working against it already."

Carefully picking their way around the patrols near the house, the pair gradually straightened their course until they were heading due west. The two tiny moons above Delta-13 hovered in the distance, casting their paltry light on the snow below. It was still difficult to see, even with the white ground reflecting it back at them. But it made the night feel a little less dark and threatening.

"Are you warm enough, my friend?" Gromyko asked once they'd hit the open expanse he'd mentioned before leaving. "I can give you my medallion for a little while if you need it."

"No, I'm fine," replied Hunt half-truthfully, unwilling to take it for even a moment from his care-worn companion. "I'll let you know if I get too cold."

The smuggler nodded vigorously and resumed walking, his feet plunging deeply into the untrodden snow.

"He's certainly gotten a lot of his old pep back," Wellesley said. "Maybe he's not as far gone as I thought."

"Let's hope so," Hunt said quietly, following in his footsteps.

The town had disappeared behind them long ago, leaving them two lonely little dots in a massive sea of white. An icy wind from the east began to beat against their backs, penetrating their gloves and the seams of their clothes. The snow caked against their pants as they shuffled through it, chilling their legs. By the time they reached the forest their hands and everything below their knees were numb.

"Come on, there's a tight little group of trees we can stand behind for a little while to get our warmth back," Gromyko said. "They will break the wind for us." He clapped Hunt on the shoulder and led the way into the dark woods.

"I hope he knows where he's going," the AI said. "We could freeze out here."

Another five minutes and the little group was reached. The two men got on the western side of it and pumped their arms and legs to keep their circulation going while they waited. Branches rattled against each other in the treetops. Far in the distance a wolf howled. The night was alive in its own frigid way, making the duo feel very small and isolated in the blackness.

More than once Rex jerked his head at the sound of a stick clattering in the gloom. He knew it was just the wind, but instinct required him to at least look. He was just wondering if his ability to inspire fear extended to animals when Gromyko spoke.

"We'd better get moving again. Stopping here hasn't helped much. But at least I can feel my feet and hands again."

Rex could just make out his shape moving away from him. But more than anything he followed with his ears, listening to the smuggler shuffle slowly through the soft snow.

"We're almost there," Gromyko eventually said in a whisper. "Be careful to follow in my tracks to avoid snapping sticks under your feet. Don't make any noise or the patrols might investigate."

Hunching low and moving silently, the two men picked their way through a densely packed growth of thorny bushes, emerging a short distance from the prison and the buildings which serviced it.

"I'll be you've never seen it from this close before," Gromyko said triumphantly.

"I have," Hunt said soberly, thinking of the last time he'd visited his father there. "But not for a long time."

"Oh, of course," replied the smuggler, regretting his faux pas but unable to redeem it. Naturally, since everyone on Delta-13 was either a prisoner or related to one, each person staying there had seen the imposing structure at least once. "Well, this is the place. The apartments are over there," he said, pointing to the north-west. "Tselitel is staying in the building closest to the prison. Her apartment faces it. What do you want to do now?"

"Get closer," Hunt said, impelled by an internal urge that he didn't understand. He started to move past Gromyko but the latter stopped him.

"Now hold on a minute," he said, grabbing his arm. "Rex, there's nothing you can do from out here, not tonight. It's late. She's probably gone to bed by now. All you're gonna do is clatter your teeth and risk getting caught."

"I have to go, Antonin," Hunt said firmly, realizing that the powerful inner drive he felt was a signal from Delta-13, just as Ugo had told him. He had to follow it, no matter where it led. "I can't explain it now. I just have to go."

"Well, alright," the smuggler said. "But double back at the first sign of trouble. We can lose them easily in these woods if we have to."

"I'll be careful," Hunt assured him, advancing into the darkness.

"*I hope so,*" Gromyko thought. "*I sincerely hope so.*"

Hunt moved quietly across the tightly packed snow. The tramping of hundreds of feet to and from the apartments had pounded it into a frozen road which crunched noisily if he wasn't careful.

"How are we gonna know which apartment is hers?" Wellesley asked. "It's not like they put numbers over the windows."

"I'll know when I see it," Hunt replied quietly.

"Boy, a few weeks with those people and you've gone full-blown mystic on me," the AI said. "Just don't start reading tea leaves on me, okay?"

Rex smiled but didn't reply, his focus diverted by a pair of guards walking slowly towards the prison from the apartments, their flashlights darting back and forth. He dropped low to the ground and waited until they had gotten very far away before risking further movement.

He reached the building and walked along it, staying about twenty feet away. He looked at each apartment as he passed, alert for any inner sign as to which one it was. Just as he passed one towards the far end of the structure he was bathed in light and froze. Someone had opened the blinds on the inside, and he hoped that by keeping still he wouldn't attract attention. At that moment he cursed the dark clothes he'd chosen to wear. They helped him hide in the shadows of the city, but he was glaringly obvious when standing before a background of white.

It was a woman who'd opened the blinds. She was about to turn away when something caught her eye and she looked again. Then she opened the window and put her head through the opening, casting a shadow over Hunt.

"Hello? Who are you?" she asked. "Please come closer. I want to talk to you."

It was Tselitel. Despite her being the whole purpose of his visit he was still shocked to see the woman from his dream standing just a few feet away. Somehow that fact hadn't been real for him until that moment, and the surprise froze his tongue. He was just about to answer when another pair of guards came around the north corner of the building, their flashlights dancing across the snow around them.

Without a moment lost he dashed back the way he'd come, running as quickly as he could manage without undue noise. Pausing briefly, he could see that none of the guards were on to him yet. But he feared they might find his tracks and put both the complex and all the police in Midway on the alert, locking him and Gromyko out in the cold night. He got back to his companion and dropped to the snow in a sweat.

"Did you see her?" he asked.

"Uh huh," Hunt said breathlessly. "But just for a moment. I could have talked to her, Antonin! She was right there in front of me! But a patrol came in sight and I had to beat it."

"That happens," Gromyko said. "I've had to abandon plenty of operations because of a chance guard in the wrong place." He stood up and jerked his thumb towards the trees behind them. "Come on, let's get out of here and back into some heat. I've had enough snow for one night."

◆ ◆ ◆

"You saw her?" Wanda asked, radiating enthusiasm as she put a hot cup of tea into his shivering hands. He sat at the kitchen table with blankets wrapped around his shoulders and a warm, flat stone on his lap that Wanda had heated in the oven. "That's great!"

"Not *too* great," Hunt said, his teeth chattering as he drank down the tea and beckoned to have it refilled. "I didn't even speak to her. She just saw me, thrust open the window, and said she wanted to talk to me."

"That's good," Ugo said from the other side of the table, slowly sipping his own cup of tea.

"How is that?" Hunt rattled out.

"Any normal woman who sees a man standing in the snow outside her apartment isn't going to make herself vulnerable by opening the only barrier between them and inviting him to come closer for a chat. She's feeling the effects of the planet as well. It is drawing her to you. It's the only explanation."

"Too bad the planet couldn't keep the patrols away long enough for us to actually talk," he said ruefully. "I spent hours in the cold tonight just to catch a glimpse of her."

"Like I said, that happens sometimes," Gromyko said, entering the room to the surprise of Ugo.

"What are *you* doing here?" he snapped in a hostile tone. His eyes shot to Hunt, and then to Wanda.

"He came with Rex," she said simply, matching his gaze with difficulty. "He was half frozen! I couldn't just turn him away."

"Would have been just as well if you had," Ugo said grumpily, downing more of his tea with a scowl.

"I gather you don't like me," Gromyko said lightly, dropping into the chair next to Rex's. "Could I get a cup of tea, too, Wanda?"

"Of course, Antonin," she said shyly, fumbling with her hands as she put a cup and saucer in front of him and poured.

Until that point Hunt had forgotten that Gromyko and Wanda had known each other for several years because of her work in the Underground's taverns. The smuggler had never paid a great deal of attention to her, as far as Hunt knew. But the portly tapster's eyes rarely lost track of him whenever he was around.

"As a matter of fact, I don't like you at all," Ugo said hotly, his usual manners overcome by some inner compulsion to speak. "And I'll thank you for leaving as soon as you've finished your tea."

"Grandfather! He can't go outside now!" objected Wanda. "Why, he'd freeze to death in this weather! And the police might catch him at any of a dozen points! He needs to stay here and rest. He's been through enough for one evening."

"I can't believe what I'm hearing!" Ugo said, standing up from the table. "This is my house, Wanda! And I'll say who stays and who goes!"

"Yes, grandfather," she said quietly. "But ours is a *healing* order. We don't turn away those who need us."

Fuming but unable to answer her, he stomped from the room and went back upstairs to bed.

"You can stay the night now," Wanda said with a weak smile. "But I'm afraid he's going to be in quite a mood tomorrow. I wouldn't stick around if I were you."

"Oh, I don't know," Gromyko said with a sly gleam in his eye as he looked at her. "I might at that."

She giggled nervously and sat down on the other side of Rex, putting a little distance between herself and the smuggler.

"I wonder why the old gentleman has such a poor view of me," Gromyko said after a few moments of silence, his jocularity replaced by a look of modest concern. Despite his devil-may-care aura he genuinely cared what people thought of him, and it troubled him to receive such a hostile reception from someone he didn't even know. "I suppose my reputation precedes me."

"It does at that," replied Wanda. "He's had an eye on you for a long time."

"Funny that I never had an inkling of it," said the smuggler, stroking his chin. "I usually know when I'm under surveillance." Then realization struck and he looked at Wanda with a wide grin. "Oh, it's been you!"

She shrunk back with an embarrassed smile, averting her eyes.

"So you've just been playing up to me, then," he said matter-of-factly, more to himself than to her. "Oh, well. It's not like it hasn't happened before. A man in my position gets chased a lot, for many different reasons."

"It wasn't like that at all!" blurted out Wanda. "I really do like you, Antonin. It's just that I also had to report your activities to grandfather because, well, I can't say."

"Because of this 'healing order' you mentioned before?" probed Gromyko. "Don't imagine that I didn't notice that. Very little passes my eye that I don't see and understand at once."

"I really can't tell you, Antonin," she said apologetically, hoping he would drop the subject. "I'm sworn to secrecy. Only higher members can initiate outsiders."

"A secret society," he mused, drumming his fingers. "Now that you mention it, I *have* heard rumors of such a group operating on Delta-13. Beyond Delta-13, in fact. They're said to have agents all over. Until now I thought they were mostly a myth."

Hunt could see the agitation growing in Wanda's face as Gromyko worked his way closer and closer to the truth. The finger drumming continued for another half minute as the smuggler thought, until Hunt finally had to step in.

"Cut it out, Antonin," he said decisively. "Can't you see you're making her uncomfortable? She made a slip earlier when she intervened for you with Ugo. Outsiders aren't meant to hear that the Order even exists, certainly not from the lips of a junior member. She could get in a lot of trouble sticking her neck out for you like that. The least you can do is say nothing more about it."

"Ah, so you're a member, too!" Gromyko said triumphantly. "Don't try to hide it! I can deduce it from your words."

"Another syllable out of you and I'll throw you out into the snow myself," snapped Hunt, half rising from his chair and raising hands to grab the insolent renegade.

"Okay! Okay!" he said, holding his hands up in a sign of surrender. "I'll shut my mouth."

Hunt lowered himself into the chair once more. The trio

sat in silence for several minutes, Hunt's anger breaking the bonhomie that had existed before.

Finally Wanda stood up.

"I guess we'd all better get some sleep," she said. "I'll make up another bed for you."

They watched her leave the room and heard the stairs creak as she ascended the steps.

"Ooh, you've got your own room here?" Gromyko needled as they stood up and made for the doorway. "Looks like you've got a pretty cozy arrangement with these two."

Anger flared in Hunt's eyes. It had been too long a day, and his nerves were too tight to put up with any more. Instantly he belted Gromyko in the mouth, sending him tumbling into the table and chairs. The table slid across the floor and slammed into the cabinets, making a thunderous crash that rattled the dishes within them. The chairs fell in all directions, clattering on the floor and adding to the noise.

Wanda hurried down the stairs and covered her mouth with her hand when she reached the kitchen. She saw Gromyko wiping blood from his mouth while Hunt stood over him, ready to hit him again if he so much as squeaked.

"What are you, some kind of savage?" she demanded, rushing to Gromyko and dabbing his mouth with a handkerchief she carried with her.

Hunt felt ashamed for what he'd done, yet he knew he'd do it again if given the opportunity. Too tired to justify himself to the frowning Wanda, he turned from the pair and stalked towards the staircase. He was halfway up them when he saw Ugo standing upon them. He had one hand resting lightly on the railing, a look of approval in his eyes. He pointed at the bloody knuckles of Rex's right hand.

"Good for you," he said in a low whisper so that Wanda couldn't hear. "If I were your age I would have done that myself already. But violence is a young man's game."

"Wanda is boiling at me right now," he said quietly.

"She'll get over that," the old man said with a wave of

his hand. "But Gromyko won't, not for quite a while. He's been making eyes at Wanda for a long time, and I've been looking for a way to put him in his place. Now you've done that for me, which I won't forget any time soon. You have my thanks."

"My pleasure," he said with a modest smile. "Antonin is a good guy. But he needs to get kicked around a little from time to time."

"He certainly does," laughed the old man. "Now, get up to bed. We all should have been asleep hours ago."

CHAPTER 8

For days Gromyko stayed with them, unwilling to leave now that he'd found a safe harbor to stay in. Each night he would slip out and get in touch with his contacts who painted a very dark picture of the campaign the police were carrying out against the Underground. Even the safehouse he'd taken Hunt to on the night of their jaunt to see Tselitel had been discovered and broken into, his meager possessions seized. Only fragments of the movement remained, and he knew they too would soon be swept away.

One evening, just as dusk turned to night, Ugo and Wanda were having yet another argument about how long the smuggler could stay with them while they washed the dishes. Hunt sat at the end of the table, eating a light dinner of soup and quietly mulling his plans for the evening. He only half listened to the argument he'd heard nearly a dozen times before. The sound of the front door opening and then closing quietly reached his ears despite the ever rising volume of his hosts. Moments later Gromyko stepped into the kitchen, snow clinging to his pants from the knees down.

"Can't you at least dust yourself off at the door?" snapped Ugo, transferring some of the argument's heat straight into its subject.

But the smuggler wore a blank expression on his face as though he didn't even hear him. Walking slowly across the kitchen, leaving a little trail of melting snow behind him, he dropped into a chair and thumped his hands carelessly on top of the table. A note was visible in his left fist, gripped tightly as though he wished to strangle it.

"Federov has betrayed us," he said after a moment. "That is how the police knew where to find us. My own second in command has delivered us to them on a silver platter. The rest of the command structure is gone. Our suppliers have all been apprehended, and the traders we pay to get artifacts off the planet will be seized upon their return. There's nothing left for us. The movement is shattered for good."

"How do you know this?" asked Ugo in a quiet voice. He couldn't feel sympathy for the smuggler's plight, nor for the demise of an organization that he felt was altogether superfluous. But his manners were much too refined to pile onto a man who was stunned and hurting.

"Federov's girlfriend," Gromyko said, holding up the note and waving it in the air before dropping his fist on the table again. "She found secret messages between him and the government. She wrote this note just before being captured herself, so the courier told me. Good woman. The cause always came first for her."

"Oh, Antonin, I'm sorry," Wanda said, wrapping her arms around his neck and hugging him from behind.

Hunt saw Ugo frown and roll his eyes at the sight. Biting his tongue, the old man turned back to the dishes he'd been drying.

"What will you do now?" Hunt asked after a few moments.

"What can I do?" Gromyko asked. "My organization is gone. All my friends have been seized. I am hunted like a rodent. There's nothing for me on Delta-13 anymore. I must try to flee on one of the transports before they capture me, too."

"That's impossible," said Ugo without turning around. "They have scanners that can detect unaccounted for passengers. You'd never get off the ground. You know that as well as I do."

"Then what is left for me?" exclaimed Gromyko at his wit's end. "Shall I bury myself in a snowdrift and save them the trouble of persecuting me further?"

"Talking nonsense isn't going to help any," Ugo said, putting away the last dish and leaning against the counter. "You'll just have to find a way to cope with the situation."

Wanda released Gromyko and looked at Ugo.

"Grandfather, couldn't we…" she said, nodding towards the smuggler significantly.

"No, absolutely not!" he said.

"I could be a great asset to you!" Gromyko said, his former life suddenly returning. "I know this city better than anyone. I'll do anything you ask! I'll even act as a lowly courier, passing messages in the darkness. Please, let me do something useful."

"Well, you might be useful," mused Ugo, savoring the idea of humiliating the former resistance leader. "We could use someone to move messages of low value around the city."

"Oh, we'd find something much more important than that for Antonin to do," Wanda said. "Think of his former position! He used to be at the top of the Underground."

"An organization that no longer exists, thanks to the folly of its leader and the choices he made," Ugo said harshly. "Federov didn't choose himself for the number two slot. The responsibility for that decision must rest with Gromyko alone."

"He's right, Wanda," the smuggler said dejectedly. "I alone am to blame for the downfall of the resistance. I'd heard warnings about Federov for years from some of our most respected members. But I ignored them."

"You made decisions," countered Wanda. "That's all any leader does. No one can be right all the time."

"Yes, but it is our mistakes that define us as leaders, as much as our victories," Gromyko said. "Your grandfather is quite right. I shall start at the bottom and prove my worth, if I have any. I'm sure they'll find a higher station for me, if in their judgment I deserve it."

Hunt saw the sincerity of his friend and was impressed, never thinking he possessed such a capacity for humility. He was always so free, so unconcerned about the consequences of his actions, that he often seemed like an overgrown child. But a change had come over him, occasioned by the defeat of the Underground. A newfound glimmer of respect for Gromyko began to glow within him.

Hunt glanced at Ugo, whose face had softened towards the deposed leader. He met the younger man's eyes and nodded slowly. He too had been impressed by the change.

An hour later Hunt stood at the door, about to depart for another trek in the snow. The inner urge to see Tselitel had lain dormant for days, and he'd taken it as a sign that it was not yet time to attempt another meeting. But that very morning a powerful urge to try again had seized him, growing stronger as the day wore on.

"Gonna be cold tonight," Wellesley said, as his friend bundled himself as thickly as he could. "Are you sure about this?"

"I've got to see her," Hunt replied, fighting to pull his boots over a pair of extra thick socks. "I can feel it."

"Well, your feelings seem to be working out pretty well so far," the AI commented. "You managed to find her apartment, after all."

"Actually, I didn't," Hunt grinned. "I was about to keep on walking when she opened the blinds. I hadn't felt a thing."

"Oh, that's reassuring," Wellesley said sarcastically. "And just when I started getting on board with your mysticism, too!"

"Don't worry about the mysticism," Hunt said. "It's alive and well. I'm convinced that she opened the blinds at that precise moment because of me. So you see, I was right: I did find it. Just not in the way I expected."

At this juncture Gromyko came out of the den and approached Hunt, holding something in his hand.

"Still going over the initiation?" Hunt asked his friend.

"Uh huh. They've got more rules than I ever thought possible. 'Don't say this,' 'don't do that.' It's enough to make me dizzy."

"Well, that's what you signed up for," Hunt said. "You've got to play the game their way now."

"Oh, I know that," replied the smuggler with a grin. "And I'll be a good little boy, don't you worry. But I won't pretend it isn't a struggle."

Gromyko stood uncertainly before him for a moment, still tightly gripping what he held.

"Got something else on your mind, Antonin?" Hunt asked.

"Yes, I do," he replied, finally making up his mind. "I want you to take my medallion, the one that helps me endure the cold," he said, holding it in front of him. "It pains me to part with it. It was such a piece of my past life that I feel I'm losing a portion of myself. But it's gonna be nasty out there tonight, and who knows how long you might have to wait to see Tselitel."

"Thank you, Antonin," Hunt said, slipping the chain around his neck and feeling the warm disc slide down his chest. "I'll take good care of it."

"Be sure you do!" he replied with enthusiasm. "I'm gonna need that when I'm carrying notes through Midway." And then, more seriously, "Take care of yourself, Rex. Remember the path we took last time and stick to it. It'll carry you where you need to go."

"I will," Hunt said, shaking his hand. Then he opened the door and stepped into the frigid night.

Carefully retracing their former steps, Hunt made his way through the night. More than once he wished that the clever smuggler was there to guide him, especially when he was forced to conceal himself in shadows as the police crunched noisily past him. However, these feelings faded once he was outside the city and traversing the wilderness. By then he was glad to be on his own, for he felt certain that he would meet Tselitel that night, and he didn't want the charming rogue around when they finally spoke. He wanted more than anything to find out what she was like, to see if she could live up to the fascinating image he carried from the vision he'd had so many nights before. And he knew he couldn't really draw her out if Gromyko was there to steal the show.

"I hope that 'inner urge,' or whatever Ugo called it, is on the money tonight," Wellesley said, once they were just short of the bushes that fringed the forest, separating them from the government complex. "It's so cold out here that *my* teeth are almost clattering."

"Don't worry," Hunt said, crouching low and feeling Gromyko's medallion against his skin, "we've got a little extra help tonight."

"Thank God for that," Wellesley said sincerely. "Otherwise I'd be seriously worried if we're gonna make it back at all."

"Well, we could always turn ourselves in if I got too cold," Hunt grinned.

"Oh hush," Wellesley said. "Don't talk like that, not even in jest."

"Where's your sense of humor?"

"I think it froze somewhere between Midway and the forest," the AI said sarcastically. "Now what's your plan for Tselitel? Gonna try her apartment again?"

"No, I'm going to wait for her here," Hunt said, kneeling in the snow, his head just poking above the bushes. "I want to intercept her."

"But what if she's already passed through? We might while half the night away just to find out she's snug in her bed."

"I don't think so. The—"

"I know, I know," cut in Wellesley. "The 'inner urge' is speaking to you."

"That's right. And it says to stay right here."

"*I hope this isn't just mumbo jumbo,*" the AI thought, as

Hunt settled in and prepared for a long wait.

Despite the wind, and the cold snow packed around his legs, Hunt was pretty comfortable. The medallion had only been barely enough to keep Gromyko warm since he'd always worn such thin clothes. But, combined with the extra layers Hunt wore, it kept the chill confined to his extremities and face

Almost half an hour passed with only the noise of a distance patrol to disturb the stillness. Suddenly Hunt jumped to his feet, squinting into the gloom ahead and trying to make out a dark shape that was walking slowly from the prison.

"I think that's our girl," he said quietly to Wellesley, slowly pressing his way through the thorn bushes and standing up to get a better view in the darkness.

"Are you sure?"

"No. Looks like her, but I can't be certain."

Stepping a few feet closer, he squinted hard in the gloom to try and make out some detail that would inform him for sure. The figure moved through the cold with hunched shoulders, trying to resist the chill for as long as possible in barely adequate clothing.

"You'd think they'd give their people better winter wear," Wellesley commented.

The duo watched the figure cross the expanse between the prison and the apartments.

"We're almost out of time, Rex," Wellesley said. "They've nearly made it inside. If it *is* Tselitel, we've got to make our move now."

"But what if it isn't?" Hunt countered. "We'll get half the complex's guards breathing down our necks if it's anyone else." He moved along the trees to try and stay parallel to the walker. Suddenly a stick snapped under his foot. The figure looked over and saw him.

"Wait! Please wait!" he heard Tselitel's voice call out. She started running towards him, seemingly making all the noise she possibly could.

"Oh, keep your mouth *shut!*" Wellesley growled, afraid

the guards would hear as Hunt turned and bolted into the forest. "Wait! Where are you going?"

"To lead her away from the sentries," Hunt said angrily. "Maybe she'll be smart enough to follow."

He dove headlong into the forest, only pausing once the lights of the prison were no longer visible. Listening intently, he heard her crunch across the hard, frozen ground until her feet hit the soft, undisturbed snow near the trees. Half a minute passed before he heard her struggling through a large drift a short distance away.

"Someone's close," Wellesley whispered. "But I can't tell if it's her or not."

"It's her," Hunt whispered. "The patrols would be flashing their lights everywhere."

"What are you going to do?"

"Lead her farther away," Hunt said, as the swishing grew near. "I don't want some chance guard to relieve himself in the forest and hear us talking."

Pushing off a tree he'd been leaning against, he walked slowly south, guiding Tselitel farther from her apartment and deeper into the wilderness, pausing periodically to ensure she was still on his trail.

"Any farther and her feet will freeze off," Wellesley said. "The sentries can't possibly find us this far out. Let's double back and get her."

"The planet agrees with you," Hunt said, a powerful intuition instructing him to retrace his steps at just that moment. Very slowly he walked back, his ears pricked for the slightest sound of Tselitel's movements.

"Just ahead, Rex," Wellesley said. "I can hear her."

"Me too," Hunt said in a loud whisper, not really caring if she heard him.

He heard her jerk in the darkness at the sound of his voice, a gasp escaping her lips.

"I think you startled her," Wellesley said.

"Good," Hunt thought, still burned at all the noise she'd

made in chasing him. He decided to get a little closer before addressing her, just in case she bolted. Moving slowly through the snow, his feet carving little valleys, he got within ten feet of her when she suddenly made a run for it. He heard three footfalls, and then a loud thwack as her head smashed against a low branch. The sound of her body falling into the snow was unmistakable. He strode up to her, seeing the slightest glimmer of light in her eyes as her lids lowered and she lost consciousness.

"I don't care how smart she is indoors," Wellesley said, "she's as helpless as a kitten out here."

"I agree," Hunt said, bending over her inert body. He slipped off his glove and slid a finger inside her right mitten. "Why, her hand is practically frozen!" He found her leg with his hand to verify an intuition. "Slacks! Indoor pants!" He followed her leg down to her feet, which were clad in shoes that stopped short of her ankle. "Doesn't the government give these people the *least* idea what they should wear on a planet like this?" Looking at her sprawled out form, he shook his head. "What did this numbskull think she was doing, running out here like this? If I hadn't doubled back she would have been lost and frozen."

"Following 'the urge,' I imagine," Wellesley said sarcastically.

"Oh, very funny," Hunt replied. "She'll be lucky not to get frostbite after this." He picked her up and started to carry her south.

"Where are you taking her?"

"To where the trees are a little thicker," he replied. "I need to break the wind if I'm gonna have a chance of saving her."

"Well, be quick about it. I don't think the planet brought you two together so you could bury her out here."

Hunt found a place where the trees were tightly packed and put her down. Slipping the medallion from around his neck, he put it around hers and shoved it down the tight neck of her blouse.

"Get me in contact with her body," Wellesley said. "I'll check out her vital signs and see what else needs to be done."

Hunt did as the ancient AI told him, sliding him into one of her mittens.

"The medallion isn't enough," Wellesley said. "Not by a long shot. I don't know how this girl has been living, but she's barely generating any heat. It's like she's been sick for weeks, or on starvation rations."

"She *is* awfully thin," Hunt observed, gently touching one of her hollow cheeks with the finger of his glove.

"She needs an external source of heat, and fast," the AI continued.

"I brought some heater packs with me," Hunt replied.

"No, those won't cut it," Wellesley said. "I think you'd better take her back to her apartment. Nothing short of head-to-foot contact with something warm is gonna make the difference."

"No, I've got a better idea," Hunt said, reaching for a small pouch behind his back. From it he drew a thin emergency blanket and a couple of chemically heated hand warmers that Gromyko had stolen from the police. Laying out the blanket like a cocoon, he activated the warmers and stuffed them in her pockets. He laid her on the edge of the blanket and stretched himself out in the middle of it. Then, taking off some of his layers so that more of his heat would radiate outwards, he pulled her on top of himself and rolled up the blanket.

"You sly dog," Wellesley said a moment later, as Tselitel's unconscious head fell against Hunt's neck.

"Oh shut up," Hunt said, knowing how it looked but unable to think of a better way to warm her up. "I couldn't let her freeze. Besides, it's not like this is very comfortable. She's almost six feet of ice cube. I'll be lucky not to freeze myself."

"All in the line of duty, I'm sure," replied the AI, barely suppressing a laugh. "But what will *she* think of your methods?"

"I don't think she's got much of a right to complain, given *she's* the one who ran all the way out here and then knocked herself out," replied Hunt. "After a stunt like that she'll just have to accept help in whatever form it comes."

Nearly twenty minutes passed before Hunt began to feel some heat radiating back from Tselitel. He sighed in relief and shifted his position slightly, his right arm having grown numb from the weight of the doctor's body. He'd lain there in dread, fearing she would die before so much as a word had passed between them. Now he knew she'd be alright.

"She's coming out of it," Hunt said, oddly tired now that the danger had passed.

"I noticed that her vitals were normalizing," Wellesley said. "I wonder how long it will be before she wakes up."

"I hope it won't be too much longer," Hunt said. "We've got a lot to do before dawn."

"I shouldn't think you'd be in too big of a hurry to call it a night," Wellesley chuckled.

"Wells, if you keep pushing on me I'll–"

"Who are you talking to?" Tselitel asked in a weak voice.

"Glad to hear you're awake," Hunt said brightly, though he'd been startled to hear her. "How do you feel?"

"Like a taco?" she replied. "Why are we...together like this?"

"Because it was all I could do to keep you from freezing to death," Hunt replied, easily imagining all the thoughts that must be circulating in her mind at that moment.

"Oh, I see," she replied dully. "Did I run into something?"

"Yeah, a branch. Didn't you see it?"

"I guess not," she replied, her head still sleepily pressed against his neck. "You know, I wouldn't have run into the forest if you hadn't bolted. Then I wouldn't have nearly frozen."

"Yeah, but I had to get out of sight," countered Hunt. "Your shouting would have alerted the patrols."

"I guess that's true," she said. "Boy, I feel awfully tired."

"That's the cold," Hunt said. "It takes something out of you like nothing else can."

"I take it you are often out in the elements?" she asked.

"All the time."

"That's good," she replied drowsily. "That's why you knew what to do."

"Uh huh."

"That's...good," she repeated, drifting away again.

"This one is a handful," Wellesley said. "You'd think she'd never seen the outdoors before."

"Probably hasn't, not really," Hunt said. Feeling a little protective of her, he slid his right arm around her back and settled in.

For the next two hours he laid there, quietly listening to the wind rustling the branches around him. Occasionally a small animal would catch their scent and move in for a closer look before wandering off again. Once something large came near, and Hunt worried that it might be the wolf he'd heard many nights before when he'd been out with Gromyko. Whatever it was stayed just outside his sight range. For over an hour it waited, neither moving nor making another sound. He began to wonder if it was some kind of manifestation from the planet when he noticed Tselitel's breathing tightening, her mind nearing consciousness.

"What's your name?" she asked after an interval.

"Rex Hunt," he replied, one ear focused on their unseen visitor. "I already know yours."

"Oh, do you?" she asked.

"Yes, Lily Tselitel."

"What, have you been stalking me?" she asked with a chuckle.

"Let's say I'm well connected," he replied evasively.

"Ooh, mysterious," she said playfully. "Tell me something, mystery man: why did you stand outside my window that night? And why were you watching me again tonight?"

"I wanted to talk with you." As he said this he felt the unseen observer draw away. It made no sound as it did so, his only indication of its departure being a sense that the air had cleared around them. Another consciousness no longer occupied the space.

"Well, I gathered that," she said. "But to talk about what?"

"The future of mankind.".

"So nothing serious, then," she replied, pulling her head back and looking into his eyes for a moment.

"Nah, just run-of-the-mill fare," he said, returning her gaze with a smile.

"That's good. I'm tired of dealing with serious stuff all the time," she said, laying her head back down and looking at the snow just outside the blanket.

"Can I ask you something?" he said after a moment's silence.

"Uh huh."

"Why aren't you freaking out right now?" he asked, an incredulous chuckle entering his voice. "Most women would sooner freeze out here than lay like this with a stranger."

"Oh, you'd never hurt me," she said with offhanded certainty.

"And how do you know that?"

"I have very strong intuitions about people," she replied. "I know when people can be trusted, when they're solid and good. I feel that about you."

"You do?" he asked.

"Yes. But there's something else, too," she said. "Something…"

"Dark?" he offered knowingly.

"Yes, as a matter of fact," she replied. "It scares me a little bit."

"I'm not surprised," he said sourly. His heart began to ache as he recalled her flight in the dream, and how he'd been unable to follow her. To spare himself more pain he tried to cut off the subtle sense of longing that had been growing within him since the moment he'd laid eyes on her that night. "Well, you won't have to stay with me much longer."

She put her hands on his chest and lifted herself just enough to look into his face easily, her gray eyes shimmering in the night.

"You've been hurt," she said with finality. "I can feel the pain within you. So much loss, so much suffering. You bear it well and hide it from others. But inside you're hurt and alone."

Her words resonated deeply within him, and caused a flood of emotions to wash over him. For a brief, brilliant moment he felt understood. A connection had been instantly formed that he couldn't explain. Somehow the woman had touched a hidden and lonely place within him, taking a share of his load onto herself.

"There, that's better," she said with a smile. "Sometimes all we need is a little understanding."

"No, it's more than that," Hunt replied firmly, unwilling to admit the idea that his experience could possibly be shared by others. He felt it was personal, unique to him and Tselitel alone. He realized that the fantasy image he'd carried within ever since seeing her in his dream had been closer to the mark than he'd ever thought possible.

"You're right," she nodded after a moment. "There *is* something more to it than just that. I guess I'm so used to explaining things in rational terms that I sometimes miss what's right in front of me. It feels mystical, like some other form of communication has taken place."

"It has," he replied. "Believe me, it has."

"I suspect I'm going to learn a lot from you," she said with an appreciative smile. "It will be nice to be taught something for a change. In my professional life I'm always Doctor Tselitel, Knower Of All Things Psychological. It's a burden as much as it is a blessing, always being the one people look to."

"I can imagine."

"But I gather now isn't the time for that," she said, her face tightening up and turning to business. "You said we've got a lot to talk about?"

"We do," he replied, matching her tone. "But there's so much for you to catch up on, I'm not sure where to start."

"Just start anywhere," she said, laying her head down again. "I'll jump in whenever I have a question."

For the next half hour he regaled her with everything he knew about the crisis growing on Delta-13. He filled her in on the organization he belonged to, having previously obtained Ugo's permission to do so. Periodically she'd clarify some point in his narrative. But mostly she listened.

"You want to know something funny?" she asked when he'd finished. "I believe every syllable. I guess I've always known something more was going on beneath the surface of human cognition, but my academic background prevented me from seeing it. After all, 'everyone knows' there's no such thing as psychic phenomena."

"I felt the same way until I'd seen it first hand," Hunt said. "But I must admit, I was a lot more skeptical about it than you're being. I'm surprised."

"So am I," she replied. "But somehow I have to believe it. It just feels right, like a revelation. It reminds me of the impulse that sent me chasing after you tonight, and why I feel safe with you now. Something is guiding me."

"Of course, the planet," Hunt mumbled.

"I guess so," she agreed. And then, in a slightly uneasy voice, "Does it control your actions? Like can it possess you?"

"No, I don't think so," replied Hunt. "Ugo told me that it guides you to what is already inside you, to inner knowledge. It seems to act more as a caretaker than anything else, helping people achieve a greater degree of wholeness. I don't think it can run you like a puppet."

"Oh, good," she replied with relief.

"Why do you ask?"

"Well, I've got some patients down at the prison who,

for lack of a better term, have succumbed to madness. Some of them are like statues, totally mute and impassive. But others are climbing the walls and screaming, like they're trying to escape some terrible fate. I guess 'madness' isn't really the right term for the former set. But that's the word they used in the official reports, for some reason or other. Anyway, I just wondered if the planet might be reaching into their minds and manipulating them. I've used every technique I can think of, even the Kuritsyn Method. But no dice. It wasn't until I resorted to basic symbology for days on end with one particular patient that I saw a breakthrough. We drew circles."

"Circles?" Hunt asked, cocking an eyebrow.

"Uh huh. You see, the circle, or sphere, often serves as a symbol of wholeness deep within the human psyche. I had an intuition that my patient, Vilks, wasn't just mute, but that he was trying to *process* something that was demanding more attention than he could offer. The predictable result being that he was so overloaded that he couldn't focus on anything else. So I attempted to reach him on a level that required no processing. And which, moreover, spoke to his condition. After days and days of drawing circles on the wall in front of him he finally responded, drawing circles with me."

"And that's a breakthrough?" Hunt asked. "Seems pretty small to me."

"On the visible scale, it is," she replied. "To the observer we're just doodling on the wall, making a mess. But it's important on two levels. First, it proves that the mutes *can* be reached, that they're not beyond hope. I must admit that the fear they couldn't be helped was growing in me daily. I possess the opposite belief as a temperamental conviction, and this seeming evidence to the contrary was turning my world upside down. I could hardly eat until I'd made *some* progress with at least one of the patients."

"And second?"

"Second, the fact he responded to the symbol of wholeness tells me that he *is* striving to overcome something.

A rogue element has broken into his psyche and upset it. He is engaged in a mighty struggle to regain balance, to integrate all his processes in one undifferentiated whole. He's trying to fix himself, to put it simply."

"Well, based on what I've learned lately, the planet is probably trying to help them in their struggle."

"That's good," she said with some relief. "They need all the help they can get. It's like a portion of their psyche has fractured, and they're trying to deal with it any way they can. The mutes are taking an introverted approach, shutting out the world and trying to handle it all on their own. The screamers, as they've been called, are taking an extroverted tack, trying to get away from their inner turmoil."

"Well, we know the government is working on mind control technology. These must be the victims of their experiments."

"That could be," mused Tselitel. "The human mind is the most complex thing we've ever encountered. Any attempt to put pressure on it, to forcibly manipulate it into a different mode or way of functioning, is certain to have disastrous results for the recipient. Actually, that idea fits rather neatly with what I've experienced with my patients. The tremendous load that they're trying to process could easily be the result of external pressure that seeks to alter their state." She thought for a moment. "So, what now? Is there some way we can end the experiments?"

"I don't know. The Order must have some plan for doing so, but I haven't been told yet. I'm still the new kid in school."

"I see," she replied. "And what about us?"

"I don't know about that, either. The planet is drawing us together for some reason. It must have some plan for us, though for the life of me I can't figure out what it is. I just know that I saw you in my dreams, and that I had to meet you."

"I'm sure we'll figure it out down the line," she smiled confidently. "I had the same urge as you, that powerful feeling that we had to meet. That's why I charged out here so senselessly. Though I guess Delta-13 knew you'd look after me, so the risk wasn't really that great after all. But I can't explain it, either. We'll just have to keep in touch and see what happens."

"About that," Hunt said. "Any ideas? You're on the inside, so you'd have a better idea than I of how we could slip messages back and forth."

"It would be hard," she replied with a frown. "They keep close tabs on all the staff up at the complex. It makes me wonder how in the world I'm going to explain my absence tonight! They must be beating the bushes looking for me, even now!"

"I know, that's why we're so far away from the complex," Hunt said. "First they'll look around the buildings, and then they'll head down to Midway. They wouldn't think of you trotting into the wilderness on your own. It would be pure suicide under normal conditions."

"But how will I get back in?" she asked, alarm growing in her voice the more she thought of it. "They have a guard stationed at the front of my apartment building, and he records everyone who enters and exits."

"Don't worry, I'll take care of the guard," Hunt grinned. "It's getting pretty late. Time for you to get back."

"But how will we talk in the future?" she asked. "We still haven't worked that part out."

"I'll meet you by the bushes in three days' time," he said. "We'll talk more then. Now, time to get this taco unwrapped."

She sat up and instantly felt the biting cold slide down her back.

"Ooh, I'd rather not," she said, dropping down once more. "It feels like ice out there!"

"Sadly, we must," he said with a smile. "Now, come on, you're a big girl aren't you?"

"I guess," she said playfully. "But I'd rather stay here."

Their eyes met for a long moment. He felt the urge to put his hands around her back, to feel her soft flesh and pull her close. But something stopped him, and the moment passed.

"Come on, let's go," he said, breaking his gaze and shifting under her.

She sat up a second time and felt the medallion bump against her chest.

"What's this?" she asked, feeling its outline through her shirt with her fingers.

"An alien artifact," he replied, helping her put on some of the extra layers he'd brought. "It helps your body withstand the cold."

"And how did it get down my blouse?"

"I put it there."

"Bold one, aren't you?" she laughed.

"Be glad that I am. You'd have probably frozen without it."

He got the rest of his kit packed away in his little pouch. Then he nodded towards the north.

"The complex is that way," he said, a note of regret in his voice. "Warm enough?"

"For the time being," she said, her long, thin form decidedly wider from the extra clothes. She swayed a little on her feet and reached out for a tree to steady herself.

"You alright?" he asked with concern.

"I think it must be that blow I took earlier," she said, rubbing her forehead with her mitten. "I guess I'm a little dizzy."

"Here, take my hand," he said, offering his right.

Silently they retraced their steps, navigating slowly through the darkness, flurries beginning to fall through the branches.

"Feels almost idyllic," she said in a whisper, as they neared the end of the forest. "I never knew the night could be so magical."

"Snow'll do that," he replied, looking down at the ground as he walked. "Makes things seem pure, clean. Like the world has been born over again, and we're starting fresh."

"Yes, the snow helps, too," she said, glancing at his face and hoping he took the implication. But he just stalked forwards, looking almost morose.

"Hold up a minute," he said in a low whisper as they reached the bushes. "Just stay here."

She watched as he hunched low and pressed quietly through the bushes to see what lay beyond. Half a minute later he returned.

"Patrols look normal," Hunt said, puzzled. "I thought for sure they would be going nuts right now."

"Maybe they don't know I'm gone," offered Tselitel. "Although I can't see how. The guard should have reported me missing hours ago."

"Let's watch for a little while and see," Hunt said. "Come on."

The pair poked their heads out through the bushes and squatted low. Within ten minutes the doctor began to shiver, and Hunt put his arm around her shoulders to offer what protection from the wind that he could.

"I can't do this for too much longer," she said, her teeth starting to chatter.

Just as she said this the guard who watched the door of her building stepped outside the lobby and looked around. Seeing no patrols nearby, he reached into his pocket and drew out a small light. He blinked it three times and then waited a moment. He repeated this two more times, and then went back inside.

"Ugo, you sly..." Hunt said with a chuckle, his voice trailing off.

"What is it?" Tselitel asked.

"Three times three," Hunt said. "It's one of the codes that the Order uses. The guard is on our side."

"Why didn't they tell you?"

"Who knows," replied Hunt. "Anyway, you'd better get going. A three-by-three means 'clear but risky.' The guard can't guarantee things will stay open for long."

Hunt helped her take the extra clothes off and threw them over his shoulder.

"I'll need that medallion back," he said, pointing at her chest.

"Oh, I was hoping I could hang onto it," she said quietly. "As a memento."

"I'm afraid not. I'll need it to make it back to Midway without freezing. Besides, it belongs to a friend of mine."

Grasping the chain and fighting the disc up through her tight collar, she handed it to him.

"Boy, that thing really does help," she said, wrapping her arms around her stomach, shaking from the cold. "I've got to get one of those for myself!"

"I'll give you the next one I come across," he chuckled.

"You do that," she smiled. "Alright, I've got to go before my lips turn blue. Three days?"

"Three days," he nodded.

She smiled again, and then started crunching her way across the snow to the lobby. He saw her go inside, chat briefly with the guard, and then disappear deeper into the building.

"Well, *that* went better than expected," said Wellesley, as Hunt turned back towards the forest and walked through the bushes. "She's got a real thing for you."

"You think so?" Hunt asked idly, almost as though the topic bored him.

"Uh, *yeah*, I do. You don't need eight hundred years of experience to see that."

He paused and looked at the medallion he still held, turning it over in his hand for a moment. Two minutes before it had hung just over her heart, and the thought fascinated him. He longed to put it on, to have her with him for the long journey back, even if only by proxy. But the same instinct that had stopped him from pulling her close when they lay together stopped him now, and he slipped the disc into his pocket instead.

"You're gonna need that," Wellesley told him.

"Later," he said, resuming his walk towards the south.

"I don't understand," the AI said. "This woman clearly has the hots for you, and you're *depressed*?"

"Just leave it alone, Wellesley."

"You can't expect me to clam up now," he said. "Not after sitting mute for all those hours while you two snuggled."

"I told you, I did that–"

"Out of necessity. Yeah, I know."

"Nobody forced you to keep quiet," Hunt said, trying to divert the conversation. "You could have spoken up at any time."

"I didn't want to cramp your style," Wellesley said.

"Don't make me toss you *back* into the snow," Hunt said testily.

"You wouldn't do that," the AI said. "But for the life of me I can't imagine why you're feeling this way. Sure, she's not the *greatest* looking woman in the world. But she's got good bone structure, and I could feel your heart jump when she looked at you."

Hunt sighed and stopped.

"You remember the dream," he said. "How she drew close and then ran away out of terror? Why, just earlier tonight she said I scared her. It's only a matter of time before she bolts."

"I don't think dreams are mandates," opined the AI.

"Well, they're doing a pretty good job so far," he replied, walking slowly and kicking frustratedly at the occasional mound of snow. "It accurately predicted that we'd be drawn to each other, didn't it?"

"Yes. But it also showed you'd rescue her from gargoyle men, or whatever they were. And *that* certainly hasn't happened."

"They were a metaphor."

"Exactly. The dream pointed to you meeting while you rescued her from imminent danger from the government, according to Ugo. You *did* rescue her from danger, but it was that of freezing to death."

"What's your point?"

"My point is the dream was right in some respects, and wrong in others. I think it's a mixture of fact and falsehood, a soup made out of your own thoughts and fears, plus whatever the planet has thrown in. Yes, you saved her life, but you painted in your lifelong fear of the government in the persons of the beast men."

"Ugo was pretty certain about his interpretation," countered Hunt.

"I don't think Ugo knows *everything*," replied the AI a little sharply. "He's been a mystic for too long and it has dissolved his point of view. He's floating, having left the sure ground of fact a long, long time ago."

"But the planet–"

"*The planet, the planet,*" said Wellesley with annoyance. "The planet is a *being*, like anyone else. Although a very *strange* being, it doesn't have the inside track. It isn't magical. Through some process or other it forms *opinions* about what will happen. So far it has been pretty accurate. But the most we can say for certain is that it tends to know who it's working with. It knows how to motivate them. A man of your temperament couldn't possibly stay away while a woman like Tselitel was in danger. So you came out here in frigid conditions at great personal risk just for the *chance* to see her. Even Ugo said that the planet just works with what's already inside you. You need to stop treating these dreams like they're your destiny, Rex. They're only that as long as you *think* they are, because you'll guide your steps by them. Consider how you're already pushing Tselitel away because of what the dream showed."

"Then you think Delta-13 is just pushing my buttons?"

"Yeah, more or less. It *seems* to do so for a benevolent purpose. Clearly Tselitel is good medicine for you, and you for her. But I think it's working you two along according to a plan only it knows about."

"Ugo's had a lot of experience working with it."

"If I hear you cite Ugo one more time–" Wellesley began.

"Okay," said Hunt. "A certain old man has had a lot of experience with it."

"Oh, very cute," replied the AI, with an audible roll of his eyes. "At least your sense of humor is coming back. That's always a good sign when you're in a mood."

"Seriously, Wellesley, he *has* worked with it for ages. That's got to count for something."

"He thinks he's the planet's prophet, Rex. He's not an independent observer, commenting objectively on the facts alone. He gets too caught up in subjective interpretation."

"You mean he isn't you?" Hunt asked with a smile.

The AI coughed for effect.

"It *does* sound like that, doesn't it?" he replied. "I guess we all favor our own viewpoint, even AIs."

"Well, don't worry about it," replied Hunt with more certainty in his voice. "I happen to agree with you."

"Not totally, I expect."

"No, not totally," admitted Hunt. "But more than I do with Ugo. He's right that the planet's got some pretty potent powers. But he does like to hop on the destiny bandwagon a little too much. I guess I've just been around him so much lately that I forgot there's another way to see things."

"That's good enough for me," Wellesley said with satisfaction. "I just didn't want you throwing away a real shot at happiness because of some bogus sense of fate."

"Thanks."

"Anytime," the AI said. "Alright, *now* will you put on that medallion?"

CHAPTER 9

The next morning Tselitel awoke to a wonderful sense of calm and security. The anxiety that had gnawed on her nerves for years was gone. Of late she'd forgotten it ever existed, so absorbed was she in her work. But once it was gone she was immediately aware of it. An elusive sense of insecurity about the outer world had vanished in the night. Ever since she was young there had been something threatening about the objects and people around her. They seemed charged with the power to drain her, to take away her vital force. Whenever she thought of it she felt ridiculous that such a fantasy should be in her mind. But all the same she felt it, and gradually built walls around herself until no one was allowed inside, not truly. Even Roy had been kept at a safe distance.

Her eyes rolled when she thought of Roy, and her betrayal at her hands. Yet somehow the sting of that betrayal seemed less potent after meeting Rex. She felt like a warm blanket surrounded her, and that it protected her from harm. Closing her eyes and thinking back on their time inside the taco, she savored the memory for a long moment. Then she stretched and sighed.

But regret soon filled her as she thought over her behavior towards her assistant. Her own feelings were difficult to unravel, for she felt both humiliated by the way she'd been treated, and simultaneously in the right for punishing Roy. To be carted off to the hospital against her will was the most outrageous thing she'd ever been subjected to. And yet, in the cool light of morning, it seemed less important than patching things up with a faithful companion who had never left her side during the years they'd worked together, especially now that her apprenticeship was drawing to a close. She slipped her feet out of bed and onto the cold floor.

"I'll have to make things right with Sadie," she said to herself. "I can't keep treating her like this."

An hour later she was standing in front of her door about to lock it when Roy stepped out of her apartment and saw her. Recoiling momentarily as though she would duck back inside, she frowned and stepped out, locking the door and walking past Tselitel without a word.

"Sadie, wait," Tselitel said when her assistant was half a dozen steps down the hall. "I want to talk to you."

"I find that hard to believe," the younger woman said without stopping.

Tselitel trotted after her, jacket thrown over her arm. She caught up with her and grasped her arm, but Roy pulled it away.

"I've hurt you, Sadie," Tselitel admitted at once, keeping pace with her as they walked out of the lobby into the frigid daylight. "I was cold and heartless, and I'm sorry."

Roy stopped and looked at her, crossing her arms over her chest.

"You haven't just hurt me," Roy said. "You've cut me out of your life. And for what? Trying to help you?"

"You hurt me terribly when you went to the warden behind my back," Tselitel said, trying to explain. "I just can't stand that kind of treatment, Sadie, no matter how good the intentions behind it were. I can't even express it."

"Well then, maybe you've got some idea of the misery you've put me through," Roy said tartly. "In any event you won't have to tolerate my presence anymore. I've requested a permanent position with the prison's psychiatric staff. It was approved just this morning."

"Oh, Sadie, please don't go," Tselitel said, reaching out an appealing hand. But Roy stepped back.

"Goodbye, Doctor Tselitel," she said formally, turning from her former mentor and walking quickly onward.

Tselitel slipped the jacket around her already shivering shoulders and slowly made for the prison, her head spinning from the shock. A dark thought suddenly rose in her that Kelbauskas was to blame for Roy's behavior. But she shook her head and rejected the notion almost as soon as she thought it.

"No, this one's on me," she said under her breath. "We've all got to pay the piper sometime."

For the rest of the day she was subdued, drawing circles with Vilks and moodily musing on the argument. When the staff came in to take him back to his cell she said nothing. She just gathered up her things and left.

When she got home she heard noises coming from Roy's apartment. The door slightly open, she slipped her head inside and saw a cleaning crew making it over for its next tenant. Her assistant had moved out.

"I'm sorry, Sadie," she thought with a sigh. "Truly sorry."

Dropping onto her bed and reaching for her tablet she began to write.

"Why does bad always seem to come along and balance out the good? I was over the moon last night after meeting Rex. What a strange, wonderful man! He makes me feel alive, secure, and a little scared all at the same time. I can't wait until I see him again. And then this whole thing with Sadie blows up! I'm not blaming anyone, though. I brought it on myself."

She stopped and looked at what she'd written. Suddenly it occurred to her that she shouldn't leave a record about Rex, since the government might find it. She deleted her paragraph and then started over.

"Things ended with Sadie today. I had held her at a distance for too long and to save herself further pain she cut me out of her life. She was the best assistant I've ever had the pleasure of working with, and I will miss her greatly. She's going to work in the prison. She'll be a great asset to them. Smart, hardworking, and

cares about her patients. I hope someday she'll forgive me for how I treated her. I'm not sure I'll ever forgive myself."

Putting aside the tablet with a sigh, Tselitel took off her jacket and went to the cafeteria for supper.

Reflexively looking for Roy when she entered, it occurred to her that she'd probably moved to the other building to minimize the risk of crossing paths with her. Feeling lower than ever, she loaded up a plate with all the comfort food it could hold and made for a table off in a corner. Idly poking her meal, she didn't notice Charlie Palmer until he spoke.

"Hi, Doctor Tselitel," he said in a friendly voice. "Care for company?"

"Oh, hi Charlie," she said with surprise, wanting to be alone but lacking the words to say so politely. "Uh, sure."

"Great," he beamed, sitting down across from her. He gestured towards her plate with his fork and chuckled. "Hungry?"

"Oh, not as much as I thought I was," she replied, taking a small bite.

"I heard that you had a major breakthrough with Vilks," he said between bites. "That's quite a feat. We'd given him up for good."

"Why is that?"

"Because he was the first to go," replied Palmer. "He's ahead of the others by, oh, eight months. Naturally we figured his case would be the most intractable, since it had been the longest."

"Naturally," replied Tselitel musingly. "But perhaps not."

"What do you mean?"

"Well, I have a theory that the victims are under a massive mental load, and that they're trying to deal with it. Some of them, like Vilks, draw in and try to process it, while the others just run from it. I guess I was lucky when I chose to work with Vilks. He's probably processed more than the others have, and thus he's closest to the surface."

"I doubt luck had much to do with it," replied Palmer with a smile. "We're fortunate to have brought you out here."

Without really paying attention to his reply Tselitel started to eat, her appetite stimulated by what she'd heard. She hoped Vilks, along with the others, would come out of their stupor and make a full recovery in time. The knowledge that he'd been under the longest gave her hope, because it offered support for her theory that their personalities were simply submerged and not obliterated as she secretly feared.

Her thoughts were interrupted by a gentle tapping sound on the table. She looked up and saw Palmer quietly tapping out a specific rhythm with his fork. Without looking at her he tapped out three sets of three. He paused for a moment, and did it again. Suddenly she realized what he was communicating and looked at him. He locked eyes with her and nodded almost imperceptibly.

"Pleasure talking to you, as always," he smiled as he got up. "I hope we'll chat more soon."

"As do I," she replied, watching him go.

"So Charlie is one of them, too," she thought. "I wonder how many more they've got working here."

◆ ◆ ◆

"Marvelous! Simply marvelous!" Ugo enthused, as Hunt told the others about his meeting with Tselitel the next morning over breakfast. "You've made first rate contact with one of the most important people on Delta-13. And she took to you! That's excellent. We'd long pondered how to approach her, especially with her academic background. We thought she'd never go along with the truth of the planet, to say nothing of all the other details you passed along to her. She must have really clicked with you."

"I imagine 'the planet' was responsible for all of that," Wellesley communicated to Hunt sarcastically, more annoyed than ever with the old man's predictable bents.

"I agree," Gromyko said slyly. "First rate *contact* are just the words I'd use. You made quite an *impression*."

"Don't be that way, Antonin," Wanda said. "You heard Rex: it was the only way to save her from the cold. To save both of them, actually. He couldn't have sat there for hours without the medallion, even if it *had* been enough to keep her from freezing. He would have just frozen in her place. Heat had to be preserved in any manner possible."

"I wish that *all* body heat could be preserved like that," Gromyko said in a joking tone that masked a hint of envy. The psychic beside him picked up his meaning at once and gave him a light smack on the arm. "I was only joking!" he pleaded in a high tone, raising his hands in protest of his innocence.

"Yes, *now* you're joking," she replied authoritatively.

Ugo watched the scene with irritation, a frown on his face as he puffed on his pipe. Gromyko and his granddaughter had quickly fallen into an easy, familiar romance. A change had come over her since Gromyko had moved in, and he noticed more distance between her and himself than ever before. He noted it with regret, but realized there was nothing he could do about it. For reasons beyond his comprehension she was falling in love with the smuggler, and that love was drawing her out of herself and causing her to mature and grow into a fuller woman. Consequently her attachment to Ugo was fading into something almost accidental, as though they were merely residents of the same house. No longer the center of her life, he felt neglected and depressed, but knew it would be wrong to do anything to intervene. It would be a purely selfish act, an attempt to stem her growth for his own benefit, and he could never do that.

He found himself warming to Hunt even more as a result. A dim light flickered in the back of his mind that he might be able to replace a lost granddaughter with a surrogate grandson.

"We've never been able to make contact with Tselitel because her position put our operatives at too great of a risk," Ugo said, steering the conversation away from the two lovebirds and back to something he could control. "If an operative made an advance and she reported it, the whole network inside the prison could have collapsed. They're always trying to sniff us out, so we have to lay low. Usually this means we can't do anything at all to stop them, making our network almost completely passive. Only on rare occasions can we actually act."

"Like the guard in front of her building?" Hunt queried.

"Exactly," Ugo said. "He fudged the log book to make it appear she'd been gone only a few minutes, just taking a stroll. The attendant at the front desk presented some trouble. But an ornamental *Kol-Prockian* artifact for his wife shut him up."

"So you guys don't actually *do* that much," said Gromyko. "What was all that holier-than-thou business you were giving me during the initiation? Looks like we in the Underground weren't doing so bad after all."

"We do a great deal more than your lot *ever* did," snapped Ugo. "Our activities may be passive, but they are effective. If it weren't for the Order's efforts the scandal about the prisoners never would have gotten off the planet. They keep a tight grip on all information emanating from the prison. Nothing of importance gets out of there and off Delta-13 without their approval. Through our efforts the scandal grew so large that the imperial government couldn't hide it any longer, and when Tselitel requested permission to come they eventually had to relent. Only her presence has halted the mind control experiments. That alone has produced more good than you people *ever* managed with your moonshine and artifact smuggling."

"Perhaps," replied Gromyko. "Or perhaps we kept them so busy chasing us that you were free to go peeping through keyholes and circulating gossip."

"It's not *gossip*!" roared Ugo, slamming his fist down.

"Well, that's all it's gonna be if things keep going the way they are," retorted Gromyko. "So you've halted the experiments for now. What happens afterwards? Your *passive* organization doesn't have weapons or soldiers. What happens when Tselitel goes home? Or say she meets with a little accident? They've been at it for too long to let her expose them. They'd put Delta-13 under martial law before they'd let word get out. They only allowed Tselitel to come because it was a safer bet than fighting it, because *that* would have been an admission of guilt. The only way to solve this problem is to destroy the technology with which they pursue their experiments. All we have to do is sneak some explosives in via your agents, and they can finish the job. Then the risk to mankind will be removed."

"You're thinking far too small," Ugo replied derisively. "The government is tottering. That's why they're pursuing mind control in the first place. The number of new colonies sprouting up every year is just too much for them to manage centrally. Unrest in the outer worlds is growing each day as they ponder why so much of their blood and sweat have to go back to Earth through exorbitant taxes. You may rest assured that we will destroy their equipment. But only after we've gotten the information we need to kick the empire into its well-deserved grave."

"How can you speak so calmly of galactic revolution?" asked Gromyko, incredulous. "Can you imagine the millions, no, *billions* of lives that will be lost? Who is to say how long it will last? It could go on for decades! And even if you *can* spark a revolution, what's to say the inner worlds will abandon the old government? They'll probably stick with it and fight the outer worlds to a standstill. And then we'll have two rival human empires, while we're surrounded by alien races that would love to reclaim some of the worlds we've taken from them."

"Everything in life comes with risk," said Ugo. "If we want to live under freedom this is our only chance. The government has backed itself into a corner with its repressive policies, and this mind control gambit is the smoking gun we need to break it."

"It would be better to blow up the prison," Gromyko said. "We'd be stuck with the old government. But at least we wouldn't have a civil war on our hands."

"No, Gromyko," replied Ugo. "Unless we overthrow the government we *will* have a civil war on our hands. The outer worlds will keep growing apart until it comes to blood. They're already establishing illegal customs unions together against the inner planets. And the word is that defensive pacts are already being discussed in secret. But if we can spread the word of what they're trying to do here, then we have the best chance of avoiding bloodshed altogether. No one will stand in defense of a government that would rob them of their own minds."

"And what happens when the government denies all this?" countered Gromyko. "The fringe worlds will eagerly seize the story as a cause for war. But the inner planets will hesitate and doubt it from the same motive: self interest. The inner planets are the ones who benefit from the milking of the fringe. They won't want to accept the story."

"That's why we'll force them to," replied Ugo in a tone of quiet mastery.

"How? Through mind control tricks of your own?"

"No, by producing evidence so conclusive that even the most skeptical loyalist will vomit to hear it," the old man said. "That is where our *passive* organization, as you called it, has been most passionately at work. At this point we are gathering indirect evidence because that is all we have available. Soon we'll have our hands on the real meat," he said, clenching his fist, his voice rising as his subject roused him. "Once we do, we'll blast it across all of human-controlled space. We'll also send it out through the authorities we've been cultivating for years. Once we're finished, there won't be a single soul standing with the government."

"I hope you're right," said Gromyko doubtfully. "Or this

will be the greatest catastrophe in human history."

"No, Antonin," replied Ugo, using the smuggler's given name for the first time. "Losing our free will will be, if we fail to stop it in time."

Once the discussion had dissolved and its members had gone their separate ways, Hunt headed for the house's back porch to think. It was walled in, with two large windows facing north. Through them he could see the hill on which the prison stood in silent judgment of the town, offering a constant reminder of why the poor and abused residents lived there.

"Not much to look at," Hunt said just to break the silence. Sometimes Ugo went out there to smoke, and there subsequently stood a stool under one of the windows so he could look out as he thought. Hunt sat on this and watched the residents of Midway shuffle through the snow, going about their tasks. Most of them were going to work, as Ugo had done a little while before. Staring out in silence for nearly twenty minutes, he eventually heard the door behind him rattle open. Gromyko stepped out and shut it quietly.

"Sunning yourself?" he asked wryly, thick clouds obscuring the sun. He walked to the other window and peeked out.

"Hey, get away from there," Hunt said urgently, bolting from the chair and grabbing his friend's arm to pull him back. "You want someone to recognize you?"

"*You're* not being very cautious, Rex," countered the smuggler, straightening the sleeve that Hunt had ruffled. "Everything thinks you're dead, yet you're showing *your* face."

"Yeah, because hardly anybody knows me. I haven't had my face plastered all over the city in graffiti underlined by the words 'Hope! Prosperity! Gromyko!'"

"I can't help it if an enthusiastic artist took it on herself to spread my legend," he said. "But perhaps I should be a little more cautious."

"Yes, perhaps," agreed Hunt, retaking his seat and watching the street once more. Several moments passed without a word from the smuggler, who stood in the middle of the porch with his hands thrust into his pockets, looking at nothing in particular. "Something on your mind, Antonin?" Hunt asked with a cocked eyebrow, surprised to find his friend at a loss for words.

"Well, now that you ask me," he began, pulling up a crate and sitting down on it between the two windows, "there *is* something on my mind." Then, glancing at the door and lowering his voice he asked, "You don't agree with Ugo, do you?"

"About what?"

"Oh, everything, I suppose," he replied. "The 'passive' approach, the idea that there won't be a civil war. You don't agree with that, do you?"

"I reckon I do," replied Hunt after a moment. "I hadn't really thought about it."

"*Hadn't thought about it!*" exclaimed Gromyko more loudly than he'd intended. He glanced at the door again and then continued. "He's gone crazy if he thinks everything is gonna play out just the way he's planned it. Nothing in life is ever that neat. There's gonna be a fight, and it'll be devastating. But if we just blow up the prison we'll sweep the entire problem away in a flash. During my initiation they said that the experiments, as far as they knew, were only being conducted on Delta-13. There's something special about this planet that makes it essential to their research."

"He's right there, Rex," Wellesley added. "The *Kol-Prockians* never managed to perfect mind control, as I told you. But it was on Delta-13 that they came the closest to doing so. Anywhere else they tried was a bust. Based on what we've learned from Ugo, I'd guess that the planet somehow facilitates the complex mental rewiring that would be needed to replace someone's thoughts with those of another."

"You mean they could only carry it out on Delta-13?" Hunt asked.

"Yes, I think so," replied Gromyko, not realizing that

Hunt was talking to the AI. "Why else would they do it here? Sure it's far away from prying eyes. But the logistics are bad. It would make more sense to do it close to Earth, where they'd have absolute control over everything. Besides, we're on the very edge of the fringe worlds. If conflict broke out with them Earth would be cut off from its secret weapon. Any confederation of the fringe would immediately seize Delta-13 and take over the rich artifact trade that comes out of Quarlac. It would just be too good to pass up." Gromyko leaned in closer. "And that is why I believe we can succeed by just blowing up the prison. Whatever work they are carrying out there is exclusive to Delta-13. They don't do it elsewhere because they *can't* do it elsewhere. So why should we burn down the house to kill a gnat? Let's just step on him instead."

"I should have thought you'd be glad to kick over the government," replied Hunt, buying a little time.

"I would have thought that as well," replied Gromyko. "But the truth is I'm terrified of the responsibility. Ugo and his set can talk all they want of freedom and whatnot. They can afford to preach lofty ideals from the sidelines. But I've been in the streets, and I know what bloody conflict looks like. I've felt the cold reality when principle meets with brutal repression. Here," Gromyko said, waving his hand to indicate the house, "Ugo can smoke in quiet safety, planning his revolution from the comfort of his fireside. But out there," he said, jerking his thumb towards the window, "there will be blood, and death, and starvation. The inner worlds *won't* go along with the fringe. There's just too much antipathy built up."

"But the evidence they'll publish–" began Hunt.

"Will be disbelieved by many," cut in the smuggler. "People see what they believe, Rex, not the other way around. I am a living legend, my friend, because people *believe* I am a legend. They think I am single handedly battling the government. This is impossible, as a moment of reflection would reveal. But they don't take the time to reflect. They don't need to. They see confirmation of their beliefs everywhere because they screen out everything else. Now, consider this: the government has a near monopoly on the sources of information accessible to citizens in the inner worlds. Even if the Order can circumvent this, they will still be battling decades of programming that portrays the government in a positive, benevolent light. And that same programming has told them for decades that the colonies are filled with revolutionaries and savages. Can a mysterious report issued from a world on the very edge of controlled space really overcome such prejudice? If the police found me and published photos all across Midway of my execution, many people would believe it was staged in order to break their will. They'd say special effects were used, or that a double was brought in. They would cling to their belief in me. The same will happen here. It will ignite the fringe because the fringe *hungers* for an excuse to break away. But the inner worlds will hold. However shakily, they will hold. The result must be war of the worst kind."

Gromyko's voice was earnestly passionate as he spoke, his eyes wide and sincere. He believed every syllable of his argument, and was striving desperately to convince Hunt. The latter eyed him for a few moments, caught between the forceful persuasiveness of the smuggler and the wise assurances of Ugo. Until that time he hadn't questioned the Order's plan. It sounded reasonable to one who had lived in a cloistered environment, as Hunt had since his earliest days. But when it collided with the gritty realism of the smuggler's viewpoint it sounded idealistic and overly optimistic. It seemed to be exactly what Gromyko had said: a scheme cooked up by people sitting safely beside their fireplaces, separated from the consequences of the real world. Hunt could easily see how it could lead to a civil war that would grind many worlds to powder before it was over.

"I can see you're thinking very hard about this," Gromyko said, breaking in on Hunt's thoughts. "That is good. Perhaps I have spurred you to reflect."

"You've certainly done that," replied Hunt.

"That's all I need for now," said the smuggler, standing up and putting back the crate he sat on. "No action can be taken yet anyhow, so your reply need not be immediate. But I want to know soon which side you are on. It will greatly impact my course."

With a roguish smile that recalled simpler days, Gromyko left the porch and went back inside.

"I didn't think he had it in him to advance a good argument," commented Wellesley once the smuggler's footsteps had receded into the house. "But that was very well reasoned. He could have been a good lawyer had circumstances been different."

"Then you agree with him?" queried Hunt.

"I didn't say that," replied the AI. "You might recall that I once fought for freedom in a drama not so different from the one we find ourselves in now. And in that case, as in this, it was a war between the fringe and the inner planets. It's odd, almost like some kind of galactic destiny repeating itself. I suppose it's just the dynamics of power: those farthest from its benefits are the first to reject it."

"You haven't answered my question," observed Hunt, looking out the window but only dimly aware of what passed before his eyes. His entire attention was absorbed by the question that now hovered before him.

"That's because I don't have an answer. Not yet. It's easy to argue in terms of slogans. 'Freedom at any cost!' 'Down with the oppressor!' But revolution, as Gromyko has pointed out, is a bloody, nasty road. The *Kol-Prockian* civil war slaughtered billions simply to maintain the status quo. Ultimately it's a question of odds, and on which side they fall. Ugo says they're in our favor, and Gromyko says no. I don't have any information to form an opinion, so whatever I'd say would just be meaningless. Not being an oracle, I'll have to bite my tongue."

"That's a big help," Hunt complained, shaking his head.

"Would you rather I gave you an opinion based on

nothing but air?"

"No, I want you to level with me," Hunt replied with an exasperated sigh. "But how am *I* supposed to decide? Like Antonin said, it's a lot of responsibility. According to Ugo I am a, or perhaps *the*, key player in all this, so my decision might very well decide the fate of numberless human beings."

"I don't envy you," Wellesley said honestly. "But I've felt the weight of such responsibility before, and I'll help you any way I can."

Hunt smiled, feeling a little better already.

"Thanks, pal," he said, rising from the stool and stepping toward the house. He stopped at the doorway and thought for a moment. "We'll proceed as planned for now," he said. "The Order has the best approach for this, as far as I can see. But I'll bail on it if necessary."

"Sounds good," agreed the AI, as Hunt left the porch.

◆ ◆ ◆

"The time has come, Rex, for you to employ your powers to practical effect," Ugo said over the dinner table that evening. Gromyko and Wanda were also there, sitting beside one another and eating quietly. A dark mood hung over the house ever since the argument at breakfast.

"Rex should use his powers as little as possible, grandfather," Wanda said. "The ability to inspire terror, while useful in a pinch, is hardly something to encourage. After all, we are a–"

"*Healing order*," cut in Ugo. "Yes, you've made that very clear to me lately. But this isn't a matter for debate. Such powers need to be used from time to time or they will build up and start to spill out. I can detect a little something already, just around the edges. I believe that is why we've all been on edge lately."

"Rex wouldn't hurt us!" exclaimed Wanda.

"Not willingly," said Ugo. "And before he accessed his power he didn't pose much of a danger. It all just swirled around deep inside, not really affecting him or anyone else. But now that a channel is open between it and the conscious mind it can flow outwards with ease. So it needs to be drained a little."

"How?" asked Hunt directly, concerned by what might happen if he didn't blow off some steam.

"I have a message for Gromyko to run tonight," he said, casting a disdainful look at the smuggler before continuing. "But it will take him into the heart of Midway, and the patrols have been particularly thick there lately. It will take his...skills, and your gift, to get through."

"Who are we taking it to?" Gromyko asked.

"A woman named Galina Peco," Ugo said. "She's an important link to our people inside the prison. We've gotten very little information out of her lately, and we need to know what is wrong. She's a channel we can't afford to let go dry, so you two will slip into her house and speak with her. She's married, but her husband is aware of her activities and supports them actively. Just be sure that you aren't mistaken for burglars and attacked. The sentries have increased in their neighborhood, and any out of place sounds might set them off."

"We'll be silent," Gromyko said with a gleam in his eye, glad to be put back in his element.

Shortly thereafter the pair departed, dressed in dark clothing so they could melt into the shadows. With Gromyko ahead of him by half a dozen feet, Hunt moved as silently as possible as he strove to keep up. But the smuggler had forgotten the disparity in their stealth skills and had to slow down before his companion lagged too far behind.

"You really need to keep up, my friend," he said, unable to understand why anyone couldn't move with the same ease he did. "We must cover as much ground as possible in a very short amount of time. The patrols are getting near the ends of their shifts. They are tired and wish to go inside where it is warm. Soon a new set will hit the streets, and they will be alert and eager for trouble. For the best chance we need to reach Peco's house in the next twenty minutes. That will give us enough time to talk and slip out again before the guards change in her neighborhood."

"If I move any faster, Antonin, they'll be able to hear us from half a block away," replied Hunt. "I've never been as quiet as you. Nobody has. We'll just have to get there when we do. I can scare off the patrols if necessary."

"Alright," replied Gromyko, unsatisfied. "Just be sure you don't miss them and hit me with some of your fear juice, or whatever it is." With this he turned and began moving again, slower than before.

Working their way along the deserted streets, their heels faintly crunching on the hard snow and ice, Hunt couldn't escape the feeling that something was wrong. It floated up from the back of his mind like a dark cloud and colored all his thoughts. Try as he might, the irrational feeling that the evening was cursed wouldn't leave him. Slowly his stomach filled with dread and his palms began to sweat. A quarter of an hour later they reached Peco's house.

"The patrols don't look as heavy as Ugo thought," Gromyko said. "Just one pair at the far end of the street."

"Doesn't this seem a little too easy?" asked Hunt, searching in the darkness for any little sign that might give away an ambush.

"Ah, the old man probably got his wires crossed," he replied offhandedly. "What does he know of actual action in the field? Come on, let's get inside before the shift changes."

Without waiting for a response the smuggler darted into the street, reaching the side of the house a few moments later. Hunt followed, watching the patrol up the street as it moved further away. He felt relief at such a thin police presence, but the fear of an ambush wouldn't go away.

By the time Hunt reached his friend the latter was tapping out a specific rhythm on Peco's bedroom window. It was barely audible out of fear that the sentries would hear it. Nearly a minute passed before the lock clicked and the window opened.

"Inside, hurry," Peco's husband said. In a flash they were inside, and the window was quickly closed and relocked. "Don't speak," he whispered. "Follow me to the basement. Otherwise they will hear us talking. The walls are thin."

Gromyko nodded in the darkness and fell in behind him, beckoning for Hunt to follow. They walked slowly through the small house, creaking their way down a narrow staircase. A cold, moldy smell filled their noses as they descended.

"I have brought them," the man said in a loud voice, once they'd reached the bottom.

Suddenly the basement was bathed in light, blinding Hunt and Gromyko. Their arms were seized from behind, their knees kicked out from underneath them. They hit the concrete hard, bolts of pain shooting up their legs.

"Hold them!" barked Galina Peco, who stood before them in a police uniform. She was short and plump, with closely cut reddish-brown hair and a square jaw. "Well, well, well, if it isn't Gromyko," she said, twirling a metal baton and taking a step closer to the smuggler. Her eyes darted to Hunt, but the cloth mask he wore to keep out the cold obscured his identity. She didn't care, anyway: the capture of the smuggler was the main thing to her.

Gromyko looked around him as his vision adjusted. Two officers held each of them, with another two standing off to the side as backup. Peco's husband, standing behind her, was incongruously dressed in pajamas to allay suspicion.

"Headquarters will be so pleased to hear we've finally nailed you," she continued with a tight smile on her lips. "Not that you posed any threat, of course. But we like to sew up all the loose ends. And you're the last."

"Well, you know what they say," replied Gromyko.

"What? 'It ain't over till the fat lady sings?'" laughed Peco patronizingly.

"I thought of that," replied the smuggler smoothly. "But out of respect for your waistline I wasn't going to say anything."

Instantly a blow from the baton crashed against his cheek and knocked him into Hunt. The guards pulled him upright again, blood streaming down his face.

"Now, what was it you were going to say?" asked Peco, thumping the baton against her palm.

"Oh, nothing much," Gromyko said with a sly grin on his lips. "I was just going to ask if you've faced your fears lately?"

At this instant a dark mist emanated from Hunt's hand and flowed into Peco. She screamed and dropped her baton, recoiling from something only she could see. Horror filled her eyes and she fled to the back wall, cowering in the corner and whimpering like a trapped animal. The guards who held them slackened their grip momentarily, stunned by what they saw.

Seeing their chance, the two men broke from their captors, Hunt snatching Peco's baton off the floor and smashing it against the skull of the officer who had held his right arm. Screaming in pain as two teeth were knocked loose, the man fell against the guard next to him, sending them both toppling over.

Hunt whipped around to see Gromyko fighting with the two guards who'd held him just as the pair on the sidelines piled onto the smuggler, overwhelming him. Hunt bashed two of them by the time the other officer who'd held him got to his feet and tackled him around the middle. Hunt's head smacked against the wall, sending his brain crashing against the inside of his skull. With stars in his eyes he rolled onto his back, the guard who'd tackled him seizing his baton arm and holding it to the floor.

In a desperate effort Hunt sent another dark mist from

his hand, this time into the guard who held him. Much like Peco he recoiled instantly, blinking his eyes at an unseen terror, his mouth agape. He shrunk away from Hunt and scrambled to the far wall, trying to crawl into the concrete.

"Rex!" shouted Gromyko, held to the ground by one guard while the other pummeled him.

Hunt shot to his feet and dropped both guards with a powerful blow to each of their heads. They fell on top of the smuggler, who struggled to free himself from their dead weight. Hunt, remembering Peco's husband, turned and saw him pressing himself against the back wall, wishing no part of the carnage.

Gromyko got to his feet and brushed his long black hair out of his eyes with his hand. Blood flowed freely down his face and onto his shirt, the wound in his cheek having widened through successive blows from the guards. He surveyed the scene and then looked at Mr. Peco.

"Spread the tale through Midway of how Gromyko defeated his captors," he said in a theatrical voice that somehow suited him. Seeing no response from Peco, he nodded towards Hunt. "Do it! Or my friend will work his dark arts on you as well."

The man looked at his wife, babbling in the corner, beside herself with fear. His eyes shot back to Gromyko and he nodded vigorously, unable to speak.

"Come on, Antonin," Hunt said, grabbing his friend's arm and pulling him towards the stairs.

In a flash they were back in the bedroom looking out the window into the night. They heard vigorous pounding at the front door in the same instant.

"The patrol must have heard the fight downstairs," Gromyko said in a whisper. "Come on! Get the window open before they break down the door!"

Opening the lock and pushing the window upward, Hunt climbed onto the sill and slid to the ground, Gromyko right behind him. They darted up the street and into the shadows. Ducking around the corner of an old shop, they glanced back momentarily before continuing.

"Strange that the house wasn't surrounded once we were inside," mused Gromyko. "You'd think they'd do that, just to ensure we didn't escape."

"Probably felt they had us in hand, eight against two," Hunt said. "Besides, hiding all those people nearby might have given them away as we approached. Now, come on. Let's get off the streets as soon as possible. It won't take long for them to put out an alert."

Drawing on his copious knowledge of the city's bypaths and secret passageways, Gromyko managed to keep their time on the streets to an absolute minimum. Clearly the call had gone out by the time they were halfway back, for the patrols tramped up and down the neighborhoods adjacent to Peco's house with a vigor that was unusual for them.

"We'll be lucky to get back now," Wellesley said, as Hunt crouched behind Gromyko in a shadow, watching a pair of sentries confer a couple dozen paces away.

Hunt closed his eyes and drew a deep breath through his cloth mask.

"They're breaking apart," Gromyko said of the sentries, as they moved off in separate directions. "We're going to–," he began, stopping when he saw his friend sway on his feet and reach out to the wall beside him for support. "Are you alright?"

"I don't know what it is," Hunt said in a voice thick with fatigue. "I just feel terribly tired."

"Well, it's been an intense night," Gromyko replied, unsatisfied with his own explanation and looking at Hunt with concern. "We'll be back soon enough. Then you can rest. Come on."

With this he dashed up the street that the sentries had just vacated, Hunt struggling to keep up. Pausing as often as he dared to allow his companion to rest, the smuggler expertly guided them home without incident. Reaching the door first, Gromyko knocked out a little code that had been agreed upon before leaving. It opened instantly, Wanda quickly ushering them inside.

"How did it go?" she asked, closing the door after them and sliding the bolt shut. She looked through the little glass window at the top of the door for a moment to ensure nobody had followed them, and then turned around. "What happened?" she gasped, seeing the dark bruise on the smuggler's face, and the frozen blood on his jacket.

"Peco turned," Hunt said flatly, dropping onto a little three legged stool near the door sighing his exhaustion. "She had six cops waiting for us."

"It was glorious," Gromyko said, as Wanda handled his face and examined the wound. "You should have seen it. They were no match for us."

"No match for Rex, I believe you mean," Ugo said, walking into the small lobby holding a steaming cup by the saucer beneath it. He held it up, inquiring with his eyes if Hunt wanted it. When he declined Ugo took a sip from it himself, apparently deciding that Gromyko didn't need it.

The smuggler frowned but said nothing.

"This needs to be dressed right away," Wanda said, taking Gromyko's hand and leading him into the house.

"Honey! The floor!" Ugo said in exasperation, wet snow falling off the smuggler's boots in large clumps. Gromyko turned and smiled at the old man just as his head disappeared around the corner, glad for a little payback.

"So, your gift saw you through?" Ugo asked, leaning against the wall next to Hunt and taking another sip.

"Yes, but only partially," replied Hunt, as he slid off his boots and put them aside. Pulling off his stocking cap and the cloth mask that covered everything below his eyes, he scratched his scalp vigorously. Ugo patiently waited until he was ready to continue. "I could only use it twice, and the second time was very hard. I thought it would be faster than that. And I feel tired. Awfully tired."

"Your connection to your gift is still imperfect," replied

Ugo, stirring his tea gently with a small spoon. "Once it's fully integrated, you'll be able to use it without any negative effects for yourself. Right now the sheer power of it imbalances your mind, causing unconscious contents to spill into places they don't belong. Then your psyche has to work to set things right, and that puts a load on you that often manifests itself in initiates as fatigue. You can think of it like water washing over the side of an old sailing ship during a storm: some of the crew have to bail the water out with buckets, and that takes them away from other tasks they could be performing. Over the coming months your connection will improve, and then you won't have side effects."

"Is that the only way?" Hunt asked wearily. "I don't see how practical of a weapon this gift is, if I'm gonna be exhausted every time I use it."

"Well, a truly powerful healer could help you straighten it out in short order," Ugo replied. "But it would place an incredible drain on them to do so. Perfecting a connection to an unconscious gift is one of the hardest things a person can do for another. It requires them to surrender themselves to the inner world of another in order to interface with it to the degree that is needed. The risk of an unconscious flood washing back over them is great, and thus only extraordinary circumstances can justify the procedure. Moreover, it tends to only be possible in the presence of a strong love bond, because that's usually the only way the ego will put itself at such risk."

"So it's the slow way, then?"

"I'm afraid so," Ugo replied, watching as Hunt reached up to feel where his skull had hit the basement wall. "I suppose the rest was knuckles?"

"Uh huh," Hunt nodded, instantly regretting his motion because of the pain it sent through his brain.

"Good thing you two are from the rough side of town," commented Ugo. "Otherwise I never could have sent you in there."

"Yeah," replied Hunt offhandedly. Realizing that

something about Ugo's statement didn't sound right, he looked up at him. "Sent us in there?" he asked. "You mean you knew?"

"Of course," replied Ugo casually. "We've suspected Peco for a long time. Luckily she never knew who anyone was. She just moved anonymous notes for us. We found out she was with the police only days ago."

"You knowingly sent us into a trap?" asked Hunt, his anger rising slowly. "Why?"

"For two reasons," replied Ugo. "First, to protect the asset that pointed her out to us. That person must remain secure, no matter the cost. They are in an extremely delicate position, and if we'd changed anything in our dealings with Peco she would have figured out who they are. We couldn't let that happen. Now they'll think it was their own blunder that gave them away. You see, I let it slip out that Gromyko would be the one dropping by. They couldn't give up a prize like him, so they had to pounce and expose themselves."

"And the second reason?" Hunt asked quietly.

"Because you needed a trial by fire," replied Ugo. "We had to see if you could really handle yourself in the thick of it. You'll have to undertake missions in the future that will make this look like a stroll in the forest, so we had to be sure of you. And more than that, *you* had to be sure of you. What you gained tonight is something that no amount of teaching or practice could ever give you. You've learned that you can rely on your gift to see you through. You've gained self reliance."

Hunt stood up deliberately, his head pointed towards the floor. He looked up slowly, his gaze falling upon Ugo with such fiery rage in them that the old man stepped back reflexively. A primitive, violent gleam was visible in his eyes.

Stepping close to Ugo and grabbing a handful of his dinner jacket, he whispered "Don't *ever* do that again," with such repressed passion that the old man stood frozen by his words several moments after he'd left the lobby.

CHAPTER 10

"Life is never what we expect it to be, is it, Rex?" asked Wellesley the next morning, as his friend shook the cobwebs out of his head after a turbulent night sleep.

"That's both philosophical *and* vague," replied Hunt in a dry, crackling voice. He hadn't touched a drop of water after coming back from his mission with Gromyko the night before, and he was parched from the dry, wintery air.

"Oh, I thought you would have liked that," Wellesley said. "You have a tendency to make broad statements. At least you used to. It seems the philosophy engine has been switched off of late."

"Guess I've got other things on my mind," he replied, rubbing his eyes and taking a deep breath which he exhaled slowly. His sleep had been bad, leaving him feeling worse rather than better. His mind swam with worries. What to do about the prison still occupied center stage. But what really tore at him was the sense of betrayal at Ugo's hands. He'd made his displeasure known in terms the old man wouldn't soon forget. But that didn't change the fact that it had been necessary to put him on notice. Just when he thought he'd found someone to trust, that trust was betrayed. Perhaps it was done for practical, sensible reasons. But betrayed it had been, all the same.

He rolled from his bed and put his feet on the creaking wooden floor.

"It's all coming unraveled, Wellesley," he said gloomily. "Ugo's playing games with me. Antonin is gonna break with the Order's plan the first chance he gets. And Wanda's so head-over-heels in love with him that I don't exist anymore. It was probably stupid of me, but I fancied I had a home here, just for a little while. It seemed like such a safe, out of the way place. And it was filled with people who understood me. Or so I thought! But what Ugo did last night burned me so badly I don't think I can forgive him. I think I have to move on."

"Move where?" countered Wellesley. "This is one of the safest places in the city. It has to be, since the Order wouldn't risk Ugo getting captured. They probably keep their ears to the ground specifically for any threats that are pointed his way. Sticking close to him is the smart play, at least for now."

"Even if I want to strangle him for what he did?"

"Yes, even then. You can't let your emotions rule you at a time like this. We're in too much trouble with the government for that. Think about it: where could we go that they wouldn't find us? The Underground is shattered, so none of their haunts will do. And we don't have any other friends we can hide out with. Not a soul in Midway would help a stranger on the run duck the authorities: the risk to themselves would be too great. And it's not like we can build an igloo in the forest and eat snow."

"I guess you're right," Hunt said with a yawn, standing up. "Forget it. Just a stupid idea before I was fully awake."

"We've all had 'em," Wellesley said, as Hunt made for the bedroom door.

He found the trio gathered around the breakfast table quietly eating. Ugo glanced at him over a book he was reading without saying a word or otherwise betraying recognition of his existence. Wanda and Gromyko looked at him curiously, not knowing what had passed between him and Ugo the night before, but aware that some major shift had occurred. They were tense and not talking.

"Good morning," Hunt said loudly, deciding to break the

ice as forcibly as possible. He was in no mood for a touchy, awkward breakfast during which they would be forced to pretend that nothing had happened.

Each of them muttered something indistinct in response.

Hunt sat down at the foot of the table, with Ugo to his left and the other two seated together on his right.

"Get you anything?" Wanda asked quietly, her eyes wide with the desire to please. She felt the strain more palpably than anyone else, and sought to make at least one person at the table happy.

"Just tea, please. Something about last night killed my appetite," he said pointedly, his eyes rolling over to the sole reader at the table.

She rose silently and poured him a cup from a kettle on the stove. Handing it to him, she shot him a look that implored him not to stir anything up.

The rest of the morning passed off uneventfully, with Ugo going to work as usual. Gromyko disappeared shortly thereafter, though whether he left the house or simply moved into another room was unknown to Rex.

Around noon Hunt was flipping through books in the den when Wanda joined him and began making small talk. He knew she was working her way slowly towards the topic that actually occupied her, and he let her ramble along until she was finally ready to broach it.

"What *happened* last night?" she asked at last. "Grandfather was practically mute all morning. Did you two have a fight?"

"Something like that," Hunt replied, before filling her in on the details.

"That's very serious, Rex," she said with a worried look on her face. "You don't just threaten a high member of the Order."

"But I thought you were a *healing* order?" Hunt replied with flippant sarcasm. "I can't be in any danger."

"Well, we're not going to *assassinate* you, if that's what you mean," she laughed mirthlessly. "But actions like yours are taken very seriously. You see, they regard themselves as a sovereign sect, above the rules and also above reproach. To be honest, the other members tend to be rather high and mighty in their dealings. This is as true of grandfather as it is of any of them."

"You don't seem too smug," countered Hunt.

"I'm one of the few, believe me," Wanda said quietly, as though some unseen observer would hear her. "And grandfather is far from being the worst. By threatening him the way you did, you pulled him down to earth, as it were. You clipped his wings and made him mortal. I don't know if he can forgive you for that."

"I think *I'm* the one who's in a position to forgive or not," replied Hunt, crossing his arms. "Ugo wasn't the one sent into a trap."

"Yes, I know that," she said, laying a sympathetic hand on his arm. "But that isn't how the rest will see it. You'll be an upstart to them, a renegade who needs to be taught a lesson. Provided he tells them, of course."

"Do you think he will?"

"I can't say. Normally he would. But I'm not sure he'd jeopardize the mission against the prison. If he tells them, there'll be no way that they'll permit you to stay in the Order, and then he'll have to find a new operative who can carry the fight to the enemy. Thwarting the government's conspiracy has very nearly become his reason for living."

"I guess we'll find out," said Hunt without concern, picking up another book and skimming it while Wanda stood there, She eyed him curiously for a moment and then spoke.

"You're awfully calm about this whole thing. I would have thought you'd be glued to the ceiling."

"Not anymore," he replied, a little surprised at his own confidence. "Something changed last night."

"It was when you used your gift for the first time,"

Wanda said. "That often happens. It's a right of passage for many, inducting them into a new world of self-assurance."

"Self-reliance was Ugo's term," replied Hunt.

"You know he didn't try to hurt you, right?" she asked. "He's just doing what he thinks is best for both you and the movement."

"I know that," Hunt responded, sliding the book back into its place and looking over the spines of the others. "But some actions are just intolerable, and what he did is one of them. I can't stand being played like that."

"Then I guess you'll have some decisions to make," Wanda replied in a subdued voice, before walking slowly from the room.

"Yeah, I guess so," he muttered once she'd gone.

That night Ugo came home from work, tired and cold from his walk in the snow. He spoke in a quiet voice to Wanda for a few minutes, and then found Hunt, still in the living room, absorbed in one of his books.

"Hi, Rex," he said in a conciliatory voice.

"Hello, Ugo," Hunt replied without looking up. He sat on the couch with a leg tossed over the other.

The old man made for the rocking chair and sat down with a satisfied sigh, glad to get the weight off his tired feet. He rocked back and forth for a few minutes, letting Hunt get used to him before speaking.

"I've been doing a lot of thinking today, Rex," he said at last, his voice a little uncertain. "And you were right: I shouldn't have sent you two in there like that. It was high handed and unnecessary."

Hunt closed his book and laid it aside, looking at the old man as though he wished to verify his words with his eyes. The meek look on Ugo's face confirmed his sincerity, and Hunt relaxed.

"I can't tolerate stuff like that, Ugo," Hunt said quietly. "Not again. It isn't in me. Another bit like that and I'll walk."

"I understand completely," Ugo said, nodding his head.

"I terribly misread you, Rex. I should have known better. You reminded me of another young man who I taught once, and that was exactly the kind of experience he needed. I should have realized it was the wrong course to take with you. You have my promise that I won't do it again."

"Alright," replied Hunt, nodding slowly. "I can accept that."

"Good," Ugo smiled in relief. "Have you told Gromyko?"

"No, I haven't. And I don't think you should either. He's a lot hotter headed than I am. But I did tell Wanda."

"We'd better tell her to keep quiet before–"

"What!" they heard Gromyko exclaim in the kitchen.

"I think it's too late for that now," Hunt said, rising from the couch just as his friend entered.

"You sent Gromyko into a trap!" the smuggler exploded, sliding into the third person as he often did when upset. "Were you jealous of his fame and trying to get rid of him?" he demanded, striding angrily towards the old man in the rocker. "Or was it the simple pleasure of tricking a man of his fame that motivated you?"

"I assure you, Gromyko, that I never–" began Ugo.

"What value are the assurances of one who would deceive?" asked the smuggler. "If you are willing to put us into the hands of eight thugs, then it is hard to imagine what else you wouldn't do. It was only through Rex's gift, and the fighting prowess of Gromyko, that we are not in shackles this very moment."

"Antonin, give him a chance to speak," replied Hunt.

"Oh, I am surrounded by betrayers!" the smuggler said, as Wanda appeared in the doorway. "First Fedorov stabs me in the back, handing the entire Underground over to the government. And now, from the hand of one from whom I sought a safe haven, comes this bitter pill! This poison! And this, after humiliating myself and accepting the lowly post of courier! Is there a plot against Gromyko? Do you conspire against him?"

"Relax, Antonin," Hunt said, putting a hand on his friend's shoulder. "Nobody is out to get you except the government, and they want us all. We're all in the same boat, and nobody is trying to push anyone out."

"That is difficult to accept, even from your lips," Gromyko replied. "I can believe only the testimony of my own eyes and ears. And what am I to think when I hear that the very organization from which I sought protection handed me over on a silver platter to our allegedly common enemy? It makes me think that perhaps the government had some extra help in breaking the Underground. That perhaps another organization, jealous of the hold we had on the affections of the people of Midway, sought to cut us out to make space for themselves."

"That's nonsense!" Ugo said sharply, his own anger rising. "The last group we'd ever be jealous of is the *Underground!*"

"The Order and the Underground worked in different spheres," Hunt said, shooting a dark look at the old man for making matters worse. "They operated in a totally separate manner from one another. There's no chance that the Order sought to undermine your people, Antonin."

"My friend, I fear that they have blinded you," Gromyko said. "What do we really know about them? They are secretive in the extreme, and operate according to their own sense of right and wrong. Already this one," he said, tossing a finger towards Ugo, "has stated that galactic civil war is not too high a price to pay for his ideals. What are you and I in comparison? To them we are mere gnats to be sacrificed at will."

"I don't agree," Hunt said sincerely. "Ugo wasn't acting on the instructions of the Order. He sent us in there on his own, for what he thought was the good of both the Order and myself. It was both an enormous risk and a terrible blunder, but I fully believe it was done with the best intentions. He and I have reached an understanding over the matter, and I'm satisfied that he won't do any such thing again."

Leaning on his right leg and crossing his arms, the smuggler cast his eyes between Ugo and his friend. Hunt could see that he was moved by his words, but much skepticism remained written on his face.

"Think about it," Hunt continued, hoping to break down the rest of his resistance. "If the Order had it out for us, they could have betrayed us long ago. Why wait until now to sell you out? They easily could have sent you to carry a message into a dark alley that was watched by a half dozen cops. And why train me just to hand me over to them? With the gift that I now wield, I'm an enormous threat to them. A smart enemy would neutralize a foe *before* he gained in power, not after."

"That's true," admitted Gromyko, nodding reluctantly.

"And what about me, Antonin?" Wanda said, pushing off the doorway in which she leaned and approaching the smuggler. "I've worked in the taverns for years, and I've seen you in them innumerable times. I could have informed the police of your whereabouts and quietly slipped out the door before they came crashing in. It would have chopped the head off the Underground in a single step. But I didn't do that, because neither I nor the Order are out to get you." She drew near and lowered her voice. "You've been on the run for so long that you don't recognize your friends, Antonin. You're still confused and hurting from the destruction of the Underground, and it has you jumping at shadows. You don't have to worry," she said, touching his arm. "We're all friends here."

Gromyko looked at Hunt for confirmation of her words, and received it in a slow nod matched with a steady gaze. The smuggler, arms still wrapped tightly over his chest, looked down at his feet for a moment and thought. Then he looked at Hunt.

"You say he apologized to you?"

"Yes, he did," replied Hunt.

Gromyko's eyes rolled over to Ugo and then doubled-back to his friend.

"And yet he does not apologize to Gromyko."

All three of them looked to the old man who sat motionless in the rocking chair, his fingers wrapped tightly around the armrests. A sour expression was on his face. The last thing he wanted to do was apologize to the smuggler. Several seconds passed silently. Wanda began to wring her hands behind her back.

"No, he hasn't," Hunt said slowly, quietly. "But he will, if he expects the continued participation of *both* of us in the Order."

Ugo's head snapped to Hunt. Surprise and fear were mingled in his eye as he contemplated the potential loss of his greatest asset. Eventually he nodded, a look of defeat on his face.

"I'm...sorry, Gromyko," Ugo said, the words coming out with effort. "It was a terrible mistake. I won't make it a second time."

"Be sure that you don't," the smuggler said. "For Gromyko is not a man to be trifled with."

The old man's eyes narrowed as his anger began to smolder within him. He was about to speak when he glanced at Hunt and bit his tongue. Nothing could be permitted to jeopardize the mission, not even his own pride. Nodding his grudging assent, he rose from the rocker and left the room.

◆ ◆ ◆

On the night of the third day since their meeting, Hunt stood in the bushes near the apartments. Darkness had fallen a couple of hours earlier and, along with it, the temperature.

"There has got to be an easier way to meet someone," Wellesley said. "You'd think in this era of high technology that the Order could outfit us with some kind of communicator."

"They don't want to run the risk of our chatter being

intercepted," Hunt said quietly, leaning against a tree with his arms crossed over his chest. He watched the goings on of the apartment buildings, and of the guards that patrolled between them and the prison. More than once a patrol had come a little too close to the forest and he'd had to retreat behind the thin, weatherbeaten branches to escape their flashlights.

"It's not like there isn't plenty of risk doing things this way," the AI said. "For starters, she has to *physically* leave her place and come out here. I don't care how many people are on the Order's payroll: that kind of risk adds up fast in espionage. All you need is a curious onlooker to report her midnight perambulations for an investigation to start. The prison authorities don't want her here anyway, so they must have their eyes open for an excuse to get rid of her."

"I doubt that," replied Hunt. "This is Delta-13, remember? There's nothing but the government complex, Midway, and thousands and thousands of square miles of snow. They'd never expect her to implicate herself in some way because there's *nothing to do here!* They'll figure her for a gadfly they have to tolerate and misdirect until she eventually gets exhausted and leaves."

The soft sound of branches rustling off to his left shut Hunt's mouth. He looked around the tree and could just make out the outline of a large fox poking about in the snow. Clapping his gloves just loudly enough to be heard, he sent the critter scurrying into the darkness.

"Wells, have you ever noticed anything...odd, on a night like this?"

"What do you mean?"

"I felt a presence a few nights ago, back when I was packed in with Lily. It came just to the edge of where I could see and simply waited, watching us. At first I thought it was an animal. But something...intuitive, told me it wasn't. When it noiselessly left the area I knew that it was something else, something immaterial. Funny that it didn't scare me at the time. You'd think it would."

"You had your mind on other things," the AI chuckled. "But no, I can't say I've ever noticed anything like that. I didn't feel anything during our entire stint with Lily, so it might be something only humans, or at least organics, can pick up." He paused for a moment. "What do you think it was?"

"I have no idea," replied Hunt, wrapping his arms over his chest a little more tightly against the wind that had begun to blow. "Could be some kind of messenger from the planet, a sort of projection into my mind. If it essentially put sounds and a feeling inside my head, like a waking dream, then that would explain why you didn't notice anything: there wasn't anything to notice."

"Makes sense," Wellesley said. "I wasn't able to come along when you and Wanda went deep diving into your head. Could be the same sort of deal."

"Could be," replied Hunt quietly, letting the conversation fade out.

The clouds overhead eventually broke up, and the dim light of the planet's tiny moons beamed down from above, casting the faintest glow on the world around him.

"Beautiful, in its own way," Hunt said after nearly an hour of stiff, frigid silence. A cold front was blowing in, and even the medallion was having a hard time combating it. "The sheer desolation of Delta-13 has a kind of appeal. It reminds a man of the emptiness in his own soul."

"Doesn't work that way on AIs," Wellesley said. "All I see is endless wastelands that can't be put to any practical use. Although I admit that its reputation as a holy world among the old priests does affect me a little more than I wish it would. It all feels a bit...mystical, even to me."

"I thought you weren't a follower of *Deleck-Hai*," said Hunt, referring to the ancient religion of most of the *Kol-Prockians*.

"No, of course not. But it was pretty popular in the fringe, even in those late days, and I came to respect it. Most of the leaders of the rebellion belonged to it, so I had to be conversant in its rules and customs."

"So you come by your feelings for the planet second hand," said Hunt.

"Yeah, I guess you could say that."

"I've always regarded the planet as something to get away from, to escape. It's as much a prison as that place over there," he said, stabbing a finger towards the walls and guard towers that stood on the peak of the hill. "But I don't know if I could be happy anywhere else. Delta-13 understands me, reflecting on the outside what I feel on the inside."

"A physical depiction of your feelings?"

"Pretty much."

"Well, I think those feelings are about to warm up a little," Wellesley said. "Here comes Lily."

Hunt's heart jumped in his chest at the AI's words. He searched the lobby but only saw the guard.

"I don't see her," he said anxiously.

"Not the *lobby*," Wellesley said. "The *window*! She's more resourceful than I thought."

Hunt's eyes scanned the darkness beside the building and saw a shadowy outline squeezing with effort out of a tiny window. A lump sat on the ground beneath the window.

"She'd better hurry up, or the sentries are gonna catch her," the AI said, watching tensely. "I think her hips are stuck."

Without a word Hunt bolted from the trees into the open, running as fast as he dared across the crackling snow. Ducking low as he neared the apartment, he slowed his pace and drew up before the half of Tselitel that was visible.

"Help! I'm stuck!" she said in an urgent whisper, panic creeping into her voice. "The guards will be along at any moment!"

Just as Wellesley had thought, her hips were stuck. Even her slight form was a touch too large to fit through the opening. She lay flat on the sill, her arms waving helplessly in the air, the flat wall of the apartment building giving her nothing to grab onto.

Hunt grasped her waist and tried to turn her diagonally to fit her through the window. But the soft fat of her hips had allowed her to squeeze through until she was jammed in tight.

"You're good and stuck," he said through gritted teeth, trying to pull her out but making no headway.

"I know that, you pinhead!" she snapped sharply. "Just get me out!"

Annoyed by her tart reply, he grabbed two handfuls of the soft flesh around her middle and shoved her back inside by a few inches. She let out a little yelp, but had sense enough to stifle it.

"What are you doing?" she asked.

"Getting you out," he said forcefully, twisting her body at a forty-five degree angle and dragging her out into the cold. He set her roughly on the ground and turned to slide the window shut when she gasped.

"Here they come!" she said, putting her hands on his back anxiously.

Hunt jerked his head and saw the sentries coming around the far end of the building, their lights flickering in every direction. Snapping up her bag in one motion, he took her arm and pulled her back the way he'd come. Keeping low, and moving only fast enough to outpace the guards, they stole across the open ground to the forest that offered them sanctuary. They kept silent as they moved inside, not risking so much as a whisper until they were far out of earshot.

They stopped. Hunt dropped her bag on the ground and released her arm.

"You didn't have to be so rough about it," Tselitel said, rubbing her stomach through the thin jacket she wore. "I think you bruised me."

"Just as well," he said. "I reckon you could use a little kicking around from time to time."

She put her hands on her hips and looked at him.

"You don't know how to treat a lady, do you?"

"I wouldn't know. I haven't met one yet," he replied.

They looked at each other for a moment. Then she laughed.

"I suppose I deserved that," she said, her hands sliding from her hips. "I'm sorry. I shouldn't have insulted you."

"Do you always get high and mighty when people try to help you?" he asked, picking up her bag and feeling it curiously in the dark. "What's this?" he asked, without waiting for a response to his first question.

"Some warmer clothes," she said, taking the bag from him and pulling out a thick jacket and some overalls. "I couldn't very well put them on and fit through the window."

"Good thing Wellesley noticed you," Hunt said. "If I'd gotten there half a minute later the guards would have been all over us."

"Who's Wellesley?" she asked, leaning against a tree and putting a leg through the overalls.

"He's an AI I carry with me. A very ancient alien artifact."

"Look, I said I was sorry," Tselitel said. "You don't need to joke around."

"I'm serious," replied Hunt.

"Let me talk to her for a moment," Wellesley said.

"Hold on a second," Hunt said, slipping the AI from around his neck. "He wants to talk to you."

"Er, talk to me?" she asked, eyeing the medallion hesitantly.

"Yes. He communicates electrically through your skin," Hunt explained, holding the medallion out before him. "Just slip it inside your mitten."

Dubiously she took the disc from him and put it inside her glove. Her eyes lit up moments later.

"It's incredible!" she enthused. "I don't believe it!" Then she fell silent, concentrating on the words she heard within. Her gaze darted between Hunt and a vacant space in front of her as she processed what the AI had to say.

"Well, don't take all night," Hunt said several minutes

later.

"Oh, of course," she replied, handing the AI back to him. Grasping the medallion, he looped the cold chain around his neck and jammed it down the tight collar of his turtleneck.

"What took you so long?" he asked with a laugh.

"Just giving her some background information," the AI replied.

Shaking his head at the cryptic answer, Hunt's eyes fell upon Tselitel.

"Are you warm enough?"

"Not really," she replied, wrapping her arms around herself for effect. "I could use that medallion, if you can spare it for a while."

Without a word he took it off and handed it to her.

"You mean I have to put it on myself?" she asked playfully, still sensing a little bit of distance between them and hoping to melt it.

"I reckon you can manage," he replied, smiling to be sociable but not really feeling it. "Put it on. Then we can walk to stay warm."

Imperceptibly a light went out of her eyes, and she did the work solo. Hunt picked up her bag and walked slowly south, deeper into the forest. She walked mutely beside him, eyes downcast as she reflected.

"So?" he asked to break the silence.

"What do you mean?" she asked, her eyes as wide as a doe's.

"So, what has been happening with your work? Have you made any more progress with the inmates?"

"No, not really," she replied. "Vilks is still drawing circles with me. Although, and I can't be sure of this, I *think* I saw a flicker of recognition in his eyes yesterday. But it might have been my own wishful thinking. I want them to recover more than anything in the world."

"The prison authorities aren't giving you any trouble?" Hunt asked.

"None whatsoever," replied Tselitel with a confused shrug. "Though I can't imagine why not. They have a great deal to lose if Vilks talks. He could say what they did to him."

"They probably figure to get rid of you before that can happen," Hunt replied. "They really can't touch him without drawing more attention to themselves, since the prisoners are under their care twenty-four hours a day. Anything that happens to them is the responsibility of the warden and his underlings. The Order would immediately spread the news, and the scandal would get worse than ever. So you're the weak link in the chain, the only one they can really afford to break."

"You mean I've been in danger here the entire time?" she asked.

"Uh huh. But I don't think they would try to kill you. Every free-thinking citizen in the empire would immediately conclude that they had you eliminated, and the storm that would follow would make the present scandal look petty by comparison. They'd probably just try to break you instead."

"A nice thought," Tselitel replied, not feeling that option to be much of an improvement. "I never realized the risk I undertook by coming here."

"Delta-13 is a dangerous place for anyone," observed Hunt. "It's just a question of where the danger comes from. Down in Midway we regularly run the risk of freezing to death, or of doing some little thing that puts the authorities on us. Just being outside after curfew, even a few steps past your own door, is a very serious crime. Talking to you like I am now would get me sent up the hill without even an hour's delay. And you'd be in deep trouble as well, though your position would protect you somewhat. They'd probably just kick you off the planet, using it as an excuse to get rid of you. Then they'd have a free hand to keep up their work on the prisoners."

"How cruel," she said.

"That's the way it is out here," Hunt replied simply. Then, shifting towards the east he said, "The Order will need your help very soon."

"How so?" she asked.

"You're on the inside in a very important way," Hunt explained. "You have contact with the victims of their mind control experiments. That is something we cannot manage on our own. Most of our agents are low-level employees because the entire upper echelon was handpicked for their loyalty to the imperial government. Even *attempting* to cultivate one of them would bring serious consequences to our entire network. But in you we have an agent who's in deep."

"But what can I do?" she asked, a little scared of the responsibility that was being thrust upon her. "Sure, I have access to the patients. But I'm constantly monitored, and the prison is an absolute maze of security doors and chokepoints. Why, two guards are watching me from behind one-way glass during each of my interviews. They'd pounce in an instant if they knew I was trying to pull something."

"I might know just the way to pull it off," he mused aloud, a bold idea quickly filling his mind. "Yes, that should do nicely."

"What are you thinking?" she asked, her curiosity rapidly growing.

"What if you could communicate with Vilks without ever saying so much as a word?" he asked cryptically.

"I'm afraid I'm not psychic," she laughed.

"I'm not talking about psychic powers," Hunt replied. "I'm talking about Wellesley."

"Me?" the AI asked.

"Wellesley?" Tselitel asked at the same time. "What can he do?"

"He can communicate with Vilks," said Hunt. "Moreover, he might be able to reach him on a deeper level than you can since he'll be sending electronic impulses straight into his nervous system. He can bypass his audio centers altogether."

"You may be right," Tselitel said, mulling the idea for a moment. "But how can I get Wellesley in contact with him?

Like I said, there are two guards who watch me constantly, to say nothing of the cameras in the room. They'll notice *instantly* if I try to pass him an alien artifact."

Hunt shook his head.

"You won't have to *pass* it to him," he explained. "Like I said, he communicates through *skin contact*. And you've already got that."

"Of course! When he takes my hand to draw the circles!" she exclaimed. "Wellesley can send the impulses through me." Then her face fell. "Provided there's enough life inside him to receive them."

"I'm certain there is," said Hunt with assurance, feeling the planet was guiding him again. "If you're right, and Vilks, along with the other mutes, is trying to process a massive mental load, then his body will be exploding with electrical impulses. The real question will be if Wellesley can penetrate all the noise and get through to him."

"I reckon I can," replied the AI gamely. "I was designed to conduct even the most delicate operations with absolute finesse. I should be able to shout loud enough for him to hear me. What you should really be wondering about is if you can get along without me while I'm palling around with this pretty little thing."

"I reckon I can," repeated Hunt with a smile.

"Don't you be too sure," replied the AI with a laugh.

"But what if Vilks starts acting strangely when Wellesley talks to him?" asked Tselitel, unsure of what Hunt was responding to but unwilling to ask and make a fuss. "We have no way of knowing how he'll react."

"That's a risk we'll have to take," Hunt said. "But the guards won't have any idea what's causing it. The worst thing they can do is cart Vilks back to his room for observation. They'd never dream that an AI was communicating with him. Most human AIs either speak audibly or interface via an implant in the user. Talking through electrical impulses is so rare that they'd never think of it." He thought for a few moments and then continued. "Having said that, Wellesley probably shouldn't communicate right away. Give it an hour or so before starting, just to throw them off in case something does happen."

"Sounds like a good idea," Tselitel said, nodding almost invisibly in the darkness. "When do I take him?"

"Tonight, as soon as we're done here," Hunt said. "We've got to learn whatever we can from Vilks as soon as possible."

They walked in silence for an interval, Hunt lost in thought and Tselitel wondering what he was mulling over.

"Can we stop for a few minutes?" she asked, stepping over a fallen tree and sitting down. "I'm not used to all this exercise."

"Sure," replied Hunt quietly, leaning against a tree a few feet away and looking west, away from her. Viewed from above, the forest which concealed them looked somewhat like a backwards C. It was long, running from north to south, but had a deep dent in the middle. It was on the inner edge of this dent that the pair rested, Hunt staring off across the great expanse of virgin snow. Here and there a little dark spot danced in the night, a creature of one sort or another prowling for a nocturnal meal.

"Do you think we'll succeed, Rex?" Tselitel asked from directly behind him. He jumped imperceptibly at her voice, unaware that she'd gotten off the fallen tree.

"I suppose so," Hunt said. "The Order seems pretty well organized, so I don't think they'll have any trouble putting the word out once we have proof. The question then will be if enough people believe it."

Unsure what else to say, Tselitel moved beside him and stood watching the wilderness. Its savage rawness struck a chord deep within her, resonating with the deepest impulses of her being. Something primitive and ancient was activated by it, an ancestral memory of long forgotten human struggles to survive in just such conditions. She felt more alive, more human, as it filled her soul and expanded it beyond the tiny confines that had defined it for so long.

"We're only truly human in conditions like this," she said at last, speaking without hesitation from the heart. "We may be safe and warm inside our little homes and offices. But it's times like this, contemplating the harsh reality of life, that we are brought face to face with our true nature. Man is a survivor. It's just who we are. We're not fully alive until we see and feel it first hand."

Hunt looked at the thin, willowy woman beside him, aware that her sentiment could easily have come from his own lips. In that moment he felt a connection with her that no deliberate act could have produced. A knot in his heart relaxed, and his feelings flowed towards her once again. He put a hand on her shoulder and squeezed it warmly. She took a step closer, standing half in front of him and staring into the night.

The wind began to pick up from the west, blowing into their faces and causing the branches above them to whisper in the night. A creature howled in the distance at the moons above, appealing to them for some inscrutable purpose. Reflexively Tselitel stepped closer to Hunt, her body bumping into his. Without a thought he put his right arm around her neck and shoulders, pulling her close and signaling his protection. She closed her eyes and savored the feeling, her heart warming at his touch.

"Are you cold?" he asked after a moment.

"Not anymore," she replied, wishing the moment would never end.

But as the minutes passed and she began to shiver, Hunt realized she was speaking from the heart and not the head. He drew her back inside the cover of the trees and shielded her body from the wind with his.

"Hang on a second," he said, digging into his pouch.

"Taco time?" she asked with a chuckle.

"Heh, no. You're not *that* cold." Pulling out several chemical warmers, he activated them and gave them to the doctor to slip into her inner pockets. He kept two for himself and worked them inside his shirt.

"Getting cold too?" she asked as she wrestled with her clothes to get the warmers inside.

"Sure, I haven't got the medallion anymore," replied Hunt casually.

"Can it help two people at once?" she asked. "Like could we both hold it and be stimulated by it?"

"I don't know. I've never thought to try, to be honest."

"No, it doesn't have the energy for that," said Wellesley. "It can only help one."

"Oh, Wellesley says no," relayed Hunt.

Tselitel just nodded and kept fighting with her clothes. Her mittens were so bulky that they made the task nearly impossible, but her hands were too cold to expose them to the open air. She sighed in exasperation and looked at him appealingly. He got her meaning and chuckled, slipping off his gloves momentarily to help.

"You must think me pretty helpless," Tselitel said, embarrassed at her plight.

"Just out here," he replied with a smile, slipping the warmers under her heavy coat and working them into the pockets of her light jacket underneath. "You seem pretty capable inside the lab. Your treatment of Vilks is brilliant."

"Oh, we all have our little talents," she said modestly, feeling his hands efficiently going about their work, sensing none of the tenderness she wished to find in them. "Out here the lab seems terribly far away and insignificant."

"I'm sure it doesn't to your patients," he replied, withdrawing his hands and slipping his gloves back on. "Anyhow, we all have our talents, like you said." Waving his hand around them, he said with a grin, "This just happens to be one of mine."

Eagerly she slid her arms around his neck and pressed her cold, shivering lips to his warm ones. Surprised but willing, he wrapped his powerful arms around her slim form and pulled her tightly against his body, relishing the contrast between them. She was so slight and fragile that instinct told him she would break if too much force was applied. And yet he enjoyed her fragility, how she couldn't resist him if she tried, because that fact, combined with her presence, implied a trust in his decency and honor that he craved above all else. It conveyed an acceptance of his intentions and thus of his entire self. So long an outcast, it was nice to feel so trusted.

After a long moment they parted.

"Your lips are cold," he said, making them both laugh.

"Of course they are. Why do you think I kissed you?" she joked, pulling him close with a chuckle. "There's something different about you. I can't put my finger on it. But I can feel it."

"Aw, I bet you tell that to all the guys who warm your lips," he replied.

"Just the ones I like," she said with quiet sincerity, turning her head and laying it against his chest. "Don't ever let me go," she whispered with sudden earnestness, closing her eyes. When he didn't reply she drew her head back and looked at him. "Will you?"

But his eyes were fixed on something behind her. She started to turn her head to look, but Hunt grabbed it and pulled it back again, covering her cheek with his hand to conceal it.

"So, Rex Hunt, the perpetual loner, has got himself a little lady friend, eh?" a voice taunted from behind her.

CHAPTER 11

"Hello, Milo," Hunt said in a flat, knowing tone, recognizing the man from his voice and outline. "What do you want?"

"Oh, nothing much," Milo said, moving a step closer. "Mostly I'm just curious."

"Curious about what?" asked Hunt, aware that the renegade was trying to get a look at Tselitel. He turned a little to the side to obscure her face all the more. She stood against him, her heart in her throat as the seconds passed by tensely. She could hear the mutual air of menace in their voices.

"Mostly about what you'd be doing out here in the middle of the night," Milo said, taking another step, this time to the south. "You see, I never bought that line about your being dead. I knew it was a lie the second I heard it."

"Lots of people have frozen in blizzards, Milo."

"Yeah, but not Rex Hunt," he replied. "You're too smart for something that stupid. Though I can see how others might have bought it. They don't know you like I do." Another step to the south was met with a further twist from Hunt. "So why the story, Rex? Were you in trouble, or just covering your tracks?"

"That's none of your business," Hunt said, his voice beginning to drop into a growl.

"Aw, come on, Rex," Milo said. "Brothers shouldn't have secrets from each other."

"Brothers?" Tselitel repeated, squeezing her eyes tight

the instant she heard her own voice.

"Ah, so she *can* speak!" Milo Hunt said, taking another step. "Why all the mystery, Rex? A dead man should have nothing to hide."

"Back off, Milo," he snapped. "I'm warning you."

"So *she's* the one who's got something to hide," Milo mused aloud, taking another step. He drew up and raised a hand to his chin, working it theatrically to indicate thought. "Now, let's see. *She* has something to hide. And you're both meeting in the forest that *just so happens* to stand between Midway and the government complex. Ah! I've got it!" he said dramatically, raising his index finger into the air as he spoke. "She's one of their employees! That puts you in a very...awkward position, brother. A man from Midway shouldn't be rendezvousing with the common enemy. Why, if word of this got across town, any number of people would be gunning for you. You know how they hate stool pigeons."

"Get out of here," Rex ordered. "And if you say one syllable of what you've seen–"

"Oh, you aren't the boss of me," laughed Milo. "Besides, someone else is bound to come across your tracks eventually. The forest isn't your personal playground, you know."

"Just nail him, Rex," Wellesley said. "He's deserved it for far too long."

"Nail him with what?" Tselitel asked in a barely audible whisper, hearing the AI's words through a patch of Rex's wrist that was pressed against her cheek.

"Yes, Rex: nail me with what?" Milo taunted.

"I see his hearing is as good as ever," Wellesley said sourly. "Keep quiet, Doctor. We're in deep if we don't play this right."

"This is your last chance, Milo," Rex said darkly.

"Oh, enough of your ultimatums," his brother laughed, walking towards them. "If you won't tell me who she is, I'll just take a peek for myself."

"Do it now, Rex," Wellesley said. "Before he sees her

face!"

"I can't take that chance," he said, not caring if Milo heard.

"Still carrying Wellesley with you, eh?" he asked, halfway to Hunt and Tselitel. "He still handing out advice like always?"

"Who cares if he's your brother, Rex!"

"It's not that," he replied, the image of Tselitel running from his gift in the dream flashing through his mind and making him hesitate.

Milo reached the pair and extended his hand to pull Tselitel away and reveal her face. At that moment Rex raised his hand and the mist flowed from it and into his brother. Terror filled his eyes as the forest turned into a scene of horror. Each of the trees transformed into a shadowy demon whose bright red eyes could see into his very soul. He felt them penetrating his deepest secrets, peeling back every layer of his mind with cruel relish. The shadows began to float and spin around him, taking swipes at him with long, vicious claws that he imagined drew blood.

"No, keep them away!" he shouted, ducking and covering his head with his arms. "Please, help me, Rex!" he pleaded.

But when he looked at Rex he no longer saw his brother. In his place stood a terrible figure made of shadows. His eyes aflame with rage, he reached forth his hand to exact punishment on Milo for a thousand crimes that were known only to himself. Morally naked before his perceived persecutor, his only open course was to flee the scene, running back to Midway as fast as his legs could carry him through the deep drifts that had built up around the forest.

"Finally got what was coming to him," Wellesley said with satisfaction, as Milo disappeared into the distance.

But Tselitel pushed away from Rex, looking up into his face with eyes that mingled fear with awe.

"You...How did you...?" she stammered, taking a step

backward.

"It is a gift of mine," Hunt said, watching her shrink back as pain filled his heart.

"A dark gift," she said, unsure and yet fascinated.

"Yes, but it has its uses," he replied, moving towards her while she continued to retreat.

"Don't come closer, Rex," she said, raising her hand to stop him. But he kept approaching.

"No, Lily, I'm not going to let you go," he said stoutly, determined to overcome the dream. "I'm still the same man you knew ten minutes ago."

"A man who can inspire terror?" she countered. "And in his own brother, no less?"

"Milo is a scoundrel of the worst sort," said Hunt, continuing to advance. "If he'd seen who you are the word would have gotten around Midway the instant he'd returned. Within hours everyone from Kelbauskas on down would have known. I had to stop him, for your sake as well as mine."

"There must have been a better way," Tselitel said, her healer's instinct tortured by the look in Milo's eyes. "There's always a better way."

"There wasn't. You've got to believe that," he said, picking up the pace of his pursuit.

At that moment she turned and bolted, running north towards the complex. She could hear Hunt's feet hitting the ground behind her, gaining with each passing moment. His hand reached out for her, grasping her jacket lightly before it slipped through his gloved fingers. She yelped and ran even harder, the cold air stinging her lungs as she gulped it down.

Another few seconds of running and she felt his fingers take a solid hold. He pulled her backwards off her feet, and they tumbled to the ground together, her landing on top of him.

"Let go of me!" she said, fighting the powerful hands that held her upper arms.

"Not until you get control of yourself!" he said through gritted teeth, striving desperately to hold on for fear she'd slip away in the darkness. She continued to struggle, so he twisted her off of him and onto her back. Sliding on top of her, his heavy frame pressing her to the ground, she finally relented, gazing up at him with fear and outrage written on her face.

"Now," he said, pausing a moment to catch his breath, "are you finally ready to listen to reason?"

"Doesn't look like I have any choice," she wheezed, his weight pressing down on her lungs.

He saw the fear begin to leave her eyes as the enforced stillness forced her to think. The outrage was still present, but it began to mix with curiosity about the man on top of her.

"I have a gift," he explained. "A dark gift, as you said. But a necessary one. There are people in this life who mean to do us harm for any number of reasons. The ability to hurt them back is rare, outside of knuckles. For some reason I have the power to strike terror into them like they've never known. It incapacitates them. But it is only the power to draw up what is already within them. I manipulate the fears they've buried in their unconscious and flood the front of their minds with them. I simply reveal what is within them already. I don't add darkness to this world."

"A subtle distinction," Tselitel said.

"But an important one," replied Hunt. "I've known pain, and I've known fear. More than most people, I expect. For some peculiar reason I can draw fear out of the depths of others. There is a darkness in me that I won't pretend isn't there, and it seeks that out in others and brings it to the surface. But it can't hurt you, Lily."

"Why?" she asked. "If you can turn it on your own flesh and blood, why wouldn't it come back on me at some point?"

"Because I'd never let it," Hunt said solemnly. "I would never do anything to hurt you. You said as much when we first met."

She felt his words as much as she heard them. Gazing deeply into his eyes despite the gloom, she knew he spoke the truth and relaxed, a great tension leaving her heart. He could feel her body soften beneath him and he closed his eyes in relief, aware that he'd achieved his aim.

Sliding off of her so she could breathe, he laid back on the snow beside her and looked at the canopy of branches above. Several minutes passed before she spoke.

"You know, my tummy still hurts from where you grabbed me earlier," she said in a mildly teasing voice to lighten the mood, rubbing her abdomen with her mitten.

"Want me to kiss it and make it better?" he replied with a grin.

"Normally I'd say yes. But it's too cold out here."

"Come on," he said, getting to his feet and offering her his hand. "We're gonna freeze if we stay on the ground any longer."

She took his hand and bounced up, holding on a moment longer and looking up at him.

"I'm sorry, Rex," she said. "I never should have run away."

"No, you shouldn't have," he replied firmly but warmly. He smiled at her. "Just be sure you don't do it again."

"I won't," she replied.

"Come on. Let's find your bag and get you back home. This evening has gone on long enough."

Retrieving her bag and walking back to the bushes on the northern end of the forest, they halted while they were still within the trees. Looking out they saw the patrols working the area normally, unaware of all that the night had contained.

"You'd better give me those warmers back," he said, glad he'd remembered them. "If those things show up in your trash people might wonder where you got them."

"Good point," she said, reaching under her jacket before she caught herself and sighed. "More help, please."

"Nah, just unzip your jacket," Hunt said, holding open the bag for her to deposit it.

"It's less enjoyable that way," she said, taking it off.

"We're not gonna have time for you to take your gear

off by the window," he said, ignoring her flirtation as his mind turned completely to the business at hand. "Ditch the overalls, too, and be quick about it. I can see the patrol that works your building is over on the southside working clockwise. We've got a few more minutes before they pass by your apartment."

In moments she was standing before him in her light jacket and thin pants, crossing her arms over her chest and hunching her shoulders against the cold. He fastened her bag shut and dropped it on the ground. Reaching for the chain around his neck, he paused momentarily.

"See you soon, old friend," he said to Wellesley. "Take good care of her."

"I will," replied the AI. "Don't get into any trouble while I'm gone."

"Heh, you know me," Hunt said.

"Yeah, that's what I'm talking about."

He raised the chain over his head, dragging the medallion out through his collar into the open air. Tselitel did the same, removing the one she wore for warmth.

"You know, I'd nearly forgotten about this," Hunt said as he took it from her. "Antonin never would have forgiven me."

Tselitel slipped Wellesley inside her collar and felt the cool disc slide to a stop just above her heart.

"Let's go," Hunt said. "That patrol isn't going to wait for us."

Moving cautiously across the snow to her window, Hunt slid it open and tossed her bag inside. Glancing northward but still seeing no patrol, he gestured for the doctor to approach. Lacing his fingers to form a foothold, he boosted her up, helping her twist through the opening and clamber inside. He glanced north and south as he waited for her to get to her feet and reappear at the window.

"Made it," she said, poking her head out and smiling at him.

"Good."

"When will I see you again?"

"As soon as you've got something to report on Vilks," Hunt said. "There's always an Order agent on hand in the cafeteria. On the morning of the day you want to meet me, just get coffee. Don't eat anything. I'll pass the word through Ugo that that's the sign for us to meet."

"That's not a very good signal," Tselitel said. "I'll be starving all day!"

"You're a big girl. You can handle it," he said, leaning in for a quick kiss and then pulling his head back and glancing all around. "Now get inside and shut that window before somebody sees us!"

"Yes, sir!" she said humorously, flashing a little salute and closing the window.

Before he had time to laugh the sentries came around the north side of the building as before, and he darted off into the darkness.

"Is he always so bossy?" Tselitel asked in a low whisper, locking the window and closing the blinds so she could turn on the light. "I've never been ordered around so much in one evening."

"Only when he knows what he's doing," Wellesley replied. "He plays it close otherwise."

She stopped and listened as the patrol crunched past her window outside, thankful that the track they'd worn in the snow over all the preceding nights hid the footprints she and Hunt would have otherwise left.

"Sounds like you two have known each other for a long time," she said, taking her clothes out of the bag and shaking the snow off before hanging them up to dry.

"Long time," agreed the AI. "We've been in just about every kind of trouble together that you can imagine."

She paused and thought for a moment.

"That being the case," she said slowly. "Maybe you could shed some light on his behavior tonight. I mean, why did he react so badly to, well, you know."

"Calling him a 'pinhead?'" Wellesley asked, determined

231

that she not forget it.

"Yes, calling him a pinhead," she said. "He seems so tough and strong. And I really didn't mean it. It was just the pressure of the moment."

"Rex is a different sort of man," began the AI. "Most of the time he really doesn't care what other people say or think of him. Towards anyone else he's just as tough as he looks. But there's one little gap in his armor where anything can get through and he can't help it, no matter how hard he tries."

"And what gap is that?" she asked, hanging up her clothes in the closet.

"The gap through which he lets the woman he loves through to his heart," Wellesley said.

She felt the blood rush to her cheeks.

"The woman he...loves?" she asked.

"Of course," replied Wellesley. "You must have known that. You're too smart not to."

"Well, I hoped," she began. "But isn't it ridiculous? After just two meetings?"

"Three," corrected Wellesley. "He saw you in a dream, too."

"Oh, those count?" she laughed.

"Why shouldn't they? His feelings towards you were the same in all three encounters. From the first time he saw you he desperately needed you in his life."

"Why?"

"To take away his pain," replied the AI solemnly. "To heal a thousand wounds that he will never be able to heal on his own. Wounds that stop him from reaching his true potential."

His words stopped her cold and struck something deep within. She'd felt the needs of her patients for years, and how they relied on her to guide them through their troubles. But she'd never experienced the need and longing of a lover. She felt centered, with a greater sense of purpose than she'd ever possessed before. After a few moments of thought she closed her closet and padded to the kitchen for something hot to drink.

"Rex is someone who falls in love in a hurry," she commented.

"Look who's talking," replied the AI.

"Is this the way you talk to Rex?" she asked. "Just nonstop repartee?"

"Pretty much," replied Wellesley simply. "But you will come to love and rely on it in time, as he does."

She laughed loudly at this, instantly covering her mouth afterward.

"I know I'm hilarious," said Wellesley. "But you need to keep it down. We don't want the neighbors to think you're nutso, laughing to yourself in the middle of the night."

"I think they already believe that," she said, putting a kettle of water on the stove for tea.

"Oh, the circle business?"

"Yeah. I'm afraid it's a little too...symbolic for their way of thinking. Most of them are from the pill pushing school of psychiatry. And to the uninitiated it just sounds crazy."

"I suppose it does," said Wellesley, as she took a stool by the counter and waited for the water to boil.

She sat with her elbows on the counter until the steam began to toot out of the pot. But she was so deeply absorbed in all that had happened that evening she didn't notice until Wellesley spoke.

"Are you...gonna get that?" he asked slowly.

"Oh, yeah," she said, coming back to herself and sliding off the stool. She walked to the pot and was about to lift it from the stove when she drew her hand back.

"The woman he loves?" she asked.

"Uh huh. The woman he loves."

She smiled and grasped the teapot, pouring its steaming contents down the drain.

"I don't need that now," she said with deep satisfaction, turning off the kitchen light and heading for bed. "I'm warm enough now."

The next morning she awoke both calm and enlivened. A new zest for life filled her bones and made her feel vibrant and free. A warm sense of security surrounded her also, giving her the stability she'd always unconsciously craved.

"Sleep well?" Wellesley asked, having spent the entire night around her neck.

She jumped at his voice, looking frantically around the room for the intruder.

"Down here," he said, when her search failed to turn up anything.

"Oh, Wellesley!" she exclaimed. "I'd forgotten about you!"

"Just what I like to hear in the morning," he said sarcastically. "'Good morning, how are you?' 'Oh, I'm fine! Remind me who you are again?'"

"It's not like that," she said, rubbing her eyes. "I'm just not used to talking jewelry yet."

"Talking jewelry!" he exclaimed. "I'm hardly an ornament to be slung around your neck! I once conducted all the logistical work necessary to keep an out-gunned rebellion intact for years!"

"I don't suppose you could conduct breakfast?" she asked.

"No, I'm afraid not," he said with an audible roll of his eyes. "Such masterful tasks are beyond my meager abilities."

Laughing and sliding out of bed, she walked to the living room and opened the blinds that covered her small window. The sight of it brought all the memories of the night before rushing palpably back, and she traced its outline with her long, thin finger.

"Do we go to the prison today?" Wellesley asked, trying to nudge her out of her obvious reverie.

"Oh, of course," she said, the dreamy look fading from her eyes. "Why wouldn't we?"

"I figured you must take a day off sometime," replied the

AI.

"Heh, not me. I never know what to do with myself."

"No hobbies?"

"When work is your life you don't have time for hobbies. Or headspace, for that matter."

"Interesting," he remarked, quietly taking note.

"Why is that?" she asked, not sure she liked his tone.

"No particular reason," he replied cryptically.

An hour later she was walking through the security checkpoint before entering the psychiatric wing. People were bustling in the halls, going about their tasks with hardly a glance in her direction. She was glad of this, because her face was red and her palms were sweating. Despite every reason to the contrary a little voice in her head *knew* that she would be discovered with Wellesley. Her hand shook as she showed her ID to the guard, who waved her through without comment.

"You need to relax," Wellesley said, monitoring her vitals minutely. "You aren't in any danger as long as you act normally. Just pretend I'm not here."

"You forget that I'm not a *spy*," she mumbled under her breath. "This isn't part of my regular routine."

"It is now," he replied. "So act casual. And don't talk to me anymore. Psychiatrists shouldn't be seen talking to themselves in public."

Something tart crossed her mind, but she heeded his advice and kept it to herself. Reaching the interview room a little before Vilks, she set down her things and sat in a chair, looking at the wall they always wrote on. Picking up a piece of chalk, she rolled it back and forth on the table in front of her, letting the minutes pass. Finally the door opened behind her, and a pair of hospital workers ushered Vilks inside.

Tselitel arose and, taking his hand, led him slowly to the wall. Then, as before, she drew a circle with the chalk.

Every few minutes she would glance at the big round clock that hung above the door behind her, anxiously willing it to move faster. But despite her insistence it kept steadily on as it always had.

"Stop looking at the clock," Wellesley ordered in one of the brief moments that Vilks' hand wasn't touching hers.

Already keyed up, his words made her jump. She drew a deep breath and tried to push every other consideration out of her mind, just focusing on Vilks and the circles.

"Rex was right: it's pure electrical bedlam inside this guy. Maybe it will clear up when I start talking to him. It might focus his mind, even a little bit."

Tselitel could feel sweat slowly collecting on her back and running down her skin, despite the cool temperature of the room. Her hands had finally steadied, though it took effort not to move with jerky, exaggerated motions.

Eventually the AI broke in again.

"Alright, it's been long enough. I'm going to communicate with him."

Tselitel's heart jumped into her throat, but she continued with the exercise as before. Drawing a circle with the chalk and lowering her hand, she trembled as Vilks' hand took hers and raised it to write.

"Can you hear me, Vilks?" Wellesley asked.

The mute's hand released hers just short of the wall, letting it fall to her side, the chalk slipping from her fingers and clattering to the floor. She gasped at the sound and froze, certain the guards would burst into the room and arrest her on the spot.

"Just pick it up calmly, as though nothing has happened," the AI directed her. "Then draw another circle."

She bent slowly at the knees and picked up the chalk. Making another circle, she lowered her hand and waited for Vilks to take it. Nearly a minute passed without any movement from him.

"He must be processing what happened," Wellesley opined. "Just as you thought, the load on his mind is incredible. There's barely enough brain power left to keep him standing there. The little that he does have to spare must be parsing my words as we speak, trying to make sense of them. Do *everything* exactly as you normally would. We don't want to give him anything else to try and figure out right now."

Slowly drawing circles until she ran out of room on the wall, she moved a couple steps to the left and continued. Awkwardly Vilks stalked after her, shuffling to the side and stopping beside her.

"Good, he recognizes you as a friend and wants to stick close," Wellesley observed. "Just keep doing what you're doing, Doctor. He'll come around eventually."

"*I hope so*," she thought, her palms sweating so much that she was moistening the chalk.

Nearly twenty minutes passed before Vilks tried to reach again, his hand making it halfway to hers before dropping limply against his side.

"See! He's coming out of it!" Wellesley said. "Just give him a little more time!"

A few minutes later he reached again, this time taking her hand and drawing a rough, scraggly circle with it.

"Vilks," was all Wellesley said, trying to keep the load to a minimum.

He shuddered at the sound of his name, but instead of releasing her hand he continued to hold it.

"*He must be trying to keep the line open*," Tselitel thought, drawing another circle while his hand covered hers.

"Help you, Vilks," Wellesley said slowly, as the mute drew on the concrete.

The hand grew stiff and paused halfway through his drawing, but continued to hold on. Tselitel took over and finished it for the guards' sake.

For several minutes Tselitel was the only one drawing, though the mute's hand continued to grip hers. Finally he drew one of his own, and Wellesley knew it was time to continue.

"Need your help, Vilks," he said.

The hand trembled but continued to draw, his ability to focus improving with time.

"Line, yes; circle, no," the AI instructed, hoping the mute would understand.

Halfway through a circle Vilks stopped. Sweat began to collect on Tselitel's forehead as she watched nervously, the chalk hovering just short of the wall. Then Vilks pressed it against the concrete, and dragged it upwards in a short, crooked line.

It took all her will to keep from screaming in delight. Vilks had been contacted, and he was able to talk back! Crudely, of course. But there was a mind inside that could process information and reply intelligently to stimuli. As she had so desperately hoped and believed, he was not beyond help.

"Is your name Vilks?" Wellesley asked, verifying that their wires weren't crossed. The hand drew another line. "Are you Doctor Tselitel?" A ragged circle was his reply.

"Good thinking," Tselitel thought, approving of the AIs thoroughness.

"Are you in pain?" Another circle.

On and on the questions went, Wellesley making them as short and direct as possible. Gradually the wall was covered with little circles and lines as the AI filled out his understanding of the mute's situation.

Tselitel watched in utter fascination as the alien construct deftly worked within the narrow confines of Vilks' ability to communicate. She envied his ability to reach directly inside, bypassing the communication portions of the brain that were clearly too greatly deemphasized by his present load to work properly.

The door clicked open behind her, and she turned to see the hospital staff stepping inside. One of them tapped her watch, indicating it was time to go.

Gently Tselitel unwound Vilks' hand from hers, and guided him slowly to his caretakers. Once they'd led him out she turned around and grabbed her jacket and a small purse she carried.

"Hey, Doc," said one of the guards as she passed through

the outer observing room with its one-way glass. "What's with the lines?"

"The lines?" she asked, startled by his question.

The guard, who had been lolling in a chair behind the glass, stood up. He was around six feet tall with dark hair and a solid build. Always quick to smile, Tselitel thought she detected a hint of attraction on his part.

"You guys seemed pretty happy with the circle bit," he continued. "Then suddenly he's making half circles and drawing lines."

"Lie to him," Wellesley ordered sternly.

"Oh, well, upwardly drawn lines are, uh, symbolic of...an upward...motion...of consciousness," she uttered slowly, trying not to sound uncertain. "Vilks is...struggling...to assert his ego. He's bathed in the unconscious right now, and I'm trying to help him rise above it. That's why he's a mute: he can't sort out his own inner psychological contents. He's drowning in notions, basically, and they're all flooding past him in a way he can't control or even stem."

"Whatever you're doing, it seems to be working," he said, moving to the doorway next to her and looking inside at the numerous markings on the wall.

"Thank you," she said, eager to walk away and get the pressure off. She started to leave when he spoke again.

"What do you think made him stop part way, though?" he asked, the slightest edge in his voice. "Until now his movements have been automatic. What interrupted him?"

"Answer him," Wellesley said, as she hesitated to turn around and face the probing guard. "He smells a rat. Pour on the charm."

She turned around and smiled in spite of her nerves.

"You've certainly been paying attention," she said in a voice a little too high, mixing tension with admiration as she stepped closer. She gripped her little purse tightly to keep her hand from shaking, hiding the other in her jacket pocket. "Are you interested in psychiatry?"

"Actually I am," he replied, his pride swelling to have it noticed. "I'm studying on the side while I work here. I specifically asked for this assignment when I heard you would be coming here, Doctor. I wanted to observe you in action and learn all that I could."

"My, how flattering," she replied with a nervous laugh.

"But you haven't answered my question," he replied, his eyes tightening a little. "Why do you think he hesitated?"

"Oh, for the same reason that he's a mute. His unconscious contents rushed to the fore and interrupted him mid-act. Lacking the ego-assertiveness to overcome the flood he just succumbed. Basically, he got distracted and lost his train of thought. That's why I kept drawing while he stood there: I knew that eventually some little part of him would bob back to the surface. When it did, I wanted to be ready to pick up right where we left off."

"Brilliant," he said with admiration, his suspicions melting away. "We're lucky to have you working here, Doctor. Even if it is to assist scum like Vilks."

"Yes, thank you," she smiled, turning and leaving the room.

"There is no one so dangerous as an admirer," Wellesley said, as the doctor's heels clicked quickly down the hall. "They notice everything."

"Paging Doctor Tselitel," she heard over the PA system. "Doctor Tselitel, please come to the reception desk."

"Sounds like our little breakthrough with Vilks has caused a stir already," Wellesley said. "Maybe they think we're making too much progress."

Dark thoughts filled the doctor's mind. But unable to reply, she just walked a little faster.

"Ah, Doctor Tselitel," the woman at the reception desk said as she approached. "I have a message from Warden Kelbauskas. He asks that you drop by his office before you leave for the day."

"Did he say why?" she asked.

"No," she smiled. "He just asked that you stop by to chat for a few minutes."

"Okay, thank you," she said.

After getting lost twice on her way to his office she finally reached a door marked 'Warden Kelbauskas.' Knocking on it with her knuckles, she heard a feminine voice invite her inside.

"Hello, I'm Doctor Tselitel," she said, approaching a small woman who sat, dwarfed, behind a massive brown desk.

"Of course," she said with a polite, restrained smile. "He's expecting you. Just go right in." Without another word she returned to the computer screen before her, as though Tselitel had ceased to exist.

"Service at its finest," Wellesley remarked.

She laid her hand on the knob and hesitated for a fraction of a second. Then she twisted it and went inside. Kelbauskas was standing in front of his desk, talking to Sadie Roy and a man she hadn't met before.

"Good to see you again, Doctor," Kelbauskas said when he saw her. "We've heard about the change in Vilks' behavior today and wanted to talk with you."

"Watch yourself," Wellesley cautioned. "They're going to try and trip you up. Talk less, listen more."

"What did you want to discuss?" she asked, stopping just short of the trio, her eyes shifting between them and settling on her former assistant. Roy eyed her with undisguised dislike, her lips drawn tightly together. Instinct told her that she had instigated the interview.

"I remotely watched your session with Vilks today, Doctor," Roy said formally. "And I'm concerned."

"She is acting as my liaison with the psychiatric section of the hospital," Kelbauskas explained. "She's so familiar with your work and methods that I thought she could provide key insights that the rest of our staff might not possess." He smiled, and then added almost apologetically, "She helps to make the whole process a little less...mysterious, to a layman such as myself."

"I'm sure she's very helpful in...*interpreting* my work," Tselitel replied.

"Were there any problems during your session with Vilks, Doctor?" Roy asked.

"No, no problems," she said slowly, pretending to give the question a good deal of reflection. "He seemed fine to me."

"Then it didn't bother you that, quite contrary to experience, he simply *stopped* interacting with you for a long period of time?" Roy probed pointedly.

"Whenever you're working with a case as complex as Mr. Vilks', there will be setbacks."

"Don't admit error," Wellesley said. "You're the authority, not her. Keep the high ground."

"Then it hasn't occurred to you that your current treatment regimen might be ineffective? That perhaps, out of a kind of boredom, he's just mimicking you?"

"I'm confident that the regimen I'm pursuing is effective."

"I disagree," Roy said.

"You see, Doctor Tselitel," Kelbauskas began, speaking as though the topic pained him, "there are those who think your methods are...esoteric. It is true that you've gotten him to engage with the outer world. But that's as far as you've gotten. Other members of the psychiatric staff would like to try different methods, now that he is interacting with his surroundings."

"It's too soon for that," Tselitel said quickly, perceiving that they were trying to slip Vilks out of her reach just as she and Wellesley had found a way to communicate with him.

"Stay calm," the AI said. "Eagerness will look like insecurity."

"Why are you so anxious to keep him under your care, Doctor?" Roy asked. "I should think you'd be open to new treatment options, especially since you've made so little progress with him."

"Because I know my patient and what is best for him," Tselitel said, regaining her composure. "It's too soon to change the treatment protocol. He's under a mental load that is far too heavy for him to tolerate any big changes right now."

"Well...there's some disagreement about that," Kelbauskas said reluctantly. "Doctor Bennet here has been exploring a new treatment option."

The heretofore unnamed man stepped forward and extended his hand.

"Doctor Bennet," Tselitel said, shaking his hand and nodding slightly.

"Please understand, Doctor, that I have the utmost respect for your work," he said, a man in his early fifties. "But we've been exploring some experimental treatments with alien artifacts for some time now. I believe that Mr. Vilks, along with the other mutes, is suffering from a peculiar state of understimulation. It's a known fact that some people take very badly to Delta-13, though most have gotten along alright. It's my belief that some of the artifacts that we've found since colonizing this world were made by the aliens to help them adapt to its occasionally strong negative side effects. We've recently discovered a device, oh, about the size of my fist," he said, holding up his clenched hand, "that has proven potently capable of stimulating the human brain. In fact, it *overstimulates* the normally functioning brain very quickly and must be switched off in a matter of minutes. Now, it could be that the *Kol-Prockians* had a very different brain than we do, and could handle the effects without issue–"

"Or, it's possibly a medical device that is meant to help cases like Vilks," cut in Roy, crossing her arms as she threw down the gauntlet before her former mentor.

"Vilks is terribly overloaded," asserted Tselitel once again. "Applying an unknown alien device to him in such a state could damage him severely. Maybe even kill him."

"According to scans of his brain, Vilks is showing almost no mental activity," Bennet countered in a polite tone.

"And it *has* been used safely on other people, but only for brief periods of time. Naturally we would take every precaution to ensure his safety, applying the device on its lowest power setting for only brief periods until we know for sure how he'll handle it."

"He's your patient, Doctor," Kelbauskas said. "And we don't want to proceed without your approval."

"I don't approve," she said firmly, crossing her own arms. "Vilks is overloaded, despite what your brain scans say."

"Ever the mystic, Doctor?" Roy asked pointedly, unable to hold in her scorn any longer. "We have scientific evidence that contradicts your opinion. Or does such proof mean just as little as it always has?"

Tselitel looked coldly at the young woman but didn't dignify her barb with a reply.

"You've asked for my approval, and I don't give it," she said, looking at the warden. "Vilks will continue under the current treatment plan."

"I understand," Kelbauskas said in a conciliatory tone. "But my first priority must be the wellbeing of those under my care."

"Meaning?"

"Meaning that if the current course of treatment fails to produce further results, I'll be forced to remove Vilks from your care and assign him to Doctor Bennet," the warden said.

"Why is it so important that Vilks specifically be treated?" Tselitel asked. "He's not the only mute in the prison."

"I would be more than willing to attempt the procedure on another patient, Warden Kelbauskas," Bennet offered in a helpful tone.

"No, that isn't possible," said a fifth voice from behind Tselitel. She turned and saw a man with a grizzled, disfigured face, half of which had been burned badly years before. A deep scar ran from the top of his head down to his chin, necessitating the removal of his left eye. The socket was covered with a thick black patch. Judging by his bone structure, she felt he must have been quite handsome at one time. Tall and powerfully built, his stride suggested something menacing, yet familiar, to Tselitel.

"Mister Lavery," Kelbauskas said, surprised by his entrance. "I'm glad you could join us."

"The device is fueled by power cells that are almost impossible to find on Delta-13," Lavery said, ignoring the warden's pleasantries. "If it is used at all, it needs to be tested on someone who offers the best chance of success. If it works, we'll be able to justify to Earth the added expense of having more brought here for the ongoing treatment of Vilks. Since he has shown the only signs of emerging from his condition, we must use it on him or wait."

"I don't want to rush you, Doctor," Kelbauskas said, looking at Tselitel. "But if Vilks doesn't improve soon I'll have to turn him over to Dr. Bennet and Mr. Lavery."

"And what is Mr. Lavery's position here?" Tselitel asked. "Is he a psychiatrist as well?"

The large, disfigured head turned towards her, its sole eye narrowing as it fell upon her. Glancing up and down her body as though storing an image of her for future reference, he paused briefly at her eyes and bored into them, seeming to find something of great personal import.

"I was once," he replied, looking away at last, his gaze sending a shiver down her spine.

"Now he helps us analyze alien technology that may be to humanity's benefit," explained Kelbauskas. "It was he who first recognized the value of the device we've been discussing."

"There's something strange about Lavery," Wellesley said. "But I can't put my finger on just what."

Tselitel glanced at the disfigured man momentarily, and then turned to the warden.

"You said I'd have to show results soon," she said. "How soon?"

"Three days," Lavery said.

"Thank you, I was asking the Warden," Tselitel replied.

Lavery drew a deep breath and moved a step closer to the slight doctor. It took all the will she could muster not to shrink back before him. Something about his presence was frightening, especially at close quarters.

"Watch it with this one, girl," Wellesley said.

"I don't want to seem unreasonable," Kelbauskas said in a smooth tone, trying to intercept Lavery's anger before it exploded onto the doctor. "But I can't justify more than a week."

"A week is barely a minute in psychiatry," Tselitel said, crossing her arms to steady herself mentally. "It takes time."

"Perhaps your method does," Roy interjected. "But psychiatry has evolved beyond the talking cure and primitive symbolism. There's very little record of mental illness among the *Kol-Prockians*, Doctor. Presumably they developed the technology to heal what nature hadn't been able to."

"Ha!" exclaimed Wellesley, unable to contain himself, knowing their struggles firsthand.

"It's a shame there aren't any *Kol-Prockians* left to ask," Tselitel retorted, directing some of her nervous tension outwards.

"Please, let's not fight," Kelbauskas said. "We're all striving towards the same aim. We each want what's best for the patients. We just disagree about the ideal method for helping them."

"We certainly do," replied Tselitel.

"Indeed," shot back Roy.

"So, as I said, you have a week to pursue your method, Doctor Tselitel. Then I'll have to give a new team a shot at it."

"I understand," she said.

"You did great in there," Wellesley said, as she left Kelbauskas' outer office and turned into the hall. "Four on one ain't easy odds. Although Bennet seemed decent enough."

"They're trying to get Vilks away from us," she mumbled.

"Well of course they are!" the AI replied. "What else

would they do? They don't want him healed for the same reason that we *want* him healed. He might blow the lid off everything."

"A week isn't much time," she said with concern.

"No, it isn't. We're gonna have to spend every second we can working on Vilks. We've got to pull out the stops, move as aggressively as we can."

"Did you manage to put together anything from your questions today?" she asked in a little louder voice once she'd gotten outside into the fresh air.

"Mhm. Not a lot. But the pieces are slowly coming into focus. It's hard, building an understanding out of such basic questions. But given another week I'm confident we'll learn what we need."

"And what is that?"

"The nature of the experiments, and the best way to end them," replied the AI, as she strode to her apartment building.

"I thought the plan was to spread the word and cause a scandal," Tselitel said in a low voice, watching a patrol out of the corner of her eye.

"That's the *Order's* plan. And Ugo's," said the AI. "But I'm not sure we're going to be able to."

"Why?"

"Because for their plan to work we're going to need irrefutable proof that the government is carrying out the experiments. And I don't see how we can do that. Sure, it's easy enough to think these things up by the fireside. But now that I've been inside the prison I don't see how it can be done."

"Then what do we do?"

"Search me," Wellesley said. "All we can do for now is keep working with Vilks and hope something turns up. But I'll be frank: it doesn't look too good."

CHAPTER 12

That evening Tselitel was laying on her bed looking up at the ceiling, her mind wandering over the events of the day. Wellesley had been silent ever since they'd reached her apartment, processing what he'd learned and leaving her to her thoughts.

Standing up and ambling into the living room, she looked over the empty space and sighed, her mood turning melancholy.

"You know, you and Rex are my only friends," she said.

"I'd say Rex is more than just a friend," Wellesley replied. "He's got to count for at least two."

She chuckled.

"Okay, I've got *three* friends: you and Rex. But that's all. I always thought there'd be more people in my life."

"Well, you've got to have some family offworld, right?"

"Nope. I was an only child. Mom and dad have been gone for years."

"And no chums of any kind?" probed the AI.

"I don't know, too much of a loner, I guess," she replied, filling up the teapot and setting it on the stove. "Even in school I didn't really socialize. I didn't really know how."

"Well, you're unique," Wellesley said. "It makes it hard to fit in."

"I suppose so," she said, walking to the little window and opening the blinds to look out. "It's funny, the nights don't seem so cold now, since I know Rex could be out there."

"He probably is. He's not much of one for sitting still. Not if he can help it."

She gazed out of the window until the teapot started to sound. Just as she turned away something caught her eye and she looked back.

"Did you see that, Wellesley?" she asked eagerly, straining to penetrate the darkness.

"I didn't notice anything," he replied casually.

"Look, right there!" she said, pointing at a dark outline. "I think it's Rex."

"Shouldn't be," uttered the AI cautiously. "He wouldn't try to make contact without getting the signal first. There'd be too much risk involved."

"Love can make you do dangerous things, Wellesley," she said, pulling up the blinds and unlatching the window.

"Yes, for himself. But not dangerous for *you*," he replied. "He'd never do anything that would put you at risk."

She was about to thrust the window upward when he said this. Pausing momentarily, she looked once again and saw the figure approaching. Suddenly a chill seized her, and she felt afraid.

"Lock the window, Lily," Wellesley said slowly. "And pull the blinds down."

She followed his instructions and then moved to the middle of the living room, feeling alone and insecure. Eyeing the window for a few moments, she wrapped her arms around herself and wished Rex was there.

"What now?" she asked quietly.

"Now we go about life," the AI said, trying to sound casual but his tone betraying tension.

"But...what about..." she began.

"He can't get in here. For starters, the window is too small, as you proved only last night. And he won't try to force his way past the guard to batter down your door. He'd have a dozen security agents on him in half a minute."

"But who is he?" she asked in a quiet voice.

"Hard to say," Wellesley replied. "It can't be someone in the government. Only a handful of high ranking people, such as yourself, are allowed out after curfew. And none of them would be staring at your apartment."

"Then it's someone from Midway," she mused. "Milo?"

"Possibly."

"No, that couldn't be. He never saw my face."

"He could have recovered from his fear and trailed you two back to the complex. We don't really know how long the effect lasts. He already knew you worked for the government, so he wouldn't even need to follow you, to be honest. He could just sit in the dark near here and watch where you went."

"I *did* get the feeling–," she began. "But no, that's too strange."

"*Nothing* is too strange on Delta-13," Wellesley said. "What did you feel?"

"Well, like it *was* Rex. But not really. A sort of family resemblance in his, I don't know, *aura*? Is that possible?"

"I imagine so," he replied. "Honestly I'd never paid a lot of attention to all the mystical happenings on this planet until Rex fell in with Ugo and his lot, so I'm not exactly an authority on such things. But if the planet can access people's dreams and draw them together, it should be able to bridge a few dozen feet and help you feel someone's nature. Perhaps your attachment to Rex gives you an affinity for the rest of his family, a sort of heightened sensitivity."

"Could be," she replied, heading for the boiling teapot and lifting it from the burner. "I sure felt *something*, I can tell you that. It was like he chilled me to the bone." She thought for a moment. "Does Milo have a gift?"

"He must, to have survived as long as he has," Wellesley said sourly. "He's got more enemies than you can imagine. Yet somehow he's never been caught or killed. He's like smoke: nobody can catch him."

"So he's a real devil?"

"Absolutely," he replied with finality.

"But what could he want with me?"

"Who can say. But whatever it is, you can be sure it isn't good."

"There's a thought to help me sleep at night," she complained.

"Just telling it like it is, Lily," he replied. "I wouldn't worry too much, though. He can't do anything during the day. And at night you're shut up in here snug as can be."

"But what if he doesn't need *physical* access?" she prodded. "What if he's got some gift like Rex, and he can just, I don't know, *fire* it through the wall?"

"We don't have any reason to believe he can attack people that way, Lily."

"But what if he can?"

"'What if' doesn't exist. We can only work with what we know," he said factually. "Now drink your tea and go to sleep. And don't worry about Milo: I'll keep my ears pricked up for him."

❖ ❖ ❖

Earlier that same night Doctor Prisk was in his office examining some patient files when Mr. Lavery entered.

"Didn't expect to see you tonight, Louis," Prisk said, turning from his computer screen. "How'd the meeting with Joris and the rest go?"

"Disastrously," Lavery said, barely controlling his anger as he paced before the doctor's desk. "Who's side is Joris on, anyway? First he lets Bennet play around with the artifact we discovered a couple months ago. That alone is reason enough to get rid of him. Then he gives Tselitel a week to work on Vilks when it's obvious she's thawing him out."

"It's that blasted Roy," Prisk said. "She's got him so that

he doesn't know what he's doing anymore. I warned him about her, told him I'd report back to Earth if he didn't play ball. But I guess he didn't listen."

"No, I guess not," he fumed. "Can you do it? Get him recalled right away?"

"Probably not," replied Prisk. "Sure, I told him that. But he's had such a good record up until recently that Earth won't act just on my recommendation. I'd have to build a case against him. And then they'd still want to send someone out to check my facts and make sure it isn't just some kind of rivalry on my part. We'd be looking at months before we lost him."

"Then it's up to us to straighten him out," Lavery said, punching his right fist into his left palm.

"It's not like we can just mug him," Prisk said, a little concerned at his associate's gesture.

"Oh, don't be a simpleton," Lavery said, shoving his hands into his pockets. "But we've got to be decisive. If he gives Bennet or Tselitel enough rope they could hang us."

"Bennet's no danger," Prisk said calmly. "I'll have no difficulty getting him assigned somewhere else."

"Immediately?"

"Absolutely."

"Then that just leaves Tselitel," Lavery said, clasping his hands behind his back and continuing to pace.

Prisk watched the large man's movements curiously. Despite his size, and lack of an eye, he moved with the ease of a professional dancer. In truth there was something almost feline about him. A dark, watchful, brooding awareness seemed to emanate from him, as though some deeper level of instinct was at work in him, plugging him into everything that went on around him. He arrived at the prison shortly before Prisk had, just after a terrible accident had taken the lives of seven inmates. Prisk had always wondered if the two events were connected.

Pacing before his desk, Lavery looked ready to pounce at the first stimulus that caught his attention. For this reason the doctor watched him move to and fro in silence. At last he stopped.

"Tselitel has got to go," he said.

"Earth was explicit on that score," Prisk said. "We've got to discredit her, not kill her."

"I know that," Lavery snapped. "But we can't risk her having a breakthrough, not now. Not when we're so close. We've got to break her down somehow, get her to leave of her own accord."

"Heh, that'll never happen," Prisk said. "She's a fanatic about her work. Joris even got me to admit her for observation at one point because she was running herself ragged. He claims it was so that I could find a medical cause to ship her home. But it was just pure softness on his part. He couldn't bear to see the good doctor tear herself apart before his eyes."

Lavery kicked over a small metal trash can that stood beside Prisk's desk, scattering rubbish across the floor.

"We could have managed Tselitel easily enough if Joris had just kept his head. But he's never had the stomach for this kind of work. Earth should have replaced him when they decided to start up the experiments again." Clasping his hands began his back, he resumed pacing. "We've got to keep up the pressure on her. We've got to *break* her immediately, before she can get any farther with Vilks."

"That should be easy enough for you," Prisk said. "Given your gift."

Lavery stopped suddenly and leveled his one eye harshly on the doctor.

"Don't *ever* speak of that," he growled. "This place is crawling with the Order's spies. The wrong word heard through a keyhole and they'll know who I am." Then he relaxed a bit. "Besides, I can't control it like that anymore," he said in a voice tinged with an unconscious hint of regret. "I'd have to physically touch her, and that's out of the question. It would put the finger on us at once."

Prisk was consumed by curiosity but knew better than

to prod any further. He'd already known that his associate's gift was out of the question. But he hoped to worm a few more details about his shadowy past out of his reaction. Inwardly he was satisfied with the breadcrumbs he'd gathered from Lavery's little outburst.

"There *must* be a way," Lavery said to himself, resuming his pacing yet again, unable to stand still for any period of time.

"There's a rumor going around that one of the civilians in Midway has the gift to inspire terror in anyone he chooses," Prisk said casually, leaning back in his chair and lacing his fingers before him, finally offering the solution he'd been quietly holding onto. "From what I understand he doesn't leave fingerprints – just results. Maybe we could get into contact and put him to work on Tselitel. If she starts coming unglued with fear she'll *have* to leave. And then we can point to her 'doodle cure' as the gossip calls it, and say the strain was too much for her. Once Delta-13 has broken the great Doctor Tselitel everyone else in her profession will think twice before sticking their noses into our business. And that'll give us all the time we need to complete our work."

Lavery paced for a full minute before offering a reply.

"It's risky," he mused, balancing the pros and cons in his head. "Bringing in an outsider might blow the lid off of everything."

"How?" asked Prisk. "Look, all those beggars down in Midway are barely scraping by. There isn't one of them that wouldn't jump at the chance to make some extra money. We'll offer him a big reward for his services, and he'll be only too happy to oblige us, no questions asked. You've got to remember that a lot of those people are *starving*, Louis. And you don't question the hand that offers to feed you when you're starving."

"How would we contact him?" Lavery asked, his movements growing slow and thoughtful as he warmed to the idea.

"The government has enough contacts in the underworld to reach just about anyone in twenty-four hours," Prisk said. "One way or another we'll get word to him."

Lavery stopped and looked at a point on the wall for a moment. Then, having made up his mind, he turned to Prisk and with two words set the operation in motion:

"Do it."

Later that night Lavery left the prison and went for a walk under the wan light of the planet's moons. An icy wind bit hard against the exposed skin of his face, but he didn't care. The walls of the prison had gotten too close, too full of frustration for him to stay there a moment longer. Everywhere at once he was hemmed in, either by the obstructions of the warden or the limitations his environment put upon his work.

"That miserable Tselitel," he growled under his breath, grinding his teeth as he thought about her. "If she hadn't gotten involved we'd be finished by now."

Leaving the path and walking through the drifts that had piled up beside the prison's massive wall, he plunged his hands into his pockets and bent his head down against the wind. Stepping heavily through the snow, leaving deep impressions where he walked, he found himself wandering towards the apartments. Recognizing his massive frame in the distance, the patrols gave him a wide berth, knowing his reputation for lashing out at anyone who annoyed him in the least.

He walked to a point between the eastern apartment building and the prison, stopping briefly to consider the latter. He was about to walk on when a light caught his attention off to the left. Turning, he saw that someone had opened their living room window's blinds and was staring out into the night. Not wanting to be seen, Lavery stood still and waited for the person to look away. Finally something caught their attention and they twisted away from the window.

"About time," he muttered, about to resume his stroll when the figure returned to the window, eagerly looking out and pointing. He saw it was a woman, and the brief turning of her face from the inner light to the window had shown enough of it to show him who it was.

"Tselitel," he growled.

In that instant a deep, savage feeling welled up inside of him. He could see her reaching to open the window's lock. Unable to control himself he began walking towards her, bent on solving the problem she posed in one moment. He could no longer use his gift at a distance: he required physical touch for the effect to be transferred into another human being. And this he was determined to get, if he had to break down her window and force his way into her apartment.

He could feel the anger rising within him as he eyed the slim silhouette at the window. He was halfway to her when she relocked the window and shut the blinds.

With the light suddenly gone, the beacon that drew him irresistibly towards her vanished. The strange spell he'd been under evaporated, and he stopped walking.

"What was I *thinking*?" he asked in self-recrimination, turning from the apartment building and moving quickly back toward the wall around the prison. "Assaulting her would kick the door wide open on us."

Once he was a safe distance away he looked back at the apartment and shook his head. He realized that something about Tselitel aggravated him far beyond her professional obstruction of his work. Resolving to leave her removal to others, he strode quickly back to the prison.

❖ ❖ ❖

The following evening Hunt sat on the porch as at other times, watching the sun descend toward the horizon and musing fruitlessly on what Tselitel and Wellesley were doing. He'd been in a state of high tension ever since turning the AI over to her, since his mere possession would instantly give the authorities cause to lock her away in the very prison she was working in. Only the thin material of her blouse stood between her and incarceration.

The realization was also growing stronger in his mind that he missed her. His mood had been low ever since their parting, and he was counting the seconds until he could see her again. The fact that he hadn't the slightest idea when that would be made matters all the worse. He had to wait on her to initiate contact via the Order's agents.

"Here you are, my friend," Gromyko said, opening the door to the porch without Hunt noticing. He saw him looking moodily out of the window and clapped a hand on his shoulder. "Don't feel so bad, Rex. We've all been there."

"Been where?" Hunt asked drably.

"Why, we've all been forced to wait on a woman at some point," the smuggler said.

Not wishing to share any more of his feelings with Gromyko, Hunt straightened up and in a clearer tone made a general comment about the weather.

Gromyko chuckled, getting the message and removing his hand from his friend's shoulder.

"It's terribly boring, being cooped up in here all the time," the smuggler said.

"It's not so bad," replied Hunt, his tone growing depressed again despite his best efforts. "Besides, you get out each day. What have you got to complain about?"

"Bah," Gromyko said, sitting on a crate. "Playing messenger boy for the Order is as dull as paste." He laughed. "And about as dangerous! No, what we need is some excitement, like we used to have."

"Wasn't that bit in the basement enough to hold you for a while?"

"Ah, that barely got the kinks out of my system that Ugo has put into it," Gromyko said, stretching his neck to illustrate his point. "To say nothing of Wanda. She wants me to be a calm, steady sort of person. You could sooner wish an iron bar into being a piece of string than make me into something stable. I am quicksilver! I dance through the night, like light shimmering off the ripples in a pond!"

Despite his mood Hunt had to smile at his friend's words. He had been '*Gromyko, the Hope of the Masses*' for so long that even his own speech had come to reflect the grandiose graffiti that had at one time covered nearly half the walls in Midway. If Hunt's memory was correct, he had read the 'shimmering light' line a couple of years before, painted on a wall on Midway's south side.

"Now, tell me," Gromyko resumed. "Wouldn't you *love* to get some adrenaline pumping through your veins? Come, you can't honestly tell me that it isn't so."

"It isn't so."

"Gah! What have they done to you?" the smuggler asked, eyeing his friend until the latter's lips turned up into a smile. "Ah, you're joking! You had me worried for a moment. I feared that Ugo's bookishness had finally worn you down. That, and that perhaps consistent meals and a warm bed had made you soft."

"It would take a lot more than that, Antonin," replied Hunt, recalling the years of struggle that preceded those few weeks of warmth and good eating. He had striven too hard, and too long, to ever have the painful memory of his fight for survival scratched out. Deep down he knew that the scars of those years would forever be with him, causing him to reflexively eat a little less at meals in order to save something for the next day. Hunger, cold, loneliness: the cursed triad of poverty. The dark hopelessness of that time would never leave his thoughts, even if its cause had long since vanished and a new day had dawned upon him, its warm rays melting the snow from his heart. He knew that all the same a little hollow place in the pit of his stomach would always remain, an almost physical reminder of his torment, his writhing, his battle to exist.

Emerging from his reverie, he turned his head from the

window and saw Gromyko looking at him expectantly.

"Alright, Antonin, what is it?" he asked with a sigh that betrayed more good humor, almost indulgence, than he had intended.

"What is what?" he asked innocently, his eyes wide.

"Come on: you're working me around to something. Now tell me."

"Well," the smuggler said, pulling the crate he sat on closer and dropping his voice. "As you know, I don't agree with this plan that the Order has to incite revolution across the empire. But these mind control experiments," Gromyko said, shuddering and shaking his head, "they are *evil*. They must be stopped at any cost. Even my life is not too great a price. But self-sacrifice is not enough. We must have the right *tools* to get the job done, Rex. We must destroy their technology, whatever it is, and scatter the ashes to the wind. They must never be able to rebuild what they have made here."

"We can't prevent that, Antonin," Hunt said. "People will always try to dominate others."

"I have found the tools we need," Gromyko said, ignoring his comment. "Some of my old contacts from the resistance still have their ears pressed to the ground, and they provide me with information that I can use. Which is more than can be said for *these* people," he said, jerking his head towards the house, indicating the Order generally. "They still treat me like a peon. I would be completely in the dark were it not for the fragments of my old network."

Despite his stated intention to be satisfied as a mere messenger, Gromyko had found the yoke too hard to bear, and had almost at once gotten to work rebuilding his spiderweb of spies across Midway. Unlike the Order, neither he nor his associates had the capacity to penetrate the government's facilities. Their information was limited almost completely to what could be gleaned from the town itself. For everything beyond its confines they relied on rumor and the occasional reconnaissance missions that hardy young adventurers would take it upon themselves to prosecute. And perhaps a very occasional bribe.

"I have found explosives, Rex," Gromyko breathed. "Not many, and they aren't very powerful. But if placed properly they should be enough to destroy the government's experiments. But there is a problem."

"The government has control of them?" Hunt asked.

"Actually, no," replied Gromyko, swallowing. "That would almost be preferable."

"You don't mean..." Hunt began, locking eyes with the smuggler and shaking his head to oppose the idea before even hearing it. He could tell by the look in his friend's eye that even he felt it was beyond the pale, and that meant only one thing.

"Yes, Rex: the Black Fang pirates," Gromyko said, whispering even though no one could possibly hear him. "Ever since the clampdown on the Underground they've been looking to pull up stakes. They'll still keep their base on the far side of the planet to intercept traffic coming from Quarlac. But with the collapse of the black market in Midway they don't need to maintain a presence here any longer. My sources tell me that the little base they maintain in the caverns south of town is almost empty now. They're carrying out everything they can under the cover of darkness. But it's certain that they'll be noticed by the police before they move it all."

"And they'll blow up whatever is left rather than let the police get it," Hunt said.

"Exactly. Now, explosives are precious this far out, as you know. So they've only left enough behind to collapse the caves. We can slip in there and–"

"No, Antonin," said Hunt. "You're nuts to even think about it. Nobody crosses the Black Fang pirates and gets away with it. They'll search for years to find who it was that let the police seize even a fraction of their contraband."

"Heh, not if they don't find out who it was," replied Gromyko, trying to sound more confident than he felt. "But, you see, I must have your help. That special power of yours is just what I need to get inside. They've left only a handful of people behind to prepare the last of the goods for shipment and detonate the charges if they are discovered. The only time that a large number of people are there is when they are loading up their transports with cargo. All we have to do is slip in when they're undermanned. You'll just zap a few people, they'll run screaming into the night, and we can grab the explosives. We'll be gone before they come back to their senses and come looking for trouble. No problem."

"You know it's never that easy," Hunt said. "You've been on enough operations like this to know that *something* always gets fouled up. Then it will be two of us against a dozen of them. And *they're* armed, don't forget that, Antonin. Why, we can barely get a *club* in Midway with things as they are. What are we gonna do when they start shooting? Throw snow at them?"

"Ah, but that is where your *power* comes in," Gromyko said, trying both to win over his friend and flatter him at the same time. "They'll never see you coming. Just a little mist from the hand," the said, making a starburst with his fingers, "and they'll run crying to mama."

"Except I can't crack it off one right after another," Hunt countered. "It takes time for me to recover. The second time I used it in the basement took all the strength I could muster. We're just lucky that was enough, 'cause otherwise we'd have been up a creek."

"Two shots?" Gromyko asked, losing some of his steam.

"That's all I can be reasonably sure of," replied Hunt. "It has been growing stronger since then. In fact, I used it once after that and didn't feel very drained at all. But I'm not a handgun, Antonin. All you could expect is two shots, with a possible third after a little bit of cool off time."

"Two shots," Gromyko muttered to himself, looking away from Hunt as he tried to square this new information with his plan. Then his eyes brightened and he looked back. "We shall only use it as a last resort! We'll fight them hand-to-hand. As I said there aren't very many of them, and they won't be expecting just two men to slip within their lines. They'll be expecting a small army of police, or nothing at all."

"We won't use it as *any* resort, because we're not going," Hunt said firmly. "Honestly, Antonin, I can't believe you're even trying to talk me into this. It's a suicide mission from beginning to end. You have the absolute tiniest chance of pulling it off."

"What I have is a chance to redeem myself," Gromyko said, his eyes suddenly serious. "After a lifetime of wickedness I have it within my power to strike a blow for humanity, one that will wash away all the wrongs I've ever done. I've lived a dirty life, Rex, you know that."

Hunt was forced to nod his agreement, involuntarily recalling some of the darker episodes in his friend's vivid career.

"And so you see," Gromyko said, sensing he'd aroused sympathy and trying to seize it with both hands, "this is a chance I must take. Never again will I have such an opportunity. And if you don't go with me," he said, rising dramatically and looking at his friend with injury in his eyes, "then I must go alone. For humanity's sake, and for my own." With this he turned and made for the door.

"Antonin, wait," Hunt said. But his friend went inside the house, leaving him alone on the porch.

Hunt slammed his fist on the windowsill, frustrated at the position the smuggler had put him in. He knew that the charming renegade was working on his feelings. But he also knew that he'd meant every syllable. Gromyko saw himself as a prophet. A soiled, tattered prophet, to be sure. But nonetheless a man predestined to deliver the people of Delta-13 from their fate. With the downfall of the Underground movement he'd seen his only instrument for carrying out that destiny swept away. Now one slight, glimmering chance hovered just before him, and Hunt knew that he would sooner die than let it slip away from him. Because if it did, Gromyko's purpose in life, as he saw it, would be at an end anyway. And it wouldn't matter to him what happened after that.

He looked out the window and wished Wellesley was there to help him figure out what to do. Then he shook his head.

"No, I already know *what* to do," he thought. "But to actually *do it!*" he exclaimed, slapping his palms down on his knees and releasing a ragged sigh, the tension building within him.

There was nothing he wanted more than to carefully guard his life and stay out of trouble. That, inadvertently, had been Tselitel's doing. By giving him someone to love he had lost the flippant attitude he'd always held towards danger. Death no longer meant both loss and deliverance for him. Before it would have emancipated him from a world that held no future. But now it would take from him the one he wanted, and needed, above all others. He craved her presence, longed to feel her touch, to see her face light up upon seeing him. He closed his eyes and savored the thought, letting it fill him. The idea of losing her was torture for a heart that had already suffered so much.

But the voice of duty whispered in his ear and told him that he couldn't abandon his friend. Before Ugo and Wanda, before Lily, even before Wellesley, there had been Antonin. Rebellious, exasperating, wily Antonin. No matter what happened, Hunt could always depend on him. And he knew that nothing less than an equal measure of loyalty would be just. Shaking his head and pushing off the stool that he'd been sitting on, he went inside.

"Wanda, have you seen Antonin?" he asked, stepping into the den.

"In the kitchen," she said. "He seemed upset about something. He wouldn't talk to me."

"Well, don't worry about that," Hunt said. "He'll get over it in a few seconds."

With a puzzled expression she watched Hunt turn and

walk out of the den. Curiously she moved across the room and stopped at the doorway, putting a hand upon it and tipping her head slightly to hear better. In an instant she learned this was needless.

"Thank you, my friend!" she heard Gromyko burst out happily. "I'm certain we'll have success!"

She was scurrying to the kitchen just as Ugo came in the front door, shivering from a bit of snow that had fallen down the back of his collar. She turned from her course and made for the lobby.

"Good evening, honey," he said, slipping off his jacket as she helped him. Gromyko was talking boisterously in the kitchen, and Ugo nodded in that direction. "Something has got him happy," the old man said. "Any idea what it is?"

"No, I was just about to find out for myself," she said, shaking the snow off his jacket and hanging it up along with his hat.

Stiff from the cold and weary from his day at work, she gestured for him to take a seat while she pulled his boots off. She nearly died each time he did it himself, watching as his center of gravity moved worryingly forward as he bent to reach his laces. She just knew that one of those times he would totter forward and break his neck. Her nerves were already too tight from all that had happened recently to endure the sight again.

"Thank you," he said, wiggling his toes in his thick socks once they were out of his boots and on the floor. He got shakily to his feet and ambled towards the kitchen with his granddaughter close on his heels.

"...sneak up from the western edge," they heard Gromyko say as they entered. As soon as the smuggler saw them he stopped and looked at them awkwardly.

"Sneak into where?" the old man asked, shuffling to the table and dropping into a chair. Wanda made for the sink to fill the teapot, hoping to pour a little heat back into his tired bones.

"You're not going to like it, Ugo," Hunt said.

"I assumed that when I heard Antonin so happy," he replied, his voice muffled as he rubbed warmth into his face with his hands. Working the cold flesh around his eyes, he paused and looked over his fingers at Hunt. "You'd better just lay it on me."

"We are going to raid the Black Fang pirate base on the south side of town," he replied.

"When?" asked Ugo without an ounce of hesitation, rubbing his face once more.

Gromyko and Hunt, having anticipated a flurry of objections, stood silently regarding the mystic for a moment. Hearing no reply, he looked up again and repeated his query.

"Why, tonight," Gromyko said. "There isn't a moment to lose. Every day that passes increases the risk that the police will find them. Then it will be too late."

"I agree. The sooner you get inside, the better," Ugo said, leaning back in his chair with a sigh and letting the warmth of the kitchen penetrate his body.

"But aren't you going to try and stop us?" asked the smuggler.

"What good would that do?" Ugo asked with a dry laugh. "You two don't listen to me, anyway. I'd just be shouting into the wind. Besides, we need the explosives to destroy the government's facilities once we've extracted the information we need."

"If you won't object, then I will," said Wanda. "What can you two *possibly* be thinking? You haven't got a chance! The base will be crawling with pirates."

"No, they're moving to a new location," Ugo said. "Their numbers are very thin."

With surprise the two younger men looked at him.

"The Order has its informants everywhere," he smiled. "Even within the pirates. As a matter of fact, we've been looking for an opportunity like this for quite some time. We've tried to barter with them for what we need. But they've absolutely refused. You see, the government hasn't gone after them with a vengeance because the pirates mostly restrict themselves to robbing commercial traffic coming out of Quarlac. Frankly the imperial presence out here is just too thin for them to willingly provoke a full on conflict with the Black Fang folks. They can't set up a major presence here without provoking the fringe worlds to act, and so they have to work with what they have. They pick and bite at the pirates, and they'll never pass up an easy catch if it drops into their laps. But they're not in a position to smash their fleet. It'd be too much for them to chew. But that's not to say the imperial government *couldn't* put pressure on them in other ways, if it chose to. So, to avoid provoking the government, the Black Fangs won't sell us the explosives. The only way forward for us is to steal them."

"Oh, this is great," Hunt said in exasperation, sitting down. "Thanks to the feelers you've put out there's no way the Black Fangs aren't going to know *exactly* who robbed them. They'll come down hard on the Order in retaliation."

"They'll try," Ugo said. "But we're very hard to catch. They'll get a few of us. But every one of us knew the risks when we signed up."

"And you're willing to live with that?" asked Hunt. "You'll be signing the death warrants of some of your people."

"Every war has casualties," replied the old man. "This one is no different. And make no mistake, gentlemen: we *are* in a war – one for the very soul of mankind. A soul that our children will never know if the government succeeds. For this reason every loss we have to suffer will be worth it."

"But this plan," Wanda interjected, pausing to find her words. "Why, it's just suicide! Two men against a base full of pirates? Okay, okay," she said, raising a hand to forestall their corrections. "Not *full* of pirates. But far more than you two can handle."

"Don't you have any faith in us?" Gromyko grinned, leaning against the counter with his arms crossed over his chest. "I've been in worse situations than this, and I'm still here to talk about it. These pirates will never expect such a small team to attack them."

"Yes, because such a small team has no chance of success!" exclaimed Wanda, growing agitated. She looked at her grandfather. "And I can't believe you *agree* with them!"

"There's no other way, honey," he said calmly. "We need the charges, and the Black Fangs won't sell them to us. We can't get weapons, so only the wits of our operatives and their native gifts can see them through. And none of our agents on Delta-13 have a gift like Rex has. So he's got to go. And Antonin knows the facility inside and out, so he's essential as well."

Gromyko's head snapped sharply to Ugo, who laughed.

"We've been watching you for a long time, Antonin. We've seen you in there before."

The smuggler's surprise turned to amusement and he laughed as well, finally starting to accept that the Order knew his movements almost as well as he did.

"Fine, then expand the team," Wanda said. "Don't just send the two of them in there!"

"To what purpose?" countered her grandfather. "Our other operatives don't have any gifts that could be of use here. They'd just be extra hands carrying clubs, making noise and getting spotted. All we'd do is increase the number of casualties. No, the best chance here is a surgical strike, one that's just as small as possible. The caverns that house the base aren't very well lit, and they're loaded with little nooks and side paths that one or two men can hide inside. The key to the whole operation is stealth. Nothing even *approximating* an assault can be contemplated."

"Then you'll both die," Wanda said flatly, looking at them. Without another word she slowly walked from the room and went upstairs.

"Give her a little time," Ugo said, as Gromyko shifted where he leaned, about to follow her. "She's upset right now. Your words won't do any good."

"I've got to say *something*," he said, pushing off the counter leaving the kitchen.

As they silently watched him go and heard him creaking up the stairs the teapot on the stove began to sound. Ugo nodded to it.

"Would you get that?" he asked. "I'm still chilled to the bone."

Hunt got to his feet and poured a cup for Ugo.

"Thank you," he said, receiving it with both hands and savoring the warmth. "Antonin can never cross his own impulses, can he? When he feels something he has to follow it through."

"Yeah, he's always been that way," Hunt said, sliding into a seat and tapping his hand on the table absentmindedly, not really listening.

Ugo watched this through the vapor of his steaming drink. He waited until he'd gotten half of it down his throat before asking Rex what was on his mind,

"Oh, this bit with the pirate base," he said with an almost helpless wave of his hand. "I happen to agree with Wanda: I think it's suicide, too. But without me Antonin doesn't have a prayer, so I have to go along. I just can't stand aside and let him get killed."

"You're not ready to put your neck on the line for the cause?" Ugo asked, eyeing him through his bushy eyebrows as he took another sip. He already knew the answer. But wanted to hear the younger man's reply anyhow.

"No, I guess not," Hunt said with a wry laugh. "I'm not an idealist at heart, not like the rest of you."

"I know that," replied Ugo.

"You do?"

"Oh, sure," he nodded, putting his cup down. "That's why we needed you. Someone cut from the same cloth as the rest of us couldn't compensate for our weaknesses. That's why you're the only one of us here on Delta who can *hurt* others with your gift. The only one within our organization, that is.

There are others who can inflict harm. But they don't have your normalcy and goodness. They get carried away by it and become twisted and vicious. We needed you because you can do what none of the rest of us can."

"I'm a weapon," he said quietly, returning to the dark notion that had often bothered him.

"Only up to a point," Ugo said.

"I guess that's why Lily means so much to me," he said, stretching his legs out and feeling uncharacteristically transparent about his inner world. Normally he would only open up about such things with Wellesley, who could scarcely fail to figure them out anyway. But a dark sense of fate hovered over him, a sense that told him he would not be returning from his mission with Gromyko, and he felt there was subsequently no risk in sharing. He wouldn't be around to be hurt by it, anyway.

"Then you've fallen for her?" the old man asked.

"In a big way," Rex frankly admitted.

"That's good."

"Why?" he asked. "Nothing has ever torn at me like the thought of losing her does now. If this mission had been planned a month ago I could do it without blinking. But now I'm scared stiff. I don't want to lose the only thing in this world that is precious to me. Especially since I've only just found her!"

"Love has a way of taking us unawares," Ugo said. "But this is something you've needed for a long time. Without an outer stimulus you could never grow. Doesn't it strike you as unnatural that you didn't really care if you lived or died?"

"I don't know," Hunt replied. "I guess I just never figured I had much to live *for*. We don't have a lot of hope on this old ice cube, you know."

"Hope has nothing to do with it," Ugo said. "The impulse to live, to strive despite the odds, is implanted in all living things. When it isn't present, it's a sign that something is drastically wrong inside. You've felt the occasional throb of this impulse, because if you didn't you would have dropped over in the snow long ago and let the cold take your life away. But its signal was so weak that you could only just hold on. Now you're stronger; now you have a reason to live, and it has awoken you to the beauty of life. *That's* why you're scared of this mission: a long dormant instinct has finally asserted itself, and it is shoving on you to back out."

"Yeah, but I can't," Hunt said almost ruefully.

"No, you can't, for all our sakes. This is the only way forward for all of us. Honestly, I was going to suggest the very same idea to you two tonight. Or, if my courage failed me in asking you to undertake a suicide mission, tomorrow night."

"I thought you were always the voice of caution," Hunt smiled.

"Only when there's no better way," he smiled in return. "So, Tselitel really trips your trigger, eh?"

"You can have no idea," Hunt said with relish, leaning back in his chair. He was glad of the chance to talk about her, to make her a little more real than memory alone could manage. His words helped him see her more clearly. "She's like a frail flower, so thin and fragile that you expect the wind to blow her over. But she's got a spirit that compensates and drives her on, like a furnace roaring in a tiny house. She touches something inside that makes me complete. I feel alive and total when I'm with her, like a new man. Before I was just built out of fragments, a puzzle with half the pieces missing. But now I can live." Then his face darkened. "Or could have."

"I think you will," Ugo said.

Before he could say more Gromyko returned, sighed in exasperation and dropped into the chair next to Rex.

"What is it with women, anyway?" he asked no one in particular.

"Don't resort to generalizations," Ugo said.

"I should have listened to you, Ugo," Gromyko exhaled.

"Excuse me, would you say that again?" the old man said, turning his head to point his ear at the smuggler.

"Oh, I'm in no mood for jokes!" he replied. "She told me not to bother returning, that she'd have to forget me if I went! The very thought of losing Gromyko is so painful, she said, that she must sever him from her heart forever!"

Hunt watched as a look crossed Ugo's face that said he would prefer it that way. But then another look, a self-critical look, passed over it. He glanced at Hunt and then spoke.

"She doesn't know what she's saying, Antonin," the old man began in an almost soothing voice. "But there's one thing you can be sure of: once her feelings take hold, they're there to stay. Right now she feels scared and helpless, and so she's doing the only thing she can to reassert control. But her heart isn't under her control, anymore than it is for anyone else. She can't just 'sever' you from her feelings, no matter what she might say."

"But the hurt in her eyes!" exclaimed Gromyko. "The betrayal! She looked upon Gromyko as an enemy!"

"Yes, because she feels you're rejecting her to go adventuring. In time she'll learn that you have more obligations in your life than just your loyalty to her. That's a lesson Rex here has already learned," he said, nodding toward him.

"Cupid is the devil himself!" Gromyko said passionately, slamming his palms down on the table. In spite of themselves his companions burst out laughing, the absoluteness of his outburst catching them off guard. "I'm glad that you are enjoying my misery," he said moodily, crossing his arms.

"Oh, it's not like that, Antonin," Hunt said in a light voice, regaining his composure. "It's just that you hit the nail on the head. We've all felt that way at one point or another."

"You have?" he asked, a little glimmer of hope coming into his eyes.

"Of course."

The smuggler turned to Ugo.

"And you really think she'll come out of it?" he asked, his hope growing a little more.

"Absolutely," he said. "I guarantee it. You've got to remember that you're her first serious romance. There's a lot of things she's learning for the first time."

"True, true," replied the smuggler, resting his chin on his palm and thinking for a few moments. "And besides, to risk losing Gromyko is a very serious matter. It would tear anyone apart."

"That it would," chuckled Hunt.

"Well, then," Gromyko said, his voice brightening along with his mood, "I guess there's nothing for it but to leave her alone for a while. It's just as well: we must plan our operation tonight. I must say that I wish your AI was here."

"As do I," replied Hunt, a little pulse of anxiety running through him as he thought about Wellesley and Tselitel.

"Don't worry about them," Ugo said, reading Rex's face. "I received word just before coming home that they are doing alright. But the pressure has been increased. In a week the warden is going to take Vilks away from her. The official excuse is that her methods aren't proving effective. But the truth is she's getting too close. Soon they'll turn him over to one of their own doctors. They must really be getting close to a breakthrough if they're this jumpy."

"Unless they know that something else is going on under the radar," offered Gromyko. "Perhaps one of them suspects the AI."

"No, they'd nail her instantly if that were the case," said Ugo, shaking his head.

"Then subliminally, perhaps," said the smuggler. "You're the one who's always saying the planet is up to this and that behind the scenes. And you've got to admit that their behavior is sudden, almost panicked. If they really are close to succeeding then the smart play would be to let Tselitel continue her work, safe in the knowledge that she could never finish in time."

Ugo thought for a moment, tracing his index finger on the table.

"You might be right," he said slowly, still tracing. "There was something else in her message, but I didn't want to add it for Rex's sake. She saw someone outside her window."

Instantly Hunt sat bolt upright, his eyes boring into Ugo.

"Don't worry, she's fine," the old man said quickly, raising a hand to calm his fears. "Both she and Wellesley are alive to the danger of their situation, and are on high alert. Nobody can attack her during the day, and she's resolved to be indoors by nightfall, even if it cuts her time with Vilks a little short."

"Smart girl," Gromyko opined.

"I've got to get to her, Ugo," Hunt said, standing up and making for the doorway.

"Hang on, Rex," Ugo said, as Gromyko grasped his arm to stop him. "There's nothing you can do now."

"I can shatter the filth who threatened her!" exploded Hunt with a fury that shocked his companions, ripping his arm away and striding out of the kitchen.

The fear of losing her, of being separated forever, had already worn down his nerves. To discover she was actually under threat was too much to bear. His instincts cried out for expression. The deep, savage inheritance of mankind rose up and called for retribution against anyone who would threaten his woman.

"Rex, wait!" said his two friends in unison.

"Don't try and talk me out of it," he said, pulling on his jacket and reaching for his boots. "I'm sorry, Antonin, but I can't rise above it. You're going to have to take the base on by yourself. I can't stand to leave her out there alone and vulnerable. There needs to be someone to protect her."

"It can't be you," Ugo said. "You're too important to the cause."

"I'm important to her, too. Or have you forgotten the value of human life in your zeal for the cause?" Hunt snapped.

"I've never lost sight of that," the old man said firmly.

"But you've got to think rationally. If they wanted to take her out there's a hundred ways they could do it while she's inside the prison. They hold all the cards, Rex. And in spite of that they haven't laid a finger on her. The fact is they can't, not without making a bigger scandal than they've already got."

"Then what do you call that guy she saw?"

"Intimidation, plain and simple," Ugo said. "These guys are professionals, Rex. They wouldn't let themselves get seen unless they wanted to be seen. They're just trying to scare her off."

"Yeah, maybe, and maybe not," replied Hunt, lacing up his boots as he spoke. "Maybe one of 'em is fed up with her snooping around, and is thinking of taking her out on his own initiative. I can't take that chance."

"Rex, she's in danger because she believes in what we're doing here," the old man argued. "If you honor what she's striving to achieve then you'll hold up your end of it. You have to play your part."

"Please, my friend," Gromyko said. "It will only be a few hours. And then you can go to her and keep watch all night. But without those explosives we cannot destroy their equipment, and all the risk she has undertaken will be for nothing."

"You've got to listen to us, Rex," Ugo said, taking a step towards the younger man. "I know what you're feeling. But you've got to finish what you've started. We can't do this without you."

Hunt reached for the door.

"Please, Rex," Gromyko said, laying a hand on his friend's shoulder. "Without you I am a dead man."

Hunt sighed and rested his hand on the knob for a moment.

"How long will the mission take, Antonin?" he asked.

"Four hours. Six at the most," the smuggler replied quickly.

"Get dressed, we're going now," Hunt ordered, withdrawing his hand. Then he looked at Ugo. "Put your best operative on guard near her place."

"But I can't–" began the old man, until Hunt reached for the knob again. "Okay, okay. I'll dispatch someone at once to keep an eye on her. But I want you to know this isn't necessary."

In a flash Gromyko was ready. They were about to walk out the door when a voice stopped them.

"Wait!" Wanda said from the top of the stairs, as she bustled down to the ground floor. "Just a minute!" She reached their level and shot past her grandfather into Gromyko's arms. Hugging him tight and swaying side-to-side, her touch conveyed more than words ever could. They embraced for a long moment. Then the sound of Hunt shifting on his feet told them it was time to part.

"I'll come back soon," the smuggler said with a smile on his lips and a gleam in his eye. "You'll see."

"Make sure you do," she said quietly, looking at him with large, round eyes that were starting to moisten. "Now go, before you see me cry."

Gromyko affectionately brushed her cheek with his hand, and then disappeared into the night with Hunt.

CHAPTER 13

"Ah, this is living, my friend!" Gromyko said once the pair had gotten past the edge of town and were traversing the wilderness. The smuggler stretched his arms over his head and filled his lungs with the frigid air. "Doesn't it fill you with vigor? Don't you feel more alive?"

But Hunt said nothing, his mood fixed at a point of absolute seriousness. The one thought that dominated all others was to complete the mission as quickly as possible so he could get to Lily. He didn't care about the air, or life, or vigor. The only thing that mattered was protecting the willowy figure who hovered dimly before his eyes as he stared into the darkness ahead, trying to make out his way.

"Are you sure this is the right direction?" he asked Gromyko.

"Of course," the smuggler said cheerily, trying to brighten his friend through his own example. "I've been this way many times, remember? It's just a question of identifying the right trees. See that one right there, with the top that's been torn off?" he asked, pointing at the shattered peak of a massive, ancient tree. "That is the beginning of our map. As time goes by we'll see other landmarks that will point the way. Don't worry: with Gromyko, you can't go astray!"

"That sounds like more graffiti," Hunt said without enthusiasm.

"It should," he laughed. "I read it just last night! Now come on."

The two men trudged into the cold night, the wind biting at the seams of their clothes as it tried to force its way inside to steal away their precious warmth. Hunt struggled to keep his mind on his task, for anything less than his full attention invited disaster. But try as he might, his thoughts always ended up back with Lily.

For nearly an hour they walked, Gromyko occasionally pointing out a landmark along the way. Finally he grew very quiet, and when he dropped into a low crouch Hunt knew they were getting close. He snuck up to a thick line of trees and squatted low before them, gesturing for Hunt to come close.

"The entrance is hidden just beyond these," Gromyko breathed in his ear, patting one of the trees with his left hand. "It will look like little more than a dark spot near some rocks. But that is by design. This place is practically impossible to find, unless you know where it is already."

Hunt nodded his understanding, and Gromyko led the way around the trees. Moving at a glacial pace, he silently worked up to the entrance, Hunt right at his heels. Suddenly he ducked into the dark hole. Hunt plunged in after the smuggler to keep from losing track of him and almost knocked him over. He felt a firm hand grasp his jacket and pull him off to the side. The hand moved to his sleeve and pulled him through the gloom until a dim light began to glow farther ahead. Soon he could make out the smuggler's general outline, and he felt the hand on his sleeve let go. Gromyko pressed a gloved finger to his lips and proceeded towards the light.

His ears alert for the slightest sound, Hunt followed closely as Gromyko expertly weaved his way through side paths, staying off the main track as much as possible. Twice they heard the sounds of footsteps ahead, and twice the smuggler had managed to find a shadowy nook for them to hide in until the pirate in question had passed them unawares. What worried Hunt was what would happen if a third or fourth pirate ambled by, and Gromyko's famed luck failed to turn up another place to duck into.

"Do you see any explosives yet?" Gromyko whispered almost inaudibly in his ear. Hunt shook his head, and the smuggler muttered something unintelligible before resuming their descent.

Soon they reached a threeway fork. Gromyko pointed Hunt down the rightmost path, being the darkest and therefore offering the least likelihood of being populated. Hunt took a few steps down it, and then glanced over his shoulder to see his companion heading for the middle path.

Hunt worked his way over three hundred feet down the tunnel, finding absolutely nothing except bare walls and shadows cast by the lights that were strung along the ceiling at great intervals. A damp, musty smell filled his nostrils and almost made him sneeze. Crushing his nose between his thumb and index finger, he managed to stifle it.

He encountered rooms of various sizes as he walked down the tunnel, each of them crudely carved out of the stony walls. But they were all empty.

Reaching the end of the tunnel and cursing his luck, he doubled back to the fork at a quicker pace. He was just short of it when he heard voices loudly echoing off the walls of the middle tunnel.

"*Antonin!*" he thought, fearing his friend was trapped. Carefully moving into the center shaft, he heard the voices growing louder until he could easily make out what they said.

"Of course I dropped by! I couldn't let my old chums leave without saying goodbye!" Hunt heard Gromyko say in a boisterous tone as he felt his way into a narrow, shadowed indentation in the wall. Leaning against it, he bent all his attention on the conversation.

"We thought for sure that you'd frozen to death by now," a high voice said. "When the police broke up your safehouses we thought it was just a matter of time before either they got you or the elements did. And when they didn't parade your body through the streets, we thought the worst."

"Nah, I have more lives than a cat," replied the smuggler

jauntily. "Though I won't pretend that I haven't gotten a little frostbite these last few weeks," he added, to the chuckles of those around him. "But, my friends, where are you going? I was so surprised to find the caverns empty that I snuck in here like a thief. I was afraid that perhaps the police had found you."

"No, certainly not," replied the high voice. "But we're leaving just as fast as we can. Most of the caves have been emptied already. And once we're finished we won't leave a trace of our having been here."

"I should have thought you would have posted a lookout near the entrance," the smuggler said. "But I didn't see one."

"Oh, we've got a few spotters stationed around Midway with radios. It's easier than watching the whole forest, and will give us enough warning to blow the remaining caves and get out of here before they're anywhere near us."

"What, you would destroy the caves?" asked Gromyko with suitable surprise.

"Naturally. The last thing we'd do is let those dogs get their hands on *our* stuff," the high voice said with scorn.

"But I didn't see any explosives," replied Gromyko with confusion in his voice.

"Oh, they're just in the last cave now. We're using just as little as possible to get the job done. The stuff is too hard to come by."

"Then why not just blow the entrance?"

"Heh, too easy to dig through. You see, we're not just burying this stuff: we want to smash it to pieces. There are some pretty valuable artifacts down here that we were going to ship out via your organization. But with that shut down we have to move our entire stock to a new network. I don't mind telling you that it's going to cost us plenty to find new runners who can get them into the inner worlds."

"What a pity," Gromyko said, his voice sympathetic.

Hunt had heard all that he needed to. Slipping out of his hiding place he made for the fork and peeked into the leftmost tunnel. He could hear someone working down at the far end of it, moving boxes around noisily and humming a tune, an old pirate song that had become popular in Midway about eight or ten years prior.

Sticking to the wall, his fingers sliding across the jagged rock, he was barely fifty feet in before his shin knocked against something in the dark. Bending over and feeling it, he found it to be a wooden crate. A little farther on his hand bumped a wire. Grasping it gently in his fingers, he followed it until it terminated in a small pouch that rested on top of a closed box.

"*The first charge,*" he thought.

Quickly he detached the wires and slipped the charge into his pocket. Finding more charges as he went, he did likewise, working his way down the shaft, the humming growing ever louder. The path twisted off to the left just as his fingers found the fifth pouch. From around the corner he could see a shadow moving ahead. Peeking with one eye, he saw a woman piling up boxes for shipment, completely absorbed in her work, her back to him. He saw a trio of charges just around the corner on a stack of crates. Evidently the woman had moved them temporarily to make her work easier.

Unsure of how many charges they would need, Hunt resolved to take them all. Looking back down the cave and seeing no one, he stole around the corner and grasped the explosives with his left hand, drawing them towards himself. But in the shadow that had half concealed them he hadn't noticed that the wires ran farther inside the shaft. When he drew back the charges the wires caught on something metallic and sent it tumbling to the floor.

The woman jerked around to see what had caused the noise. Seeing Rex, she reached for the pistol on her hip. But as her hand touched it a dark mist flowed from his hand, striking her in the forehead and sending her scrambling against the wall. She began to swipe at something in front of her, muttering pathetically for it to keep back as he dashed around the corner and hurried back to the fork.

Upon reaching the intersection he stopped and listened,

the noise of his own breathing making it difficult to hear. The sound of Gromyko and the others still talking was audible to his left. Straining to hear what they said, he didn't notice a pirate coming down the main tunnel from outside until he was nearly on top of him. Hunt pressed himself flat against the wall when he heard him, but it was too late.

"Hey, who are you?" he barked, simultaneously reaching for a pistol that hung from his hip.

Shoving away from the wall, Hunt tumbled into the massive man and knocked the gun out of his hand. Getting to his feet first, he kicked the pirate in the face and dove for his weapon. But in a flash the other man was on his feet and tackled Hunt, sending them both crashing into the stony wall. Narrowly missing the wall with his head, hitting the ground on his stomach, he saw the gun lying a few feet away. He stuck out his hand to grab it, but the pirate jumped on his back and restrained him.

"You shouldn't have come here, friend," the pirate taunted, pinning Hunt to the floor.

Straining against the man's iron grasp, Hunt managed to twist his hand around in his assailant's direction and release his gift.

Instantly he rolled off of his back, screaming as he shrunk away in wide-eyed amazement at what he saw.

"Keep them away!" he shouted. "Don't let them get me!"

Pressing himself against the wall he grabbed Hunt and tried to drag him in front of himself as a human shield. Twisting where he lay, Hunt whipped out a hard right punch that cracked against the man's nose and drove his skull against the wall. With a thwack his head made contact, and instantly the pirate lost consciousness, slumping forward over Hunt.

Shoving him away, Rex stood up just in time to hear voices running towards him from the middle tunnel. He dashed across to the right tunnel just moments before half a dozen men and women emerged from the center shaft with pistols drawn. Gromyko followed up the rear.

"We're under attack," the high voiced one said, a woman in her forties with black hair and deep set eyes.

"Police?" Gromyko asked.

"No, they'd flood in here like ants," the woman said. "It must be a solo operator, or at most two or three people." Her eyes narrowed and she turned her weapon on the smuggler. "What a coincidence that this should happen while you're keeping us busy with your endless talk."

"You don't think *I* had anything to do with it?" he asked in shock, raising his hands.

"We'll find out," she said. "Two of you check each of the tunnels," she ordered.

Hunt knew in an instant they'd discover him hiding around the corner of the right tunnel. Suddenly an impulse welled up within him and he dove around the corner, striking the hard floor with his shoulder as he shouted, "Duck, Antonin!"

The smuggler hit the ground just as a flat wave of mist flowed from Hunt's hand, striking each of the pirates and sending them into fits. They began shooting and fighting each other as Gromyko crawled on his hands and knees out of their midst. Keeping low, Rex joined him in the main tunnel, and together they dashed for the entrance.

Hearing the noise of the battle within, a pair of pirates ran inside, dashing past the two intruders who had just managed to hide in a shadow before being spotted.

"Come on!" Gromyko said once they had passed. "Now is our chance!"

Running at full tilt they exploded into the night air, bolted through the trees, and put hundreds of feet behind them before they collapsed into the snow, completely out of breath.

"My friend," Gromyko gasped. "You were wonderful! I never knew you could do that!"

"Neither did I," panted Hunt, trying to catch his breath but unable to in the frozen air. His lungs began to sting.

Drawing up the cloth mask that had fallen loosely around his neck, he tried to obtain some relief.

"We had better get moving," the smuggler said, standing up and looking over their backtrail. "Once they figure out what happened they'll be after us. Don't you think–" he started to say, stopping mid sentence when he saw Hunt collapse on the ground, wheezing.

"What's wrong?" he asked, dropping to his knees and putting his hands on Hunt.

"I don't know," Rex whispered, unable to speak more loudly. "I...I can't...."

"Don't worry, my friend," the smuggler said, grabbing Hunt's arm and dragging him to his feet. "Gromyko will get you home."

Slowly the two ambled through the snow towards Midway, stopping every few hundred feet so Hunt could recover what little strength he had left. Every time they paused, Gromyko anxiously looked behind them, certain that at any moment the pirates would come into view. It wasn't until they were halfway home that he began to relax.

"You must have really done a number on them," the smuggler said approvingly, as they rested again. "I thought for certain they'd have search parties after us by now."

"Why...would they?" panted Rex, lying in the snow. "The six I struck are...probably dead..."

"Of course!" Gromyko said. "Why didn't I think of it before? I'd just assumed that the fear would wear off and they'd come after us. But the ones you hit probably finished themselves off by the time those last two showed up. And then there'd be no one to tell the tale. So, we're home free!"

"At quite a cost," Hunt mumbled, as Gromyko dragged him to his feet once more.

"Oh, you'll recover," the smuggler said with certainty. "Just need a little rest and some hot food in you."

"No, I meant the six that are dead. I killed half the base to get these explosives," he said, patting one of his bulging pockets.

"Casualties in war, as Ugo would say," the smuggler replied almost casually. "Don't think any more about it. They would have drilled both of us once they knew what we were there for. It was them or us."

"I suppose so," Hunt replied.

Once Midway was in sight Gromyko lowered his friend into the snow and laid down himself. A tall drift ran east-west, offering some protection from the wind that had begun to beat against them from the south.

"I can see the city now," the smuggler said brightly, trying to encourage him. "Before long you'll be sitting by the fireplace with a drink in your hand and a blanket around your shoulders."

"It's gonna be tough getting inside Midway," Hunt replied, shifting on the ground to test his strength. But he was as weak as a newborn kitten, and in frustration he smacked his balled fist against the frozen turf.

"Relax, my friend. Relax!" said Gromyko. "There's no use getting upset. Besides, most of the danger is behind us," he said, jerking his thumb over his shoulder. "All we have to do is dodge a few patrols on the way back."

"That's gonna be tough when I can barely stand," replied Rex, straining off of his back and onto his right side. "I think we'll get caught if we try it."

"Nah, that'll never happen. You're with Gromyko, remember?" he said brightly, making Hunt laugh in spite of himself. "Now, come on. We still have a long way to go."

Once they reached the outskirts of the city they began weaving their way indirectly to Ugo's house. Twice they were nearly detected. But through the smuggler's skill they managed to reach their destination without serious incident. Gromyko gently kicked at the front door with his boot, looking anxiously around. Hunt's arm was stretched across his shoulder, and he now bore most of his weight.

Hearing snow crunch under a pair of nearby boots, the

smuggler glanced to the right and saw the beam of a flashlight shimmering off the icicles that hung from the rooftops across the street. Any second the sentry to whom the boots belonged would come into view.

"Come on," he muttered under his breath, kicking at the door as loudly as he dared.

Finally it opened and he dragged Hunt's almost unconscious form across the threshold. The instant they were through Wanda shut the door and locked it.

"What happened?" she asked, taking Hunt's other arm and helping to drag him into the den. "Was he injured?"

"No, just overused his gift," Gromyko said, as Ugo came down the stairs and tightened the drawstrings of a robe.

"Did you get the explosives?" the old man asked, as the other two took Hunt to the den and deposited him on the couch.

"Rex is in a bad way, grandfather," Wanda said disapprovingly.

"Oh, he'll be alright," Ugo replied. "Like Antonin said, he just overused his gift. It was bound to happen sooner or later, and the only thing for it is rest and quiet. Needless concern won't help him."

With a frown Wanda made for the kitchen to heat some broth. Gromyko worked Rex's boots off and covered him with a thick blanket.

"We're lucky to have gotten back," the smuggler said, suddenly tired now that the stress and adrenaline were fading from his system. He sat down on the couch's armrest and peeled off his stocking cap, scattering half melted ice crystals across the floor.

"Did you get them?" Ugo repeated.

"Yes, we got them," he replied wearily. Looking up and seeing the old man watching him with anxious anticipation, he sighed and got to his feet. He pulled back the blanket momentarily and drew the pouches from Hunt's pockets, tossing them to Ugo.

"Hey, careful!" he said, afraid to drop them.

"Oh, they won't blow you up," Gromyko said, sliding to the floor in front of the couch, using it as a backrest. "They're very safe."

"Get the fire going, grandpa," Wanda said as she reentered the room and knelt beside Hunt.

"Just get those things out of here first!" Gromyko said with a laugh. "Explosives and fire don't mix."

With a frown of his own Ugo ambled from the room, annoyed to be ordered around in his own house. Moments later he returned and knelt before the fireplace.

"Is he going to be alright?" Wanda whispered to Gromyko.

"Oh, sure," he replied, nodding his head with certainty. "Just exhaustion."

"No, it's more than that," Ugo said, his hearing as good as ever. "Although that's true to some extent as well."

"Why do you have to talk in riddles?" Gromyko asked, his head sloshing lazily onto his own shoulder, his arms resting on the worn cushions of the couch. "Most other people find it easy to say what's on their minds."

"Yes, Rex is tired," Ugo said, ignoring the smuggler. "But he has also had a powerful encounter with the unconscious. You must remember that that is ultimately where his gift resides, no matter how much control he comes to have over it. And when you funnel as much psychic energy from the unconscious as he did, it can burn you. In some cases, badly."

"You said he'd be fine!" exclaimed Gromyko.

"And he will," replied Ugo, turning around and sitting on a little shelf of red bricks that ran along the front of the fireplace. Weakly the fire flickered behind him, casting the beginnings of a gentle warmth. "Rex is strong, and his ego won't be easily overwhelmed. A lesser mind would be in a bad place right now. Perhaps even in a coma."

"Why didn't you warn us about this?" the smuggler asked.

"Warn you about what? That sometime Rex would push things too far? There's no way to protect against that. The balancing of the ego and the unconscious is a purely organic matter, worked out differently in every individual. There's no program or blueprint. And there's absolutely no way to know when an episode like this will occur. What was I to do?"

"Nothing, I suppose," admitted Gromyko. "But how can you be sure he'll be alright?"

"Because I feel it," Ugo said, raising his hand towards Hunt and closing his eyes briefly to illustrate. "He's been singed a little by the unconscious outburst, but that will ultimately prove a good thing. It'll improve the relationship his ego has with it. For the most part he's just tired and cold."

"What *did* happen?" Wanda asked, turning to the smuggler.

"The pirates had me cold," he replied with a shrug. "Then Rex jumped into the open and discharged a wave of his...darkness, or whatever you want to call it, into them."

"You mean he didn't target just one specifically?" Ugo inquired.

"Nope. He emitted it like a radio. He would have hit me too if I hadn't ducked in time."

"This is incredible," Ugo said.

"What is?" Wanda asked.

"His rate of progression. First of all, I never thought he'd be able to discharge his gift into several assailants at once. That alone is a minor miracle. Having said that, it's completely unheard of for someone to progress as quickly as he has. He must be getting a lot of outside help."

"The planet, you mean," Gromyko said.

"Exactly. But I wonder why it's pushing things ahead so quickly. If that discharge had been a little more powerful Rex would certainly have been in danger. Something is wrong, something we don't know about."

"It must be the experiments in the prison. We know they're getting close."

"No, I feel that it is much more than that. Something is making the planet push things at a breakneck pace. I just wish I knew what it was."

Rex awoke to find himself surrounded in darkness. With a soft mattress below, and a warm blanket above, he knew that his friends had looked after him. The last thing he could remember was shuffling into the house and seeing Wanda. Beyond that, only the hazy fragments of a dozen dreams served to tell him that time had passed.

Taking a deep breath and exhaling slowly, he was glad to find the room almost hot. After his ordeal getting back from the pirate base he preferred anything to the cold that had penetrated his bones and stolen away his breath.

"I must've been asleep for hours," he thought, climbing out of bed and shuffling towards the door in the dark.

As he ambled down the stairs he passed a little window with a white curtain stretched across it. Pulling it back and looking out, he saw flurries falling gently from the night sky. The sight, once so pleasant, now gave him a chill. He slid the little curtain back into place and resumed his descent.

"Anything hot to drink around here?" he asked, walking into the kitchen in socked feet, making no sound. His voice startled the three people who sat there.

"Rex!" exclaimed Gromyko, jumping to his feet, moving to his side and clasping his hand. "It's good to see you up and about!"

"It's good to be up," Hunt said, a little confused.

"Are you feeling alright?" Wanda asked, rising also and pressing a hand to his forehead.

"I could ask you two the same question," Hunt replied with an awkward laugh. "What's got into you two? I was only asleep for, what, maybe six hours?"

"Try two days," Ugo said, retaining his composure as he watched from the table.

"Two days!" repeated Hunt.

The old man nodded.

"Why don't you sit down, Rex?" Wanda said, ushering him to a seat across from Ugo. "I'll warm some soup for you."

"I'd prefer a steak," Hunt said, watching her move away, heedless of his comment.

"Light fare is best for the time being," Ugo said, as Gromyko took the chair beside him. "You don't want to rush things."

"I swear, it feels like it's been just a few hours," Hunt said, rubbing his forehead and closing his eyes. "I can't believe it's been that long."

"It was unleashing your gift that wiped you out," Gromyko said. "You weren't ready for it."

"No, I guess not," agreed Hunt. "To be honest, I'm not really sure what happened. A sudden impulse just came over me and I acted, almost without thought."

"I'm certainly glad you did," replied the smuggler. "Or I'd be buried in some snowdrift by now."

"Oh, Antonin," chided Wanda. "I wish you wouldn't say such things."

"It's the truth, darling," he replied, his term of endearment visibly grating on the old man next to him. "I can only speak the facts as they are."

"Yes, well," interjected Ugo, taking control of the discussion, "you're lucky to have had Antonin with you, or we'd have lost you somewhere between Midway and the wilderness. That, or the police would have you, which would be even worse."

"Perish the thought," replied Hunt. "What's been happening since I've been out? Any word from Lily?"

"Yes," replied Ugo slowly. "But you'd better get a little something into you first."

"What is it, Ugo?" Hunt said, his voice becoming low and firm, his question almost an order.

"She's making good progress with Vilks," Gromyko answered instead. "Wellesley is piecing together the inside of the prison from what he's learning."

"But?" prodded Hunt when his friend had stopped.

"But, she's been suffering panic attacks, nightmares, and constant anxiety," replied Ugo. "She's coming apart at the seams, Rex, and we don't know why. She's doing the best she can to hold it together. But the strain of the work with Vilks, plus the constant risk she's running by carrying Wellesley with her, well, I think it's breaking her down. She's not used to the kind of ordeal she's being put through."

"It must be those devils in the prison" Gromyko said slowly, as the thought formed in his mind. "They must be doing it to her."

"And how can that be?" asked Ugo. "They never lay a finger on her. And it's not like they're tampering with her food or water. Our people in the cafeteria are being extra careful to protect her."

"It is amazing that I should have to school you, of all people," Gromyko said to Ugo, shaking his head.

"School me about what?" he asked, more surprised than annoyed.

"Why, isn't it obvious? They are assaulting her *mind*, with a mind of their own! Someone with a gift like Rex must be attacking her. That is why there are no concrete traces. No fingerprints."

"There's no proof of that," replied Ugo. "To my knowledge Rex is the only person in Midway that can inspire fear."

"Your organization doesn't know everything," Gromyko said.

"*Our* organization, Antonin," Ugo replied, to remind him of his obligations.

"I've heard rumors of another one who can inspire fear," went on Gromyko. "At first I dismissed them because I thought they were about Rex."

"They *are* about Rex," replied Ugo with certainty. "We've heard them, too. The timing matches up so perfectly that it can't be anyone else."

"Not unless Rex is a woman," Gromyko said with a sly look in his eye, unveiling his trump card.

"What are you talking about?" asked Ugo.

"I put one of my best men on the case as soon as the rumors began cropping up," Gromyko said with satisfaction, glad to be the one with all the information for a change. "I wanted to be sure there wasn't a leak in the Order, one that was putting Rex at risk."

"There's never a leak in the Order," replied Ugo with annoyance. "That was unnecessary."

"So it proved," agreed Gromyko. "But in the meantime my man put together a great many facts. More, it would seem, than your people have been able to do."

"And you're only mentioning this now?"

"I only learned this information last night," explained the smuggler. "And I didn't link it to Tselitel's condition until this moment. I'm sorry, Rex: it simply didn't occur to me until now."

"You were supposed to be protecting her, Ugo!" snapped Hunt, glaring at him.

"We didn't know we were up against something like this," he replied. "The government has never employed the gift of a Midway resident before. They've always used their own people, and generally in very prosaic ways. Hiring an outsider to scare Tselitel out of her wits is the last thing we expected."

"Obviously," retorted Hunt, standing up and making for the doorway.

"Where are you going?" Gromyko asked.

"Where I should have gone two nights ago," Hunt replied over his shoulder.

Gromyko started to rise when Ugo laid a hand on his arm and pulled him back down.

"Let him go, Antonin," the old man said, gazing through the empty doorway. "There's no stopping him this time." Turning to Wanda he said, "Wrap up the biggest hunk of meat we've got, honey. He's going to need some nourishment to carry him through."

❖ ❖ ❖

Mr. Lavery stood in the shadow of a small government building near the prison that same night. It was late, the clouds overhead obscuring every ray of light that the stars and moons could have provided, making the darkness almost touchable. He heard a sound behind him, like a whisper in the wind.

"It's about time you showed up," he said gruffly to Camille Bodkin. Turning, he saw her slight form standing before him, just concealed in the shadow. She was small and narrow of figure. A cloth mask concealed her face, revealing only a pair of dark brown eyes and a wisp of black hair that lay across her forehead.

"I had a tail," she explained. "Couldn't lead 'em to you, could I?"

"Took care of him?"

"Oh yeah."

"That's more than can be said for Tselitel," he said acidly. "Two days and she still hasn't broken."

"I can't explain it," replied Bodkin. "I'm giving her everything I can. She just won't crack. Something is protecting her."

"*Nothing* can protect her from a gift like you have," he said irritably. "What do you think she has, some kind of lucky charm?"

"I don't know," she replied defensively. "But nobody has ever taken what I've given her, I promise you. Something is interfering. She ought to be climbing the walls with fear by now."

"Well, she isn't," replied Lavery, taking a step closer. "But I'll tell you something: if she isn't broken by tonight, someone else *will be*. You're failing me, Bodkin. And I don't tolerate failure."

"Don't think that I can't turn this against you," she said hotly. "I can–"

Before she finished he took another step towards her and clamped his massive hands onto her shoulders, crushing her flesh between his powerful fingers. She could feel a terrible darkness within him, and it was slowly flowing into her body, overpowering her will and forcing her to her knees. Just as she was about to blackout he released her and let her fall face first into the snow.

Squatting beside her and roughly seizing her chin, he raised her head until he could look into her eyes.

"Don't *ever* threaten me again," he said. "Or I'll crush you like the maggot you are." He squeezed her chin until she began to squirm from the pain. "Finish the job you were hired to do. If you haven't broken her by dawn, I'll shatter you by dusk." Standing over her and scoffing, he turned and walked towards the prison.

"One day soon," she muttered, struggling to her feet as she watched his outline shrink into the darkness, "I will kill you for this!"

CHAPTER 14

Standing just inside the forest, Hunt watched the apartments for nearly forty minutes, working out the paths of the patrols before proceeding. Their routes had changed, and they seemed to spend less time around the apartments themselves. Most of their patrol kept them watching the open ground that surrounded the buildings.

Leaning against a tree, still feeling weak from his recent ordeal, he thanked his lucky stars for the thousandth time that Gromyko had given him his medallion for warmth. Though even with it the cold pressed into his body from every side, taking advantage of his reduced state.

Having worked out the best time to move out, he waited patiently for the sentries to rotate through their circuits. Several of the routes interlaced, making it impossible to leave cover without being spotted. There was a brief moment when they each had their backs turned to each other, and it was for this interval that he was waiting. He could see it approaching, and moved out of the trees and crouched low by the bushes. Finally the instant arrived, and he bolted across the snow as quickly as noise would allow, reaching the shadow of Tselitel's building just as the sentries turned and faced each other once again.

Letting out a sigh of relief, he moved slowly along the building until he came to her little window. He tapped gently on the glass, keeping his back to the wall and watching the darkness for patrols.

Tapping twice and getting no response, it occurred to him that she might not realize it was him. He switched to the familiar code of the Order, three taps times three, and moments later heard the latch on the window open.

"Oh, Rex!" she exclaimed a little too loudly, sticking her head out of the window and pressing it against the cold arm of his jacket. "I've been terrified! You can have no idea!"

"Ugo told me," Hunt replied tersely as he turned towards her, still angry with the mystic.

"I can't explain it," she said, almost to herself. "I'm coming apart, Rex! I'm shattering to bits!"

"No, you're under attack," he replied firmly.

"But by who?" she asked, confusion in her eyes.

"So, the good doctor has a boyfriend," sneered a female voice from behind him.

He turned quickly and saw a small figure in the darkness twenty feet away. She stood cocked on one leg, one gloved hand hovering just above her thigh.

"You're the one who's been attacking her," Hunt said, moving slowly away from the window to protect Tselitel from any collateral damage. He felt her hand tug on his arm as he moved, wishing him to stay with her.

"The one and only," she said, bowing slightly but never taking her eyes off him. "And who are you?"

"Nobody important," he replied in a low voice, his anger slowly swelling up from the deepest recesses of his mind.

"Oh, I think you're someone very important if you're talking to *her*," countered Bodkin. "She's causing those scum in the prison enough trouble that they want her gone, and they've paid me plenty of money to ensure that happens. So I figure you've got to be her handler."

"Wrong," said Hunt, keeping her talking so he could move farther away from Tselitel, who watched anxiously from the open window.

"That's far enough, Mister," she said. "Another step and I'll give the doctor a good firm blast."

"You do and it'll be the last mistake you ever make," growled Hunt.

"Ooh, so the boyfriend has *teeth*," she taunted, looking him over. "Well, you're unarmed, and the distance is too far for you to attack me physically, so I'd say I hold all the cards. So stop blowing hot air at me, Mr. boyfriend, and answer my question: who are you?"

"Your darkest nightmare," he replied.

"Oh, that won't work on me," she laughed. "You see, I know all about the nightmare business." With this a faint mist poured from the tips of her fingers and struck Tselitel, sending her cowering from the window. It was only a small blast, enough to send her skittering away.

At that instant Hunt let loose a mist of his own, narrowly missing Bodkin as she dove to one side.

"So *that's* your game!" she exclaimed, jumping to her feet. "Well, two can play that way!"

She fired at him and caught him in the chest, knocking him onto his back. He looked up and saw himself falling down a shaft, at the top of which stood Tselitel. She grew smaller and smaller as he fell into loneliness and despair.

"No!" he growled, shutting his eyes and pushing away the vision. Struggling to his feet he faced Bodkin, who had closed the distance to about ten feet.

"Well, you're stronger than the others I've encountered," she said with a touch of respect in her voice. "But it won't help you."

Again she fired, but this time Hunt threw himself to the ground. Her mist floated harmlessly over his head and dissipated in the darkness.

Discharging a shot of his own as his body hit the snow, he struck her in the leg. She began to retreat before the vision that clouded her eyes, but like him she was strong and soon fought it off.

"We're pretty evenly matched," she said, regaining her composure. "We could keep this up for half the night."

"We won't," he said with grim determination.

"You're right! Because I've got the perfect way to tip things back in my favor!" she said, pointing her hand towards the open window. "Now surrender, or I'll drive her out of her mind with fear."

"Don't even try," he said.

"Well, as you like it," she said, the mist rising from her hand and sailing into the window.

At this Hunt felt a tectonic shift in the very core of his being as the fearsome power of his gift arose within him. Raising both his hands he discharged a thick black smoke towards Bodkin. She relinquished her assault on Tselitel and dodged to the side, cracking off a shot as she did so. It caught him in the stomach. Fearful figures began to rise on the sides of his vision, little goblins that clambered over the windowsill and threatened to carry away Tselitel. But he shoved the vision aside and caught Bodkin with his blast, pouring everything he had into her.

"Please! No!" she gasped, writhing on the ground as the smoke poured into her body and darkened her eyes into orbs of pure blackness. She watched helplessly as he approached, seemingly growing larger with each step, until he was a dozen feet tall. His eyes burned like twin flames, and in his hand was a sword of judgment. "I'll leave her alone! I'll never come back!" she pleaded.

But he was deaf to her appeal. Pouring it on until he was just before her, he shifted to one hand which he laid upon her forehead.

"Please," she mumbled pathetically one last time, as her ego began to fade beneath the torrent of nightmares that reached up from the unconscious and pulled at it. Slowly her body relaxed against the snow, her head tipping back until she stared uncomprehendingly into the clouds above.

Hunt removed his hand and stood up, looking down on the woman who lay before him. Shaking his head at her, he turned towards the window and approached.

"Lily, are you alright?" he asked, leaning on the sill for support. Already his strength was beginning to ebb.

"Is she gone?" Tselitel asked, looking nervously around as she fought to keep back the fears that still gnawed at her.

Hunt leaned to one side so she could see the body in the snow.

"Is she dead?"

"No. But she might as well be," replied Hunt, resting both elbows on the sill and sighing. "Are you alright?"

"I have no idea," she whispered, afraid that the figures who ran around the room would hear. "I see things, Rex. Terrible things. I can't get them out of my head."

"They'll pass," he replied heavily. "She didn't do enough harm to leave any permanent damage. But you won't sleep well tonight."

"I haven't slept well since coming here," she said with a little smile. "What's another night?"

"That's my girl," he said, his head sinking as he spoke.

"Rex, what's wrong?" she asked with alarm, instantly forgetting her own troubles. She reached out of the window and grasped his face with her hands.

"He must have exhausted himself fighting with her," he heard Wellesley say. "I'm not reading any damage to his body."

"How have you been, buddy?" Hunt asked weakly.

"Just fine. She doesn't get me into trouble like you used to," he said, joshing in the hope of inspiring a little spark. "How about you?"

"Same as always," he chuckled.

"That bad, eh?"

"Well, ever since you left me for this pretty little thing I've had to get along on my own."

"That's true," replied the AI.

"I've got to get you inside," Tselitel said. "You need care, right now."

"Not like...I can fit through here..." he said, beginning to fade. His face slipped out of her hands as he fell back onto the snow with a low groan. He tried to get up, but couldn't find the strength, his whole body growing lethargic.

"No, but I can," she said with as much determination as she could muster, rushing past the ghastly shadows that walked through her apartment. They were like dark, animate robes that floated above the floor, wailing whenever her eyes fell upon them. Grabbing a modest duffel bag, she entered her closet and began to fill it, tears of fear sliding down her cheeks as the figures started to circle around.

Two of them approached from either side and wailed in her face. Their mouths, dark as midnight, opened to a hideous extent, occupying half their faces. The fear ran through her that they were trying to take her soul. Reflexively she covered her face with the jacket she'd been packing, sobbing in terror.

"They're not real, Lily," Wellesley said, unable to see them but inferring their position by her behavior. "You've got to be strong, for Rex's sake."

Gritting her teeth, she lowered the jacket and shoved it into the bag along with a few other items that were close at hand. Two minutes later, dressed as warmly as the window would permit, she pushed the bag out into the cold and climbed out after it. Dropping into the snow with a crunch, she turned and slid the window down. The figures floated out through the wall and inhabited the darkness around her, keeping their distance now that she had gotten control of herself.

Slinging the bag over her shoulder, she wrapped her slender hands around Rex's arm and tried to pull him up.

"Come on, Rex," she said, straining fruitlessly. "You've got to help me. I can't do this alone."

But he lay inert, unable to hear her.

As her fear of failure grew, the figures that had followed her outside began to draw near.

"Put me around his neck," Wellesley said. "I've got an idea."

Quickly slipping the AI off, she got the chain around

Hunt's neck and slid the medallion into his shirt. She watched for half a minute, unsure what to expect. Then his eyes slowly opened, and he struggled to get up.

"Here, here," Tselitel said urgently, slipping under his right arm and giving him support.

Together they moved along the apartment building, stopping just short of the corner as the patrols came into view.

Pulling off her glove with her teeth, she slipped her fingers inside Hunt's sleeve to make skin contact.

"Keep watching them, Lily," Wellesley said. "I'll let you know when to go."

Anxiously the minutes passed as the two of them stood in the shadow of the building. Hunt was barely conscious of what was happening around him, it all coming to him like the echoes of a far distant dream. Eventually he heard Wellesley order them to move, and slowly they made their way across the open ground to the forest beyond. As soon as they were hidden in the trees Tselitel dropped to her knees, Hunt's arm slipping off her shoulders as he tumbled into the snow.

"Rex!" she gasped, grabbing his jacket and rolling him onto his back. "Don't leave me, Rex!"

Realizing she would need all the help she could get, she put Wellesley back on.

"Great job, Lily," he said encouragingly. "Now get the rest of your clothes on before you freeze out here."

"Right," she said, opening the bag and layering up in a flash.

"Did you get any better idea what's wrong with him?" she asked, putting her ear close to his mouth to convince herself he was still breathing.

"It reminds me of Vilks. He's struggling with a massive outburst of unconscious thought and it's pushing his ego aside. That, and just sheer physical exhaustion. I believe the two are interconnected."

"But what can we do?" she asked desperately.

"I have no idea," the AI said frankly. "But we'd better

think of something fast."

"Why?" she asked with alarm.

"Because he's getting worse. I was able to temporarily boost his conscious awareness by virtue of what I've learned working with Vilks. But that petered out just short of the trees. He was on autopilot for the last fifty feet or so. Just before you took me off of him I felt he was sliding inwards. We're losing him."

"No!" she exclaimed, looking at him pleadingly and trying to figure out what to do. As her fears grew the night seemed to darken, and the shadow figures drew closer. They all gathered near his head and shoulders, extending spindly black arms and laying long, vicious fingers on his body, as though they would pull him off into the forest. "No! I won't let you take him!" she said, throwing herself at them to shield him. They retreated momentarily and contemplated her. Then, with one consent, they advanced again.

"They'll take him if you don't stop them," Wellesley said, upping the pressure deliberately.

"But what can I do?" she cried.

"Dig deep and *act*," the AI ordered. "Don't *think*, and don't *wait*. Act!"

Putting aside her rationalism, she listened to an inner voice of primitive magic that urged her to touch him. Turning around and facing his head, she ripped off her gloves and put her bare palms on his cheeks, touching her inverted forehead to his. Closing her eyes, she willed energy and strength to enter him. Feeling ridiculous, yet afraid to disobey the wisdom of the ancient AI, she continued even as the monsters gathered around her, their mournful, soulless moaning filling her ears.

At her wits end, and fearing she would lose him, she began to sob. With her chest convulsing and her body trembling, she wrapped her arms around his head and kissed him.

At that instant she became aware of a warm, peaceful glow reaching up from the back of her mind. It guided her instinctively, directing her to touch him as she had before.

Replacing her hands on his cheeks, and pressing her forehead against his, she began to feel the dark conflict within him flow into her own body. As poison is drawn from a wound, so the unconscious excess that threatened Hunt's sanity began to leave him, giving his ego the opening it needed to reassert itself. And she felt more: a shifting of his internal workings into a healthier state. The fractured connection he'd had with his gift started to heal. Her head began to swim as her own psyche struggled to grapple with the dark, mysterious psychic contents she was heedlessly gulping down. The instinct of self-preservation arose, urging her to stop the procedure for the sake of her own safety. But she shoved aside such notions, doubling down until every last vestige of bleedover from the gift was gone. Growing weak as the last drops of strength left her body, she smiled faintly with satisfaction as her head rolled off of his into the snow.

"Good girl," she heard Wellesley say.

Unable to lift her head, indeed barely possessing the strength to breathe, she lay helpless in the snow. The wailing of the figures began to recede until all she heard was the rustling of branches and the calm, steady breathing of the man next to her. Several times she tried to rise but lacked the energy. Somehow she had the presence of mind to slip her gloves back on so her hands wouldn't freeze off.

"You're totally spent," Wellesley said. "Don't try to get up. Just recover as well as you can."

"But...Rex..." she mumbled, her lips unwilling to move.

"Is alright now," the AI said with certainty. "You got him through, Lily. You got him through."

"I got him through," she repeated, as her eyes grew dim and the wind in the trees faded away.

After an interval Hunt's hand began to move. The fingers spread out, feeling the snow beneath them. Then they tightened into a fist. Bolting to his feet and looking around for enemies, he saw none. Smacking his head to shake some memories loose, the last thing he could recall was the fight with Bodkin. He took a couple of steps as he tried to remember how he'd reached the forest. Then his boot hit something soft and he heard a groan.

"Hey, I'm sleeping here," he heard Tselitel say with a weak laugh.

"Lily," he said, dropping to his knees and feeling her body in the dark. "What's wrong? Are you hurt?"

"No. But I've never been so...tired," she said with a yawn.

Slipping his glove off and holding the back of his hand to her cheek, he found her very cold.

"Put me on, Rex," Wellesley said, taking advantage of the skin contact.

"Yeah, put him on," Tselitel said. "He's gonna have a lot to tell you."

"That can wait," Hunt said, picking Tselitel up and carrying her deeper into the forest, away from the eyes and ears of the sentries. He was confused, unable to understand how he had recovered so quickly. From the look of the night he deduced he hadn't been out very long. No more than twenty or so minutes, he guessed. And yet he felt more robust than he had in years.

Going just as short a distance as he could manage, he put her down and busted out the emergency kit he kept in his pouch. Packing her pockets with heaters and laying out the blanket as before, he bundled them up as he had on their first meeting.

"So we've come full circle," she said slowly, half-consciously. "From first to last, a taco."

"Very funny," Hunt replied, worried sick that she'd gotten too cold. "How do you feel now?"

"You know," she said dreamily, ignoring his question, her voice almost a singsong, "you always hit me before snuggling up. First you hit me with that tree. And then tonight you kicked me in the stomach. Is this some way of making up?"

"Wellesley, is she alright?" he asked seriously.

"Well. Rex, she's–"

"Oh, I'm alright," she replied, her voice a little clearer. "In fact I feel wonderful. I'm just a little cold."

"Very cold," Wellesley said. "Another few minutes and even the 'taco,' as she likes to call it, wouldn't have been enough. But I think she'll be alright now. Just keep her pulled close."

"Doctor's orders!" Tselitel said with mock officialness before snorting.

"Is she drunk?" he asked the AI.

"More or less," Wellesley said. "She drew an enormous amount of dark matter out of your mind, and now she's trying to deal with it. She'll probably be like this for a while."

"You didn't answer my question," she said. "Are you making up, or what?"

"I'm trying to save your life," he replied with annoyance.

"Oh, always so serious," she said, looking up into his eyes and frowning exaggeratedly.

"Only when I need to be," he said, putting his hand behind her head and pressing it back down against his chest to keep it warm. "Besides, you hit yourself with that tree. I didn't do that."

"You scared me until I didn't know which way I was going," she said. "But let's not argue," she purred, releasing a long sigh. "I just want to lay here and rest."

After several minutes of silence Hunt heard a low rumbling sound. Shifting his head to discover its location, he realized it was coming from Tselitel. She was snoring.

"This woman never ceases to amaze me," Wellesley said.

"You and me both," Hunt whispered, trying not to disturb her. "So just what did happen?"

"Well, you passed out just after you'd finished with what's-her-name. Lily was seeing monsters and whatnot after the attack she'd suffered, and was coming unglued. But she managed to get into some warmer clothes, and together we got you over here."

"Together?"

"Yeah, I dragged you back to something like consciousness. You don't remember?"

"Not at all."

"Well, anyhow, you were fading fast. In fact, your unconscious was about to swallow your ego whole. At least that's what I could make out of it, given my recent work in the prison. But I'm not a professional."

"I'd say you've gotten a pretty good crash course on this sort of thing," replied Hunt.

"Tell me about it."

"But how'd you get me past those sentries? They were thick as gnats when I came through."

"Honestly, I have no idea," replied the AI. "By rights we shouldn't have. I could have sworn that one of them turned toward us. But nobody blew the alarm."

"Well, that woman said she was being paid by the government to take out Lily," Hunt mused. "Maybe they were under orders to let a dark figure pass."

"Nah, that would leave their fingerprints all over her sudden madness," replied the AI. "The whole point of hiring an outsider would be to keep their hands clean."

"Well what's your answer, then?" countered Hunt.

"Not to sound like Ugo," Wellesley said, "but I think the planet helped us."

"What did it do? Make the sentry blind?" laughed Hunt.

"I'm sure I wouldn't know," replied the AI tartly. "But all the same we got through when we shouldn't have. I can't explain it any other way."

"Ugo will be glad to hear you've come over to his side," smiled Hunt.

"Oh, *bah!*" he exclaimed. "I'll come over to his side when I'm a pile of rust, and not before!"

"Just as acerbic as ever I see," Hunt said. "I thought she'd mellow you out a little bit."

"Can't teach an ancient AI new tricks, I suppose," Wellesley replied. "Besides, someone's got to keep you on your toes."

"That's true," chuckled Hunt. "Alright, so you got me to the trees. Then what?"

"Well, Lily was going nuts, seeing things. I told her you were fading fast, and that she had to do something in a hurry, or we were gonna lose you."

"You mean she did this?" he asked.

"Uh huh. Of course, I sent her looking in the right direction. Told her to just act on instinct and do what occurred to her. But she took hold of your head and after a few moments something started to happen. She drew the chaos out of your body like a syringe. Eventually she dropped into the snow and passed out. I tried to wake her but couldn't for some reason. It wasn't until you kicked her in the stomach thirty-seven minutes later that she finally revived."

"She laid in the snow for forty minutes?" he asked, fear shooting through his stomach. His head began to swim as he thought of how close he'd come to losing her. Only the accident of waking up when he did saved her from freezing to death.

"Uh huh. A few more minutes and it would have been game over. At that point we couldn't have generated enough heat to bring her back."

"Oh, Lily," Hunt mumbled, looking down at her unconscious head and stroking it gently. He double checked that Gromyko's medallion was pressed tightly against her skin, just as when he'd first bundled them up. Drawing the blanket over her head and tucking it under his chin, he looked at the dark, waving branches above and thanked his lucky stars that he'd awoken in time.

"So Lily has a gift, then," he commented.

"Indeed. Apparently she's some kind of healer. At the very least she can help restore the balance of the conscious and unconscious portions of the mind. Though admittedly this was an extreme case. It remains to be seen if she can do this for people generally, or only those she's attached to.."

"Ugo would know," Hunt said, more to himself.

"Ugo knows everything," the AI replied sarcastically.

"Oh, he's not as bad as all that," said Hunt. "Not after I set him straight."

"Wait, you set him straight?"

"Uh huh."

"And just why did you do that?"

"Because he sent Gromyko and I into a trap."

"That miserable scoundrel!" exploded Wellesley. "So, he's betrayed us, then?"

"No, nothing like that. He sent us in for our own good, as you'd expect. I told him never to do it again, and he got the message. He's been a little easier to live with since then."

"Given what you did to that woman tonight, I can see why," the AI said, impressed. "I look forward to seeing the new Ugo."

"The change is subtle," Hunt replied. "Don't expect too much."

"Oh, I won't," laughed Wellesley. "So, what else has happened?"

"Antonin and I attacked a pirate base and stole some explosives," Hunt said casually.

"Sounds reasonable," Wellesley said.

"Aren't you going to chew me out for taking a risk like that?"

"It's not like it would do any good. Antonin wants to blow up the facility, and he's your friend. The last thing you'd do is let him go off on his own for a mission like that. The one thing you can't say no to is your friends. Well, unless it's me."

"Oh, you're more than a friend," Hunt replied.

"I agree. I'm really a father to you."

"I'd say more of a cantankerous uncle."

"And yet you ignore what I say. Haven't you got any respect for your elders?"

"I suppose not," Hunt said.

"No, I suppose not," agreed Wellesley. "So, did you get the explosives?"

"Uh huh. Eight little charges. Should be enough to blow up the equipment."

"More than enough," replied the AI. "You see, it's not 'equipment,' per se. It's a room."

"A room?"

"Yeah. Something the *Kol-Prockians* left behind. The machinery is embedded in the walls around the room – a very efficient design. I've worked out where it is, and how to get to it, from Vilks. But there is a problem."

"What's that?"

"It's embedded in the lowest level of the prison. The regular workers don't even know it exists. You have to gain access by one of two special doors that are completely hidden when closed. And this would be after fighting our way through a sea of guards and at least a dozen security checkpoints. You'd have an easier time opening an egg without cracking the shell."

"You mean the brilliant war AI *Allokanah* can't figure out how to get us inside?" asked Hunt lightly.

"Well, you must consider what I have to work with," Wellesley said with an audible roll of his eyes. "I was built to achieve victory with *Kol-Prockian* warriors, not a bundle of ragamuffins led by an aging mystic."

"I'm pretty sure he resents the term mystic," Hunt said.

"I'll be sure to use it the next time I see him."

"So what do we do?" asked Hunt, growing serious once more.

"Well, the room is *Kol-Prockian*, like I said. It's part of an older structure that the prison was eventually built on top of. Maybe it has an entrance that we can access from outside the prison."

"Like a tunnel or something?"

"Sure. Mind control wasn't any more popular then than it is now. They could have had secret entrances, especially since the building was already underground. But it's equally possible that the entrances were located on top, and that the prison now affords the only access point."

"In which case–"

"In which case you should enjoy your freedom of thought while you've got it. That, or hope that the fringe independence movement gets going in the next week."

"The next *week*?"

"Just an estimate, of course."

"A pretty sour one," Hunt said uncomfortably.

"I'm a glass-half-empty kind of guy."

At this point Tselitel moaned and turned her head the other way. Her snoring stopped, and she breathed slowly and smoothly.

"What about her?" Hunt asked. "Does she need to go back tomorrow?"

"No, I've learned everything I need to know. And I can't help Vilks anymore," he added, a touch of regret entering his voice. "His initial improvement has slowed to a crawl. It would take months to get anywhere with him at this rate. Maybe when this is all over I can do him some good."

"Then we're taking her back with us to Ugo's," Hunt said firmly.

"Great. It'll be good to get everyone together. I've missed Wanda's chubby face." The AI thought for a moment. "But won't they think it's odd that she's disappeared?"

"They'd also think it odd if she simply showed up for work the next day and the woman they sent after her vanished into thin air. It's too dangerous to leave her there anymore. If they can find one wretch with a gift to send against her, they can find another one."

"The Order might not like it," cautioned Wellesley. "They might figure you've put the mission at risk for your personal feelings."

"The Order doesn't have to like it," Hunt said darkly.

"I'm glad to hear that," the AI said with satisfaction. "I just wanted you to be clear on the risks."

"Consider me clear," Hunt replied. "But there's one thing I'm not clear on," he added in a more normal tone.

"What's that?"

"How in the world a single room can threaten all of mankind. What are they gonna do, ship us here like cattle to get brainwashed?"

"That's a long story," Wellesley said.

"It's not like we don't have time," Hunt replied, patting the still sleeping Tselitel on the back. "Go ahead."

"Alright. Well, the problem with mind control isn't the actual controlling of the mind: it's finding a frequency of emission that matches the recipient adequately. You see, the room isn't really a mind control chamber. It's that too, of course. But in the main it is a *calibration* chamber. The peculiar nature of Delta-13 permits the government's scientists, as it did the *Kol-Prockians* before them, to delve more deeply into the minds of their subjects than they could anywhere else. This room, indeed the entire planet, is just the staging area. Once they've dialed in their equipment correctly they can build devices en masse and spread them throughout the empire."

"Then why haven't they done so already?"

"Because the process of tuning their equipment just right is exquisitely delicate. If you go overboard, like they did with Vilks and the rest, you flood the mind with noise. Essentially you cause a rupture in the balance between the conscious and unconscious mind, allowing the latter to flow uninhibited into the former. It's like trying to breathe with a gale blowing in your face, but worse. You never get a moment to pause and process your thoughts. An endless sea of data flows into your mind, drowning you. Soon you simply succumb to the flood, like Vilks and the other mutes. Or you run from it, as the so-called screamers do. You see, the screamers are just as unconsciously dominated as the mutes. But instead of halting all interaction with the outside in an attempt to deal with the internal flood, their instincts take over. Perceiving themselves to be under attack, as in fact their ego is, they explode outwards, trying to get away from the threat inside."

"Then Vilks and the rest are just guinea pigs?" Hunt asked, his anger rising.

"Yes, I'm afraid so."

"Will they ever recover?"

"I can't say. The torrent is so great, and they've been affected by it for so long, that their ego is buried. I could only talk with Vilks because of my ability to bypass his main communications centers and interface directly with his nervous system electronically. In the absence of that, there would have been little hope indeed. Lily probably could have pursued her method for months without effect."

"You said earlier you thought the government was close to a breakthrough," Hunt said, redirecting the conversation. "What makes you say that?"

"Two things," Wellesley said. "First, some of the information I got out of Vilks made me think that he'd noticed changes in some of his fellow inmates. Deep in a little pocket of his mind he was trying to come to terms with some subtle, but significant, changes in a cellmate of his. Understandably he couldn't make sense of it. These memories seemed to have formed just before Lily arrived on Delta-13."

"So they'd gotten close," Hunt said.

"Yeah, terribly close. It wasn't true mind control yet. The prisoners still maintained their autonomy. But it was possible to slip suggestions into their minds that altered their behavior in meaningful ways."

"And the second point?"

"That has to do with Lily again," Wellesley said. "I'd been thinking about why they'd wanted her gone, why they were willing to hire an outsider to get rid of her."

"And?"

"And I realized it was because of the experiments. You see, they don't have their machinery dialed in *yet*. They have to run quite a few more people through it to find the ideal way to target mankind as a whole. And they simply can't move that many through it while she's here to snoop around. Like I said, most of the workers in the prison haven't the least idea this is going on. It was clear from what I learned from Vilks that they secreted him away with the utmost caution, permitting no one to know outside of a very narrow circle. If they started herding bodies into the room–"

"Then someone in the prison might get concerned and blow the whistle to Lily," finished Hunt.

"Exactly. The workers are keyed up as it is, afraid that they might succumb to the 'madness' of the prisoners. Anything too out of the ordinary would easily get their attention and set the rumor mill running overtime."

"So they're playing it safe," Hunt said. "That's why they put a third party on her. Especially a third party that could do her job literally without leaving fingerprints."

"It's clever of them," Wellesley said.

"And evil," Hunt replied ominously. "Once I get my hands on them," he began, unconsciously digging his fingers into Tselitel's back.

"Hey, you've got your hands on me right now," she said, causing him to instantly release his grip.

"Oh, I'm sorry!" he said quickly, smoothing her back with his hand and lifting the blanket so he could see her face. "Did I scratch you?"

"Ah, it was terrible!" she said, writhing around. "Like that time you hit me with the tree!"

"Oh hush," he replied.

"Then you're not going to kiss and make up?" she asked, closing her eyes and pursing her lips.

"Not until you're good and sane again," he said, pulling her head down once more and covering it with the blanket.

"What are you doing? Trying to snuff me?" she asked, her voice muffled.

"That's not a bad idea," he laughed.

"If you're going to be mean to me I'm just going to go home," she said.

"Fine, go ahead."

She popped her head out from under the blanket and shivered as the night air hit her.

"Well, I guess I can stand this *brutal treatment* a little longer," she said with a wink, pulling the blanket over her head again. "Besides, you two were talking so smartly that I'd like to keep listening."

"You hear that, Wellesley? She thinks we're smart."

"I've never been so proud," the AI replied humorously.

"Just carry on like you were before," she said whimsically. "Pretend I'm still asleep."

Hunt smiled and patted her affectionately, unable to remember where they'd left off because of the glow of good feelings that were running through him. He could feel warmth emanating from her body and flowing into him, assuring him that she would be alright. His mind at ease, it began to wander until it hit upon a memory from many weeks before.

"Didn't you say the *Kol-Prockians* never got mind control to work?" he asked Wellesley.

"Uh huh."

"Then how is the government getting so close?"

"Oh, that has to do with the differences between human and *Kol-Prockian* psychology."

"What, were *Kol-Prockians* smarter than us?" laughed Hunt. And then, after several moments of silence, "Well?"

"Smarter isn't exactly the right term," Wellesley said. "Humans are a little more...mono, than *Kol-Prockians*. The difficulty in controlling the latter was that their minds were so chaotic, so quick to jump from one thing to the next. This meant that before you could really implant an idea, they had already moved onto something else. It proved too much to realistically manage. Oh, once in a while they'd have a breakthrough with a single individual. But the time, and expense involved, made it pointless."

"So it's possible with us because we're simpler?"

"If you like, yes," replied the AI. "It's still difficult. But unlike with the *Kol-Prockians* it's actually feasible. All the government has to do is isolate the ideal approach to reach the majority of humans, and then they can begin to snuff out civil discontent once and for all."

"Cheery thought."

"Indeed." Several minutes passed silently before Wellesley spoke again. "When do you want to get out of here? She's out of danger now."

"I'd rather wait until she's come back to her senses before chancing the patrols in Midway."

"Hey!" objected Tselitel.

"Quiet, you're asleep," he said.

"Well I'm not *that* asleep!" she replied. "I'm ready to go whenever you are, Mister."

"I reckon now is as good a time as any," Wellesley said. "There's no telling how long it'll take for those effects to wear off. If they ever do."

"What?" asked Hunt with alarm.

"We don't know what might have changed inside her, Rex," the AI replied calmly. "Most likely she's just fine. But there could have been a permanent shift in her psyche when she drew all that dark matter into herself like that. Only time will tell."

Fear began to nag at his heart. But he pushed it aside and got Tselitel on her feet and the emergency kit put away. She was still light headed, but clearer than before. He took her hand to keep her close in the darkness, and made for the south.

They paused at the edge of the forest and looked across the open expanse of snow before them. The clouds had finally broken overhead, and a pale, hazy light shone down.

"Doesn't anyone leave a light on at night?" Tselitel asked, observing the dark silhouette of the city in the distance. "It's like a ghost town."

"Nobody can afford to," Hunt replied, squeezing her

hand a little tighter and setting off into the open.

Crouching low as they neared the buildings, they moved quickly and silently through a little fenced in yard with a broken gate. Reaching the back, Hunt climbed over the wooden fence and dropped onto the other side. Seeing no sentries, he whistled low for Tselitel to follow. Clambering up the horizontal supports that braced the wooden wall, she got half her body over the top when a bootlace got caught and she slipped, falling head first into Hunt's arms.

"I promise I'm smarter than this with my patients!" she whispered with a laugh, her leg still pointing upward.

"Hold on to me," he said, and as she took hold of his waist he reached up and untangled her lace.

Lowering her to the ground, he took her hand again and moved quickly away from the fence and up a nearby alley. It stank of refuse and the odd dead animal, but for this reason it was all the more preferable: the patrols, disliking the stench as much as anyone, avoided such paths whenever possible.

"How far from our destination are we?" Tselitel asked as they paused at the end of the alley and surveyed for sentries.

"It'll be a while yet. At least an hour."

Looking carefully around, doubly cautious since she was with him, Hunt resolved to take the safest path possible back to Ugo's. They saw fewer patrols than usual, but he nevertheless stuck to the shadows, keeping Lily close to him at all times. The journey was longer than he expected, and it was nearly two hours before they were in the vicinity of the house.

"We're close now," he whispered, pressing his back to the corner of a house and looking around it. At the end of the street he could make out a tiny sliver of Ugo's place that was visible between two other houses. A pair of dark shapes crossed this gap, moving from right to left. "We've got patrols close by."

"How many?" she asked.

"Can't tell," he whispered. "Wait here."

In a flash he released her hand and disappeared around

the corner. She was perfectly still, her ears straining for the sound of snow crunching under hostile boots. Several minutes passed before she edged up to the corner and peeked around. Seeing a face right before hers, she jumped and released a little yelp. Recognizing Hunt she covered her mouth with her hand and eyed him apologetically, moving back down the wall.

"The lights are on inside the house. I don't like it."

"Why not?"

"Because we use blackout curtains after dark so the sentries can't see what we're doing at night," he explained. "Technically it's illegal, but too many people do it for the government to step in and stop us. If the curtains are up then something is wrong. I think it might be a signal for us to keep away."

"But where can we go?" she asked, a little scared at the idea of spending the entire night outside.

"I don't know," replied Hunt. "They've broken into most of the safehouses I know of."

"Well, we can't stand around here thinking about it," Wellesley said. "Let's get away from those patrols."

Nodding silently and switching to Tselitel's other side, he took her hand again and moved slowly back the way he'd come. Just as he reached the opposite corner and was about to take a peek, a dark figure shot around it, nearly walking into him.

"Ah, my friend!" Gromyko said in a delighted whisper. "It's about time I found you. And your lovely companion," he added, as his eyes fell upon Tselitel.

"Hello," she said with a nervous smile.

"What happened back there?" Hunt asked, nodding toward Ugo's.

"Oh, there's no time to explain that now," the smuggler said. "Quick, come with me."

Without another word he darted into the night, setting his usual lightning pace through the city. He led them by twists and turns out of Midway, taking them into the trees off to the east.

"Where are we going?" Tselitel asked as they disappeared into the thick foliage.

"I have no idea," replied Hunt quietly.

Now that they were out of the city and away from prying eyes, Gromyko stood up straight and walked jauntily through the forest ahead of them, whistling a low tune as though he hadn't a care in the world.

"Who is this guy?" she asked.

"I am Gromyko," the smuggler replied, somehow hearing her whispered inquiry. "But beautiful women may always call me Antonin, from the very first meeting."

"But what shall *I* call you?" she replied humorously.

"Oh, tut tut," he said, looking over his shoulder and winking.

"Where are we going, Antonin?" Hunt asked.

"To a little hideaway I recently found, courtesy of an old friend of yours," he replied cryptically. "Ugo got word through one of his contacts that the government was about to close in, so we abandoned his place. I'm glad you got our message with the curtains before trying to get inside. I'd been circling the area for hours, trying to intercept you. The police are planning to break in just short of dawn."

"But how could they know?" Hunt asked.

"I guess the Order isn't as leak free as Ugo likes to think," the smuggler said. "Somewhere along the line we got sold out. They couldn't have found out about Ugo by accident. His cover was too good."

As time wore on and they penetrated deeper into the forest Gromyko grew thoughtful and very quiet. Glancing to and fro, and pausing periodically to get his bearings, he moved along ever more slowly, as though he feared walking past something important in the darkness.

"I hate to be a bother," Tselitel whispered to Hunt. "But I'm getting very cold. I thought we'd be indoors by now."

"Just a little longer," Gromyko replied. "I think it's just

up ahead."

"You think?" asked Hunt tensely, anxious for Tselitel's sake.

"Oh, don't worry," the smuggler said with a careless wave, "Gromyko will get you to safety." Then, grinning over his shoulder, "And if not, you can always bundle up again."

"You told him about that?" Tselitel asked, her cheeks turning red.

But before he could reply Gromyko clapped his hands in satisfaction.

"Ah, I told you it was just up ahead!" he announced, stepping off to the side and gesturing grandly to a little mound of snow a short distance away.

"An igloo?" Tselitel asked.

"Wait and see," Gromyko said, striding quickly ahead and stopping at the mound. He waited for them to catch up and then walked to the opposite side. Ducking his head, he disappeared.

"A showman to the last," Wellesley observed, as Hunt and Tselitel walked around the mound and saw a small wooden door ajar. Warm light shone from within, and the sounds of several voices could be heard.

Looking to the woman beside him and shrugging, Hunt pulled the door open and saw a narrow set of stairs that descended a dozen feet into the ground. Releasing Tselitel's hand, he bent over and got through the door, standing up once he'd gotten deep enough.

The sight inside astonished him. It wasn't an igloo at all, but a cozy, well-built bunker. The stairs descended into a little mud room where various boots and jackets had been left, the snow on them gradually melting and running down a drain in the concrete floor. Peeking his head farther inside just as Tselitel reached the bottom of the stairs, he could see a hallway that connected to a half dozen rooms, three on each side.

"Come on inside!" they heard Gromyko call from one of the inner rooms.

"But leave your things there!" they heard Wanda add. "Don't track snow in here!"

With a chuckle they did as they were bidden, and then followed the sounds of voices to a room at the far end of the hall.

"Rex!" Ugo said, rising from his chair and shaking his hand. "Glad you got back alright." At that moment Tselitel entered behind him, and the old man's face fell. "What is she doing here?" he asked flatly.

"I brought her with me," Hunt said.

"I can see that," he replied darkly. "Rex, you shouldn't have done that."

"Too late to worry about it now," Hunt replied, walking past him and giving Wanda a hug. There were a few unfamiliar faces around the table and he nodded to them collectively. Then his eyes fell upon one figure sitting alone at the end of the table. "Milo!" he growled angrily, bolting to him and seizing him by the shirt. "I ought to crumple you up and shove you out the door to freeze!"

"Hold on, Rex," Gromyko remonstrated, taking his friend's arm and pulling him back. "He's working with us now."

"Oh, very likely!" Hunt retorted, grinding his brother against the wall. "And what occasioned *this* change of conscience?"

"You did, Rex," Ugo said, laying a firm hand on his shoulder. "Now, let go of him. We don't have time for this."

"Maybe you don't," Hunt said through gritted teeth. "But I do."

Jerking Milo away from the wall and shoving him into the hallway, he dragged him to one of the empty rooms and slammed the door behind him.

"Alright, now spill it!" barked Hunt. "And make it good," he added, a faint mist hovering between his fingers.

"I will! I swear I will!" Milo said, dropping to his knees. "Oh, please, don't do that to me again! I can't take another nightmare like the one you put me through out there!"

"It was less than you deserved," said Hunt. "Now talk!"

"Well, I don't expect you to believe this," Milo began, regaining some of his composure and trying to concentrate. "But when you...struck me that night, it changed something inside. In a flash I saw myself punished for all my crimes, for everything I'd ever done. I guess I always imagined I'd get away with it. But deep down I was afraid of being caught, and that fear drove me. Talking to Ugo, I learned that you brought me face to face with my own conscience. As he put it, you acted like a therapist for me. It was the most horrible experience I've ever had, believe me, Rex. But I wouldn't trade it for anything. You helped me to stop running."

"And why should I believe you?" asked Hunt implacably, crossing his arms and leaning on one leg. "After everything you've done I'd be an idiot to trust you again."

"Believe me, I understand," Milo said, his eyes wide and his face open and frank. "In your position I wouldn't trust, either. Too much history would stop me. But I'm hoping you'll be a better man than I would be."

Hunt frowned, believing that Milo was just pushing his buttons.

"After you struck me with that nightmare, I was beside myself. It was like a thousand judges surrounded me day and night, striking their gavels in condemnation of my past life. No matter what I did I couldn't escape it. I'd heard over the years that Ugo was some kind of shaman or mystic or something, so I sought him out. I guess it was fate that drove me to him."

"Uh huh," nodded Hunt.

"Well, when Gromyko burst in with the note saying that the police would raid the house in the morning, I offered them sanctuary here. It's an old pirate base that they abandoned years ago when they set up the southern location. It was too small for their purposes. But it's a perfect hideout for a handful of people on the run. Ugo had Wanda examine me psychically, and when she gave the all clear they packed off this way at once."

"You know I'll check out every detail of this with them," Hunt said.

"Please, do," Milo said. "Anything for you to see that I can be trusted."

Looking at him skeptically Hunt left, closing the door behind him. Several minutes later he returned.

"Your story checks out," Hunt said. "But you've got a ways to go yet before I'll trust you."

"I understand that," nodded Milo. "Believe me, I'll do anything to set things right. I've got a lot of years of wrong to make up for. I guess once they dumped us on this planet I just gave up on doing the right thing. I didn't care anymore."

"Save the analysis for Ugo," Hunt said, holding up his hand to stop further revelations. With this he stepped from the room, leaving the door open behind him to signal his brother that the interrogation was over. Seeing Ugo in the dining room across the hall, Hunt frowned and shook his head, taking a right and walking back towards the mudroom.

"Where are you going?" Wellesley asked, as his companion put on his boots and outerwear.

"I need some air," Hunt said tersely, climbing the narrow stairs and stepping outside.

The wind had picked during his brief time inside the bunker. Through the canopy above he could see a straight line of clouds blowing in from the east. A storm was on the way, and judging from the way it bit into Rex's face, it would be a nasty one.

Striding away from the bunker and clenching his fists, he suddenly shouted into the night air and fiercely kicked a tree that stood beside him over and over again.

"Have you *ever* had retribution taken from you?" he growled to Wellesley, his foot aching when he was done. "Have you ever thought over and over again what you'd do to someone if you ever caught up with him, just to have the chance taken from you?"

"That's what's upsetting you?" he asked evenly, trying

not to provoke him further.

"Yeah, that's what's upsetting me," replied Hunt, wandering back to the bunker's entrance and leaning against it. "That miserable little piece of filth does everything he can to harm me over the years, but he always slips away somehow. Then suddenly he turns over a new leaf. Intent on atoning for his past deeds, no less." Hunt slammed his fist against the bunker's roof. "And what can I do? It wouldn't be just to do anything against him now. Provided he's playing it straight."

"I think he is," commented Wellesley. "My read is that he was sincere. And I don't see how he could trick Wanda, what with her jumping into his mind and all."

"That's it, then," Hunt said sourly.

"I should think you'd be happy to see him turn his life around," the AI said.

"I'm way past caring about what happens to him," he replied.

At this moment the door to the bunker opened, bathing the snow in yellow light that was partially obscured by a silhouette. It belonged to Tselitel.

"Hey, you're gonna freeze out here," she said, closing the door and wrapping her jacket around her shoulders. "Everyone is worried about you. Milo looks like he's about to eat his last meal." She brushed a little bit of snow from a part of the bunker entrance and leaned beside him. "What happened between you two? Why do you hate him so much?"

"Why don't you ask him," replied Hunt. "I'd like him to live through the shame of it again."

"I'd rather hear it from you," she said. "I think it would do you some good."

"What, confessing it to my psychiatrist?" he retorted.

"No," she replied quietly. "Sharing it with your other half. Don't forget that part of you is inside me now."

He put his arm around her shoulder and pulled her close.

"I'm sorry, baby," he said, kissing her hair.

"That's alright," she smiled. "But tell me: what did he do?"

"Oh, a lot of things," Hunt said with a sigh. "Honestly I wouldn't know where to begin."

"Why not at the beginning?" she asked.

"Well, we came here when we were very young. Dad was put away on trumped up charges by the government, and as per policy we were shipped off with him. Mom was dead by this time, so the government put us with a foster family. Instead of sticking with me Milo took to the streets when he was old enough, hanging out with all kinds of riff raff and getting into trouble. I was older than him, and I always took after dad. He never made a secret of how he hated dad for getting us shipped out to Delta-13, and I guess he took it out on me. That's all the sense I could ever make of it. For whatever reason he took every chance he could get to sabotage me, upsetting deals for artifacts, and one time even tipping the police off to a hideout of mine."

"*No*," said Tselitel with feeling.

"Oh, yeah," nodded Hunt. "Twice he's tried to kill me to take artifacts I'd recovered. And a few years ago he even spread the rumor that I was trying to pass off phony artifacts. Fortunately that last one came back on him, and ruined his reputation with the underworld. They wouldn't have much to do with him after that. In order for the black market to function in an environment as hostile as this we need to have a basic level of honesty. It finally became clear to everyone besides myself that he couldn't be trusted."

"What happened then?"

"Well, he became an artifact scavenger himself. He'd disappear for weeks, penetrating deep into the wilderness. And just about the time I'd come to hope he wouldn't be coming back, word would pass through Midway that he'd found a stash of some kind and he was rolling in dough. Early on I figured he was stealing them from someone and reselling them. But after a while it became clear that he was running a legitimate operation. I didn't see too much of him after that."

"Until that night in the forest," Tselitel said.

"Yeah, until then."

"I see why you hate him," she said.

"You do?" he asked, surprised.

"Oh, sure. Anyone treats you that badly and you're bound to hate him. You'd almost have to be more than human not to."

"And now I can't even settle the score with him," commented Hunt, quietly hitting his hand against the entrance again.

"I'd say you have," she replied. "You must have scared him to the brink of insanity to make him change like he has. Sure, you only hit one blow against him. But it rattled him to his very core. He'll never mess with you again, not when you could do that to him at any time. And if Ugo and the rest are right, you'll never have to. So it's a win-win: you got your retribution, and the Order got an agent."

"I can't imagine he'll be of very much value to them," Hunt replied. "Outside of letting them use this place, what can he do for them?"

"I wouldn't know," Tselitel said, shaking her head. "But one thing I *do* know: I'm freezing out here! Can we go inside now?"

By way of answering he opened the door and ushered her down the stairs ahead of him. Quiet talk was flowing down the hall from the dining room, too low to be understood. They took off their things and then joined the rest of the group.

"Ah, you're back!" Gromyko said, trying to put a bright face on things. "I didn't think you two could neck forever."

Milo glanced furtively at Rex while he bent over a bowl of steaming soup, guilt and fear written on his face. The rest of the table eyed the pair with looks that combined curiosity, apprehension, and friendliness. Most of them were tense from the way Hunt had hauled his brother from the room, and he knew it would take a while for them to settle down.

"What can I get you two?" Wanda asked, trying to second Gromyko's brightness.

"Anything, as long as it's hot," Hunt replied, taking a seat at the table, Tselitel sitting to his right.

The meal passed off uneasily, with Gromyko trying to stir the rest into conversation. When that failed, he fell into a monologue about his past exploits, regaling them with story after story, and sometimes explaining the backgrounds for the more memorable graffiti that was spread around town.

"Now, one that caused me a *lot* of trouble ran like this: *There is a song in my heart, and Gromyko is the singer.* 'But why should that cause you trouble?' you'll ask. Well, I'll tell you: it was painted on the inside of the police station on the north side of Midway! Don't ask me how, but one of my most ardent followers, a very short woman of twenty-five, somehow managed to slip inside and accomplish the deed before they knew she was there! I suspect she climbed through the ventilation system. She couldn't have been more than four and a half feet tall. Just the right size to fit! 'Such a short woman!' you'll say. 'Whatever happened to her?' Well, I'll tell you..."

On and on he went, supplying both ends of the conversation himself until the diners began to trickle out of the room and off to bed.

Finally it was just the original foursome, with the new addition of Tselitel. It was clear that something was in the offing, but each of them was reluctant to begin. Finally Ugo cleared his throat.

"My dear," he said, looking at Tselitel, "would you excuse us, please? There's something we need to discuss."

"Oh, of course," she said, starting to rise.

"Anything you want to say can be said to Lily," Hunt said firmly, putting his hand over hers on the table.

"As you like it," the old man nodded, waiting for her to retake her seat. "Rex, you shouldn't have brought her here. The only thing holding up the experiments was the threat of her blowing the whistle on them. With her gone they can resume as early as tomorrow."

"No, they can't," replied Hunt. "You're right, they won't know where she is. But they'd be insane to jump right back into their tests. They'll wait a few days and conduct a thorough search for her. Once that turns up nothing they'll brace for the scandal of her disappearance. Only after things have quieted down will they resume."

"I agree with you, my friend," Gromyko seconded. "Simple human nature will cause them to duck their heads and wait for fallout. They won't try anything until the ground stops shaking beneath them."

"I *don't* agree with you," Ugo said. "And neither does the Order. Now, it's early enough that we can slip her back into her apartment before they know she's missing. Dawn is still hours away, and with this latest storm blowing in we'll have extra cover."

"The agent they sent after her won't be the last," Hunt said. "It's a miracle she didn't break Lily in the last few days."

"And yet she didn't," Ugo said. "You must think of this from a broad perspective, Rex. She is the only one capable of holding them up. We can hope and *assume* that they'll react to her disappearance the way you think they will. But she's the only guarantee we have. We can't let an advantage like that slip away. We have to play every card we hold."

"Even if it puts her in mortal danger?" Hunt retorted.

"We're all in mortal danger," answered the old man.

"I can't go back there," Tselitel said. "Oh, I want to be brave, believe me. But the things that woman put inside my head! I can't help shuddering when I think about them. I couldn't sleep at night from the terror of it all. And it would last for hours after reaching the prison. The shadow creatures would wail and moan at me all throughout my time with Vilks, pressing their long fingers into my body, like they were extracting my organs." A cold shiver ran down her spine at the memory. "Only about midday would they finally depart. And then with nightfall they would start again. It was only

Wellesley who kept me sane. Frankly I'm surprised I got through it. I'm sorry, but I couldn't handle another encounter like that."

"We all have to be stronger than we think we are at a time like this," Ugo said. "We're faced with the total domination of mankind by the most nefarious conspiracy ever devised. Don't forget that they are on the cusp of a breakthrough. Who knows if a few weeks is all they need to finish their work? They can keep your disappearance quiet for that long. And then it will be game over. Doctor, you must go back, no matter the risk."

"No," cut in Rex firmly. "I'm not putting her in a position like that. Not again."

"The Order isn't going to give you a choice," Ugo said in a low voice.

"Grandfather!" Wanda said in shock. "You can't threaten Rex!"

"I'll threaten whoever I have to!" flashed Ugo. "Don't you understand? One misstep and we're all going to tumble into the ravine together. This is no time to let our personal feelings cloud our judgment. We must be just as ruthless as our enemies."

"Then what, pray tell, makes us better than them?" asked Gromyko.

"Oh, don't be a simpleton," snapped Ugo. "We serve totally different aims. The two can't possibly be compared with each other."

"When you sacrifice people like sheep it's hard to tell the difference!" retorted the smuggler. "You hold human life as cheaply as our enemies do!"

"Evil has always been stopped only through the heroic actions of the few!" replied Ugo, his voice rising. "That's why they're heroes: they're outnumbered and outgunned, and the odds are always against them. For that reason they must make sacrifices that other people don't."

"And yet you seem to be bearing none of these noble

risks," countered Gromyko. "Just when do you play the hero? Or are you content to watch this drama unfold from the sidelines?"

"I've borne more risks than you'll ever know!" shouted Ugo, standing up out of his chair and slamming his fist against the table, making the utensils jump. "Don't you *ever* presume to lecture me again." He turned to Hunt and Tselitel with fire in his eyes. "She goes back tonight. The Order has decreed that it be so."

At that moment several of the people who'd sat at the table earlier crowded the doorway that led into the hall. Hunt looked at them and saw nervous anticipation in their faces. They were ready for a struggle, several of them holding clubs.

"She stays with me," Hunt said, slowly rising to his feet and turning so he could watch both the group and the old man at the same time. He put his right on Tselitel's shoulder and gave her a little squeeze. "And anyone who thinks otherwise will learn the true meaning of fear," he added, dark smoke beginning to float around his left hand.

"Indeed," Gromyko said, taking a position beside Hunt and cracking his knuckles.

"The Order will never forget this, Rex," Ugo said ominously, waving off the others and retaking his seat. "I regret the day I brought you home with me. I thought you were wiser than this. But you're just as blind in your passion as that miserable smuggler."

"Come on," Hunt said, taking Tselitel's hand and drawing her to her feet. Ushering her out the door ahead of him, he paused and looked into the old man's eyes for a long moment. Moving off down the hall, he found a room devoid of people and followed her inside, closing the door after them.

"I can't believe that just happened," she whispered, trembling with anxiety. "He would have ordered those people to attack you!"

"Without any hesitation at all," Hunt said, looking around the room. It was little more than a supply closet, the walls packed high with goods. A narrow cot stood along the back wall, and they walked to this and sat down, still clasping each other's hand.

"Maybe I should have gone back," Tselitel mused guiltily.

"The man is a fanatic," Wellesley said, chiming in at last. "No possible good could be served by your going back there, Lily. You've been marked. Not that Ugo cares, of course. He'd be more than willing to throw your life away on the chance that it would do some good. He hasn't got any other use for you, anyhow."

"He's right," Hunt said. "Don't give it a second thought."

"But what do we do now?" she asked. "If the Order is against us, we have nowhere to go."

"We go anywhere I say we go," Hunt said with a grim smile, raising his left hand and flexing his fingers. "Besides, despite what he said tonight, Ugo and the Order still need me. I'm the only hope they have. He'll remember that once he's cooled off."

"*If* he cools off," Tselitel said. "You saw that look in his eyes."

"He'll cool off," Hunt said with certainty. "If he was about to sacrifice you for the cause, he won't let his own emotions get in the way. By morning he'll be surly, but reasonable."

"I hope you're right," she said, leaning up against him. "Because right now I feel like we're between two fires."

CHAPTER 15

As night turned to morning the storm hit Midway. Much worse than the blizzard that had supposedly ended Hunt's life, it blanketed the area with snow. Harsh winds stole the heat from exposed flesh in moments, and even those who were bundled up could stand its wrath for only a few minutes at a time. The entire town was paralyzed as everyone hunkered down, prepared for a long wait.

Deep within the bunker, dozing on the cot with Tselitel half beside him, half on top of him, Hunt could hear the wind whistling through the cracks in the meager wooden door, sending ghostly howls down the hallway. Unconsciously hearing this sound and associating it with the figures that Bodkin had called up in her mind, Tselitel drew Hunt a little closer in her sleep and sighed.

Another hour passed, and people could be heard moving outside their room. Hunt tensed as he listened, wondering if Ugo would stoop so low as to try and snatch Tselitel while they slept. More than once shadows appeared under the door as unseen figures exchanged words in low tones in the hallway. But each time they would move away, heading either for the mudroom or the dining room.

Unwilling to awaken her after the ordeal she'd been through, Hunt lay quietly and thought. Questions popped into his mind that he wanted to ask Wellesley. But he stifled his tongue for her sake.

Eventually her eyes slowly opened, and she smiled and

yawned.

"What time is it?" she asked.

"Pretty early yet," he replied. "Sleep well?"

"Mmm," she replied ambiguously. "My body is stiff. I guess I didn't move around much last night."

"There isn't a lot of room on this thing," he said, indicating the cot that barely fit him alone. "And I'm afraid I don't make a very good mattress, regardless."

"You're the best mattress for me," she said, laying her head on his chest and sighing. "I guess we'll have to go out and face them now. I've been dreading this moment all night, even in my sleep."

"Yeah, I've been thinking about it, too."

"I can't help but feel that this is my fault," she fretted. "If I could have held out longer against that woman–"

"That would be a tall order for anyone," interrupted Hunt. "She was good, very good. She hit me a couple of times, and it took everything I had to shove it aside and concentrate."

"But to crumble like that!" she persisted. "And now I've made a mess of things here. I've jeopardized your relations with the Order, and with Ugo. It would have been better if I hadn't come to Delta-13 at all. There are others who could have come to investigate the condition of the inmates. The screamers in particular have made quite an impression in the middle and inner planets, and there were plenty of candidates for the task. But I had more pull than the rest, so I got the job. If I hadn't been so egotistical, someone tougher could have made the journey."

"You're tough enough for me," he smiled.

"You're being sweet," she said. "But I'm serious. I've bungled things badly."

"Not for me," Hunt said. "You've been everything I've ever needed, and more. Try and take a little solace in that."

"I do take solace in that," she said, her head still laying against his chest. "But I hate that I've made things harder for you here."

"You didn't: Ugo did. Once he's made up his mind there's no arguing with him. Wellesley said it right: he thinks he's the planet's prophet. It makes him self-righteous and, to his thinking, incapable of error. When you meet up with someone like that, only force will suffice. That's why I pushed things as far as I did last night: there was no other way. And the responsibility for that is entirely on his shoulders."

"I couldn't agree more," Wellesley added. "Let it go, Lily."

"I'll do my best," she said. "So, what's our next move?" she asked a moment later.

"I wish I knew," replied Hunt.

"While you two have been blissfully resting I've been thinking, as usual," Wellesley said. "And I've got an idea. But it involves Milo."

"Oh, great."

"I've been scouring my memory for hours, and it occurred to me that he might be able to help us get access to the mind control chamber."

"How?" asked Tselitel.

"Well, the chamber didn't start as a mind control chamber, exactly. It was originally made by the *Kol-Prockian* priests who worshiped here and administered the religion. Their belief system was structured around finding balance in life, to oversimplify to an incredible degree. That's why Delta-13 was central to their beliefs: it helped them do this."

"So they thought they'd throw mind control on top of it to spice things up?" asked Hunt wryly.

"Oh, very funny. No, it was quite different than that. You see, the priests were benevolent and generous, always helping anyone who came to them for aid. Mostly this was psychological aid. In many ways they held your function in society, Lily: they helped those who were all tangled up inside to find inner harmony. But there were some cases that even the priests, with the planet helping them, couldn't resolve. They ended up in government hospitals to keep them off the streets, where they lived out their days making as little trouble as possible."

"I don't see where this helps us," Hunt said.

"I'm getting to that," the AI said impatiently. "As *Kol-Prockian* technology advanced, some members of the priesthood saw in it a way to help those cases that had proven incurable. Naturally this caused a split in their ranks, with many of them sticking to the old ways, regarding the journey into the psyche as a purely spiritual affair. They felt that adding technology to the mix would lead their followers into a kind of materialistic pragmatism, undermining them in the long run. In essence they were afraid that religion would become psychiatry, losing the mystic hold it had possessed for millennia. Those who supported the use of technological aids in achieving wholeness were derisively called the *Prollok-Hee*, which is milder than a heretic, but not by much."

"*Wellesley*," said Hunt.

"Fine, fine, I'll jump ahead. As generations passed the views of the old guard came to be seen as passe, and those of the *Prollok-Hee* became dominant within the priesthood. It was they who built the original building upon which the prison now stands. The room, along with all of its technology, was built and paid for by the priesthood in the hope that it would provide greater insight into the workings of the *Kol-Prockian* mind. As time went on they even developed technology with which they attempted to plant ideas in the minds of their patients in the hope that they could help the toughest cases over the humps that had held them back."

"This all sounds a little...suspicious?" said Hunt.

"Which is why they kept it a secret, telling only those members of the priesthood who needed to know. They realized it would be regarded as a conspiracy to reassert the dominant role of the priesthood in *Kol-Prockian* society, which had been on the wane for centuries. This was not the case, of course. But such slander would be all too tempting for the unbelieving to seize hold of. Moreover they feared that the government would try and take what they'd developed, using it for its own purposes. So they kept the project a secret. Even their patients didn't know what they were being subjected to."

"That's pretty high handed," Tselitel said.

"They weren't as big on informed consent as humans tend to be," Wellesley said. "If something worked, people didn't tend to ask questions. Besides, those who sought out the help of the priests tended to treat them almost like shamans or medicine men. They pretty much did what they were told."

"Wake me when he gets to the point," Hunt teased, laying his head back and closing his eyes.

"The point is this: Milo has been scavenging for artifacts for years. Time and again he would return with a massive haul of them and survive off the proceeds for months at a time. He *must* have found some kind of stash. And there's only one place in my data banks that can fit that description: the great temple of *Berek-Po*. I think he stumbled into it, and has been living off of its riches. Now, this temple was the headquarters of the *Delek-Hai* religion. If anywhere on this ice cube would have some kind of map or blueprint of the facility under the prison, it's there."

"So what do you want to do? Squeeze it out of him?" asked Hunt sourly.

"I was planning to just ask him," replied Wellesley. "If he really has changed he'll be all too happy to let us know where it is."

"And hand away his riches? I don't think so."

"Well, let me try all the same," the AI said. "If he proves difficult, I'm sure you can loosen his tongue."

"Come on, baby," Hunt said with a sigh, patting Tselitel and gesturing for her to get off his chest. "Our brilliant war AI has a plan."

Stepping into the hallway together, they made for the dining room. Only Gromyko, Wanda, and Milo were there.

"I want to talk to you," Hunt said, standing in the doorway and pointing at his brother. Milo swallowed hard and rose slowly, his eyes fixed on Hunt as he navigated around the table. He stopped just short of him. "Come on: there's someone who wants to talk with you," he said, leading him back into the hallway to the storage room.

"Good morning, dear," Wanda said with a warm smile, crossing to Tselitel and taking her arms in her hands. "Did you sleep well?"

"Eh," Lily replied with a seesaw motion of her hand. Seeing the tension written on Wanda's plump face, she intuited that she'd slept poorly herself. "Has Ugo been to breakfast yet?"

"Oh, yes. He's come and gone. He's holed up in his room now."

"Good," said Tselitel with relief. "Oh, I'm sorry! I didn't–" she began. But Wanda held up her hand and smiled with sweet understanding.

"He's a handful, I know," she said confidentially. "And last night he was simply outrageous. I'm glad Rex stood up to him."

"As am I," Tselitel said quietly.

Wanda affectionately squeezed her arms and went to get her some breakfast.

She walked to the table and sat down near the end, a few places from Gromyko.

"So," Gromyko said, sliding into the seat next to hers, bringing a steaming bowl of porridge with him, "I trust you and Rex passed a pleasant night?"

"Not really," Tselitel said.

"Ah, Rex was never much of a man with the ladies," the smuggler said philosophically, pausing to work something from between his teeth with a small pick he carried with him. "Now, Gromyko..."

"You presume a great deal!" Tselitel said, her face growing red. "I'll have you now I haven't–, I mean, we haven't–."

"Don't feel you have to tete-e-tete with this renegade," Wanda said with a laugh, setting down a bowl of porridge in front of her. "He'll say anything to get a reaction out of you. But his heart is solid gold."

"That's what you think," the smuggler said slyly. "Perhaps on the inside I'm just as roguish, charming, and irresistible as I appear."

"Don't forget I've seen your insides, back when you were initiated," Wanda said, tapping her temple and smiling. Then, looking at Tselitel, "Whenever a new member joins the Order, they must pass a psychic evaluation. It's the only way we can be certain of our operatives. The government is constantly trying to infiltrate our ranks."

"If you keep up like this you'll ruin my reputation as a scoundrel," Gromyko complained. "I shall have to work overtime to compensate." Turning to Tselitel, he grasped her hand and kissed it. "And now, my dear, seeing as Rex is away, perhaps you'd like to go somewhere a little more...private?"

But the doctor just laughed good naturedly at his display, and he withdrew his hands with a harrumph.

"See? Thanks to you I can't make her uncomfortable anymore! I'll never be able to flirt with her again!"

"Good," Wanda said, turning from the table and walking to the small kitchen that stood in the back of the room. "You should just be flirting with me by now, anyhow."

"It's no fun flirting with your own girl," he protested. "There's no danger! No mystery!" He turned to Tselitel. "She is trying to make an honest, productive man out of me. But I swear to fight her tooth and nail. Should she succeed, Gromyko will no longer be a symbol, a beacon of hope to the downtrodden masses. He would degenerate into a common, everyday drudge. It would be the death of me!"

"And the beginning of something stable and reliable," Wanda said, bringing a cup of tea to the table and sitting down across from them. "You can't be a symbol forever. Eventually the sheen is going to fade from that black hair of yours, and you'll be forced to live something normal like the rest of us. What will you do, then? It'll be too late to change your ways."

"It was too late to change them the instant I was born," Gromyko replied. "Why, when I sprang from the womb and slapped the doctor, the world knew what kind of man it was getting! Now, who am I to fight destiny? I could never be so arrogant as to oppose fate! Some men are born to be drudges, and some are born to be great. But I am the only man who was born to be Gromyko!"

"He likes to exaggerate," Wanda said, shaking her head. "He's been building his legend for so long that he's come to believe it, I'm afraid."

"All legends have a grain of truth," replied Gromyko, leaning back in his chair and roguishly working his teeth with the pick. "That is why the masses believe them. But in my case it is more than a grain: it's an entire sack!"

"Sadly his is a legend you can never *shut off*," Wanda replied, stressing the last two words to make them an order.

"You would never have fallen in love with me if I was anything less than I am," the smuggler replied confidently. "We humans love the whole being, not just what we consciously consider the good parts. That is why we never fall in love with the person who would be 'good for us:' they don't appeal to the dark side we carry within. We want a little bad mixed in with the good. I am an egotist: I admit it freely. If I weren't, you never would have noticed me. You like a little bit of naughty mixed in with the nice."

"Oh, hush you!" Wanda said, her cheeks glowing red as he hit a little too close to the truth for her comfort. Tselitel recognized this and glanced away, fighting a little smile off of her lips to spare Wanda embarrassment.

"I venture to think the same is true of you and Rex, dear doctor," Gromyko said, pleased that he had made his point with Wanda and eager to follow it up by making another. "He carries wells of darkness within that make me look like a placid little lapdog by comparison. He could bathe half of Midway in the shadow that follows him like an obedient servant, always at his heels."

"Antonin!" exclaimed Wanda. "What a way to talk about your friend!"

"And we should be glad of that fact," continued Gromyko. "Mightily glad. It was only the threat of that darkness that stopped Ugo and his henchmen from dragging you off by force last night."

"I should hardly call them 'henchmen,'" Ugo said from the doorway, his mouth drawn into a scowl. "They are loyal servants of a cause that is above all our conceptions of petty self-interest. They would willingly sacrifice their lives without hesitation, if need be."

"That seems appropriate," replied Gromyko easily. "Given that they are so willing to sacrifice those of others."

"Where's Rex?" the old man asked Wanda, ignoring the smuggler's remark.

"He's talking to Milo."

"What! And you let them go off alone together?" Ugo asked no one in particular. "You know how he feels about his brother! He could just as easily kill him as lay eyes on him. Where did they go?"

"Rex doesn't want to hurt him," Tselitel explained. "Wellesley had something he wanted to discuss with him."

Ugo frowned at her, wishing to hear from her least of all. He was about to say something tart when a door opened down the hall and footsteps were heard coming their way. Rex and Milo entered the dining room, the former moving past Ugo without acknowledging him, while the latter shuffled meekly by and returned to his seat in the back of the room.

Hunt crossed to Tselitel and leaned against the table next to her. He wished to conspicuously make the point to Ugo that they were a package deal. Crossing his arms, he stood silently.

"Well?" asked Gromyko after a few moments. "What have you got for us?"

"Wellesley has a plan that might carry us into the old *Kol-Prockian* facility beneath the prison."

"Impossible," Ugo said. "There's no way inside."

"There is an ancient temple that may hold a clue as to how we can enter. But it's several days from here, and only Milo knows the way," he said, tossing his head disdainfully in his brother's direction. "He's been there numerous times, and has agreed to take us."

"Rex, there is no external way inside the facility," Ugo said, approaching the table. "The Order has looked a thousand times over the years. Rambling off into the wilderness on a wild goose chase like this will only waste more time, to say nothing of the risks you'll endure along the way."

"Naturally I will come with you," Gromyko said, nodding his head with certainty.

"No, you'll stay here," replied Hunt. "Someone has to watch the store," he said, his eyes falling on Ugo.

"I'm sorry, my friend," Gromyko said. "But I cannot permit you to walk into the unknown with only this reprobate to guide you. There's no telling what he may do once he is beyond the view of watchful eyes. He may betray you when your back is turned."

"Of that you need have no fear," Ugo said. "We have very thorough methods for examining those we trust. And Milo came back perfectly clean."

"So thorough that the police managed to learn your location only yesterday," retorted Gromyko. "No, I trust what I can see. And I intend to keep Milo in sight at all times."

"You're adamant on that point?" Hunt asked the smuggler, his eyes still on Ugo.

"Absolutely."

"I thought you'd be," Hunt said with a faint, appreciative grin.

"We'll send a team of operatives with you," Ugo said. "The Order is familiar with the writing and architecture of the *Kol-Prockians*. We may be of immeasurable help to you."

"No, I only want people with me I can trust," Hunt said acidly. "Wellesley can provide any translations that we may need, and his knowledge of *Kol-Prockian* society and religious customs is unmatched."

Seeing that he was totally cut out of the process, Ugo turned from them and left. They heard the door to his room click shut moments later.

"What about me?" Tselitel asked.

"You'll have to come with us," Hunt said. "I'm sorry to put you back into the elements. But I can't leave you behind for the Order to drag off."

"But, Rex," Wanda said, rounding the table and standing beside him, "she isn't up to a days long trek into the wild. Just look at her: she looks like a coat rack."

"Thanks, Wanda," Tselitel laughed.

"Oh, you know what I mean," Wanda said. "You're not used to roughing it. How can you possibly hold up out there? It's gonna be an ordeal for these two," she said, gesturing towards Hunt and Gromyko. "And they've lived here almost their whole lives. It would be awfully dangerous."

"Milo has some artifacts that will help us," Hunt said, his eyes sliding to his brother for a moment. "He's got at least a half dozen of the medallions that Antonin has used to withstand the cold."

"Outstanding!" exclaimed the smuggler. "I'd long feared that I'd found the only one!"

"No, there's more of them around," Hunt replied. "We'll each take one along for the journey. That'll help to cut down the risk."

"Yes, but not eliminate it," replied Wanda dubiously.

"I'll be alright, Wanda," Tselitel said, rising from her chair and warmly taking the other woman's hands. "Don't worry."

"Well," Wanda said, unable to come up with another argument and growing a little flustered. "Well, what are you going to eat along the way?"

"Snow, unless you get busy packing!" said Gromyko with a laugh.

The blizzard worsened as they prepared to leave, blanketing the countryside in more snow than it had seen in years. The wind piled this against the door of the bunker, forming a great drift that reached halfway to the squat entrance's roof.

Shortly before noon they were ready to depart, each of them sporting the warmest clothes the bunker could offer, and wearing a medallion around their necks.

"Alright, it's gonna be nasty out there," Milo said, his voice a mixture of solicitousness and confidence born of experience with the elements. Whenever he spoke he looked reflexively at Rex, as though obtaining his permission for each sentence he uttered. Each time Rex offered neither encouragement nor condemnation, simply returning his look and leaving him to stand on his own two feet. "I'm going to attach a rope to my belt," he said, affixing one as he spoke. "The person behind me will tie it on, and then string one back from *their* belt to the person behind them, and so on. This way if one of us falls down in the snow the rest will know at once."

"I should think we'd simply hear them cry out in that case," replied Gromyko doubtfully. "Why go through all this nonsense?"

"Because the simplest precautions are the difference between life and death in a situation like this," Milo said. "With the wind blowing and our hoods pulled up, you'd be surprised how little you can hear. And visibility will be near to zero out there. I need to be sure you guys are alright, and following close behind me."

"Go ahead: tie it on, Antonin," Hunt cut in. "Lily will attach to yours, and I'll follow up the rear."

"Alright," Gromyko said, not eager to be tied to Milo but unwilling to fight Hunt over it.

While the smuggler worked the rope around his belt and Milo watched, Hunt drew Tselitel a few feet away.

"Don't push yourself too hard out there," he whispered, sliding his hand between her hood and her head, brushing her cheek. "It's easy to overdo it in conditions like these." Regarding her thin face, topped as it was by a little bit of white hair that poked down from her stocking cap, he was struck by how cute she looked and couldn't resist giving her a little kiss.

"Is that meant to keep me warm?" she asked playfully.

"Nah, that was just for me," he smiled, kissing her again. "Now, *that's* meant to keep you warm."

Realizing the other two were awkwardly waiting for them to finish, he tied his rope around Tselitel's belt while she attached herself to Gromyko's. This done, they ascended the stairs one by one, Milo fighting at the top to push the door through the snow that had accumulated.

As the first three filed out into the storm, Hunt felt the urge to look behind him one last time before leaving. He was surprised to see Ugo standing in the doorway, leaning against it with his arms crossed.

"Bring her back alive, Rex," he said in a voice just loud enough to be heard over the roar of the storm outside. "She's a fine woman."

"What difference does it make to you?" Hunt asked, turning his back and ascending the last few steps. "If I don't she'll just be another one of your noble sacrifices."

Before Ugo could respond Hunt was out of the bunker and pushing the door shut behind him. Shaking his head with a regretful sigh, he turned and walked back down the hall.

Despite the fact it was midday outside, the world around the foursome was a dark gray. Shielding their eyes with their hands, the three looked to Milo, who mutely gestured in an exaggerated manner into the trees. Shuffling into the white shroud, his rope tugged on Gromyko's belt, pulling him into motion. Tselitel and Hunt fell into line behind them, walking slowly.

With the wind blasting harshly against his face, Hunt, like the rest of them, watched his feet most of the time. Periodically he would glance up briefly to see what Milo was doing. But his brother was a mere silhouette in the storm, a two-dimensional figure slowly, deliberately, pushing his feet through the snow. Occasionally he appeared to be consulting something that he held, but Hunt could never be sure, and chalked it up to his own suspiciousness.

More often his eyes fell upon Tselitel. Initially she'd shown great energy in charging through the drifts and keeping up with the other two. But soon her strength waned, and she fell into a stiff shuffle. Hunt tried to deduce if she was growing too weak, pushing herself too hard in an effort not to hold the others back. But such information couldn't be gleaned from her movements, and he resolved to wait on her to ask for a break, provided she needed one.

For several hours they walked, the three followers moving along the path that Milo cut with his feet.

"We're starting to track a bit northward," Wellesley observed, expecting no answer because of the storm.

Suddenly Tselitel's boot slipped and she fell face first into a drift. Gromyko felt her rope yank against the back of his belt and stopped, looking back as Hunt stepped forward to help her up.

"I guess I slipped," she said breathlessly, as Hunt brushed the snow off her face and jacket.

"Are you alright?" he asked, looking into her tired eyes.

"Oh, yes," she said, trying to sound game. "I'm just...a little short of breath. It's hard to breathe with all this...wind in my face."

"Is she alright?" Milo called from ahead, taking a few steps back until he was beside Gromyko.

"Yes, she's alright," Hunt said over the gale. "A little winded."

"Oh. Well, we'll be taking a break in a few more hours," Milo said, glancing at the clouds above. "Sooner, if we can pick up the pace a little. I want to get out of this before it gets worse." Then he turned and resumed his slow walk.

"It's gonna get *worse*?" Tselitel asked Hunt.

"Come on," he said, turning her around and giving her a

little push. "Let's keep moving."

An hour passed, and the trees around them were bending with the wind, their branches shaking wildly. A thick powder blew across their feet, destined to settle into deep drifts hundreds, if not thousands, of feet away.

"It's been a long time since I've seen a storm this bad," Wellesley observed. "Not since before I knew you. I don't think Lily can take much more of this. She's been stumbling for the last twenty minutes now."

"Yeah, but if we stop I don't think she'll be able to start again," Hunt said, barely loud enough to hear himself over the gale. "She'll have to tough it out."

"Guess you're right," he replied. "But I wish I could check her vitals about now. She's got enough spirit to push on until half her body is frozen."

"I'll check on her in a little while," Hunt replied, glancing at her briefly before tipping his head down once again.

Later, while eyeing Milo, he saw Tselitel slip again, this time landing on her rear. She let out a little cry when she hit, and was still for a moment.

Pushing through the snow that separated them, Hunt slid to his knees and looked at her.

"Think I...hurt something...that time," she panted, trying to sit up. But her face tightened with pain and she eased back onto the snow.

"Let me check her out," Wellesley said, and in an instant Hunt slipped him off and pushed him inside her mitten.

"Is she alright?" Milo asked, as he and Gromyko reached them.

"We'll find out in a moment," Hunt replied.

"He says I'm alright," Tselitel relayed. "Probably pulled a muscle in my back, though."

"Can you stand?" Gromyko asked.

"She'll have to," replied Hunt, putting Wellesley back around his neck and packing him down his shirt. "Come on, give me your hand," he said, slipping his right arm around her back and helping her up. He looked at Milo, who stood watching them. "Let's get moving."

Mutely nodding, his brother resumed his position at the front of the line, this time clearly consulting something in his hand.

"I'd like to know what he's looking at," Gromyko said suspiciously. "Every little while he looks at that thing."

"We'll find out soon enough," Hunt said. "Better get in line, Antonin."

The smuggler nodded, looked at Milo as though he was distasteful, and then resumed his former position.

"I'll walk with you for a while," Hunt said, seeing how unsteady Tselitel was on her feet. Holding the rope that was strung between them in his left hand so they wouldn't trip, he kept his right around her middle, giving a little extra push whenever a thick drift happened along.

After several more hours they reached Milo's first checkpoint.

"This is it," he said, stopping before a mound of snow.

"This is what?" asked the smuggler, as the other two caught up.

"This is where we'll recuperate for the next few hours," Milo explained, walking towards the mound and pressing his hands into the snow. Brushing at it energetically, he revealed a dark metal door with a large handle. He looked at Gromyko. "Give me a hand, will you? The hinges get stiff."

Shrugging, the smuggler grabbed the handle and began to pull against it. Straining at it for a few moments, it slowly creaked open, revealing a dark space within.

"Come on," Milo said between breaths, nodding the rest inside while he stood beside the door.

"After you, Mr. Guide," Gromyko said, gesturing toward the opening.

Milo's face dropped a little and he complied, stepping into the darkness and turning on a light he held in his hand.

Gromyko looked at Hunt and nodded, cautiously following Milo inside. Moments later he emerged, waving for them to come inside and closing the door after them.

The air inside the structure was perfectly still, as though it hadn't been disturbed for centuries. The wind outside sounded quiet, far away, like a distant memory. The structure was cold, but the break from the wind was more than enough to satisfy them.

"What is this place?" asked Tselitel, looking around. She saw stone enclosures stacked on shelves against either wall, running the entire length of the small building. On the face of each enclosure were elaborately carved figures. Their faces inhuman, she concluded this was yet another alien construction.

"It's a *Kol-Prockian* mausoleum," Milo said, sliding off his cap and scratching his head. "I found it a few years ago when I was hunting for the great temple. Found it just in time, too: another hour and I'd have frozen to death." Walking along the stone coffins and rubbing his hand across several of them, he commented, "Must have been a bunch of poor people they put here. I checked for artifacts but didn't find any. Not so much as an ornament or a piece of jewelry between them all."

"Grave robber," Wellesley said.

"Cheery place to spend the night," Gromyko said, looking around him cautiously, as though a ghost would spring out at him. "Sleeping with the dead."

"Oh, we won't be here long," Milo said, setting his backpack down and fishing for something to eat. "We're just going to wait for the storm to ease off in a few hours. Then we'll resume."

"And what makes you think it will?" asked the smuggler. "It's been getting worse all the time."

"I just do, that's all," he replied.

"Alright, let's have it, Milo," Hunt said.

"Have what?" he asked innocently.

"This, perhaps?" Gromyko asked, snatching up the

device that Milo was using as a light.

"Hey, give that back!" Milo said, jumping to his feet.

"What do you think, Rex?" Gromyko asked, tossing the device to his friend once Milo had gotten close. "Government issue, I'd say."

"Mhm," Hunt said, looking it over, still standing beside Tselitel.

Reflexively Milo rushed towards him, stopping halfway when he saw the look in his eyes.

"Government?" she asked. "You mean he's working for them?"

"No, or he'd have turned us over when the police chased us out of Ugo's place," Hunt said.

"That's a WTD-600," Gromyko observed. "Actually, a WTD-600G, the government model. It's a real fancy piece of tech."

"Tells you the weather, your location, vital signs," Hunt said. "It can even process visual data and provide on the spot analysis. Artifact hunters love them."

"And so does the government," added Gromyko, "because each one is fitted with a *tracker*."

"What?" asked Tselitel. "You mean they've been following our progress the entire time?"

"Of course not!" said Milo. "What kind of an idiot do you think I am? I had it taken out years ago."

"The tracker in a 600G is notoriously hard to remove," Gromyko said. "It's designed to stop working if you mess with it."

"I know," said Milo. "That's why I had it fitted with a dummy tracker. The device can't tell the difference."

"A lot of people have thought over the years that they'd outsmarted the failsafes," the smuggler said, crossing his arms. "But sooner or later the police came crashing through their front door."

"Well, I must have gotten it right, because they've never come for me," Milo said. "And I've done enough to them that they wouldn't be able to resist nailing me if they had a bug on me the entire time." He looked between Hunt and Gromyko and saw they were still unconvinced. "Look, if their data showed a guy was making repeated trips out of town to a specific location, and within days of his return the black market was doused in artifacts, don't you think that would be too good to pass up? They've been trying to crush the illegal artifact trade for years! They're too smart not to put two and two together and pounce on me if they knew."

Gromyko glanced at Hunt.

"I guess that makes sense," he said.

Hunt held out the 600G, which Milo eagerly snatched.

"Then why were you so touchy about it?" the smuggler asked, once Milo had returned to his backpack.

"I've got a lot of data saved in that thing," Milo admitted reluctantly. "Our entire trip to the great temple is plotted in it, plus dozens of other high value locations. Hideouts, smuggler bases, and everything in between. If the police came for me tomorrow I could conceal myself in any number of hidden places that they'd never be able to find, and with supplies extensive enough to last for years. I'd sooner part with my arm than lose that thing."

"I can see why," Gromyko said, wishing he had it. And then, with a sly glance at Hunt he added in an insinuating tone, "I bet the Order would love to know about it."

Milo's head snapped to the smuggler.

"You wouldn't!" he said. "I-I just went to them because I needed help. I never joined up or anything. They don't own any piece of me!"

"Have you made that clear to Ugo?" Gromyko countered, leaning against one of the stone coffins. "He has a way of...appropriating what belongs to others. For the good of the cause, of course."

"Look, I'm not part of his cause," Milo said defensively. "And I don't want to be. I'm just trying to survive on this snowball. If they take the 600G and use the information in it, burning through my supplies and drawing attention to my hideouts, I'll have nowhere else to go! The police would have me in a matter of days! It would be no different than if you clubbed me and threw me into the snow to freeze to death."

"From what I hear, it would be poetic justice," Gromyko said indifferently, drawing the pick from his pocket and working it between his teeth once more. "I should think plenty of people would consider it a just end, given how you've lived up till now."

"But that's all past!" Milo pleaded. "Don't you understand? I'm trying to atone for all that now. I don't know if I ever can," he said frankly. "But I'm doing my best to try!"

"If you really want to start setting things straight, then play things square with us," Hunt said. "No more secrets. No more games."

"No more secrets," Milo nodded sincerely. "I promise: no more."

"Alright," Hunt said, glancing at Gromyko to signal he should stop pushing on him. The smuggler grinned his recognition and put the pick away.

"Was that really necessary?" Tselitel asked quietly as Hunt rejoined her. "Why'd Antonin put the screws to him like that?"

"To show him he has to commit one hundred percent to us," Hunt said, slipping off his backpack and unzipping the main flap. "Milo might have turned a corner, but a lot of old habits are still with him. His first impulse is to put just as little of himself into this as possible, keeping his options perpetually open. He's got to know that he can't be halfway in the door and stay there. He's got to commit, throw in his fortune with ours."

"I see," Tselitel said, looking over Hunt's shoulder at Milo. He was trying to eat a biscuit that Wanda had packed, now totally frozen from its time out in the cold. "I'd say you rattled him pretty well," she commented. "He'll break his teeth before he gets any nourishment out of that thing. He's too preoccupied to realize that."

Hunt's eyes followed hers, and he chuckled when they fell upon his brother.

"He'll get over it," he said, turning back to his pack. Seeing her eyes wide with sympathy he sighed. "Antonin," he called over his shoulder, "bust out the stove you found in the bunker."

"I prefer a cold camp, myself," the smuggler said, stifling a laugh. "But if you insist."

Twenty minutes later they were all seated around Gromyko's small portable stove, warming their hands and some of the little tins that they'd carried with them.

"Ooh, I thought I'd never feel warm again," Tselitel said, holding her hands near the tiny flame, savoring the heat. "I'll never be able to look at a snowglobe without shivering after this. I don't know how you guys can handle it so well."

"You get used to it after the first few decades," Hunt said offhandedly, carefully picking up his little boiling tin of meat and trying to eat it.

"Indeed," assented Gromyko. "Eventually the snow becomes a part of you. Knowing it will be there even after you are gone, you come to respect it."

"Not me," said Milo, finally starting to relax. "I can never get out of it fast enough."

The other two men said nothing, making as though they hadn't heard him. He got the message: he wasn't part of the group yet, and ought to keep his mouth shut.

"So, when do we leave?" Tselitel asked, ending several minutes of silence that had followed.

"Well, Mister Guide?" Gromyko asked after an interval.

"According to the 600G, the storm will weaken in two hours or so," he said meekly. "A lull will ensue for about six hours, at which time it will strengthen once more. Our next stop is a little over five hours from here."

"That's a pretty tight window," Gromyko commented, looking at Hunt. "Do you want to risk it?"

"Hard to see that we have much choice," Hunt said,

setting his empty tin down and leaning back on his elbow. "We need to get inside the facility as quickly as possible and take out the room."

"But I thought you said that they'd be too scared to start things up right away," Tselitel said. "Why the rush?"

"Because he's not as certain of that argument as he intended Ugo to believe," Gromyko answered for Hunt, a grin slowly forming on his lips.

"It's true," Rex said frankly. "I haven't the least idea if they'd behave the way I said. I just needed to throw something at Ugo at the time."

"Then they could be conducting experiments even now," mused Tselitel, looking away and reflecting anxiously.

"I wouldn't worry about it," the smuggler said. "They're bound to wait at least a few days, until they're reasonably sure you won't come walking through the front door while they're processing their victims. We've got that much time, at least."

"Which isn't much," added Hunt, looking at Lily. "So I've got to ask you: can you go on?"

"My pride says yes," she replied, shifting painfully as she spoke. "But the rest of me says no. I ache from head to foot."

"She'll make it," Gromyko said with assurance. "But it would be good to catch a nap while we're waiting. Do you think you could sleep for a little while, if we keep it down?"

"Yes, I think so," she nodded.

"Alright, we're finished eating, anyway," Hunt said, gathering up the tins so nobody would kick them by accident and make a racket while she slept. "Stretch out by the stove here. We'll wake you just before it's time to go."

Leaving her near the front of the building by the tiny flame to rest, the three men gathered in the back, too tense to follow her example. Sitting on the floor, their backs against the wall, each of them occupied himself with his own thoughts.

"They built this place very well," Gromyko opined after an interval. "Not so much as a draft disturbs our comfort. Pretty nice place for poor priests."

"That's because they weren't poor," Hunt said after a little while.

"I'm sorry?" asked Gromyko.

"Wellesley has been bending my ear for the last two minutes," Hunt explained. "The *Kol-Prockian* priests who are buried here *weren't* poor, not by a long shot. This mausoleum was built for the high priests."

"Really?" Milo asked.

"Yes. The reason there aren't any artifacts is because the high priests were required to take a vow of poverty before ascending to their office."

"But this place isn't very, I don't know, *impressive*, considering who's buried here," Gromyko said.

"That's part of the poverty vow," Hunt replied after a few moments, relaying the AI's words. "No adornments, because such things would not be required by individuals who'd truly achieved wholeness within themselves. Just simple stone caskets in which to lie. That's why this place is built so well: it was required to be made of the most basic materials as a reflection of their lack of any materialistic needs. But, being high priests, they had only the best workmanship."

"I'm glad of that," the smuggler said, moving away from the wall and stretching out on the floor, his hands cupped under his head. "Otherwise this trip would be a lot nastier."

"It isn't over yet," replied Hunt darkly.

"Just what is our next stop, Mister Guide?" Gromyko asked, closing his eyes and wagging his feet as though he lay comfortably atop his own bed back home. "Another burial site?"

"No, a minor shrine," he replied. "It's smaller than this place, so we'll be packed in pretty tight."

"Wonderful," Gromyko said, not wishing to be at close quarters with Milo. "And you're sure we can beat the storm there?"

"As long as we maintain my usual speed, yes," replied

Milo.

"I don't think we can assume that," Gromyko said, opening his eyes and peeking over his boots to where Tselitel lay. "She's already had it from the first leg of our trip. I don't see how we can put her through another five hours."

Hunt slammed his fist on the stony floor. Milo looked at him, but knew better than to comment. Finally the smuggler spoke up.

"Something the matter, boss?"

"It's that blasted Ugo," Hunt growled. "If he hadn't been so high handed with Lily I never would have needed to drag her along with us. I hate putting her through this."

"We could leave her here," Gromyko offered. "Pick her up on the way back."

"No, we don't know what we'll find at the temple," replied Hunt, shaking his head. "That's why I brought the explosives along in my pack: if we can get a straight shot into the facility, we're taking it without delay. If anything happened to us, she'd be stranded out here, without the least idea how to get back to Midway."

"Guess Wanda was right about her not being suited to this sort of thing," Gromyko said, watching the subtle rise and fall of the doctor's jacket as she breathed.

"Of course she was right," Hunt said. "But there wasn't any other way."

The minutes ticked slowly by, with Milo periodically checking the 600G to ensure they didn't overstay their time. With fifteen minutes to go the men arose and made for the front of the building.

"Does Ugo know that you brought the charges?" Gromyko asked as they approached where Tselitel lay peacefully breathing.

"No," Hunt said, pausing momentarily before waking her. "He'd have piled bodies up to the ceiling before letting us out of there with them. He'd never let us blow the room before he's achieved his propaganda coup."

"Then you've come to see the matter as I do?" the smuggler asked, drawing a step closer and lowering his voice. "You consider a civil war to be *madness*?"

"I don't know," Hunt said, dissatisfied with his own answer. "But I know we don't have time to pussyfoot around. The technology is *Kol-Prockian*, so Wellesley should be able to interface with it and extract some pretty damning information. If he can, I'll give him the chance to gather what he can before I blow the room to Earth and back. But my absolute priority is destroying the room, with or without the data."

"But Ugo will use it to incite *war*!" Gromyko said, viewing his friend doubtfully.

"Only if Wellesley and I let him," Hunt said, dropping to a knee beside Tselitel. "I'm just keeping my options open, Antonin. He'll never know we have the data unless we tell him. Until then, it will be our secret."

"Quite a secret," Gromyko muttered, as Hunt put his hand on Tselitel and gently shook her. "It has the power to kill untold millions. In fact, billions."

"Is it time to go already?" Tselitel asked, looking up into Hunt's face with dry, tired eyes.

"We've got about ten more minutes," he said soothingly. "Take a minute to wake up."

"Alright."

Soon she was on her feet, and each of the men had their packs on their backs as before. Once they were roped together, they gathered by the door.

"Ready?" Milo asked, his hand upon it.

"Go for it," Hunt said.

As soon as Milo pushed the door open the wind caught it, nearly ripping it from his hand. The four moved slowly into the cold, blustery night.

"I thought you said it would be better by now!" Gromyko said, as Milo struggled to push the door shut. "This is worse than ever!"

"We're a bit early," he replied, glancing at the 600G. "Give it another few minutes and it will calm down." Shuffling ahead of the other three, he assumed his former position in the lead, invisible in the darkness.

Gromyko was about to say something to Hunt when the rope yanked on his belt and he started to walk.

"I can't see a thing," Tselitel shouted to Hunt over the wind.

"Just follow the rope," he yelled back, tugging on it to make sure it was securely attached.

So the long walk into the night began. Barely able to see as the storm drove snow into their eyes, they walked cautiously forward, totally dependent on the ropes that bound them together. Hunt despised the utter helplessness of his position, for Milo could betray them at any time, if he so chose, and disappear into the night. The three of them would then be completely lost, feeling around in the dark without the least idea where to go. Even Wellesley, dependent as he was on Rex's own senses to observe the world, would be no help. His stomach churned as he thought on this, realizing that their lives, and perhaps the future freedom of the human race, now rested in the questionable hands of his brother.

"This would be the perfect time for Milo to bolt," Wellesley said tensely, his thoughts running parallel to Rex's. "I guess this is going to prove him, one way or the other."

It took a little longer than Milo had thought, but the storm finally lost its ferocity. The wind at last ceased forcing its way down their throats, half choking them despite the cloth masks that covered their mouths.

Fruitlessly Hunt studied the darkness ahead of him, trying to catch some little gleam of light from the 600G that would reassure him that Milo was still there. He knew that he must be, or Gromyko would have called out. But the irrational fear that they were following mere air continued to grow within him until it was strong enough for him to shout ahead, just to make sure his brother hadn't abandoned them.

But just as he inhaled to do this, he pitched forward into the snow, having tripped over Tselitel. She had slipped moments before, and he walked into her before she'd had a chance to warn him.

"You're always hitting me," she joked, unable to resist the opportunity.

"Just wait until I get you home," he teased, pulling her to her feet.

"Ooh, do you always play so tough with skinny little coat racks?" she asked.

"Just when they trip me," he said, dusting her off.

"Everything alright?" they heard Milo ask from the nearby darkness.

"Yeah, we're fine," Hunt said. "She just tripped, is all."

"We can rest for a few minutes if you need to, Doctor," Milo said solicitously. "We're making better time than I expected, so there shouldn't be any problem reaching the shrine."

"No, let's keep moving," Hunt said before she could answer. "There's no telling what else we might encounter before we get there."

"Alright," Milo said doubtfully, moving off to the lead again.

"Thanks a lot!" Lily said, a touch of exasperation mingling with her usual good humor. "I could have used the chance to catch my breath."

"You're a big girl, aren't you?" Hunt said, giving her a little nudge to get her going.

"Not as big as I was this morning," she mumbled, picking up her feet as Gromyko's rope yanked on her.

"Pushing her pretty hard, aren't you?" Wellesley asked, as Hunt's rope went taut and he began to walk. "I don't see where a few minutes would have hurt our progress any."

"She's starting to peter out," Hunt said. "I could hear it in her voice. If I'd been nice to her she would have needed a break in twenty minutes. Now that she's a little mad she'll go farther."

"You're a crafty one, aren't you?" laughed Wellesley.

"Only when I need to be."

Falling silent and following the rope, he listened carefully to the sounds of the night. Occasionally he heard an animal in the distance, but nothing close enough to cause alarm. He wondered what creatures the storm might be concealing. Indeed, he reflected, they could have passed several without either party being aware of it.

Eventually the rope went slack ahead of him. Pulling it tight with his hands, he followed it until he gently bumped into Tselitel.

"Just need...a breather..." she explained.

The other two seemed to intuit this and didn't bother doubling back, simply pausing where they stood.

"How much...farther?" she asked.

"I reckon we're about halfway there," Hunt said. "Maybe a little further."

"Oh...goody!" she exclaimed sarcastically. "This is the worst...vacation ever!"

"Glad you haven't lost your sense of humor," Hunt said, smiling in the darkness. He waited a few moments. "Good to go?"

"Good as I'll ever be," she replied, tugging on the rope ahead to indicate she was ready. "My muscles are burning so badly that I feel like I'm on fire," she complained, shuffling away from him.

With the exception of a few more pauses for Tselitel's sake, the rest of the journey passed off uneventfully. Several hours later Milo paused in the snow, waiting for everyone else to catch up.

"This is it, the shrine," he said when they'd gathered around. Activating the light on the 600G, he illuminated a tall, narrow structure that loomed incongruently out of the snow and trees around it. Shaped like a pyramid and made of perfectly cut stone blocks, it bore no markings except for a trio of circles that were etched above a small door. Milo pulled it open and gestured for them to enter.

"Circles," Tselitel said when she saw them. "I wonder if they symbolized wholeness in their unconscious as well."

"They certainly had simple tastes for such an advanced race," Gromyko observed, ducking his head as he passed through the doorway. "And they seem to have been a short lot, too!"

Milo showed them inside and closed the door, bringing his light to the center of the building. It was totally empty within. The pyramid had three sides. Beside two of them deep ruts were cut into the ground beneath the structure and paved with dull gray stones.

"Incredible," Tselitel said, running her hand along the stone wall. "I don't know what it is, but something about this place speaks to me." She looked at the others and smiled apologetically. "Oh, I know that sounds hokey–" she started to say.

"Milo, give me the 600G," Hunt said abruptly.

Slowly his brother handed it to him, reluctant to part with it but knowing better than to argue.

"What are you doing?" Gromyko asked, as Hunt drew Wellesley from his shirt.

"Wellesley thinks he can interface with the 600G and speak through it," Hunt said. "These things work as communicators as well, and he thinks he can use the speaker to talk."

After a few moments a crackly voice came through the device, a bland, artificial monotone.

"Can you hear me?" the AI asked.

"Yes, we hear you," Hunt said, surprised to hear him through his ears for the first time in his life. "You sound...different."

"I had to synthesize a voice for this thing to broadcast," he explained. "It's not my natural voice, of course. But it'll have to do."

"Well, I don't know about you guys," Gromyko said, dropping his pack and busting out the little stove, "but I'm *hungry*. Let's get some food going."

"Always thinking with your stomach, Antonin," Wellesley said. "Can't you appreciate the place you're in for a few moments? This is an historic find. Honestly I doubted any of the *Kol-Prockian* shrines still stood since there was no one to take care of them."

"Oh, this is all beyond me," Gromyko said frankly. "I have no head for all this mystical mumbo jumbo. I'm just a simple man, really."

"One with a hero complex," Wellesley said sarcastically, to which the smuggler exploded with laughter.

"You've got to remember you're audible now, Wellesley," Hunt said.

"What makes you think I didn't mean to say that out loud?" the AI asked. Then, changing the subject, "Lily, you're right to feel that this place speaks to you. It is meant to. The old priests had a deep intuitive knowledge of the unconscious mind, and the symbolism by which it communicates. Naturally the human and *Kol-Prockian* mind differs considerably. But there's still a lot of overlap, and many of the symbols are profoundly meaningful to both races."

"Fascinating," she said, touching the stones once more. Then she looked down at the ruts. "What are those for?"

"They're meant to facilitate meditation. Being below the surface, they promote closeness to the planet and were thought to boost its power to assist those making the journey toward wholeness."

"And the circles above the doorway?" Tselitel asked, her excitement growing. "Are they meant to signify wholeness, just like for us?"

"Yes, the symbolism is the same," explained the AI. "The reason for three rings is that three, to the *Kol-Prockians*, represented mind, body, and spirit. It was in shrines like this that they sought to unite the three in a wholeness that would harmonize their lives. You probably haven't noticed, but there are three circles etched on the insides of these walls, reaching all the way around the room at different heights, equidistant from each other."

"You're right," Milo said, his mouth agape as he looked up at the one near the top. "I'd never noticed that before."

"Not surprising," replied the AI.

"But why stone?" asked Gromyko, setting several tins on a grill above the tiny flame that now flickered from his stove. "Surely a race as advanced as they could have managed something a little more...premium?"

"It was probably that 'vow of poverty' thing he mentioned earlier," Milo chimed in.

"No, it wasn't that 'vow of poverty' thing," Wellesley replied with annoyance. "That pertained only to the high priests, although many of the lower priests voluntarily took such an oath upon themselves. No, it was because stone is a part of the natural world. It symbolized the simple, organic completeness they sought through spiritual growth."

"You mean they held up rock as a role model?" chuckled Milo, squatting beside the stove and tapping one of the tins to see how hot it was.

"That's not so very far fetched," uttered the AI. "I know people whose entire *heads* are made of stone."

"You don't have to get nasty," objected Milo. "It was just a question."

"And you don't have to disrespect the customs of *Delek-Hai*," replied the AI. "These people dedicated their lives to finding wholeness, for themselves and others. You don't have to practice what they believed to respect them for their conviction."

"You've got to admit that stone isn't much to aspire to," pointed out Milo. "They sound simpleminded."

"I'd say a *wretch* like you isn't in much of a position to judge other people's aspirations," the AI said, the monotone somehow conveying a surprising amount of emotion.

"Wellesley," Tselitel cut in, trying to take a little of the heat out of the discussion, "I take it this shrine was built before the technologists became dominant in *Delek-Hai*?"

"Smart girl," Wellesley said with satisfaction. "Yes, that's precisely right. The *Prollok-Hee* had little use for places like this and abandoned them over time. Their view of the ancient ways eventually degenerated into outright scorn and contempt. They saw the old masters as blind primitives who had for too long rejected what technology could bring to the table. But it wasn't just that. The nature of *Kol-Prockian* society was changing. *Respect for the natural world*," he said, aiming his emphasis at Milo, "seemed passe and superstitious in the face of the dominance science had given them over their environment. They became too self-important for such things, and their religious life came to reflect that. Honestly it became little more than a covering for their materialism. You humans went through the same thing."

"Yeah, a long time ago," Hunt said, having read a little about the subject.

"Too bad," the AI said.

After their meal they split up. Gromyko, quite uncharacteristically, decided to try his hand at a little meditation. Settling into one of the ruts, he bowed towards the wall, humming in low tones. Milo, meanwhile, sat against the opposite wall, alone with his thoughts.

"Antonin will never make any headway like that," Wellesley chuckled quietly. "His entire knowledge of such practices is just a bundle of cliches."

"At least he's trying," Hunt said, his arm around Tselitel's shoulders as they sat against the cold wall that held the door. "I never thought he'd go in for something like that."

"It'll pass," opined the AI. "Like indigestion. He's a hardcore materialist. He's just a little intrigued by the spiritual life because of our surroundings."

"You're quite the old conservative, aren't you, Wellesley?" Tselitel asked after a few minutes.

"What do you mean?"

"Well, you don't practice *Delek-Hai*, but you respect it. You certainly get mad if anyone treats it lightly. And from the drift of your conversation I gathered that you regretted the loss of the old ways. Your sympathy seems to lie with them, despite the fact you wouldn't even exist without a very high degree of technological development."

"Never let this girl go, Rex," Wellesley said. "She's too smart!"

"Don't I know it," he said, drawing her close and kissing her head.

"But to answer your question," the AI said, "yes, I suppose I am. That was one of the things I relished about the *Kol-Prockian* fringe worlds: they still retained many of the traditions of their ancestors. *Koln* had been steeped in *Delek-Hai* from his earliest days, though his impulsive soul wasn't very fertile ground for a religion so harmonious. Our mutual appreciation for the past was a bonding point for us. I guess you could say we were both old conservatives. What about you?"

"Me?" Tselitel asked. "I don't really have a philosophical slant. People are going to do what they do, and I try to help them go about it in a healthy way. I try to help them find wholeness, like your priests."

"That's a rather uncommitted approach to take," Wellesley opined. "I should have thought you'd have a more concrete idea of how people ought to live."

"It's a big, swirling galaxy out there," she said with a chuckle. "And I'm just one girl trying to get through it with a level head."

"That's reasonable enough," the AI replied. "Can't bite off more than you can chew."

"I can't tell you how spiritual I feel right now," Gromyko said some time later, walking to them and stretching his arms over his head. "Everything seems to be at peace. But I must admit I now have a crick in my back that won't go away."

"The road to spiritual growth is long and hard, Antonin," the AI said, barely suppressing a laugh.

"Tell me about it," the smuggler yawned. "Anyway, I'm going to get some sleep. I'm beat."

"That's a good idea for all of us," Hunt said, squeezing Tselitel's shoulder and heading for his pack for a couple of thin emergency blankets. Laying one out on the floor, the two of them stretched out on top of it, covering themselves with the other.

"What about him?" Gromyko asked, speaking low and nodding toward Milo. "I hate to leave him ambling around while we're all asleep. Maybe we should take turns so one of us can watch him."

"No, don't do that," Wellesley said. "The 600G has cameras on the front. Just prop me up in the corner so I can watch the entire room. I'll let you know if he does anything."

The smuggler glanced at Hunt, who nodded his approval of the plan. Shrugging, he took Wellesley and put him in the corner. Returning to where Hunt and Tselitel lay, he put down his blankets a few feet away, positioning himself so he could watch Milo until he fell asleep.

"You know," Gromyko said without turning around, "I can't believe we forgot to bring extra flashlights. That little doohickey," here he stabbed a finger at the 600G, "is the only light we've got."

"That's why I hate leaving anywhere on short notice," Hunt said, rolling over and turning his back to Milo and the smuggler. "You forget the most obvious things."

"Heh, tell me about it!"

"Don't you want to keep watch with them?" Tselitel whispered, laying on her back, her eyes sparkling from the dim light the 600G cast from the corner.

"What for?" he asked quietly, settling as comfortably as he could on the hard floor. "If those two can't manage it between them, then a third set of eyes won't make a difference."

"Oh, I just meant you seem so suspicious of him still," she replied, raising her head slightly to look at Milo over his hip. "I think he's proved himself to us. He could have betrayed us a number of times now, and he hasn't chosen to do so. But you three are still pushing on him."

"Call it an instinct," he said. "We've lived on the edge so long that we've developed a kind of sixth sense. On a planet like this you either have it or you end up dead. It's a nose for trouble, and Milo stinks. But," he added, "on very rare occasions it's wrong. So far he hasn't misbehaved, so we're giving him a little more rope as time goes by, letting him stretch his wings a bit. We ought to have him figured out by the time we're finished at the temple."

"Why there?"

"Again, just an instinct," he smiled. "Now, go to sleep."

Hunt saw her close her eyes and fold her hands on her stomach. Too tense to fall asleep quickly, he listened to the sounds of the storm outside. It had regained much of its former ferocity since they'd been in there, more or less following the prediction of the 600G. His mind wandered over the events of the day, sticking uncomfortably on their walk through the darkness with Milo at the lead. His skin crawled as he thought afresh on how totally they'd been within his power; how at any moment he could have left them to their fate had he chosen to. And yet, he hadn't. Hunt had to admit that was a point in his favor, for there was no way the situation could have escaped his wily brother's attention. The idea made him frown. Deep down he *wanted* to find his brother guilty, to receive confirmation of his suspicions. But Tselitel was right: so far, he'd acted well.

Thinking of her made him smile, and he opened his eyes just to watch her breathing peacefully in the near darkness of the shrine. Her face relaxed and serene, she reminded him of a delicate flower blooming in springtime. Unconsciously his breathing began to follow hers, and before he knew it he was drifting away to sleep.

He seemed to have slept for only a few moments when he felt a hand on his face.

"Wake up, Rex," Tselitel said tensely. "We have a visitor."

CHAPTER 16

In an instant Hunt snapped to his other side, searching the room for the intruder but seeing no one. All he could see, besides the unconscious smuggler, was Milo lying on his back, petrified in his blankets.

"No, Rex," Tselitel said quietly, patting his shoulder and pointing to the peak of the structure. "Up there."

Looking up he saw a whitish-gray mist floating above them all, its outer edges undulating ceaselessly like ripples near the shore.

"*Kolak. Pree nol freh selehnah,*" Wellesley said in a low voice.

"*Keewah, belen poh fahfal selehnah,*" replied the mist in a hauntingly childish whisper.

"They've been talking like that for several minutes," Tselitel breathed in his ear. "I was too scared to move until now, or I would have awoken you sooner."

"*Peeleth, morraw feelee porum tass felek toro bahn vee?*" the AI asked in his monotone.

"*Pran!*" the mist whispered emphatically. "*Farna ollakuth breenith porafon!*"

"Is it friendly?" Tselitel whispered to Hunt, unable to rip her eyes from the insubstantial figure.

"Decidedly so," Wellesley answered quietly, before darting off another quick sentence in *Kol-Prockian*. "It's incredible," the AI said. "But his name is *Selek-Pey*. Well, it's not *actually Selek-Pey*, but a sort of imprint that he left on the planet."

"And who was *Zelek-Pey*?" asked Hunt.

"*Selek-Pey!*" whispered the figure harshly, causing Tselitel to jump behind him.

"He's particular about his name," Wellesley explained. "And he has a right to be. *Selek-Pey* was the greatest of the old masters. It was he who originally discovered the true power of Delta-13. He didn't found *Delek-Hai*, but his designation of this planet as a holy world, and the enlightenment that followed, made it the dominant force in *Kol-Prockian* society for thousands of years."

"So what are we talking to? Some kind of planetary memory?"

"Exactly. You see, for most people Delta-13 only gives. It helps them process their inner world and receives nothing in return. But something about *Selek-Pey* appealed to Delta-13, and it kept a record of him from his day down to ours. You can think of it as a sort of virtual version of him. He communed on a daily basis with this world for decades, so you can bet that this is a good representation of what he was like."

"But why is he here?" Tselitel asked, still very much concerned.

"A better question would be to ask why *we're* here," Wellesley said. "In effect, we're in his house, and he wanted to know why. This shrine was dedicated to him long ago, and it is one of his favorite places to stay, after the great temple of *Berek-Po*."

"I-I've never seen him here before," Milo stuttered. "I never would have st-stayed here if I knew it was haunted!"

"It isn't *haunted*, you dummy," Wellesley snapped. "A homeowner isn't a squatter in his own house, and *Selek-Pey* can't *haunt* his own place of learning and reflection."

"What in the world is *that?!*" exclaimed Gromyko, nearly jumping out of his blankets when he saw the mist.

"Calm down, Antonin," Hunt said evenly, regaining his composure before the rest. "He's a friend."

"Some friend!" he replied, trying to make sense of what he was seeing. "Am I asleep? Is this a dream?" he asked himself, rubbing his eyes and looking again.

"You're very much awake," Wellesley said. "Now relax and quit gawking at him. You're going to upset him.

"Him? The fog comes with a pronoun?"

"It's a long story," Hunt said. "Just relax."

He looked uneasily at Hunt and then back at the mist, venturing a doubtful wave of his hand to *Selek-Pey*.

"*Poroth veree mollotrom!*" the fog whispered excitedly. "*Voth korosat beelay porumadach!*"

"What did he say?" Gromyko asked, not sure he wanted to know.

"He says he likes your mustache very much," Wellesley translated. "And that he recognizes in you a kindred spirit."

"Really?" the smuggler asked

"*Reth gorodalan vieth varan*," continued *Selek-Pey*.

"Yes. He's been watching you in particular ever since we came here. You see, *Selek-Pey* was a very…passionate figure in his time, not known for restraint. But he breathed *Delek-Hai* to the very marrow of his bones, and lived it with every ounce of his being. Surrendering completely to it, he achieved a deeper connection to the inner world than anyone among my people has ever been known to. That is why he left an imprint on the planet: he was the high water mark of all the beings who have come here over millennia."

"And he likes Gromyko?" the smuggler asked.

"I said he recognized a kindred spirit," the AI said punctiliously, "not that–"

"Tell him that Gromyko is honored to meet such a worthy figure," cut in the smuggler importantly.

"I will do no such thing," Wellesley said emphatically. "I'm not going to play messenger boy for a–"

"*Malack dereth 'G-Groomeekah'*," said the voice. "*Valan en valan.*"

"What did he say?" Gromyko asked eagerly.

"Wellesley?" Hunt prodded when several seconds of silence ensued.

The AI sighed.

"He said he wishes to speak with Gromyko privately," Wellesley said slowly. "'As one brother to another,' were his exact words."

Selek-Pey slowly descended from the ceiling and made his way to Wellesley and the 600G. In an instant Gromyko was on his feet and huddled in the corner with them, talking quietly with the fog, the AI acting as interpreter.

"Looks like we've been squeezed out," Hunt said philosophically, rolling onto his back. "Antonin is the man of the hour."

"Odd that it should choose him," she replied, watching the trio a moment longer before emulating Hunt's position. "I just hope Antonin doesn't say anything to tick him off. I'd hate to have a million year old ghost as an enemy."

"I wouldn't worry about it. He clearly likes Antonin."

"What are they doing?" Milo asked, skittering across the floor to them, his eyes fixed on the trio.

"They're just talking, Milo," Hunt said dismissively.

"But about what?" he asked. "And what's he doing here tonight, anyway? D-Do you think he wants revenge for all the artifacts I've taken over the years?"

"If that's all he wanted he would have acted by now," Hunt said, closing his eyes and folding his hands on his stomach. "Now be quiet, or go back to your corner and wait. This could take a while."

Muttering something to himself, Milo backed away from his brother and returned to his blankets, watching the fog the entire time.

"His conscience is really bothering him," Tselitel observed, once he was out of earshot.

"It ought to," replied Hunt coldly.

As the minutes passed slowly, Tselitel kept anxiously glancing up at the fog. Finally she settled onto her back.

Drawing one of Hunt's hands off his stomach, she gripped it with both of hers, working it nervously with her fingers.

"What, is your conscience bothering you, too?" he chuckled, considering such an idea utterly impossible.

"It's not that," she said, stealing another look in spite of herself. "It's just…"

"Just what?"

"*Selek-Pey* reminds me of the nightmare figures that woman put into my head," she whispered, barely making a sound from the fear that they would hear her and return. "I know it's irrational. But the voice, the immateriality of him! I can't get past it!"

"Fear itself is irrational," Hunt replied. "You can't argue it down. You can only push it aside until it loses its power over you."

"I don't think I can," she said, twisting to look again before lying flat. She pulled her hood over her head as though she'd like to crawl in there and stay.

"Then just lie here," Hunt said, slipping his arm under her head and around her shoulders, "and don't look anymore." His move was meant to comfort her. But it had the added purpose of pinning her to the floor so she couldn't keep looking and adding to her own fear.

"But what if it comes over here?" she asked.

"Then I'll deal with it," Hunt said, raising his hand, a little bit of smoke dancing between his fingers. "Now, hush."

He hadn't the least idea whether the mist was susceptible to his gift or not. But it had the desired effect of calming her down, which was all he sought to accomplish.

Eventually they heard footsteps approaching, and Gromyko's head appeared over them.

"Our friend has left for the day," the smuggler said, holding Wellesley and the 600G in his hands. Squatting down beside Rex, he put them on the floor. "What a character he is! You'd think he'd be some kind of foggy mystic, always talking in proverbs and whatnot. But he's just like you or I!

Perhaps moreso, in fact, seeing as he has no material concerns to hold back the full expression of his personality. It's a curious thing, the effects that everyday pressures have on our personalities..." he said musingly.

"What did he have to say?" Hunt asked, trying to get his friend back on course.

"A lot," Gromyko replied, dropping onto his rear and resting his elbows on his knees. "But not a lot that is relevant for our present journey."

"Mostly they caught up like a couple of old school chums," said Wellesley tartly, envious that the illustrious *Selek-Pey* had chosen Gromyko instead of himself as his compatriot. "A great deal of flattery was exchanged, and very little business was conducted."

"The forming of strong personal bonds is never frivolous, my friend," Gromyko said philosophically. "They are the foundation of any effective collaboration. And that will be important when we reach the great temple."

"And why is that?" asked Hunt.

"Because there is a chamber in the temple which holds what we seek. *Selek-Pey* wouldn't elaborate on just what it was. But when we told him our situation he said the 'secret of the temple' would guide our path. But we're gonna need him to help us find it, because they put the chamber inside a hopelessly complex labyrinth."

"A labyrinth?" asked Tselitel. "It's like something out of ancient mythology."

"It was a rite of passage," replied Wellesley. "You see, every path looks exactly the same. There is no way to memorize your way through, or figure it out. One would have to call upon the planet for assistance, and only those who had achieved wholeness could do so at will. It was the final step before attaining the rank of high priest, so it was almost impossibly difficult."

"But after I explained our situation to him, *Selek-Pey* agreed to guide us through," Gromyko said proudly.

"Did you ask him if there's a tunnel into the facility?" asked Hunt.

"Yes, but he didn't know," replied Wellesley. "It seems he can't access this 'secret' that is supposed to guide us. Probably because of his immaterial nature he can no longer interact with whatever it is and extract the data it holds."

"Well, what brought him out tonight?" Tselitel asked. "Was it Antonin's meditation?"

"Certainly not!" exclaimed Wellesley with a laugh, the idea beyond ridiculous to him. "It would take more than a little humming to get *Selek-Pey*'s attention."

Gromyko frowned at the AI but said nothing.

"Was it me?" asked Milo, drawing a little closer to the group and looking persecuted.

"Why would he want you?" asked Wellesley, genuinely surprised. "No, it was…something else."

"What?" asked Tselitel. "Was it something bad?"

"He said he wanted to know who had brought darkness into his shrine," Gromyko answered, looking at Rex. "He said he'd never seen such a shadow follow in the wake of a single individual before. Your capacity to inflict suffering is greater than anyone he's ever known, he said, with the possible exception of one man."

"Who was that?" Hunt asked.

"I don't know," the smuggler said with a shrug. "I asked, but he wouldn't tell me."

"I take it he didn't approve of my being in his shrine?" Hunt asked with a knowing look on his face.

"I wouldn't say that," Wellesley replied. "But he was awfully curious about you. I told him as much as I could, before the mutual admiration society kicked into gear and all productive conversation ended."

"Hey, don't talk that way about *Selek-Pey*," Gromyko chided the AI. "He's fantastic. And he clearly knows a quality individual when he sees one."

"How would you know?" retorted the AI.

"That's enough," Hunt said firmly, ending the argument. "Is he going to materialize again, or will he meet us at the temple?"

"He wasn't clear about that," Wellesley said. "But I think we'll see him before we go tomorrow."

"Alright," Hunt said, looking at the 600G. "It's only a few hours until dawn. Everyone get as much sleep as you can. We move out as soon as the weather breaks."

Gromyko put Wellesley back where he could watch Milo, and then moved his blankets off to another corner so he could lie awake and talk animatedly to himself in whispers about his conversation with *Selek-Pey*. He was just far enough away that Hunt couldn't make out his mutterings.

"I think *Selek-Pey* has made a buddy for life out of Antonin," Tselitel said, chuckling at the spectacle.

"Most likely," Hunt said without interest, pulling the blanket over himself and turning towards her. "Now, do *you* intend to stay up all night talking, or can we get some sleep?"

"I'll be quiet," she said with a little grin, closing her lips and making as though she was zipping them shut with her fingers.

"Good," he replied, putting his hand on the stomach of her jacket and drawing her close. Within minutes he was asleep.

As night transitioned into morning the storm continued to batter the region. Everything for miles around was painted white, the trees showing not so much as a twig that wasn't caked with snow. The wind continued to blow hard from the east, cruelly draining the heat from any creature that had been unwise enough to venture out into the dim morning light.

Hunt was the first to awaken. Surprised to find his hand still on Lily's stomach, he drew it back slowly and got up, silently making his way to Wellesley.

"Sleep well?" the AI asked quietly, careful not to wake the others.

"Good enough," Hunt replied, squatting down and looking at the 600G. Flicking through the menus on its display, he found the weather setting. "I can't believe the storm is still blowing like this," he muttered, more to himself. "It's supposed to weaken pretty soon. But it'll strengthen sometime after nightfall." He glanced at Milo, who slept facing the wall, his back to the rest of them. "Did you rip the rest of the data from this thing?" he whispered.

"Oh, yeah," the AI said with satisfaction. "Even the stuff he thought he'd deleted. These government models are really tenacious about holding onto data once it's been entered. We have a complete record of every hideout, stash, and Underground pub he's ever saved to this thing."

"Good. Never know when it might come in handy."

"You planning to turn him in or something? Hand this data over to the Order?"

"I wouldn't give them a bucket of warm spit," Hunt said. "Not after they threatened Lily."

"Then what's all this for?" the AI asked.

"Call it insurance, just in case things get nasty once we blow that room," Hunt said. "There's no telling how the government will react. They'll certainly scour Midway looking for us, and when that fails to turn us up they'll spread out into the forests nearby. We might need a hideaway deep in the wilds to wait for things to blow over."

"If they ever do," Wellesley said. "If they end up with the least idea who was responsible they'll hunt you for life, you know. All of you will be outlaws till your dying day."

"Better than mindless slaves," Hunt said.

"How did we go from working in a greenhouse and snatching the odd artifact to this?" the AI asked. "We used to live such a bland, boring, stupid life. I kinda miss it."

"We're just lucky, I guess," Hunt said.

"Guess so," agreed Wellesley. "But I'll be glad when we can part company with half of this lot. Oh, I love you and Lily, as you know. But the other two…"

"I can see Milo," Hunt said, glancing at his brother as he spoke. "But what's got you so bent out of shape with Antonin? You've never liked him, even after all he's done for us."

"He's too flashy, too in love with his own legend," the AI said. "Why, half the time he was talking to *Selek-Pey*, it was 'Gromyko thinks *this*,' and 'Gromyko would like to express *that*,' and so on and on. What kind of idiot talks in the third person? I'm surprised *Selek-Pey* didn't realize what a pompous little blowhard he really is. His so-called 'movement' has long since collapsed, and he's still strutting around like some kind of royalty. Whatever tiny claim to recognition he once had has vanished forever, and he ought to have the sense to pull in his plumage."

"That's something he'd never do," Hunt replied. "It'd be the death of him. He needs the attention just to feel normal."

"Heh, some normal," Wellesley said dismissively. "But for the life of me, I just can't understand what *Selek-Pey* sees in him!"

"He has that effect on some people," Hunt replied with the certainty of personal experience. "I guess his mystique reaches beyond the human race."

"A high priest should know better," Wellesley said. "I studied the life of *Selek-Pey* back when I served the fringe independence movement. The middle and inner worlds had long since fallen under the sway of the *Prollok-Hee*, and only the outer planets held true to the old masters of *Delek-Hai*. And *Selek-Pey* was our patron, Rex. Even those of us who didn't actually believe looked to his life and example during the darkest days and found strength." The AI sighed. "But I guess the old saying is true: you should never meet your heroes."

"I wouldn't say that," replied Hunt with a grin. "After all, you've met me, haven't you?"

"Very cute," the AI said sarcastically. "I could understand if he'd grown attached to you: you're purposeful and honorable, though apparently your darkness is something that people can detect from a mile away. And Lily would make sense, too, especially with her background as a healer. In fact, they ought to be bosom companions, especially after she helped you achieve greater balance between you and your gift. In that regard she has acted just as Delta-13 itself acts. But he chose *Gromyko*. Of all people, why *Gromyko*?"

"I guess some things are just inscrutable," Hunt said, trying to back subtly away from the topic. He wanted to let the AI air his grievances. But his loyalty to the charming smuggler kept him from listening indefinitely as he was beaten upon without being able to defend himself. Wellesley got the message and backed off.

"When do you plan to wake the rest of them?" he asked.

"Not for another hour yet," Hunt said, leaning against the wall and sliding to the floor. "We've got a long road ahead, and I want them ready for what's to come. Especially Lily. I don't think she's really recovered from the assault she was under when I rescued her. She said last night that *Selek-Pey*'s misty form reminded her of the figures she saw."

"I'm not sure anyone could recover from that, not truly," said the AI frankly. "To have your world penetrated by a vile assassin and then filled with all the darkest fantasies of your unconscious would be shattering. Everything you held to be stable in the world would vanish in an instant. The instinctive fear that the figures could return at any time would haunt anyone, especially someone like Lily. She couldn't kid herself that the figures were just a product of her imagination like some people: she knows the nature of the unconscious too well. She knows they're always inside her, waiting in the eves for the right stimulus to spring forth once more. An experience like that would be transformational, for good or bad."

"She *does* seem more vulnerable lately," reflected Hunt. "Not as sure of herself. She's sticking to me like glue. Of course, that could just be the environment we're in. She's been out of her element ever since she left her apartment." He paused for a moment. "What do you mean, 'for good or bad?' What good could possibly come from an experience like that?"

"Sometimes our worst experiences help us grow the most. Pain tends to be the best teacher, and not just for humans. Most of the *Kol-Prockians* who came to Delta-13 to get help from the priests had suffered some kind of terrible blow and were trying to recover. It shook them out of old thought patterns and made them grapple anew with life. It might be the same for Lily. To be honest she never seemed very happy to me while I was with her."

"She was scared out of her wits that she'd be caught!" laughed Hunt quietly. "You can't hold that against her. Playing amateur spy while under constant surveillance would be enough to twist anyone out of shape."

"Sure, but there was more than that. I sensed a dull lack of stimulation, even in her work. Naturally she was happy with the progress Vilks had made. But deep inside something failed to move. I think at one time she *lived* for her work, you know, really drawing every breath in its service. But that must have run out along the way, and the lack of any other outlet left her empty inside. I suspect she came to Delta-13 for more than humanitarian reasons. I think she sought an escape."

"What could she have to escape from?" asked Hunt, glancing at her sleeping form, her chest rising and falling slowly. "She was a celebrity in the inner worlds. Shoot, we'd even heard of her way out here."

"None of that matters if it doesn't feed your soul," Wellesley replied. "That's something about both humans and *Kol-Prockians*: you both have instinctive drives that must be satisfied. And the rarefied nature of the technologically advanced societies that humans, and formerly, the *Kol-Prockians*, both inhabit keeps you from satisfying them. You're stuck trying to wring what you can out of success and accolades. But it doesn't work very well. Only on a planet like this, where the authorities artificially keep the technology level low to facilitate your imprisonment, can anything like a normal life be led."

"And you think she sought us out for that purpose? A sort of 'retrograde vacation' from a life that no longer proved satisfying?"

"Plenty of other people have done that," the AI replied. "People from both our races. Ever heard of hobby farms?"

Rex eyed her for a while, letting his mind wander over their mutual history before he spoke again.

"What do we do about her gift?"

"I haven't the slightest idea," Wellesley replied. "It's incredible. The old masters would have envied her ability to return balance to an individual who'd been overwhelmed by the unconscious. In all honesty she probably saved your life, or at least your sanity. But she was only able to embrace it because you were in mortal peril. The fact that her unconscious was already being forced to the surface, though in a very negative way, probably helped. Her gift likely hitched a ride on the stream of content that flooded up from the back. It's too bad neither of us know enough to help her develop it. I take it you consider the Order–"

"Out of the question," cut in Hunt decisively. "Even when all this is over, who knows what those snakes will have up their sleeves. They want revolution. Their 'mission' doesn't end when we blow up that room. They'd probably try to twist Lily to some purpose of their own, one that we couldn't see coming until it was too late."

"You know," Wellesley said after a few moments, "*Selek-Pey* might be able to help her."

"Really?" asked Hunt, intrigued.

"Sure. It would put a lot more pressure on Lily, not being guided hands on, as it were. There'd be no Wanda to jump inside her head and help her make a connection, like you had. But he might be able to guide her along."

"Provided he gets past his fascination with 'Groomeekah,'" Hunt laughed.

"Naturally," replied Wellesley, irritated to be reminded. "But I can't imagine that will last long."

"Well, ask him next time he pops up," Hunt said, closing his eyes and leaning his head against the wall. "Could be the old gentleman will help us."

"Could be," seconded the AI. A few seconds passed silently. "Would you do me a favor?"

"Sure," Hunt replied, rocking his head back and forth against the wall.

"Would you unplug me from this thing? It's all well and good being able to talk out loud. But I prefer the privacy of communicating through skin. I feel naked talking like this."

An hour later the group left the shrine. *Selek-Pey* didn't return, to the chagrin of Gromyko, who'd tossed and turned all night in nervous anticipation of another conversation with him. With great reluctance he closed the small door to the shrine once the other three were outside.

"I thought we'd see him again," he said with disappointment.

"Don't worry," Tselitel said, laying a hand on his arm. "We'll see him again at the temple."

"How far away is it, Mister Guide?" the smuggler asked, as Milo walked past him to assume the lead.

"Two days," he replied without looking at him. Once they were roped together he mutely began his march. Gromyko fell in behind him, looking downcast.

The wind had finally ceased, save for an occasional breeze that swept little handfuls of snow off the glimmering white ground beneath their feet. The sun shone blindingly upon them through a chance hole in the clouds.

"Two more days," Tselitel said, walking beside Hunt, holding the rope in her hand. "Honestly I didn't think I'd make it this far. There were a couple of times yesterday that I nearly collapsed."

"Couldn't have known that from the way you lit up inside the shrine," he said.

"In a different life I would have been an archeologist, I'm sure," she replied, taking his hand and swinging it between them. "I like old stuff."

"I guess that's why you like me," he replied with a grin.

"You know, I've never asked about that. How old are you?"

"I don't know. Thirty, thirty-five, maybe," he said offhandedly.

"What, you don't know?"

"It's not like birthdays are very important around here. Most of us just live until we die, anyway. And with no family to celebrate with, well, it's just not something to get excited about. What would I do, anyhow? Gift myself a snowball?"

"Everyone should remember their birthday," Tselitel said firmly. "It's the beginning of your story."

"Mine's never been a story worth knowing about," Hunt replied factually.

"Don't say that," she said, pulling on his hand and looking into his eyes. "Don't ever say that." She was silent for a moment to let her point sink in. "Do you remember what date you were born on?"

"Honestly, I don't."

"Then we'll just have to pick one and celebrate," she said in a brighter voice. "Once this is all over, of course."

He squeezed her hand tightly, warmed by her tender, generous sentiments.

Except for a stop shortly past noon, the group walked all day, their journey eased by the gap in the storm. Eventually the sun dropped towards the horizon, and the dense clouds many miles away blocked it from view. As their surroundings grew dark Milo addressed the group.

"Our next stop is at least four hours from here. According to the 600G the storm will hit us again in a few hours. If we hustle we should just make it. It's gonna be bad, so we'll have to keep pushing until we're under cover for the night."

"And you're only telling us this *now*?" Gromyko asked.

"The opening in the storm was bigger a few hours ago,"

Milo explained. "I checked the 600G from time to time, and it looked fine. Something made it tighten up all of a sudden."

"Sounds like it could use a tune up," the smuggler said moodily, adjusting his hood against a light breeze that had begun to blow against them.

"That, or the planet is getting temperamental," Wellesley commented, as the group got moving again.

"Can it do that?" asked Hunt. "Mess around with the weather?"

"Who's to say it can't?"

"Wellesley thinks it's Delta-13 doing it?" Tselitel asked, looking up at him.

"He thinks it's possible," he replied, squeezing her hand and pulling her along. "Come on: we're falling behind."

CHAPTER 17

"Just a little bit further!" Milo tried to shout over the gale that buffeted them. But it stole his words the instant they left his mouth.

"What?" bellowed Gromyko with equal success.

Gesturing for the group to close in on him, Milo put his hands on their shoulders and drew them close.

"The temple is only a little bit further," he yelled at the top of his frigid lungs.

The storm had redoubled around them, dropping the temperature until even the veterans of Delta-13 were shivering from the cold. Tselitel was numb in her limbs, her face ghostly pale. Packing her close against his side to protect her from the wind, Hunt kept his arm around her back, half-dragging her willowy form through the snow.

"It shouldn't be more than ten or fifteen minutes!" Milo shouted, before turning around and walking shakily into the hail of massive flakes the wind drove against them.

"It's like the planet doesn't want us to get to the temple," Gromyko yelled to Hunt. His jet black mustache had long since frozen with snow, making him look forty years older. "Why would it do that?" he asked, not expecting a response. Twisting in the snow, he held his hand before his eyes to keep the flakes out of his vision until he found Milo. Seeing his silhouette recede into the swirl of white ahead, he struggled after him.

"It's not just us," Wellesley said, his voice incongruently

calm in the tempestuous weather. "When I interfaced with the 600G a few hours ago, the weather was the same all across the planet. Something has Delta-13 upset. I'd bet my life on it."

The information intrigued Hunt, but he had something more pressing to think about: keeping Tselitel from becoming an ice sculpture before they reached the sanctuary of the great temple. Like clumsy clubs her arms and legs wagged awkwardly as she walked. Often the only thing keeping her upright was Hunt's powerful right arm wrapped firmly around her slender middle. Afraid that each icy moment in the cold was carrying her closer to death, he moved as quickly as the added burden of her form would permit. Panting from exhaustion, it took all the strength he had to keep from collapsing into the snow himself. His awareness of the world around him shrank to the ground immediately in front of him. His face long since numbed, he no longer felt the sting when the wind hurled hard, icy flakes against his skin.

"A little further, baby," he muttered, too weak to raise his voice loud enough to be heard. "Just a little more."

Putting his chin against his chest and closing his eyes, feeling his way with the rope, he gave every last ounce of effort he could muster. It wasn't until he felt hands feebly grasping at him and Tselitel that he looked up and saw they'd arrived.

A covered stone entrance, surrounded and hidden in a dense growth of trees, stood before them, rising out of the ground. Behind it, as far as he could see, were only more trees. Milo and Gromyko, their own hands numb, attempted to guide him and the scarcely conscious Tselitel inside the protective overhang it provided. The floor of the entrance was also made of stone and slightly raised off the ground. Hunt's boot caught on the lip that this formed and he fell down hard against it. Gromyko snatched Tselitel before she tumbled down with him.

Unable to get up, his own limbs nearly useless by this time, he crawled farther inside and rolled onto his back panting.

"What is...this place?" he asked, his voice barely audible

over the howl of the wind tearing past the edges of the enclosure. "Where is the temple?"

"This is it," Milo said, dropping to the ground next to his brother once he and Gromyko had helped Tselitel inside the enclosure. Exhausted himself, he lay still and breathed for a few moments before continuing. "This is the entrance. The temple is underground."

"Underground?" Hunt asked in disbelief, having always imagined a massive, impressive structure like he'd seen in books about such buildings on Earth. "Why?"

"Search me," his brother said. "But it'll be warmer in there. Let's get you two inside."

With the smuggler's help Milo managed to get the ancient door open and the barely ambulatory members of the group inside and down the long flight of stairs that followed. Together they collapsed in a large antechamber.

"It's surprisingly warm in here," Gromyko said, pushing his hood back and feeling the air. "In fact it's downright hot!"

"The temple was ingeniously built to take advantage of a nearby geothermal vent," Wellesley said, once they'd slipped him off Rex's neck and connected him to the 600G. "It provides natural heat to the entire structure."

"I'd always wondered how this place stayed warm with no one to take care of it," Milo said, slipping off his hat. "Frankly it used to give me the creeps."

Slipping off his gloves and feeling the warm stone beneath him, Hunt struggled to get Tselitel's outerwear off so she could warm up faster. Floating on the fringe of consciousness, she tried to help but mostly got in the way.

"Just let me do it," he said through rubbery lips. "It'll just be a minute."

Soon they were all stretched out on the floor, letting the stones radiate their heat directly into their bodies. The blood quickly returned to their extremities, flooding them with exquisite sensations. Quickly they fell asleep, their exhaustion complete.

Hours later Gromyko awoke to the sound of talking nearby. Through half-open eyes he saw the familiar form of *Selek-Pey* floating above them all, whispering quietly to Wellesley. He jerked upright, about to speak when he remembered the others. Moving quietly to the two talkers, he waved to the mist and picked up Wellesley and the 600G. Carrying them to a far corner of the barren stone room, followed closely by *Selek-Pey*, he sat down, his back against the warm wall.

"They could make this place into a resort," he said, closing his eyes and savoring the warmth for a moment.

"A shameful end for such an important structure," Wellesley said in his monotone.

"Oh, I didn't mean it like that," Gromyko said. "I just meant they knew how to build things back in the old days."

"May I continue with *Selek-Pey*?" Wellesley asked impatiently. "Or do you have more to say?"

"I'm done," the smuggler said, shutting his eyes with a frown.

"Thank you," the AI said, returning to his conversation in *Kol-Prockian*.

The smuggler listened for several minutes, recognizing a word here or there that he'd heard back in the shrine. Not a patient soul, he began drumming his fingers and wagging his feet as the minutes passed. Finally he spoke.

"Are you finished, yet?" he asked with exasperation. "I didn't bring you two over here just to listen."

"*Pralelat, boro meen Groomeekah,*" *Selek-Pey* said.

"What did he say?" the smuggler asked excitedly. "I heard my name in the midst of all that gobbledygook."

"*Poroth, vahn borom veen corothonea,*" replied Wellesley.

"*Nigath borbor vahn, deetoth kahn morranee, Allokanah,*" said the fog, as though reasoning with the AI.

"Wellesley!" prodded Gromyko.

"Will you shut your mouth for a moment?" he snapped. "There's more to this conversation than just you." And then, "*Nelegeneth, porat bleren keeso Delek-Hai. Vee borum kee Tehsaleetahl, Hoont. Meren seylat.*"

For several seconds the mist was silent. Gromyko looked up at it through his dark eyebrows, recognizing the names of his friends and dying to know what they were talking about.

"*Selek-Pey* has misgivings about Rex and Lily," Wellesley said with concern. "I've told him that they are both friends, but he is doubtful. The darkness he finds in Rex has come to trouble him greatly. And he's all but made up his mind that he shouldn't be in the temple at all. Strangely enough, he feels the same way about Lily."

"What darkness could she possibly be hiding?" asked Gromyko, genuinely surprised. "She's about the nicest woman I've ever met."

"I as well," replied the AI. "But *Selek-Pey* isn't the sort to make this up. He must know something we don't."

"Like what?"

"If I knew that, *I* would be the master, and not *Selek-Pey*. But he refuses to help us as long as they are among us. He fears that the secrets of the temple will be misused by them."

"Let me speak to him," Gromyko said, standing up and looking into the mist. "Perhaps a brother can make the matter clear."

"You're not his brother, Antonin," Wellesley said. "He only said–"

"Just translate what I say, alright?" the smuggler cut in. "*Selek-Pey*, sickness is the road to health."

"What in the world are you talking about?" Wellesley asked.

"Translate, or I'll toss you out into the snow!" growled Gromyko with instant passion. "Sickness is the road to health."

"*Perek, boolath merik dur foan balan.*"

"When the body is attacked, it makes itself unwell, that it may *become* well," the smuggler continued.

"*Bef tahr solofon, boyn morthath derendalik, duff tatratorn.*"

"The world makes itself dark, that it may shine on the morrow."

"*Jelek wosumik lupason hee, rugnan elioamanta valnu iturnash.*"

"*Quervan,*" the mist replied thoughtfully.

"'It is so,'" Wellesley translated.

"Rex and Lily bring darkness..."

"Are you out of your mind?" exploded the AI. "You want to argue his point for him?"

"Just say it!"

"*Tehsaleetahl en Hoont lupason nar...*" said the AI reluctantly.

"That darkness, in swallowing darkness, may allow the morning light to shine brighter."

"*Mesat lupason, wevor san lupason, beret elioama terleth sahfon rilalion.*"

For several anxious moments the smuggler watched the mist. Its edges forever undulating, it gave off the impression of being perpetually in motion even when stationary.

"*Pren, viloth corva, Groomeekah,*" it said at last. "*Ur sallan hetheth mallol.*"

"Your words are wise," the AI translated. "Yet in the mouth of any but Gromyko, I should not have been moved."

"*Should not have been...*" said the smuggler to himself, trying to work out his meaning.

"He believes you," Wellesley said. "It seems you really *do* have an effect on people, even if they're only a memory. Every argument I could muster before fell on deaf ears. Although he doesn't seem overly convinced. I think he still has his doubts."

"You mean *that's* what you were talking about earlier?" he asked.

"What did you think we were doing? Exchanging recipes?"

"I hadn't any idea."

"That's not unusual for you," the AI said. But in spite of the tartness of his words, he felt a faint glow of respect for the smuggler beginning to grow within him. In a few eloquent sentences he'd done more than the AI had managed in twenty minutes of cool, well-reasoned argument. It was the appeal of emotional, poetic imagery that had won the day, he decided. It reminded him of some of the more flowery graffiti that was spread about Midway.

"Then he will still guide us through the maze?"

"Yes. Once the others are awake we can all proceed."

"I'll get them up," Gromyko said, moving abruptly towards them.

"Just hang on a minute," Wellesley said, stopping him. "A few more hours won't make a difference to our mission. But it'll mean a great deal to them. Let them recover for a while."

"But how can I rest when we're *so close* to our goal?" replied the smuggler. "I would go now, except the others would never forgive me."

"There's nothing to stop you from exploring the rest of the temple if you want to kill some time. Just leave the maze alone. Without *Selek-Pey* you'd get hopelessly lost."

"What, you don't think I have the necessary wholeness to make it through?" asked Gromyko.

"*You?*" laughed the AI, feeling no further reply was necessary.

He knew it was a ridiculous question even before he'd asked it. But his pride was wounded all the same, and he wandered away from Wellesley grumbling under his breath.

The temple was dimly lit by ancient lights that the technologists had left behind. At one time they must have illuminated the massive space brilliantly. But centuries of neglect had left most of them broken, leaving much of the structure in darkness. Carefully probing the gloom with his foot whenever he encountered it, Gromyko walked slowly from room to room, gawking like a tourist at the architecture. The rooms were vast yet simple, meant both to humble their occupants and to draw them into the natural world.

Hearing his feet echo as he walked, he was unable to

resist the temptation to whistle, howl, and make a general ruckus once he'd gotten too far for Wellesley to hear him. Hearing the sounds reverberate off the barren walls and double back on him again was the most fun he'd had since before the Underground fell. Getting carried away with his fun, he didn't notice *Selek-Pey* behind him until the ancient memory whistled himself.

"*Dahhhh!*" Gromyko exclaimed, bouncing nervously on his feet as he turned to see what was behind him. Seeing the mist, he grew self-conscious of all the racket he'd been making. "I-I didn't mean to disrespect the temple..." he began, unsure what else to say.

Selek-Pey drew up alongside him. The smuggler swallowed hard, unsure what to expect. Suddenly the fog released a loud, rapid fire chirping sound that bounced off the walls like a thousand tiny balls, all of them echoing back on the pair and drowning them in noise. Gromyko barked out a laugh.

"You're as bad as I am!" he said. Then he cupped his hands around his mouth and tried to beat the mist at his own game, chirping rapidly with his tongue.

As the noise died down the mist drew inwards and exploded with such a deafening roar of noise that it nearly staggered him, the chirps seemingly pressing through his skull straight into his brain.

"Okay, you win that round," Gromyko laughed, once the noise had subsided. "Any more of that and I'll lose my hearing!"

"*Prona van, Groomeekah,*" he replied, floating slowly forwards.

The smuggler watched him until he'd gotten about twenty feet away. Then it shifted slightly and repeated itself with greater emphasis.

"*Prona van, Groomeekah!*"

"Oh! Come with you!" he said, clicking his fingers and darting after him. Once he'd gotten alongside him he slowed his pace. "You've got to remember that I don't speak your language." He walked a few steps and then laughed again. "Ha!

Look at me talking! You don't speak my language, either!"

Mutely *Selek-Pey* led him through the temple to the priest's quarters in the back, a series of small rooms with scarcely enough space for a bed and a tiny nightstand.

"You guys sure didn't live in splendor," Gromyko mused, intuiting the purpose of the rooms as he walked slowly through them. "That, or you were all midgets. I'd get claustrophobic if I had to stay here."

One chamber was a little larger than the rest and located between all the others. The fog floated through the open doorway, followed closely by Gromyko. One tiny orb above the door emitted a low glow that was just enough to see with.

"What's that?" he asked, pointing at a brightly painted mural on the wall. Depicted were a series of humanoid figures swirling in a bright orange pool, despair written on their tiny faces. Another figure stood on the shore with a rope, drawing them out onto solid ground. This figure looked small, with gray hair, a thin, human-like body, and widely spaced eyes.

"*Selek-Pey*," the fog said, floating near the figure with the rope. "*Nazath Selek-Pey*."

"So this is you, eh?" Gromyko said, drawing closer to the mural and tapping his finger on the *Kol-Prockian* on shore. "*Selek-Pey*?"

"*Kee*," the figure replied. "*Nazath Selek-Pey*."

"Never took you for a lifeguard," he muttered, looking for a long moment. "Ah, it's a metaphor," he mused. Noticing that several figures were already on shore behind *Selek-Pey*, their hands clasped together with a look of serenity on their faces, something began to stir in the back of his mind. "Well, you're more or less the founder of *Delek-Hai*, and this *is* the great temple. So I guess you're rescuing them from…too much stress? Nah, it's got to be something more than that. Chaos, perhaps?" He looked at the undulating form of his companion and sighed. "Too bad you don't speak English."

Turning from the mural and slowly leaving the

chamber, he put his hands on his hips.

"Where to now?"

Without a word *Selek-Pey* floated past him and disappeared around a corner.

"That way, apparently," Gromyko said to himself, jogging to catch up with the mist.

Slowly they worked their way back to the rest of the group. The human half of the pair quickly grew bored with his surroundings, the minimalism of the priests' lives leading to a monotonous lack of variation in their decor. Each room was massive, with high ceilings and made from skillfully carved stone blocks. But that was all. Not so much as a ragged old rug lay piled in a corner to shake up the look.

"There you are," Wellesley said when they reentered the antechamber. "I thought perhaps you'd gotten lost."

"Nah, I had my pal here to guide me back," the smuggler said with a grin, aware that referring to *Selek-Pey* that way would burn the AI. "I thought the others would be up by now."

"As did I," replied Wellesley. "But I suppose they lack your boyish energy."

"Well, they've rested long enough," he said, walking towards them and waking each in their turn.

"Couldn't you have left us a bit longer?" Milo grumbled as he yawned, stretching his arms over his head. "The secret chamber isn't going anywhere."

"And neither are we, if we don't get moving," the smuggler asserted boldly. "Come on, let's get at it."

"Can't we at least eat something first?" Tselitel asked, rubbing her stiff neck. "That last walk really took it out of me. I hardly feel strong enough to stand."

"I suppose," replied Gromyko. "But let's be quick about it. I want to get into that maze as soon as possible."

"Why the rush?" Hunt asked, as his friend hurriedly busted out the tiny camp stove and lit it.

"We've spent days getting here, and it'll take days to get back," he replied, pulling tins of food out of his pack and opening them so they wouldn't burst above the flame. "With the government closing in on a breakthrough we can't afford to waste even a minute."

Unconvinced by his reply but unwilling to push further, Hunt sat down beside Tselitel and watched as the smuggler hastened to warm breakfast, trying to place the little tins as advantageously as possible so as to shorten their cooking time.

"What's gotten into him?" she whispered, drawing her knees up to her chest and resting her chin upon them.

"I have no idea," he replied.

Selek-Pey disappeared for a few minutes while they were eating, causing Gromyko to fret that they would be delayed in setting off. But he returned just as they were packing up their bags.

"Alright, let's go," the smuggler said, slinging his pack over his shoulder and picking up Wellesley. "Tell *Selek-Pey* we're ready for the maze now."

"Who made you boss?" asked the AI.

"Just do it, Wells," Hunt said, picking up his own bag and taking Tselitel's hand.

The AI sighed and then complied.

"*Selek-Pey, irfum falolon massik del baska.*"

"*Prona van,*" the mist replied, moving to the end of the room and hoving by a doorway.

"Let's go," Gromyko said determinedly, taking the lead.

❖ ❖ ❖

"This is the place," Wellesley said much later, after *Selek-Pey* had guided them through a confusing array of corridors and side rooms, all the while taking them lower and lower into the structure.

"The temple itself is a maze," Gromyko said, putting

down his pack and wiping sweat from his brow with the back of his hand. "I wish it wasn't so hot down here."

"It's because we're closer to the geothermal vent that warms the building," Wellesley explained. "It has the added bonus of putting aspirants to the office of high priest through an even greater ordeal, testing their merit yet further."

"Some bonus," Milo opined, taking off his shirt and stuffing it into his bag. "I'll melt down here if we stay much longer."

"Pity," muttered Wellesley.

"So what's next?" asked Hunt, looking at the ancient door that separated them from the maze. "Just open it and go in?"

"We'd better ask *Selek-Pey* what he thinks," Wellesley replied. "He might be...particular about who goes in."

"Why would he be particular?" asked Hunt.

"It's a long story," replied the AI, not wanting to discuss it in front of the others, particularly Milo. "Just let me ask him."

"Be my guest," Hunt said, gesturing towards the mist and taking a step back.

"*Selek-Pey: pororum uitel baska roupe dahn po?*"

"*Groomeekah. Yulam Groomeekah.*"

"He says only Gromyko may enter."

"Is this what you meant about 'being particular?'" asked Hunt. "Come on, Wellesley: spill it."

"We talked this morning," the AI said reluctantly. "And he's concerned about the darkness you carry within. He's worried that you'll use the secrets of the temple for bad purposes."

"But I changed his mind!" exclaimed Gromyko.

"Well, apparently he changed it back. He only trusts you to go inside."

Looking at the cloud sternly, Gromyko said to it, "*Selek-Pey*, as you and I are brothers, so Rex is my brother."

"*Illifon melik valan, uit ro Hoont tele valan.*"

"And if the brother of Gromyko cannot enter, then

Gromyko *will not enter*!" he said stoutly, crossing his arms and looking away from the fog.

"*Jeladof mik valan tuo Groomeekah, tann rol nerek uitel Groomeekah.*"

"Just go ahead, Antonin," Hunt said in a low voice. "You can find what we need on your own and bring it back to the rest of us."

"No, we've been through too much together to stop now," he replied. "We do this together, or we don't do it at all."

"Antonin," began Tselitel.

"*Groomeekah oit remna valan*," the fog said, cutting her off.

"Gromyko is loyal to his brother."

"*Yur talaknofan no teek po vasan kash.*"

"But his brother descends from evil."

"Evil? What possible evil?" exploded Gromyko. "You insult him! And you insult me! How could there–"

"Take it easy!" Wellesley said. "We'll never make any progress yelling at him. Now, gather your thoughts and give me a reply."

Gromyko drew a deep breath and thought for a moment.

"*Elet poray vum derasat kash*," *Selek-Pey* said.

"His father works much evil."

"My father is dead," replied Hunt, taking a step towards the mist. "He died, years ago, in the prison."

Wellesley translated Hunt's words.

"*Elet vanan ito nom. Qant feri pomi fyr holutan. Belek darfan moh trus.*"

"Your father lives," Wellesley said. "Even now he strives to dominate your kind. The planet has seen this."

"That's impossible," Hunt said. "My father is *dead*."

"Oh!" exclaimed Tselitel, covering her mouth with her hand, looking as though she'd seen a ghost.

"What is it?" Milo asked.

"Wellesley, do you remember that night at the window,

before all the trouble with that woman started?"

"You mean when Milo was staring at you?" asked the AI.

"I never stared at you," he said with surprise. "I never even knew what apartment you were in."

"Sure you did," replied Wellesley. "There's no use lying about it now."

"I'm not lying," insisted Milo, taking a step closer. Then, looking at Tselitel, "I never had the slightest idea that it was you Rex was seeing until I saw you both much later, at the hideout with Ugo and the rest. How could I have? Rex nearly drove me out of my mind with fear that night. It's a wonder I didn't freeze to death out there."

"Oh, come *on*," replied Wellesley. "Look, you can't tell me–"

"It was his father in the snow," Tselitel said in a tone of revelation. "I told you then that there was something familiar about him. I called it a 'family resemblance,' remember?"

"Yes, I do," agreed the AI. "But there's no way that Rex's father could be working for the government. Why, the Order would have seen him long ago."

"Not if he was horribly disfigured," Tselitel said quietly.

"You mean..." began the AI.

"Yes, Wellesley," she said slowly. "It's Mr. Lavery."

"I don't understand," Hunt said, trying to make sense of what he was hearing. "Who's Mr. Lavery?"

"A bad man, Rex," Gromyko said. "Not a lot is known about him. He stays in the prison mostly, only venturing out occasionally. In the Underground we only knew bits and pieces about him. But it was enough for us to give him the widest possible berth. Some say that he can drive people insane just by touching them."

"It made my skin crawl to be near him," Tselitel said. "I can't explain it. But I felt that at any moment he could burst forth on everyone in the room. And then, when I saw him through the window, something terrible began to happen. It was like my world started to shake from its very foundation upward. All I wanted to do was hide. I closed the blinds, and for some reason he just went away."

"I know this must be shocking, Rex," Wellesley said.

"I don't think anything can shock me anymore," he replied grimly, turning once more to the mist. "So, *Selek-Pey* thinks I'll go the same way that my father did?"

"Apparently," replied the AI.

"Tell him that the planet he reveres has chosen me to end this evil," he said.

"But, Rex," said the AI slowly, "he's your father."

"He threatened Lily," he said, his voice cold, his eyes deadly serious. "Now, tell him."

"*Hoont goran fal nosta*," the fog said before Wellesley could speak.

"Hunt is determined to end this evil," the AI translated.

"What, he can understand us?" asked Gromyko.

"Only bits and pieces, I suspect," replied the AI. Then he translated Hunt's words just to be sure they were on the same page.

"*Dalam fel toree sab teekorna*," *Selek-Pey* replied. "*Doloth pree uiot porlaff ohn.*"

"Okay, turns out he understands us pretty well," Wellesley said. "Apparently he's been pretending not to understand so we'd feel safe chatting among ourselves. This permitted him to verify our intentions."

"Clever," said the smuggler. "So, he can speak with us, then?"

"Not really. He understands most of what we say, but can only speak a little."

"Yes, I am determined to end this evil," Hunt said, addressing *Selek-Pey*. "Now, will you guide us to the secret chamber?"

"*Kee*," replied the cloud.

"That means yes," Gromyko said, gesturing to Hunt and Milo. "Come on, help me pry this door open."

But despite nearly breaking their backs, the door,

unopened for many years, proved unwilling to move. Even Tselitel pitched in, but it was no use.

"I doubt this thing has been touched in centuries," Gromyko panted, sliding down the wall to the floor, his face soaked with sweat.

"What do we do now?" asked Milo. "Blast it open?"

"Are you out of your mind?" asked Wellesley. "Desecrate a monument like this?"

"It was just an idea."

"Some ideas aren't worth the air they're breathed on," said the AI. "If you had any sense you'd know that."

"You know, I've had just about enough of you riding me day in and day out," snapped Milo through gritted teeth. "You lecture us like you're some kind of sage. And you treat me like I'm *dirt!* What's it going to take to–"

"*Kalar booran meklethan varvi,*" interrupted *Selek-Pey*.

"*Nolar! Pafan deren deeth portrashon uitan!*" replied Wellesley quickly.

"*Navan do'kloth fasam doruthalum,*" replied the mist.

Several seconds of silence ensued before the AI spoke.

"He agrees with you," he said unwillingly. "He says to use one of the charges on the door. To use his exact words, 'sentiment must give place to necessity.'"

"I love this guy," Gromyko said, jumping to his feet and rummaging through Hunt's pack for a charge. "Everybody get around the corner," he said, nodding to the edge of a stout stone wall a few feet away. "I'll have this thing wired up in no time."

Gromyko laid the charge at the bottom of the door and carefully led the wires around the corner, squatting down once he was protected from the blast.

"Open the battery compartment for the 600G," he said to Milo, holding the two wires apart in front of him. "Alright, now set it on the floor. Each of you had better cover your ears."

"What about you?" Tselitel asked. "That blast is going to be deafening from this range."

"Not like we've got a better option," he replied. "Now, cover up!"

Her hands had barely reached her ears when an enormous roar exploded around the corner, shooting bits of rock and dust everywhere. *Selek-Pey*, beyond harm in his state, had elected to stay near the blast so he could watch. He emitted a high squeal of delight just after the explosion, thrilling to the sheer destructiveness of the charge.

"You two really are brothers," Wellesley said disapprovingly, as the mist rejoined the group.

"Huh?" Gromyko shouted, cupping his hand near his ear.

"He said–" began Tselitel.

"Oh, nevermind what I said. Let's just get inside that maze and get this over with."

A wave of warm air washed over them now that the door was gone. The temperature inside the maze was much hotter than the already sweltering temple.

"I don't think I can make it in there," Milo said, standing next to the opening and wilting from the heat. "I'm beat as it is."

Ignoring his brother, Hunt looked to Tselitel with inquiring eyes. Her clothes were already soaked through with sweat, and she looked weary and in need of a long rest. She approached the hole and raised her hands to it, immediately stepping back before the heatwave that vented itself upon her.

"Wellesley, how long will it take to traverse the maze?" she asked.

"At least several hours," he replied.

Drawing near to Hunt, she shook her head. "I can't do it, Rex. All those days in the snow have wiped me out. It wouldn't be an hour before you'd have to carry me."

"I don't want to leave you here with him," Hunt said quietly, putting his hand on her shoulder and caressing it. He looked past her head at his disheveled brother, who sat with his back against the stone wall, fanning himself with his shirt.

"I'll be alright," she smiled faintly, as sweat ran down her forehead and collected on the tip of her nose. "He's turned over a new leaf, I'm sure of it. Besides, you'll only be gone for a few hours. He won't dare try anything knowing you'll be coming back."

Hunt glanced doubtfully at his brother, who finally became aware of the attention he was getting. His cheeks flushed and he looked away.

"Just go," she said, kissing his warm, damp cheek and hugging him. "We have to get this over with."

Glancing between Tselitel and his brother, Hunt sighed and nodded his head reluctantly.

"Are you ready, Antonin?" he asked, as the smuggler looked inside the hole.

"What?" he bellowed, turning around and tripping over some of the rock that had been blown loose, falling on his face next to Tselitel. Hunt bent over to help him up, but the smuggler shook him loose when he was half erect. "Oh, I'm alright," he shouted, immediately falling down again from disorientation.

"As good as always," Wellesley said, both he and the 600G tucked under Hunt's arm.

"Come on, old friend," Hunt said, pulling Gromyko to his feet once more and guiding him to the opening. "Time to swallow your pride."

"Nah, there's no way I could have *died!*" he shouted in reply. "Nothing could have blown through that wall we were behind!"

"Oh, this is going to be fun," mumbled the AI, as Hunt, Gromyko, and *Selek-Pey* moved into the pitch black maze.

"I can't see a thing in here!" roared the smuggler, tripping over some shattered pieces of stone that lay on the floor, almost smacking his head into the wall. "Can't you hit the light, Wellesley?"

Without a word the 600G's flashlight flicked on, and Hunt shined it all around to get his bearings. He saw three paths leading away from the door.

"Alright, which way do we go?" he asked *Selek-Pey*, looking at him.

"*Prona van*," he said, floating slowly into the leftmost tunnel.

"Left it is," Wellesley said, as Hunt began to follow, his hand still gripping Gromyko's arm.

Thus began a slow walk down a seemingly endless series of paths, each of them looking exactly the same. With no lights, and almost no air moving, it felt like they were moving through ancient catacombs. Their sense of direction lost almost at once, they were totally dependent on their immaterial guide.

"It's so hot down here," Gromyko said loudly after an hour, following Milo's example and taking off his shirt. His hearing had finally begun to normalize, though a constant ringing was still audible. "It's like an oven. I wonder if any of the fellows who tried to become high priests ever died of thirst down here."

"Several, in fact," replied Wellesley. "Actually, one of the last aspirants to the office met his end like that. He had more ego than brains, and thought he could master these tunnels before he was truly ready. Funny how often you meet people like that."

"Did he say something?" Gromyko mock yelled to Hunt, pointing at his ear.

"*Heh heh heh*," *Selek-Pey* chuckled from a little ways ahead.

"Glad to see someone appreciates your humor," the AI said sarcastically.

After another hour had passed Hunt called a stop. Sitting down on the floor, he busted out a canteen and handed it to Gromyko. The smuggler took a deep drink and then handed it back.

"You've been awfully quiet ever since we came in here," he said, eyeing Hunt curiously. "You scared we won't make it?"

"No, I'm sure we will," he said, glancing at *Selek-Pey* as he downed a couple of swallows.

"It's the business with your father?" asked Wellesley.

"I'd hardly call it 'business,' Wells," Hunt said, screwing the cap back on and tucking it away in his pack. He quietly thumped his fist against the stone floor before continuing. "Nobody threatens Lily," he said, looking at them with eyes as cold as death, smoke beginning to dance between his fingers. "Absolutely nobody. I don't care if it's my father, or my brother, or any other kind of blood relation. I'll shatter anyone who lays a finger on her, no matter the cost."

"I understand," Wellesley said quietly, though the fervent intensity of his friend disturbed him. He could hear in his voice a dark note that he didn't like, as if Hunt was in the grip of something more powerful than he realized. He felt that he would welcome a chance to batter his father, perhaps even destroying him, if circumstances warranted. And while that may prove satisfying to him in the moment, the AI wondered how his friend would process such an action once his emotions cooled and he had a chance to come to terms with what he'd done.

Without another word they got to their feet and resumed their journey.

"*Relafass bree owat*," *Selek-Pey* said an hour later, halting just short of a dead end.

"We have arrived," Wellesley translated.

"But this is just a wall," said Gromyko, walking up to it and extending his hand towards it. To his surprise it passed right through. "What the!" he exclaimed, jerking his hand back. "Ah, a hologram! But isn't that a little–"

"Advanced for the temple?" asked Wellesley. "It must have been left behind by the *Prollok-Hee* as a final test. Remember, this was their temple, too, once they'd become dominant in *Delek-Hai*."

Hunt approached the hologram and passed his hand through it as Gromyko had done, just to convince himself it wasn't solid. Then he stepped through, closely followed by the smuggler and *Selek-Pey*.

The room they found was small, square, and dimly lit by a tiny crack in the ceiling that somehow permitted daylight to reach the underground space. Tapestries covered the walls, recounting the glories of former high priests and other luminaries. Beside one such tapestry *Selek-Pey* muttered something in a disapproving tone.

"Not a friend of yours, eh?" Gromyko asked, standing beside him. The tapestry depicted a sole *Kol-Prockian* holding a bright light over his head, driving away a swirl of darkness that surrounded him.

"That's *Bena-Foe*, the first *Prollok-Hee* high priest," explained Wellesley. "He was also one of the most aggressive of the technologists. He destroyed thousands of scrolls of writings from the ancient masters, seeking to erase their influence from *Delek-Hai* forever. If a handful of the lower priests hadn't been loyal to the old ways and hidden what was left of the ancient texts, almost nothing of true *Delek-Hai* would be known today. But once *Bena-Foe* had died he was followed by high priests who were less revolutionary. They permitted the old texts to be returned to the temple and preserved."

"Fascinating," the smuggler said.

"But what about what we came here for?" asked Hunt, looking around the room. "All I see is tapestries."

"*Bere tollashon volu par*," the mist replied.

"Look behind the tapestries," the AI translated.

Three of them hung from each wall, and they gently lifted them up to peek behind.

"Over here," Hunt said, raising the lower edge of one and seeing a small notch that had been cut into the wall. "Looks like some kind of keyhole."

"And this," Groymko said, raising an ornately carved crystal that he just found behind a different tapestry, "must be the key."

"Stick it in," Hunt said, holding up the cloth and stepping aside.

The smuggler did so, slipping it in slowly and giving it a gentle clockwise twist. They heard a loud click on the other side of the wall, but nothing else.

"*Taslana koul atar*," *Selek-Pey* said, hovering near them.

"Push on the door," Wellesley told them.

Putting Wellesley down in the center of the room, the 600G's light shining on the wall, they placed their hands on opposite edges and pushed on it without effect.

"*Tot um salan.*"

"Both on one side."

Hunt joined Gromyko on the left side of the door, and with their combined effort it began to twist open, rotating in the middle.

"We were fighting each other before," Gromyko said, his voice tight with exertion.

"Just keep pushing," Hunt said, sweat pouring off his body and wetting the floor.

Little by little the massive stone wall turned until it was open enough for them to slip inside. They slowly released their pressure on it, unsure if it would swing back the other way. When it held steady they leaned against the wall and panted.

"Can't see how a…skinny high priest could have…pulled this off…alone," Gromyko said between gasps.

"The machinery must have decayed with time," Wellesley said. "That, or the *Prollok-Hee* messed up the original design when they automated it."

"You mean this thing used to open on its own?" Gromyko asked, feeling all his efforts had been needless.

"Apparently. *Selek-Pey* told me about it while you two were getting it open. Now pick me up, and let's take a look inside."

Grabbing Wellesley off the floor and returning to the half open door, Hunt stepped into the darkness just beyond it. All at once the adjoining chamber was filled with light.

A hologram of Delta-13 floated in the middle of it, with innumerable little places lit up in red across its surface.

Selek-Pey launched into a long explanation, speaking for several minutes without pausing. When he'd finished, both men looked at Wellesley.

"Give me a sec!" he laughed. "I'm trying to remember everything he said and put it in the right order. It was easier when he spoke in single sentences."

"Take your time," Hunt said, looking around the room. Beneath the hologram stood a dark pillar about three feet tall, apparently emitting the massive orb that took up nearly half the space. Cables ran from the device out through the walls.

"Funny that this is all that's in here," Gromyko said to Hunt, walking around the orb. "It's like a big map."

"That's exactly what it is," the AI said at last. "According to *Selek-Pey*, the technologists had cleaned out the ancient writings long ago, and had turned this into a sort of command center for the revitalization of their religion."

"I don't understand," Hunt said.

"Sorry, I'm still working out what he said," Wellesley replied. "Alright, let's try it like this. With the rise of technology, and the materialistic society it produced, people lost faith in *Delek-Hai* and its base of followers shrunk drastically. This problem was aggravated by the *Prollok-Hee*, who through their rationalism had stripped away all the mystical elements of the faith. This kept it from acting as the counterpoise it otherwise could have been, and cost it followers all the more quickly. Those who sought refuge for their souls in an age of dry materialism couldn't find it, and splintered off into a thousand other forms of belief. In some cases, they even attempted to revive some of the ancient local religions that had predated *Delek-Hai*."

"Seeing this, some of the priests tried to revitalize the faith through a scientific approach. They attempted to establish a rational basis for the ancient practices of *Delek-Hai*. They called themselves the *Kah-Delek-Hai*, or Rebirth of the Path to Wholeness. They tried to study and document the effects of the planet in order to convince the populace to return to the faith. Contradictory as it sounds, they tried to legitimize faith through science."

"Can't imagine that worked very well," commented Gromyko.

"Not to revitalize the faith. Its position had slipped too far for anything to save it. But they made many fascinating discoveries into the nature of the planet and how it worked. For one, the ancient builders of the temples and shrines all used stone quarried from a very great depth, known as *kral*. *Kral* possesses a kind of affinity for Delta-13's consciousness."

"You mean we're surrounded by psychic rocks?" asked the smuggler, looking around curiously.

"In a sense," replied Wellesley. "*Kral* enjoys a special connection with the planet. It has been 'charged,' if you will, by millennia of contact with it. Its special affinity permits a greater connection. Intuitively the old masters knew this, and thus all their structures were made out of *kral*. When the *Prollok-Hee* came to power they continued the practice simply because it had been a custom since time out of mind. That's good for us, because they made the facility beneath the prison out of *kral* as well."

"How does that help us?" Hunt asked.

"Because *kral* gives off a very distinct signature. And the machinery in this room can track it, among other things. This means we can use the hologram to work out if there are any other ways into the facility."

"But how do we control it?" asked Gromyko. "I don't see any kind of interface."

"The *Kah-Delek-Hai* left such data oriented tasks to their AIs," Wellesley replied. "I should be able to interact with the map if you place me against the device that's generating it."

Hunt ducked beneath the massive hologram and placed the AI, along with the 600G, against the dark pillar. Climbing out from underneath it he watched Delta-13 begin to swirl around as Wellesley got his bearings. Soon it centered on a particular section, and a portion of the hologram magnified many times over until the prison was visible.

"A familiar sight to us all," the AI said darkly. "Now to get a look underneath it."

A moment later the view of the prison was replaced by the outline of a subterranean square structure rendered in bright orange. The fringes of it looked broken down, like it had suffered some kind of collapse over the centuries that left only the interior intact. Two long lines stretched away from it, one to the east, and one to the north.

Quietly the two men watched as Wellesley traced the northern route.

"That'll never do," he muttered.

"Why?" asked Hunt.

"Because it's broken down in a dozen different places. It'd take a week for us to blast our way through all the debris. And we don't have enough explosives for that, even assuming the tunnel could take that kind of abuse."

"What about the other one?" asked Gromyko.

"Checking that now."

The view shifted back to the facility and slowly traced the eastern tunnel all the way to the point at which it terminated.

"Well, that's troubling," the AI said.

"What?" asked the smuggler urgently. "Is this tunnel broken, too?"

"No, the tunnel is fine. But it might not do us a lot of good. I'm getting massive lifesign readings from the area it ends in. It's connected to the caves that the old pirate base on the edge of town was built in."

"Human lifesigns?" asked Hunt, stepping closer to the hologram and watching as a tight cluster of little red dots glowed in and out at the edge of the tunnel of *kral*.

"No, the computer identifies them as *karrakpoi*," replied Wellesley. "That's *Kol-Prockian* for massive, soul-sucking spiders. They live off the life energy of the planet like so many ticks on a dog. Usually they live in a state of quasi-hibernation since they can only get a little bit of juice out of Delta-13 at a time. But if something warm, breathing, and packed with vitality like a human should walk past, the chance is very high that they'd wake up and pile onto him, sucking him drier than a raisin."

"Not a very fun way to go," Hunt said.

"*Karrakpoi fal bo!*" exclaimed *Selek-Pey*, following the statement with a spitting sound.

"I'm pretty sure you both got the gist of that," commented Wellesley. "The old priests hated the *karrakpoi*, seeing them as devils that sucked the precious life from their holy world. They exterminated them whenever they found a hive. For a long time they were thought extinct, but clearly a few of them survived to reproduce. It's odd: the computer identifies the *karrakpoi* as an invasive species, as though they're not native to Delta-13. Maybe someone brought them to the planet millennia ago."

"But what are they doing there?" asked Gromyko.

"They're using the *kral* as a conduit to feed off the planet. It can't be very effective for them, since they're used to feeding at much greater depths. But it appears to be enough to keep them alive, even permitting procreation. But I'd wager they're pretty emaciated down there."

"So they're just camped out in front of the tunnel," Hunt said, looking at the map. "Why haven't they moved inside of it to get better access to the *kral*?"

"Looks like there's a door blocking their entry," Wellesley said. "It's not very thick; I can barely make it out on the scanner. But we should thank our lucky stars for it all the same."

"As long as we can get it open," Hunt said. "Is there anything else we need here?"

"Just give me a few minutes to download some more data," Wellesley replied. "Never know what might come in handy."

❖ ❖ ❖

"I wonder if they got lost," Milo said, leaning beside the labyrinth's entrance and sticking his head inside. "It *is* a maze, after all."

"I'm sure they're fine," Tselitel said, not half as confident as she sounded.

"Who can say, with only a ghost to guide them," said Milo, jumping to his feet and kicking a chunk of rock that the explosive had knocked loose hours earlier. Pacing around like a caged animal in front of the hole, he stole the occasional glance at her, which she pretended not to notice.

"How did you find any artifacts in here?" she asked, trying to direct his attention away from herself. "I haven't seen one the entire time we've been here."

"Oh, you have to go lower for those," he said. "There are chambers on the other side of the temple that still have tons of them. I guess they dumped them there for storage purposes, or something. There's just boxes filled with them. Most are just ornamental, though. I guess the aliens didn't have much use for them when they packed up and left. It's pretty rare to find any that are useful, like this," he said, handling the one that hung against his bare chest. "Too bad the ornamental ones don't bring much of a price. If they did I'd have been a rich man long ago. Of course, it's pretty much impossible to trade in artifacts now, since the government has shut down the Underground. It really wouldn't matter if I stumbled across a fortune in artifacts at this point."

"So you relied on the Underground?"

"Oh, sure," he said, walking to where she sat against the wall and leaning against it. "Gromyko's bunch had contacts a guy like me could only dream of. It takes years to earn the trust of the handful of traders who are willing to run contraband offworld. Especially with undercover cops constantly trying to bait them into incriminating themselves. It wasn't until the Underground had built up a sizable reputation in the sector that doors finally began to open for them. That's clout you can only get with an organization at your back."

"I'd always been under the impression that the Underground was very badly run," she replied, uncomfortably aware of his proximity.

"You must have been listening to that chatterbox that's wrapped around Rex's neck," he said with a laugh, squatting down beside her, his knee just brushing her leg. "The problem with him is he's too uptight. That's probably why Rex hangs out with him: they're both stodgy."

"I like Rex just the way he is," she replied, growing a little warm.

"Oh, he's alright, I guess," he replied. "But he's more grim than a prisoner in front of a firing squad. With a man like that," he said, leaning a little closer, "you'd be old before your time." In an instant he crossed the foot or so that separated them and locked his lips onto hers. She struggled ineffectually for a moment, panicking and unsure what to do. Suddenly she scratched her nails down his chest, drawing blood from his exposed skin. He drew back his head with a yelp as she shot to her feet.

"Why you little," he said, standing up and taking several steps towards her as she retreated across the hot stony floor. "What'd you do that for? It was just a little kiss!"

He saw her face turn white, her eyes widening with fear as she reached the reverse wall. "No, please don't!" she said.

"Oh, come off it, Doctor," he said with annoyance, following her up to the back wall as she shrank away. "What do you take me for, anyway? Some kind of monster?" He drew his fingers across his chest, gathering a little blood. "It's not like I didn't get your message.".

"She isn't talking to you," he heard Wellesley's

monotone drone out behind him.

Just as he whipped around to look, Hunt seized him by the throat and slammed him against the wall next to her.

"Please, Rex!" she pleaded, taking hold of his free arm and trying to pull him off. "He doesn't deserve that kind of punishment!"

Smoke gathered around the fingers that held Milo's neck and flowed into him. His face twisted up with terror, his eyes turning dark and otherworldly. His body grew slack as his ego receded before the horrors that surrounded it.

"Another few moments and he'll never come back from this," Wellesley said impartially, neither encouraging nor censuring his action. "The rest of his days will be a living nightmare."

Implacably the hand remained on his brother's neck, slowly filling every inch of his soul with darkness.

"Please," Lily said quietly, releasing his arm. "For me."

Hunt looked at her for a moment and then faced Milo. The flow of darkness slowed until it ceased. He released his grip and let his brother slide to the floor.

The instant Milo hit the ground his hands went reflexively to his throat as though he was trying to draw the psychological poison from his own body. Pressing himself against the wall in a futile attempt to get away from Hunt, he began whimpering like a wounded animal, unable to talk.

"Shh," Tselitel said, slipping her hand onto his neck and closing her eyes. "Shh."

Even in his irrational state he recognized in her a friend who sought to help, and he didn't fight her gentle hold. She began drawing the darkness into herself. It took several minutes, but the blackness faded from his eyes and they could see he was back.

"Rex!" he exclaimed, jumping to his feet and stumbling along the wall away from his brother. "I didn't–. I mean, there wasn't any–."

Hunt grabbed Milo by the arm and dragged him away

from the rest of the group, driving his powerful fingers into his flesh.

"If...you...*ever*...touch her again," he said quietly, his voice trembling with rage, smoke unconsciously gathering around his left hand.

"I won't! I swear I won't!" he said in a desperate whisper. "Please believe me! I-I don't know what came over me!"

"I'll let you go this time," he said, "out of consideration for Lily. But next time neither she, nor my conscience, will hold me back. Is that understood?"

Gromyko watched them talk, unable to hear what was said, yet nodding slowly.

"That's why *Selek-Pey* saw darkness in Lily," he said quietly to Wellesley. "She must have drawn some out of Rex at some point. Just like she drew it out of Milo. What an amazing gift."

"Of course!" he exclaimed. "In the forest, after the battle outside her apartment! When she helped him achieve balance she soaked up some of his darkness as well!"

"What happened?"

"Oh, Rex was fading fast and she rescued him. It wiped her out and she nearly froze to death. Once we got her warmed up she became, well, inebriated. Totally unfamiliar psychic contents were floating through her mind, and she had no way to cope with them at the time. She was off-balance, bubbly, and struggling to integrate a whole new world."

"I wonder if she'll be like that again," Gromyko remarked, watching her as she nervously observed the two brothers talk. "We've gotta get out of here in a hurry. We're not going to have time to wait for her to sleep it off."

"*Roluna, tlel nok bemiu san tvora lupason.*"

"Our illustrious friend doesn't think that will be necessary," Wellesley said. "He believes that the load she took from Rex initially was much, much larger than what she just extracted from Milo. Add that to the fact she isn't a completely green beginner now, and there's a good chance she'll be a little wobbly, but otherwise okay. She seems to learn fast, and I think that's just as true for her unconscious gift as it is for her more front-brain activities."

Wellesley had just finished saying this when the dialogue between the two brothers broke up. Ashamed to look at any of them, Milo kept his eyes down as he returned to the group. Hunt went to Lily and put his hands on her shoulders

"Are you alright?" he asked gently.

"Yes, I'm fine," she said quietly. "Darling, you can't go off like that whenever someone does something to me. All he did was kiss me!"

"I don't care if he *breathed* on you," Hunt said, sliding a hand to her neck and caressing it. "Anyone who touches you touches me. I will not tolerate the least insult against you. You're my soul, don't you understand? You're my very life."

"I'm a woman, Rex," she replied in a whisper. "I can't be more than that. I'm just a person like anyone else."

"Not to me you're not," he said earnestly. "You're my very breath."

Seeing the odd fervency in his eyes that Wellesley had noticed earlier in the labyrinth, she quietly nodded and yielded the point.

◆ ◆ ◆

Hours later they were back at the antechamber in the front of the temple. Night had long since fallen outside, and the storm that had followed them there continued to beat against the door of the temple.

"Not going anywhere tonight," Gromyko said as he broke out his little stove for a late meal. Despite his eagerness to leave he was silently glad to have an excuse to kick back and rest. The ordeal in the labyrinth took more out of him than he cared to admit, and all he wanted to do was sleep.

"We'll leave at first light," Hunt said with grim

determination, holding Tselitel's hand as he had ever since they'd left the labyrinth behind. Eyeing his brother angrily, Hunt guided Tselitel to one of the steps at the bottom of the stairs that led outside and sat down.

"Agreed," said the smuggler, stretching out beside his stove, propping himself up on one arm. "I'll be sad to leave you behind, *Selek-Pey*," he said to the mist. "But one leader understands the need of another to leave his personal feelings outside his calculations. He must direct his course by the needs of those he serves."

"*Kee, quervan.*

"Yes, it is so," translated Wellesley, rolling his eyes internally.

"But I suppose we'll see you again at the shrine," mused Gromyko. "Provided we stop there."

"*Yol wruest nelem barna. Kyo tele sanloma kirilin.*"

"He says that is not likely. He must commune with the planet and find out what is troubling it. If he finds out in time he will try to catch up with us and let us know."

"That's a pity," Gromyko said.

"*Poliu, faryala tee coraku. Tayal chee tolak, voyu valan Groomeekah.*"

"He wishes us well, and looks forward to many more interesting discussions with his brother Gromyko."

The fog bobbed back and forth for a moment, and then drifted slowly out of the room.

"It's gonna be hard not having him around," the smuggler said with disappointment. "I've gotten used to him." He glanced at Milo. "Besides, it was always good having an extra set of eyes on that rascal," he added quietly.

Only Wellesley, laying on the ground next to him, could hear his remark. He chuckled his agreement to which Gromyko grinned, not thinking he'd spoken loudly enough to be heard.

"It's gonna be a long way back to Midway," Hunt said sourly, eyeing his brother from the staircase.

"You shouldn't be so hard on him, Rex," Tselitel said.

"After all, I'm pretty hard to resist."

"This is no time for jokes, Lily," he said with annoyance. "You of all people should be mad at him right now. Doesn't it burn you that he took liberties with you?"

"No, it really doesn't," she said, stretching her legs out across the floor and leaning back on the hard steps, trying to find a comfortable position. "Look, I'd only care that much if I was insecure in my own skin, which I'm not. Our experience in the *taco* should have proven that to you. So he stole a kiss! Big deal. There's a lot worse things he could have done, which he didn't. And even if given the opportunity, I'm sure he wouldn't. Yes, he's a ruffian. Frankly, I think he'll always be one. He has a crass lack of principle that grates on honest souls. But he isn't *evil*, Rex. You can't paint him into a corner as though he's one of the truly dark ones. He's not–," she started to say, stopping herself.

"My father?" Hunt asked.

"I'm sorry. I didn't mean to bring him to mind."

"He hasn't left my mind since the moment I learned the truth about him," Hunt said, mimicking her recumbent posture. "How could Ugo have been so wrong about him, Lily? He said he was a hero! That he'd been the one who'd drawn him into the Order back in the day!"

"Maybe he *was* back then, but something changed him afterwards," she suggested. "People *do* change, you know," she added, glancing at Milo.

"Not that much," he said in a low rumble. "It's not like *I* could change that much. Or you. Or Antonin. People don't just flip over like that. Ugo told me that he worked to undo the damage that the government had done to some of its victims. He said that was the entire reason they sent him up in the first place. Did he lie to me? Make dad into a hero so that I'd have an easier time joining the Order?"

"I guess that's possible," she replied after a moment of thought. "But we can't know for sure until we talk to him."

"Ugo? I don't intend to speak with him ever again. Not if

I can help it."

"I doubt you'll have any choice," she said. "There's going to be a maelstrom once we blow up that room."

"That's what I think, too," he said quietly, picking at a little crack in one of the steps with his thumb nail. "We've seen to that as well as we can, Wellesley and I." Leaning close and dropping his voice he added, "He downloaded all the data from the 600G. We know the location of every hideout he's ever punched into that thing."

"I thought you did," she whispered back, a smile slowly crossing her lips as his face lit up with surprise. "I've known you long enough to see something like that coming a mile away. You never leave things to chance if you can help it. I'm just surprised Milo didn't put up more of a fuss."

"He's just glad to be breathing, after what I did to him the first time," Hunt said, his face souring. "He knew better than to make a ruckus." Then his face lightened again. "But I'm surprised at you! I didn't think you could be so suspicious."

"I guess you're rubbing off on me," she laughed. "Actually, that really seems to be true," she added a moment later.

"What do you mean?"

"Well, you remember that little scene in the snow?"

"Just what you and Wells have told me about it," he replied.

"After that moment, I've felt different. Looser, somehow. Some part of you got inside me at that moment and changed how my gears spin. I've been trying to make sense of it ever since."

"I've noticed that you've been more withdrawn," he said. "Even hesitant."

"Yes, I have been. It's like someone gave my perspective a quarter twist, and I've been relearning how to view the world ever since. It's jarring, Rex. I'm a forty-two year old woman. I never expected to have things turned upside down this way. But I'm glad for it, too. I see a darker side that always escaped me before. It's exciting, and a little scary, at the same time. But I wouldn't trade it for anything. It's the purest kind of enlightenment to be shown another person's world, especially when it contrasts so completely with your own personality."

"I'd say you got the worse half of the deal," he laughed.

"Don't say that," she said seriously, locking her eyes on his. "Don't ever say that."

"Come on, Lily," he said offhandedly, shifting where he lay as the steps began to gouge his back. "You can't tell me that experiencing my mind is any kind of treat. It must have been a pain in the neck to set me to rights out there in the snow. Dumpster diving is never any fun."

"Is that what you think your mind is like?" she asked.

"Can't see what else it could be like."

"Then you really don't know yourself at all."

"I know all that I want to know," he replied with certainty.

"Not enough to make a fair assessment," she said with a deep-seated sincerity that moved him. "The problem with you is you don't see any value in yourself. Though for the life of me I don't see why. A man who loves as much as you do has something wonderful to give."

"I've never thought of myself as a lover," he laughed, considering the idea ridiculous. "A harbinger of woe, perhaps. Certainly anyone who's felt my gift would agree with that!"

"You're wrong," she said, shaking her head slowly from side-to-side. "Oh, you're wrapped in a shell of threat and danger. Anyone who wants to do wrong sees that at once, and they're rightly afraid. You have immense power to hurt, but only those who deserve it." She grasped his hand in both of hers and held it. "Look at this hand: so strong, so dangerous to those who work wrong. Yet it is gentle, harmless to me," she said, raising it to her cheek, brushing the calloused palm against her soft, thin skin. "You're a gentle man with a kind heart, Rex. But you've been hurt, and you've put on violence to protect yourself. Your decisive stride; your cold, hard eyes;

even the way you dress is a subtle warning to anyone who would threaten you. You're a sensitive man living in a violent, nasty situation that would kick you to the ground and keep you there if you let it. Subsequently your persona is one of almost existential seriousness. You're determined not to let anything past your carefully constructed shell. But it's just a shell, darling! You've lived it for so long that you've forgotten that fact. You hate it because it's your opposite. But it's a necessary opposite. Without it, living in Midway would have broken you years ago."

Rex's feelings were confused. He was relieved to be understood, even to be shown more about himself than he'd realized on his own. And yet it was disturbing to have his mask pulled away, exposing the raw vulnerability of his soul to the outside world. Before he could find the words to reply she smiled with sweet comprehension, seemingly reading his mind.

"Don't worry, your secret is safe with me," she said quietly.

◆ ◆ ◆

Three days later they were just on the verge of the shrine in which they had first met *Selek-Pey*. Their progress had been painfully slow, the ferocity of the storm above forcing them to seek shelter whenever they could find it.

Within hours of leaving the temple it had become clear that they couldn't endure the elements without protection. Subsequently they had been forced from the direct path back to Midway, working their way through one stretch of forest after another. Only brief periods in the open could be tolerated. Even an hour shuffling across the vast fields of snow was enough to rob them of their precious warmth.

"Not far now," Hunt said to Gromyko, who walked beside him through the trees.

No longer trusting Milo to perform even the most minor task, he had taken over navigator duty. Periodically he drew the 600G from his pocket to get his bearings. Now that they were close to their destination he kept it out continually, careful that they not walk past the shrine in the gloom. For they were shrouded in darkness, the snow-laden branches blocking out the scanty light that managed to penetrate the storm.

"Thank God for trees," Gromyko said sincerely, glad to feel a little warmth return to his numb cheeks. The last stretch of open ground had blown all the heat from his body, despite the best efforts of the medallion that slid back and forth over chest with every step.

So dense was the woodland through which the foursome moved that scarcely a breeze could be felt from the raging tempest that bent lone trees until their branches snapped, leaving them to sag helplessly against their trunks. An eerie quiet prevailed, magnified by the thick bed of snow that had gradually slipped off the branches above and fallen to the ground.

"I think I see something ahead," Tselitel said in a voice hollow with cold. Pointing forward with her glove, they followed it with their eyes to a dim triangle that was just visible in the light of the 600G.

"She's right," Milo seconded. "It's the shrine."

Frowning at the sound of his brother's voice, Hunt picked up his pace, eager to get Lily out of the cold as quickly as possible.

"I never thought I would be so happy to see this place again," Gromyko said, dropping to his knees once they were inside. Pulling back his hood and pushing his stocking cap off the back of his head, he quickly got his pack off his back and set to work establishing camp. "I wonder if we'll see *Selek-Pey* while we're here," he said.

"Probably not," Wellesley opined. "With the planet as agitated as it is, I doubt he'll be able to make heads or tails of what's bothering it for at least a week. Delta-13 doesn't turn corners very fast, if you will. It takes a while for it to make itself comprehensible to other creatures. After all, a thousand years to a world like this is scarcely a moment in its lifetime, when you compare it to ours. Or yours, I should say."

"When you consider that, it turns corners pretty fast," Gromyko said, pausing to think for a moment and then resuming his work. "All the same, I hope we see him before hitting the room. Who knows what will happen then."

"Indeed," agreed Wellesley.

Milo mutely watched the smuggler unpack his kit for a moment, then he shuffled a few feet away and sat down against the wall.

"You alright, baby?" Hunt asked Tselitel quietly, a few feet from the others. Slipping her gloves off, he rubbed her icy hands between his to warm them up.

"I'll live," she smiled, her teeth almost clattering. "Especially if Antonin can get some hot food going!" she said a little louder, hoping to spur him on.

"In a flash!" he said in a jocular tone, his mood for some reason an inversion of the temperature outside. "Wellesley, have you ever noticed how a survival situation always brings out a person's true colors? Oh, I've seen it many times before. Why, when I was running the Underground, I would never trust someone until I had personally seen him in mortal danger. It's only then that you get the true read of a person's nature and intentions. The whole self comes out, and not just the pleasant mask we wear for the benefit of others."

"I would agree with that," the AI said. "Most of the time. But sometimes it's when they think no one is watching that you get the clearest image of a person's nature.".

"You're right," he replied, pointing at the AI with a long, narrow tin of meat. "Absolutely right. I guess different natures require different tests to prove them."

"How true."

"Those two seem to be getting chummy all of a sudden," Tselitel whispered to Hunt as he continued to rub her hands. "Back in the temple Wellesley took every shot he could manage at Antonin."

Hunt glanced at them for a moment and chuckled.

"They're united by a common enemy," he said quietly, putting his mouth close to her ear. "They've briefly forgotten their differences. In fact it's more than that: they're willing to *highlight* them in each other, so long as they go against Milo. They're too temperamentally different to ever really get along. But they're both solid to the core, and they both hate a scoundrel."

"They'd better back off on him," she said with concern in her voice, looking at Milo as he tried to shrink into the wall, painfully aware of their censure. "At this rate he'll throw himself out in the snow from pure self-loathing."

"Not like he'd be missed," Hunt said matter-of-factly.

She turned back to him.

"You don't mean that," she asserted, studying his cool gaze. "Not deep down. That's just your shell talking."

Without altering his expression he glanced at his brother and then down at her hands. "Pretty good?" he asked, ceasing his rubbing and holding them for a moment.

"Yes, they're much better," she replied with a little smile, letting the matter drop.

Once they'd eaten they settled down to sleep. Hunt and Tselitel camped out near the door. Gromyko lay a little farther inside. And Milo, bundled up in his blankets, pressed himself against the far wall.

"I wish the morning would never come," the smuggler said, climbing into his blankets and yawning. "I could use at least twenty hours of sleep after today's walk. There's something uniquely exhausting about the cold. It saps all the strength from your bones." He yawned again. "Or at least mine, anyway." Within moments of his head connecting with his backpack, which served as a makeshift pillow, his face slackened and he drifted off to sleep.

"He does everything at one hundred percent," Tselitel chuckled quietly to Hunt. "Even sleep!"

"Yeah, he's high strung, no matter what he's doing," Hunt said, twisting his neck to look at the unconscious smuggler before turning back to her. "But at least–" he began, halting when he saw her gazing at Milo.

"We can't leave things like this," she whispered, more to herself than to him. "I'm going to talk to him," she said, pushing the blankets aside and getting to her feet.

"No, Lily–" he started to whisper. But she was already out of earshot and moving on quick, silent feet across the structure. Milo's back was to her, and when she touched his shoulder gently he nearly jumped out of his blankets.

"What? What is it?" he asked with alarm, twisting around and expecting to see Hunt. When he saw Tselitel his anxiety, if anything, increased. "Please go! If he sees you over here–"

"He *knows* I'm here, Milo," she assured him, sliding to her knees, folding her legs under her. "I wanted to talk to you."

"Please leave me alone," he said, turning away from her and pulling the thin blanket up around his neck.

"I'm not going to leave until I've spoken to you," she said, her voice gaining a touch of firmness.

"Nobody's stopping you," he replied.

"Milo, I'm not angry about what you did," she began. "A little confused, perhaps. But not angry."

"What's there to be confused about?" he asked evenly. "I was bored, and you were beautiful. It's pretty simple math to add the two together and get a little spice, don't you think?"

She chuckled.

"Go ahead and laugh," he said sullenly.

"Oh, I'm not laughing at you," she said quickly. "I was just thinking about how similar you and Rex are."

"Ha!" he exclaimed, a little more loudly than he'd

intended. He glanced across the shrine and saw his brother's eyes boring into him, causing him to look away instantly. "When was the last time you saw me flood a man with terror, destroying every ounce of hope within his soul?"

"Oh, not like that," she replied. "But you both have a point blank logic that makes the most of circumstances as you see them. You see a situation, add it up, and *act* according to your own understanding of what is desirable. In that you're both the same. The difference lies in what you consider a desirable outcome."

"I don't understand," Milo said, turning onto his back so he could look at her. "And what does any of this matter, anyway?" He stole another glance at his brother and then continued. "Those two hate my guts. Three, if you count the AI. Nothing is going to change that. I've committed my crimes, and it's off to the executioner's block, as far as they're concerned. So why don't we call it a night and get some sleep?"

"I just wanted you to know that I didn't hold what happened back in the temple against you."

"Nothing *happened* back at the temple," he corrected her. "It's not like it was some random accident. I *acted*, deliberately. I hate myself for doing it, too. I really think I was starting to make a little bit of headway with those guys," he said, nodding subtly towards the others. "But when I see a juicy plum hanging from a tree I just have to grab it. I never think ahead. Rex was always the one who could hold himself in, keeping his hands off things even if he wanted them desperately. I used to hate him for it, and I made his life miserable every chance I could for it. He's so *holy* all the time," he said, his teeth grinding. "What chance has a guy like me got beside him? I mean look at me! I couldn't even keep my hands off you after what he did to me that night in the forest."

"You're impulsive," she said soothingly.

"Oh, don't patronize me," he snapped, growing ever more angry with himself. "Just leave me alone, will you, Doctor? You've said your piece, now let me get some sleep."

With this he turned away from her, facing the wall as before.

"Alright," she said quietly, silently rising to her feet and padding slowly across the *kral* floor to Rex.

The next morning she felt a hand touch her shoulder, gently shaking her awake.

"Is it time to go already?" she asked groggily.

"Milo's gone," Hunt said flatly, causing her to jolt upright in an instant.

She quickly scanned the shrine, her eyes confirming his words.

"And he took the 600G, too," Gromyko added with disgust. "Heh, little did he know that we don't even need it anymore, since Wellesley copied all his data!"

"Actually, he did know," replied the AI. "He was going to leave without it so we could use it. But I told him to take it and explained about the data. He managed to pop the speaker out of it without waking you guys so I could keep talking. He said he didn't need it, anyway."

"Oh," replied the smuggler, his face clouding over with doubt. "Maybe he wasn't such a..." his voice trailed off, unwilling to finish his thought out loud.

"Yes, perhaps not," agreed Wellesley. "Turns out he also had a small flashlight on him as well. He left it so we could see without the 600G."

"We should go after him!" Tselitel said urgently. "He could die out there on his own!"

"There'd be no use," replied the AI. "He left nearly three hours ago. The instant he leaves the forest his tracks will be obliterated by the storm. Besides, he's survived out there for years on his own. If anyone can make it, he can."

"Ran away again," Hunt said, shaking his head.

"What?" snapped Tselitel, her face flushing deep red as she turned on him. "Implacable as ever?"

"No," he replied, surprised by the violence of her expression but standing firm. "He's never owned up to anything in his life. He had to run, sooner or later. It's just who he is."

"What else could he be, if his own brother won't give him a chance?" she said sharply.

"He burned through all his chances years ago," Hunt replied stoutly. "Right around the first time he tried to kill me."

Unable to answer him further, she huffed and strode across the shrine, crossing her arms and staring at the wall.

"Guess I'll get breakfast started," Gromyko muttered, signaling his exit from the conversation.

"I'll help," Wellesley said, prompting the smuggler to pick him up along with the speaker and set to work with the stove.

Hunt watched Tselitel for a minute before slowly crossing the shrine to her. Crossing his arms and leaning against the slanted wall, he waited for her to speak.

"I'm sorry," she said, still facing the wall. "You're the last person I ever want to be angry with. But poor Milo! He'll die out there!" She turned around with tears in her eyes. "I don't know if he'll bother to take care of himself. He was so angry with himself last night."

"Wellesley talked him into taking the 600G," observed Rex. "If he wanted to wander out and die he would have left it behind. I'm sure we'll see him again, once the shame has worn off."

"Shame, justice," she said with frustration. "Is there any mercy on Delta-13? Any grace? Does every crime need to be punished? Every wrong righted? How can we keep from tearing each other apart when such relentless standards prevail? Don't you people know how to *forgive*?"

"We've gotten along pretty well so far," Hunt said, surprised to find a touch of pride swell in his heart over the functionings of a penal colony. "We have so little margin for error out here that there simply isn't room for forgiveness. Most of the time."

"But do you need to punish *yourselves*?" she persisted. "Milo persecuted himself more than you three ever did. It was his own conscience that drove him out there," she said, pointing to the door. "If he dies, it'll be because of his own standards; standards that he adopted from a harsh community that he could never live up to."

"A community that must be tough with itself in order to survive," he replied, growing heated. "We're on the brink, here, Lily. There's nothing in Midway that we haven't made ourselves. You come here and think we're some kind of displaced, otherwise normal village. But you're wrong: we're an army; an army of survivors. And like any army we must exist according to an ironclad set of rules that we enforce on ourselves as much as on each other. There's no other way to live. Half of Midway could die tomorrow and the government wouldn't lift a finger to help as long as it didn't get into the news and cause a scandal." He began to cool off and his tone lightened. "I don't expect you to understand. We're unlike anything you've encountered before. But you must respect why we do things the way we do. Our customs grew up in response to circumstances we couldn't control. It doesn't do any good to attack us for them."

"You're right," she replied, nodding her head slowly. "I'm sorry, I shouldn't take out my feelings on all of you. I just feel like I could have done more for Milo. He was hurting so badly last night and I didn't help at all."

"Ultimately we can only help ourselves," Hunt opined grimly. "And if we reject help that's generously offered, that's on us. You couldn't have done more."

"I hope you're right," she said doubtfully, turning with him towards the others as he put his arm around her shoulders.

◆ ◆ ◆

"The place looks quiet," Gromyko said several days later, surveying the entrance to the old pirate base through a pair of field glasses. He'd been watching it for hours, patiently waiting for any sign of life before they ventured inside. Laying on the ground, peeking under the snow coated branches of a large bush, his breath rose up before him and fogged his lenses. Rubbing them on his sleeve, he held them up to his eyes again.

"It's a miracle they haven't blown the place yet," Hunt said, settling in beside his friend as the last vestiges of light faded from the sky. The storm was blowing as fiercely as ever, obliterating tracks almost as soon as they were formed. The trio had dug a hole in a massive drift a couple of hundred feet away, hidden within a line of trees to keep Tselitel out of the wind.

"Probably haven't got any more explosives to spare," the smuggler replied. "We must have taken what they had left near Midway. Anything else they'd have to ship in, and that's just too much work to be worth it."

"Hope you're right," Hunt said, pulling his hood around his face to try to hold back the bitter bite of the wind. "Can you see anything through those?" he asked, squinting to keep the barrage of little white flakes out of his eyes.

"Oh, sure," Gromyko said, offering him the binoculars lazily, which he took. "Not much, mind you. But you'll be able to tell if there's any light in that little hole," he added, nodding towards the entrance. "That's about all we can hope for: a stray glimmer bouncing off something deeper inside. The pirates aren't gonna let themselves be seen otherwise, unless one of them gets claustrophobic!"

"Can't count on that," Hunt said quietly, looking at the hole and wishing above all else that he could know for sure what was going on inside.

"I wouldn't worry about it too much," Gromyko said, seeming to read his mind. "After the treatment you gave them last time they probably got out of there as fast as they could. Still, it doesn't hurt to be careful, especially with Lily here."

"She's not coming with us," he said, handing the binoculars back.

"Does she know that?" the smuggler asked, cocking a chilled eyebrow as he grasped the glasses and drew them near. "I don't think she's gonna let you go in there on your own."

"I don't plan to give her a choice in the matter," he said in a low voice. "You ready to go?"

"Uh huh," he nodded.

The two men slithered away from the bush on their bellies, staying low until they were out of sight of the base.

"How do things look?" asked Wellesley, as they climbed into their makeshift shelter. Already the storm had deposited a sizable mound of snow at the entrance, which they mashed flat when they crawled over it.

"Looks clear," Gromyko said, crossing his arms tightly over his chest, glad to be out of the wind at last. "Can't know for sure without heading inside, though. Too bad we haven't got a clairvoyant with us!"

"When do we leave?" Tselitel asked, as Hunt double-checked his pack, making sure the explosives were intact and safe from any snow that might get in and melt once they were inside the caverns. Without answering her he detached Wellesley from the speaker and handed him to Gromyko.

"Take Wellesley," he said. "The room is filled with *Kol-Prockian* technology, so hopefully he can interface with it and download whatever data it might have stored about the experiments. We're sure to have company, so I'll keep them busy while you set the explosives and get the data."

"What'll I do?" asked Tselitel, already gathering the drift of his thoughts. Milo's light flickered in her hands, on its last legs.

"You'll stay here," he said without looking at her.

"No way. I'm coming with you," she said stoutly. She looked to Gromyko for support, but the smuggler averted his gaze. He'd recognized the look in Hunt's eyes and knew it was no use for him to speak. "You can't cut me out of the team now!"

"I'll cut you out whenever I see fit!" snapped Hunt,

turning on her with fire in his eyes.

"I'll wait for you by the tunnel," Gromyko said, crawling out of the shelter, wishing no part of the argument to follow.

"Why are you doing this?" she asked, moving closer to him.

"I don't want to talk about it," he said, zipping up the backpack and slinging it over his shoulder.

"Well you're going to have to," she said, grabbing his arm as he started to crawl out.

"Stay here," he ordered her slowly. "I'm warning you."

"Or what?" she asked. "It's not like you can cuff me to the snowbank. No, I'm coming with you, and that's that. I've got to make sure you're alright. The only way you can stop me would be to fill me with terror, and I know you won't do that."

"Don't think I won't," he said in a voice that nearly growled.

"You couldn't," she said with certainty, shaking her head back and forth.

In an instant he turned on her, seizing the side of her face with his left hand, smoke rising beside her head but not entering it. His eyes dark and wrathful, his jaw implacable set, he knew it would take only the slightest flick of his will to drive her into petrified stillness. For hours she would remain, unable to move, unable to speak, until his task was done. She would be safe, though at a terrible price.

Without fear her pale gray eyes regarded him, looking up into his face with steady assurance. Slowly she raised her hand to his, squeezing it against her cheek.

"I told you once that these hands could never hurt me," she said slowly. "And I know they won't hurt me now, even for what you think is my own good."

For several moments they watched each other in this fashion. Gradually the smoke receded back into his hand and he drew it away.

"You don't understand," Hunt said. "I'm going to encounter my father in there. And I'm not coming back. He's too strong."

"You don't know that," she replied, reaching out and putting a hand on his arm. "You're just nervous about the mission."

"No, it's more than that," he said. "I had a dream last night, Lily. Actually, it's the continuation of a dream I started having long ago. In it I am a wizard, and I'm battling a massive red dragon. For as long as I've been having it the two would battle, with neither of them winning. It seemed to be stuck in some kind of cycle, like the dream didn't have an ending. But last night I found the ending: the dragon wins."

"But that's just a dream," she said with a reassuring smile. "It can't tell the future."

"It's not just a dream: it's a message from Delta-13," he said with certainty. "The planet has sized up my father and myself, and decided that I will lose. I guess it didn't know for sure before, and that's why the dream kept looping. But last night I saw it just once and the result was swift and clear." He looked at her with eyes full of tender emotion. "I'm not coming back, Lily. I don't think Antonin is either, but he knows the stakes and is willing to run that risk. But you've got to live on after me. I have to feel that some little piece of myself will go on, even if it's as dubious as the hint of darkness that you now carry within yourself. I need that anchor."

"And I need you," she said, drawing him into her arms, wrapping them around his neck and talking quietly into his ear. "Don't you see that? I need you just as much. I was lost before I came here. If anything happened to you my life would be over. I don't think I could on breathing knowing you were gone."

"You would," he replied with grim certainty. "And you'd be better off, too."

"There you go running yourself down again," she laughed, even as tears began to stream down her face. "Oh, silly man: don't you realize that you're perfect for me? Darkness and all? Every inch of you is just what I want. And that's why I'm coming with you, to make sure you come back."

"You can't do any good in there," he said, gently pushing her away. "Lavery is too powerful for anyone to handle."

"Anyone *alone*," she corrected him. "Remember, your dream showed you battling the dragon all by yourself. But you won't be alone with me there, see? I'll have your back."

"And what can you do?" he asked.

"Well, I think I was pretty handy after you'd finished with that woman outside my apartment," she said. "Maybe I can keep you in the game long enough to finish with Lavery. Or at least until we blow the charges and bury him under a thousand tons of rubble and dust." She fixed him with her eyes. "But one way or another, I'm coming with you. Even if I have to chase you around like an unwanted puppy."

The word picture made him laugh in spite of himself and broke the tension of the moment. With a resigned sigh he nodded and crawled out into the blustery night, Tselitel right behind him.

"Glad to see you two could make it," Gromyko said as they slid up to him on their stomachs by the bush.

"Anything?" Hunt asked.

"Not a thing." He glanced between his two companions. "Ready?"

Hunt looked at Tselitel, who smiled and nodded.

"Ready," he replied.

"Alright, stay close," the smuggler said. Jumping to his feet and dashing across the open space, he paused beside the hole, his companions right behind him.

Holding up his hand for them to wait, he stole a look inside and then bolted around the corner. For several anxious moments they waited, until his head popped out. "Come on!" he hissed, wondering why in the world they were waiting.

"Give me that light," Gromyko whispered to Tselitel once they were all inside. Wrapping his hand around the end of it to limit its spread, he shined it carefully at the ground under them. "Nobody has been in or out for some time," he observed, pulling his hood back to hear better. Pointing at the heavy dusting on the floor, he added, "The wind hasn't blown in this direction for about a day now, so all this snow is at least that old. And I don't see any tracks except our own. We're probably all alone down here." As he said this the flashlight flickered and went out. He tried to start it several times, but it was dead. "Couldn't Milo have left us a better light?" he grumbled, sliding the useless stick into his pocket

"Let's go," Hunt said, slipping past the smuggler and taking the lead, moving cautiously inside.

"I'm surprised they left the lights strung up in here," Gromyko muttered as the trio passed through the wan light of one that hung overhead. "I would have thought they'd take them out."

Reaching the fork, Tselitel gasped when she saw the blood of the pirates that had nearly captured Hunt and Gromyko. Unfortunately someone had taken the weapons they'd dropped.

"What *happened* here?" she asked in shock, pointing at the blood which had gotten everywhere.

"Long story," Hunt whispered, closing the issue. Looking at the smuggler and nodding down the left tunnel, he and Tselitel took the center one. Finding nothing, they met up again at the fork and searched the right tunnel, but found nothing there, either. Slowly they returned to the fork.

"They must have cleared out in a hurry," Gromyko said. "There's still some supplies in the left tunnel. At least they took out their dead," he said musingly, kicking a bit at the dried blood on the ground. "I guess they didn't forget their manners, no matter how bad you scared them!"

"What, *you* did that?" Tselitel asked.

"No, I think something else drove them out, Antonin," Hunt said, ignoring her question as he squinted at the dark ground beneath their feet. "Take a look at these," he said, kneeling in the thin layer of dust that covered the floor. "They look like big scratches in the dirt."

"What are they?" Tselitel asked, crouching down to look at them.

"Spider tracks," Hunt said seriously.

"Yep, no doubt about it," seconded Gromyko.

"But I thought they were farther inside," Tselitel said. "What would have brought them out now?"

"Maybe the same thing that's got the planet in such a huff," Gromyko said, squatting beside her and tracing one of the scratches with his finger. "Big. About like a large dog, I would think."

"That's what I figured," agreed Hunt, standing up and looking at the walls, searching for their point of entry. "Where'd they come in," he muttered thoughtfully, instinct sending him back down the right tunnel, his companions following at a slight distance. "Something tells me this is the place," he said before shrugging. "But I don't see any openings."

"Wellesley suggests that we look up," Gromyko said, looking at Hunt and pointing his finger upward.

Hunt glanced at him and then followed his finger. A hole was just barely visible in the darkness that prevailed at the end of the tunnel.

"So, that's how they got in," he said, trying to peer into the opening. "Well, it'll save us a charge, anyhow."

"A charge?" she asked.

"Sure," Gromyko said, straightening up. "If it wasn't for this hole, we'd have blasted one open."

"But that would have awoken the spiders," she objected.

"Well, it wasn't a *perfect* plan," the smuggler grinned. "It was just the best we had."

"Antonin, you'd better head back to the main tunnel and find something we can stand on," Hunt said. "That hole is about ten feet up. Try to find a large crate we can turn on end. We'll keep watch here."

"On it," Gromyko said, hastening back the way they'd come, his footfalls quickly receding.

"You know, I just thought of something," Hunt said,

crossing his arms and leaning against the rocky wall of the tunnel after a minute or two had silently passed. "Does my power work on animals? Especially something as simple minded as a spider?"

"Why wouldn't it?" asked Tselitel, joining him at the wall and mimicking his posture.

"Well, it's not like I spray people with a fear hose. My gift unlocks the fears that already rest within their own psyches. Within their unconscious, specifically. But do spiders even have an unconscious? Do they even have fears like we conceptualize them?"

"I haven't any idea," she said, her voice thinning as she looked up once more at the hole. "Maybe it–"

"Shh!" he cut in, holding up his hand and listening carefully. "Do you hear that?" he whispered.

She shook her head in the negative, her eyes glued on the ceiling.

"Not up *there!*" he said in her ear, taking her arm and pulling her further around the corner. Taking her place at the edge of the dead end, right where it curved into the tunnel that led back to the fork, he waited in perfect stillness. Soon Tselitel could hear faint footsteps and the sound of metal clinking against metal. It was too soon to be Gromyko, she realized. It had to be someone else.

Hunt raised his hand for her to be quiet. Then, just as a dark figure rounded the corner, he leapt from his hiding place and seized him by the throat. The figure gasped, dropping half a dozen pieces of metal pipe that fell to the stony floor with a deafening clang as his body was slammed against the wall.

"Who are you?" Hunt demanded, smoke rising around his hand, his voice a low growl.

"M-Milo!" the figure choked out from behind a frosty cloth mask. "I-It's Milo!"

"Milo?" Tselitel repeated, as Rex let his brother go. The latter straightened his clothes and took a deep breath. "What are you doing here?" she asked.

"I came to help you," he said simply, pulling down his mask.

"We don't need any help from you," Hunt said, as footsteps came running quickly towards them.

"What was all that racket?" Gromyko asked in a harsh whisper. "Are you trying to wake the dead?" Then his eyes landed on Milo. "Oh, you again."

"These pieces of pipe are the best I could do for weapons on such short notice," Milo said, picking them off the floor. "If I'd had time I could have–"

"Get lost, Milo," Hunt said, turning from him to Gromyko. "Get something for us to stand on," he said firmly to the smuggler. Nodding without a word, the latter turned and disappeared into the darkness again.

"You need every hand you can get, Rex," his brother said.

"Every hand I can *trust*, Milo," Hunt replied, turning on him and grabbing a handful of his jacket. "Now *beat it!*"

"No!" he said, ripping his jacket out of his hand and taking a step back. "I'm here to see this through. I'm done running."

"You won't be done running until you're dead," Hunt snapped, walking towards him.

"Well I'm here to tell you that I am," he said through gritted teeth, moving back towards the rear wall. "And nothing is going to get me out of here!"

"I'm sure *this* will do the trick," Hunt said, raising his left hand.

"Rex!" exclaimed Tselitel.

"And what will *that* prove?" Milo retorted as his brother advanced within a step of him. "That's playing dirty, and you know it. Sure, you can zap me with your fear ray if you want to. But you're gonna need me."

"I don't need you," he said.

"Yes, you do," replied Milo. "Because you can't take Dad alone."

These words made Hunt pause. Slowly he lowered his hand, to Milo's visible relief.

"There's nothing you can do to help," Hunt said, turning away. "You don't have a gift, and that's the only way anyone could stand against him."

"A piece of pipe upside the head will do just as well, no matter how powerful he is."

"Don't talk nonsense," Hunt replied.

"I'm not," Milo said, walking after him. "Look, I figure he can only attack so many people at once, right? So if we hit him from as many sides as possible, we might just have a chance."

"That's pure assumption."

"So is believing I can't be of any help. Come on, four people are better than three. And with the stakes what they are, you can't afford to throw away any advantage you can get."

"He's right, Rex," Tselitel said quietly.

"Just one question," Hunt said, facing him again.

"Absolutely. Just name it," Milo replied openly.

"Why the change of heart? Why did you come back?"

Milo's eyes flashed briefly to Tselitel before landing on his brother.

"Because she helped me to realize that I could be better," he said quietly. "For those few minutes we talked in the shrine she treated me like a human being. That was more than even I could do at that point, and it made me hope. I don't know, maybe even *hope* is too strong a word. It made me hold out the *possibility* of redeeming what I'd made of my life." He laughed mirthlessly. "That, and the fear you put into me outside the labyrinth entrance. It completed what began in the forest weeks ago. It closed the circuit. You don't have to worry about me sliding anymore."

Hunt eyed his brother for a long moment, weighing his words against his assessment of his character. Eventually he nodded. "Go help Antonin," he ordered, tipping his head towards the tunnel.

"Already done," he replied, taking a few steps and then

pausing. He reached into his pocket and drew out the 600G. "You might want this," he added, before scurrying down the tunnel.

"Didn't expect to see him again," Tselitel said quietly, once he'd gotten out of earshot. "Guess I helped him more than I thought."

"Guess so," Hunt replied without enthusiasm, turning on the 600G's light and shining it at the hole. "Looks like it's part of a tunnel that runs over top ours," he said, moving around to try and see inside. "We're lucky: if it was any narrower we couldn't fit through it."

"I suppose now is a bad time to tell you I'm deathly afraid of spiders?" she asked playfully.

"Nothing better for a phobia than the exposure cure," he replied with a grin, catching a little bit of her good humor and glad to have it.

"Ooh, cruel man," she replied, shoving her hands into her pockets and scrunching up her shoulders like it was cold. "I might have to break up with you."

"What again?" he asked, shaking his head. "I guess some people just can't see a good thing when they've got it."

"That's true," she said, wrapping her arms around his middle as she continued to gaze upward. "After all, where else could I find a man who loves me so much he'd hit me with a tree?"

"Maybe you'd like to be the *first* one up through that hole," he said in mock anger, thrusting his thumb towards the ceiling.

"No, I'll be good," she said, giving him a little squeeze and then backing off as she heard the other two coming down the tunnel.

"It isn't much," Gromyko said, lugging a tall, narrow crate into view with Milo's help. "But it'll give us five or so feet."

"That'll do," Hunt said, helping them maneuver it underneath the hole.

"I don't think I'm strong enough to pull myself up,"

Tselitel said doubtfully.

"We'll pull you up," Hunt said, putting his hands on the crate. "Hold it steady."

"No, you'd better let me," Milo said, stepping up beside him and grabbing the crate himself.

"You're not running things here, Milo," Hunt said darkly.

"No, but you're too important to go first. We need you for Lavery. If any of those bugs are up there," he said, bending over and snatching up a piece of pipe, "let me nail 'em first."

"Alright," Hunt said reluctantly, stepping back so his brother would have enough room to climb.

Unbuttoning his jacket and sticking the pipe into his belt, Milo clambered up the box. Crouching atop it, he slowly extended his legs until his head disappeared inside the hole.

"What do you see?" Gromyko asked impatiently.

"Can't see anything," Milo said, carefully ducking his head out of the hole, and doing his best to steady himself by putting his hands on the craggy ceiling. "It's too dark. Hand me the 600G."

Carefully crouching in order to take it, he stood straight once more and put it through the hole, sticking his head in after.

"Well?" prodded the smuggler.

"It's clear," he whispered without withdrawing his head. Gently he tossed the 600G into the tunnel and, getting a firm hold of the edges of the hole, pulled himself up after it. They saw the light dash to and fro for a few moments as he double checked for *karrakpoi*. Then his head appeared in the opening. "Alright, come on up."

"I'll go next," Hunt said, sliding two pieces of pipe into his belt, after his brother's example. "Antonin, go last and give her a hand up," he said, nodding to Tselitel.

"Absolutely," he said, flashing a quick grin.

Rex, broader than his brother through the shoulders, barely made it through the hole the spiders had scratched in the ceiling. Only with Milo's help, which he was reluctant to accept, did he manage to squeeze through.

"Alright, Lily," he said, peeking through the opening. "Come ahead."

"Okay," she said doubtfully, looking at the crate.

"Here, allow me," Gromyko said, knitting his fingers together and giving her a foothold. "Just be careful once you reach the top. Give me a chance to steady it before you try to stand up."

Soon they had her up through the hole. The wiry smuggler had the easiest go of it, slipping up through it like a monkey.

"Well, that certainly gets the blood pumping, doesn't it?" he asked once he'd joined them.

"Let's go," Hunt said, nodding soberly down the tunnel. Slipping the pipes from his belt, he handed one to Tselitel. Looking at Gromyko he said, "Cover the rear. Lily, stick close to him."

"Ready, brother?" Milo asked, taking his place beside and a little behind Hunt.

The latter looked at him and nodded.

"Carry the light," he said, handing Milo the 600G. "I'm going to need both hands free."

With infinite care they moved slowly down the dark tunnel, its hard stone walls echoing with their footsteps. Frequently they stopped to listen for the subtle sound of long, thin legs pattering along the floor. After nearly two hundred feet the tunnel narrowed and split into two more, one rising upward, and one descending.

"Which one do we take?" Tselitel asked, her almost inaudible whisper sounding intolerably loud in her anxious ears.

"Wellesley says that one," Gromyko said, pointing with the pipe toward the downward path. "But watch it: he says it gets pretty steep."

Hunt nodded and turned into the tunnel indicated.

Their pace grew ever slower as they advanced, the steepness of the grade increasing until it was hard to keep their footing. Craggy outcroppings began to appear on the sides of the path, large enough to hide a small animal. Warily they checked around them before passing by, their progress slowing to a crawl.

Briefly the tunnel leveled out. Then a steep drop followed, at the top of which they paused.

"Easy, people," Hunt said, sliding the pipe back into his belt and turning around so he could crawl backwards down the path. Reaching the bottom, he looked into the darkness before him and strained his ears for any sign of life. But he could hear almost nothing, the sound of Milo's boots sliding through the soft dirt that covered the stony path being too loud. Once at the bottom the younger Hunt flashed the light around, revealing a large cavern before he pointed it back over his shoulder so the others could see.

"Looks empty," he whispered to Rex, as Tselitel noisily worked her way down towards them.

Hunt had just opened his mouth to respond when a scream tore through the air. Jerking his head back towards the tunnel, he saw Tselitel had lost her grip and was sliding on her rear down the path. Frantically she was pointing at Gromyko, who was wrestling with something around his head.

"Down here!" Hunt shouted to the smuggler, who instinctively threw himself down the decline and tumbled to the bottom, crashing into Tselitel boots first. A large spider had its legs wrapped around his head and was attempting to draw itself against his scalp. In an instant Rex swung his pipe and tore the creature from his friend's head, mashing part of its body with the force of the blow.

Clattering to the wall upside down, it hissed defiance as it righted itself. In a flash it was on its feet, feinting to and fro between the foursome, trying to confuse them as to its target. Gromyko had just gotten to his feet and laid fingers on his pipe when it settled on him. Letting out a high screech, it bunched up its legs and lunged at him. Swinging the pipe like a bat the smuggler nailed it on the face, sending it flying against the opposite wall. Oozing a yellowish fluid, the spider made feebly for him one more time. But a vicious downward blow from his pipe smashed it to the floor, the sound of the impact reverberating down the tunnel and out into the cavern. It twitched several times, trying to drag itself forward before it finally lost motor control and lay still.

"How horrible!" Tselitel said, looking at the mashed remains.

"You're telling me," Gromyko replied, wiping some of the yellowish fluid off his pipe and onto the wall. "I had no idea it was behind me. I just heard your scream and then felt it hit me."

"Yes, it jumped at you," she said, her face tight with pain, her left hand held gingerly at her side. "I saw it when it was already airborne."

"You alright?" Hunt asked, stepping to her. "Let me see your hand."

"Antonin hit it with his boot when he slid into me," she explained, drawing a sharp breath as Hunt worked her glove off and looked at it.

"Does this hurt?" he asked, carefully examining her hand.

"Like crazy," she winced, biting her lip.

"I think it's broken," Hunt said, slowly sliding her glove back on to protect it from the cold. "Nothing we can do about it now. It'll have to keep until we can get back to the surface."

"I'm sorry, Lily," Gromyko said sincerely.

"Oh, forget it," she said with a wave of her other hand, trying to be as bright about it as possible. "You had other things on your mind."

"We'd better move," Milo said. "That scream might have awoken the rest of them." He pointed at the dead spider. "If we're lucky, this fella was just out for a walk and happened into us."

"I wouldn't bet on it," Hunt replied seriously, resuming the lead position and walking boldly into the cavern. "Let's hoof it. Anything nearby knows we're here now, anyway."

Hastening through the cavern, they found another tunnel on the other side. This one was much smaller, requiring them to stoop and walk in single file as they entered.

"Don't like this," Gromyko muttered. With the light pointing forward most of the time, he was forced to listen as well as he could for any sounds behind him that might foretell danger. But this was nearly impossible with four pairs of feet marching through the tiny, claustrophobic passageway. Every sound they made was magnified until he was certain an army of spiders could be following them without his being able to hear them.

The tunnel grew ever more narrow until Hunt, with his large frame, had to twist sideways to fit. The 600G, still carried by Milo, cast long shadows off his body.

"If it gets any...*narrower*," Milo said, sucking in his stomach to slip past a bulge in the wall, "we're gonna be trapped."

Just as he said this the tunnel expanded into another wide cavern. They all filed out, none so quickly as Gromyko, who dashed into the open space, glad to no longer be the human shield covering the rear.

"Wellesley says we're almost there," the smuggler relayed to the rest of the group in a whisper. "He also says we're close to the highest concentration of spiders, according to the map in the temple."

"Absolute silence," Hunt replied, looking at everyone in their turn to fix his point in their minds.

Gromyko put his hand on Tselitel's shoulder to keep track of her as he walked, his head turned perpetually to the side to listen behind.

After twenty more minutes of cautious movement through the cavern, Wellesley spoke up.

"Tell them to stop," he said to Gromyko. "The *kral* tunnel

is just ahead."

"Stop," he whispered, to which they all slowly complied. "The tunnel is just ahead. The spiders should be near us now."

Milo flashed the light around but all they saw was the empty cavern stretching away from them in all directions. Hunt moved on until he saw a massive door of *Kol-Prockian* make emerge from the gloom. Suddenly his heart jumped into his throat, feeling that the *karrakpoi* must be near. Again Milo darted the light around, but still saw nothing.

"Looks like the computer was wrong about the spiders," Milo said quietly, approaching the door and laying his hand on it. "Maybe they all cleared out through the same hole we came in by."

"Get the door open," Hunt ordered, taking the light from his brother and turning his back to the door to watch the darkness that surrounded them.

"How?" asked Milo, dwarfed by the nearly ten foot door. "I've tried the handle, but it won't budge."

"The door is locked," Wellesley said to Gromyko. "They usually have a small indent where an AI can be inserted to open it. It should be right next to the handle."

Slipping Wellesley from around his neck, the smuggler felt in the darkness for the indent with his fingers, unwilling to take the light from Rex because of the spiders. Finding it, he clicked the AI inside. Little grooves began to glow blue in the door, running from the indent out into the *kral* frame. A subtle grinding sound became audible from the other side of the door, and it slowly began to open.

"Hurry it up, Wells," Hunt said tensely. "I hear something coming towards us. Lily, take the light."

No sooner had he said this than little shapes became visible just on the edge of the light. Spiders, dozens of them, were gathering around them. Forming a half circle, they began rhythmically tapping two of their back legs against the stony floor.

"Get behind me," Gromyko said to Tselitel, pulling her

towards the door and taking her place, his pipe held high. "Let us know the second that thing is open."

Milo moved off to the other side and thumped his pipe against his palm. Several of the spiders made a dash for the foursome. But a few quick blows sent them retreating towards their fellows oozing yellow. Another such sortie was attempted with the same result.

"They're feeling us out," Gromyko said, taking a swipe at one that had gotten a little too close. "Trying to see what we're made of."

"No," Hunt said, shaking his head as he heard heavy steps approach from the darkness. "They're holding us in place."

The spiders ahead of him parted to either side to permit a massive one to approach. Its eyes as large as his fist, it was broad and stood as tall as he did. Raising one of its front legs, it took a swipe at him, narrowly missing as he jumped back. Smacking it with his pipe as it passed by, the spider hissed and dove at him, crashing headfirst into the wall as he rolled underneath it.

Gromyko and Milo rushed it and began smacking it with their pipes while it momentarily lay dazed. Quickly recovering, it swept out a powerful leg on either side, knocking theirs out from under them.

"Back off, guys," Hunt said, as the spider turned around without attacking them further. "It's me she wants."

"She?" Milo asked, getting carefully to his feet.

"Queen," Gromyko said, moving so he stood between her and Tselitel. "Get over here, Milo. Let Rex do his thing."

Hunt pointed to the queen, and then made sweeping motions with his hand towards the spiders that flanked them. She got his meaning and screeched to them, causing them to move off into the darkness, clearing the playing field. The second they were out of the way she dove again, holding two rear legs in readiness to stab him should he roll under her a second time. Anticipating this, he leapt to the right, smacking her with the pipe but doing no harm.

"Use your gift, Rex!" Gromyko said.

Hunt discharged a bolt of dark smoke from his left hand, striking the creature in the face. She shuddered and stumbled for a moment before shaking her head and charging at him furiously, slicing the air around him with her sharply pointed legs.

"Bad idea," Hunt shouted, dashing to the side as the beast charged him and rammed into the wall where he just stood, shaking bits of rock loose. She compulsively slammed into the wall several more times, as though he was still there.

"I think you've confused her!" Milo yelled, the spider's legs slipping as she turned around, her eyes searching desperately for Hunt. "Hit it again!"

"She's mad enough already!" Hunt retorted as the multitude of eyes fell on him, finally picking him out of the mass of shapes that crowded her vision. Coiling her legs beneath her, she leapt into the air and landed just short of him. Still confused, she took several swipes at him but failed to reach him, unaware that he was farther away than he appeared.

"Get her, Rex!" Milo yelled enthusiastically. "Finish her off!"

The queen turned sharply toward the sound of his voice and screeched. Rearing back, she rushed for the trio by the door. Milo and Gromyko dove off to the sides. Having no time to move, Tselitel dropped to the ground, allowing the creature to sail over her and smash into the door behind.

"Get away from her!" Hunt yelled to Tselitel, as the queen regained her senses. Aware that one of them was under her, she began fitfully stabbing at the ground directly beneath her, forcing Tselitel to roll back and forth to avoid getting hit. She dodged three blows before a fourth sliced into her arm. A scream pealed out from between her lips, and the queen knew she'd found her target.

"No!" roared Hunt, running for the beast and jumping

onto her back as she raised two more legs to finish the job. Pulling himself up her hairy back and wrapping his left arm partially around her, he gripped his pipe like a dagger and drove it deeply into one of her eyes.

Squealing in pain, she jerked side-to-side, trying to throw him off. But the motion only served to work the pipe deeper, until it was against the back of her socket. Laying both hands on the pipe he drove it inward, crushing the thin wall of bone that separated her eye from her brain. The moment the cool iron connected with the modicum of gray matter that controlled her massive body, the latter went limp, crashing to the ground just moments after Tselitel had crawled clear.

The body reflexively twitched as Hunt slid off, his pipe raised for the dozens of her progeny that still surrounded them. But instead of advancing the horde dissolved into the darkness.

"Guess they've had enough," Gromyko said as they skittered off.

Once the sounds of their feet died away he turned to Tselitel. Milo had dragged her to the wall so she could rest against it, and was seeing to her arm.

"How is it?" Hunt asked, kneeling beside her.

"Just sliced the flesh," Milo said, tearing a piece of his shirt to use as a bandage. "Honestly it's not that bad. Just grazed her."

"It burned like a hot knife!" Tselitel said, surprised to find the wound so minor. "I thought I'd had it."

"You had, until Rex got on top of her," Milo said without looking up. "She'll be ready to move in a minute," he added, glancing at his brother while his fingers made quick work with the bandage.

"Alright," he said, standing up and walking to the door that was still slowly opening. Pulling his glove off, he pressed a finger to Wellesley. "Can't this thing move any faster? We almost bought it out here waiting for it."

"This thing is powered by the energy present in the

kral," Wellesley said. "Its output is understandably very low. It's nearly a miracle that they devised machinery that could run on it at all. We'll just have to be patient."

"Provided we live long enough," Hunt said, turning from the door and searching the darkness again to make sure the spiders hadn't changed their minds. Picking up a piece of rock that the queen had knocked loose, he tossed it into the dark to see if anything moved. It sailed out of sight and clattered to the ground far away, casting hollow echoes back over them. But no other sound followed. No pattering of feet. No surprised screeches.

"What'll they do now?" Gromyko asked, joining him by the door and looking into the darkness with him. "Elect a new queen?"

"Search me," he replied, walking past the smuggler and returning to Tselitel. "Can you walk?"

"Oh, sure," she said. "It'd take more than this to stop me."

"Good girl," he said, squeezing her good arm.

They all gathered at the door and waited, tensely watching as it crept open. Twice Milo tried to squeeze through, but couldn't quite make it.

"Just wait," Hunt said after his second attempt. "You can't do any good in there yet, anyway."

"Could scout around, at least," Milo replied, crossing his arms and leaning against the wall, watching the door with annoyance. "I wish these fellas had put in a hand crank, or something! Anything would be faster than this!"

Gromyko smiled as he thought of what Wellesley must be saying to himself in reply to that comment.

Once it was wide enough for them to enter, Gromyko pulled Wellesley from the door, causing it to stop.

"Will it close without you in there?" he asked. "I don't want to get shut in."

"No, it will just stay put," replied the AI.

Nodding to himself, Gromyko slipped the chain around

his neck.

"We're good to go," he said to Hunt.

"Alright, Antonin and I will go first, followed by Milo. Lily, don't come out until we've secured the room."

"Okay," she said, nodding nervously.

Twisting so he could fit between the door and its frame, Hunt shined the light back until the rest had made it through. Moving quietly but quickly, they advanced through the pristine tunnel of *kral* until they came to another, smaller, door.

"If this one is as slow as the other one, they'll know we're coming for half an hour," Milo said.

"Insert me into the door," Wellesley said to Gromyko, who mutely followed his instructions. After a moment of interfacing with the ancient technology he said, "I don't know why, but this door is unpowered. It's just held on by a number of locks. Perhaps they were replacing the machinery but never finished for some reason. In any event, I can release them and the door will fall into the room instantly, provided you give it a little push."

"Do it," Hunt said, once the smuggler had relayed Wellesley's words.

Just after saying this four loud clicks sounded from within the doorframe. Standing beside Gromyko, Hunt held up three fingers, counting down with them. Upon hitting zero, they both kicked the *kral* door, sending it crashing into the room.

CHAPTER 18

The only light in the room was provided by the 600G. Everything else was dark.

"Looks like nobody is home," Gromyko said, as he moved towards an ancient *Kol-Prockian* terminal that stood near the door. The center of the room was outfitted with a number of chairs and an empty table. Along the walls were computers, both human and alien. "Over here, Rex. I can't see anything."

Hunt moved towards the smuggler, shining the light on the terminal.

"Stick close to Wellesley," Hunt told him. "I'll start placing the charges. If we have to get out of here in a hurry don't forget to grab him first."

"Gotcha," Gromyko said, clicking the AI into a disc shaped indent on the terminal.

Quickly Hunt took the pack off his back and set it on the table, fishing out the charges and their attendant wires.

"Let me help you with those," Milo said, taking half the charges that he'd put on the table. When his brother eyed him doubtfully, he added, "Look, you've got to trust me sometime. Besides, I've seen the pirates use these things."

"When?" asked Hunt skeptically, handing him the wires for the explosives.

"Well, not recently. But it's not the sort of thing you

forget." With this he made for the left side of the room. Hunt shook his head and made for the right.

Before they were halfway done a door opened at the top of a short flight of stairs and a single man was silhouetted. He flicked a switch next to him, bathing the room in light and blinding them momentarily. Yet he didn't take advantage of that fact. Feeling himself the master of the situation, he saw no need to.

It was Lavery.

"Well, well, Doctor Tselitel," he said, taking a few easy steps towards them, the door shutting automatically behind him. "I always knew there was more to you than the little bookish doctor routine you had going. And Gromyko! It'll be good to finally nail your carcass to the wall." His sole eye darted between Hunt and Milo. "And who are you two? More disgruntled 'freedom fighters?'"

Hunt was speechless. The face was so disfigured that he never would have recognized it. But that voice! It's distinctive sound instantly carried him back to the last time he'd seen him as a child. It was jarring to hear it come from a man who no longer looked anything like the father he'd known. Only the massive frame recalled his previous appearance.

For once Milo hesitated to speak, feeling that his older brother had the floor. Anxiously looking between him and his father, his palms began to sweat as he realized that his sole weapon, the piece of pipe, had been carelessly left on the table when he grabbed his share of the charges. Trying to look natural, he shifted his feet and stepped sideways towards the table.

"Just hold it right there, junior," Lavery ordered, his eye fixing him in place. Then it rolled back to Hunt. "What are you? A mute?"

"You don't remember us?" Hunt asked.

"No," he said, his tone implying a question as to why he should. "I can't keep track of all the trash that runs around with that renegade," he said, tossing a finger towards

Gromyko, who smirked in reply.

Twisting on his feet, the smuggler leaned his hand on the terminal as though to support himself. But in the process he put his palm across Wellesley to conceal him.

"Talk to him," the AI said the instant contact was made. "Stretch it out. I need more time to download all the data."

"Too bad Wellesley couldn't be here to see this," he said to Hunt. "But he's still busy."

"And who's Wellesley?" Lavery asked.

"You wouldn't know him," Hunt said, taking the smuggler's meaning. "It seems your memory is as bad as your appearance."

"Don't press me," Lavery growled. "The only reason I haven't flattened all of you already is that I'm curious as to how you got in here." He nodded toward the square hole in the wall, and the door that lay before it. "Evidently you found another way inside. What I want to know is *how*."

"There'll be time for that later," Hunt replied. "But first I have a question."

"You're not in much of a position to set the agenda," Lavery replied, crossing his arms and leaning against the thin metal railing that ran alongside the steps. "But I suppose I'll humor you. Shoot."

"I'd like to know," Hunt began, his anger slowly rising within him, "how a good man like Maximilian Hunt turned into a miserable wretch named Lavery."

Instantly Lavery's face went blank with shock.

"How did–how *could* you possibly know that?" he asked with surprise.

"It'd be a poor son who couldn't recognize his own father," Hunt replied through gritted teeth.

His formerly wide eye narrowed as he studied him minutely.

"Rex?" he asked at last. Then, looking at his brother, he added, "Milo?"

"Yes, Dad," Milo nodded, seizing the chance to take

another step to the side. "I'm surprised you don't remember us. You always had a good memory for faces."

"I don't believe it," he said, flabbergasted. "But what are you doing here?"

"The Order recruited us," Hunt replied. "We've come to destroy the room, once and for all."

"That's out of the question," he replied, instantly snapping into his old mode, but with a touch of shock still visible in his face. "The work being done here is too important."

"What work?" asked Tselitel, taking a step forward. "Brainwashing people? Shattering their minds like poor Vilks?"

"I don't expect you to understand," Lavery said with a dismissive wave of his hand. "You're too soft to accept the hard reality of what needs to be done for the good of humanity."

"And what good is that?" asked Gromyko. "The good of being enslaved by their own government?"

"Is that what you think this is all about?" Lavery chuckled dryly, as though the smuggler had asked the stupidest question in the world. "Do you think this is just a petty matter of internal discord? Of the government trying to squash unrest? This isn't about politics: it's about survival, on the most fundamental level. Oh, it started out as a way to enslave the population. That's why I opposed it and got sent here. But times have changed, as you'll learn in time. Such...domestic ambitions ended years ago." He looked at his two sons. "I thought you two knew me better than that."

"So did I," Hunt replied.

"Ugo told us you were a hero!" exclaimed Milo, taking another step. "A member of the Order, no less!"

"Ugo is an imbecile," Lavery said. "And so are you, if you take one more step towards that pipe. Now get back to where you were standing before," he said, pointing to the place. "Son or not, I'll flatten you if I have to."

Reluctantly Milo obeyed.

"Seventy percent," Wellesley said to Gromyko. "Just buy me a couple more minutes."

"I don't understand," the smuggler said, putting his hand to his chin as though thinking. "Why the change of heart? What made you throw in with the government?"

"They opened my eyes to what we're up against," Lavery said. "They showed me the absolute necessity of the work being done here. Humanity is on the brink of crumbling apart. The fringe movement, to say nothing of the discord in the middle worlds, is unraveling us as a race. And just at a time when we can't tolerate any divisions. Dark times are coming, and we have to stand as one to overcome them. But humans are perverse, and they never accept the hard choices as long as they can kid themselves about their necessity. They have to be shunted like cattle into the course that serves their interests in the long run."

"And who gets to decide what those interests are?" Gromyko asked. "You?"

"Those who have the courage to act have always set humanity's course," Lavery replied in a didactic tone. "And the weak have always followed, like sheep, in the direction indicated."

"And just what are these 'dark times' you've hinted at?" Tselitel asked.

"That's above your paygrade, Doctor," he said contemptuously.

"Answer her question," Hunt ordered in a low voice, smoke gathering around his hand.

"I saw what you did to the woman we sent after your lady friend here," Lavery said, a touch of fatherly pride entering his voice in spite of himself. "But don't let that give you a swelled head. I could have crushed her like a gnat."

"*Could* have," Tselitel said, taking a few steps towards him. "But Rex actually *did* crush her."

"You have an annoyingly persistent personality, Doctor," Lavery said. "It's what got you in the government's crosshairs in the first place. If you'd just left well enough alone with Vilks, you could have gone home without all the unpleasantness. But you forced our hand, and we had to get you out of the way."

"And how can you possibly justify such a step?" she asked, continuing to move towards him, attempting to distract him so the others would have an opening to act.

"That's far enough, Doctor," he said, when she was six feet short of him. "Now get back to the others."

"Why?" she asked, taking another step. "Are you afraid of a frail woman with a broken hand?" she asked, holding up her left.

"You're the last person I'd ever fear," he laughed scornfully. "You're nothing but an idealistic dreamer."

"Download complete," Wellesley said.

Noiselessly Gromyko popped the AI out of the slot and slipped him into his palm.

"Four on one aren't great odds, my friend," the smuggler said, pushing away from the terminal and taking a couple of casual steps towards Hunt. "Especially now that Wellesley is done."

"Again with this Wellesley," Lavery said with annoyance. "Just who is he?"

"The one who kept you breathing this long," Gromyko said with a dark smile. "Duck, Lily!" he shouted.

Dropping to her knees just as a dark trail of smoke sailed over her head, she saw it strike Lavery in the chest, causing him to stagger backwards and hit the wall behind him. Shaking his head to clear it, he growled.

"Now you're going to get it."

Another two bolts hit him, but he brushed them off. Grabbing Tselitel by the wrists, he jerked her up in front of him, using her as a shield against the dark blasts. Hunt held his ground, his hand raised to discharge another shot the instant an opening appeared. The other two were rushing towards Lavery with hands outstretched to peel Tselitel from his grasp when he barked, "*Stop!* Or I'll drive her out of her mind!" halting them instantly.

Writhing in pain as he ground her wrists between his powerful fingers, she twisted around to look at Hunt.

"Don't listen to him!" she yelled.

"Have it your way," Lavery said menacingly, a gray aura flowing out of his hands and into her body. She screamed, losing control of her arms, the effect quickly spreading to her shoulders.

"No!" shouted Gromyko, who reached him at the same time Milo did. But the instant they touched him to rip him away from her, the effect was channeled into them, numbing their bodies and dropping them to the floor. Desperately they struggled to stand, but couldn't.

"Say goodbye to her, Rex!" Lavery taunted, as the aura penetrated every inch of her body and threatened to overwhelm her soul. "I've wanted to do this for a long time, Doctor!"

A desperate impulse from the deepest reaches of his psyche seized Hunt. His eyes turned black as midnight as everything in the room but Lavery ceased to exist for him. Raising both his hands, the mysterious word *khollaforta* unconsciously escaped his lips. Possessed by a power he no longer controlled, the entirety of his spirit exploded onto the tiny portion of Lavery that was exposed. A dark stream, formed from two smaller ones that flowed from each hand, knocked him onto his back, causing him to release Tselitel. Limply she fell at his feet.

Slowly Hunt approached his father who twisted on the ground, attempting to resist the terrors that strove to dominate him.

"You can't do this, Rex!" Lavery said, aware he was losing the battle. "Humanity needs me!"

But Hunt was not there to be reasoned with. The power had overtaken his will and buried it deep within. Only the ferocity of his gift remained. Lavery's threatening of Tselitel had given it the necessary opening to thrust itself forth without restraint, because that was exactly what Hunt wanted.

"*Rex! Don't!*" pleaded Tselitel.

Hunt knelt beside his father, placing a hand on his head as he'd done with Bodkin. In moments the violent air of defiance left his eyes, replaced by a blank lack of comprehension.

This done, Hunt slowly arose, turning towards the tunnel entrance as though he would leave.

"Stop, Rex!" shouted Gromyko, standing with the help of a nearby chair. "Don't leave!"

The black eyes turned to the smuggler, their lack of humanity shocking him to his very core.

"*Khereteth*," Hunt said, raising his arms in preparation of launching an attack.

"Rex!" said Tselitel, struggling to her feet and stumbling towards him. "Friend, Rex! He's a friend!"

"*Khereteth*," he said in reply, turning toward her as she neared. Upon seeing her he hesitated briefly, some slight hint of recognition flashing across his face. Once she was within arm's length of him smoke began to gather on his hands. Taking them in hers, she pressed them to her cheeks and looked up into his face.

"I told you once these hands could never hurt me," she said, her pure gray eyes looking into his dark orbs. "And they won't hurt me now."

"Lily, that's not Rex!" warned Milo.

"He will be again," she said, pressing her own hands to his cheeks.

"*Khereteth*," he said one last time, in a low, slow rumble.

"Shh," she said, closing her eyes and drawing forth her own gift, it rising within her like a blossoming flower. She felt its power flow through her body into his, realigning the balance within his mind. The dark force within him strove against her, but gradually yielded to the combined power of her gift and his rapidly reasserted will. In moments the blackness faded from his eyes, and Hunt had returned.

The instant her task was completed, Tselitel dropped to the floor in sheer exhaustion.

"Lily!" Hunt exclaimed, hitting his knees and lifting her head off the hard stone. "Are you alright?"

"Just need...a little rest," she smiled weakly, rubbing her head against his hand lovingly before drifting out of consciousness.

Hunt lifted her up and laid her on the table, using his backpack as a pillow.

"Is she gonna be alright?" Milo asked with concern, standing beside his brother.

"Wellesley thinks so," Gromyko said, joining them. "She'll be out for a while, but she should be okay." The smuggler looked over the table to where Lavery lay. "Can't say the same for him, though."

Following Gromyko's eyes, Hunt looked at the prostrate form of his father for a few moments before walking over to him.

"Is he dead?" Milo asked, as Hunt checked for a pulse.

"Uh huh," he replied grimly. With his fingers he gently drew the lids down on the vacant eyes that stared at the ceiling. "Died of fright, I suppose."

"You did what you had to do, Rex," Milo said, putting a hand on his brother's shoulder. "He didn't give you any choice. He would have killed Lily."

"I know that," Hunt said. "But that doesn't make it any less terrible." Drawing a breath and slowly exhaling it, he stood up. "Let's get the charges placed and get out of here. Antonin, check the tunnel and cavern for *karrakpoi*. I don't want to blow this place just to find out we're trapped."

"On it," the smuggler said, grabbing the 600G and making for the tunnel.

Quickly placing the remaining explosives, they led the wires back to the tunnel, reaching it just as Gromyko popped his head back through it.

"We're clear on this end," he said. "Not a sign of them anywhere."

"Good," Hunt replied, handing him the coiled up wires. "Lead them down into the tunnel. I'll get Lily."

"What about him?" Milo asked, pointing at Lavery. "Should we just leave him here?"

"It's better like this," Hunt replied somberly. "Nobody but us knows his real identity. This way Maximilian Hunt will be remembered for who he was, and not for what he became."

Milo looked at him for a moment and then slowly nodded his agreement. Taking the 600G from Gromyko, he shined it into the tunnel as the smuggler began working the wires out of the room.

Hunt gently brushed his hand across Tselitel's forehead. She smiled in her sleep but otherwise didn't stir. Slipping his arms under her body, he lifted her light frame off the table and carried her to the tunnel.

"Gimme some light," he said as he stepped into the dark passageway, unwilling to risk tripping and hurting her. Instantly Milo had the light on him, and he reached them moments later. "Run the wires as far as they'll go. With any luck they'll reach the cavern."

"I hope so," Milo said. "'Cause this tunnel is gonna be like standing in the barrel of a gun when it goes off. All the force will travel this way."

"I know," Hunt replied, watching as Gromyko quickly unfurled the wires, which stopped twenty feet short of the door.

"Uh, that's a problem," Milo said ominously. "Now what?"

"One of us stays behind and sets it off," Gromyko said.

"I'll do it," Hunt said. "One of you take Lily and get her into the cavern."

"No dice, Rex," Gromyko replied. "You've got to keep breathing, for her sake, if nothing else. Besides, I've got more lives than a cat! If anyone can pull this off, it's me."

"And what about Wanda?" asked Hunt. "It'll tear her apart to lose you."

"She knew what she was signing up for when she fell for the likes of me," Gromyko said soberly.

"No, let me do it," Milo said, snatching the wires off the floor and gripping them tightly in his hand. "I don't have anyone waiting for me. Besides, it'll give me a chance to make up for all I've done."

"I hate to interrupt all this noble self-sacrifice," Wellesley said to Gromyko. "But I've got a better way."

"And what's that?" he asked, looking at the ceiling and placing his hands on his hips.

"Let *me* do it. I think I can emit just enough of a charge to set off one of the explosives. That'll trigger the others, and the chain reaction will take out the room. But you'll need to disconnect all the other explosives so that the slight charge I can generate won't be spread too thin."

"And what'll happen to you?" the smuggler prodded.

"I'll be shot out of here like a bullet, naturally," the AI replied calmly. "But I think my body is strong enough to handle the shock. And anyway, it's better than what you guys are planning. Now get to it."

Gromyko relayed the AI's words and quickly went about following his instructions. Laying the golden disc on the floor of the tunnel several minutes later, he gently placed the exposed wires against it.

"You sure about this, Wells?" asked Hunt, laying a finger on the disc.

"About eighty percent," the AI replied factually. "It's hard to calculate how much force the *kral* walls inside the room will absorb, so I can't be absolutely certain."

"Good luck," he said sincerely.

"Thanks. Now get moving. I'll give you sixty seconds before I blow the charge."

Hunt and Gromyko hurried out of the tunnel and

around the door. Running along the wall, they reached Milo and the still unconscious Tselitel. Shining the light towards the door in the hope of seeing where Wellesley might fly, they waited tensely for the time to count down. Suddenly an explosion rumbled within the room, almost instantly followed by a massive roar as all the other charges went off.

"*What the?!*" exclaimed Tselitel, the noise waking her up.

Just as she said this Hunt saw a tiny glimmer of gold shoot out the door into the cavern. Taking the 600G, he ran as fast as he could in the direction it flew. Milo jumped to his feet and chased after him, while Gromyko followed more slowly with Tselitel.

"Where are you? Where are you?" Hunt muttered under his breath, shining the light back and forth, desperate not to walk past his friend.

"Wait, Rex!" Milo called from behind, catching a faint reflection on the very edge of the light. "Over here!"

Hunt turned and ran towards him, reaching the place indicated just as Milo dropped to his knees and picked up the battered medallion.

"Let me see that," Hunt said, snatching it from his brother's hand and turning it over. There was a nick in the edge where it had ricocheted off the door before sailing into the cavern.

"Are you alright, Wells?" he asked anxiously. "Wells?"

"Boy, what a rush," the AI replied in a daze. "I never knew bullets had it so good!"

"Glad you enjoyed yourself," Hunt said sarcastically, as relief washed over him. "Are you alright?"

"Right as rain. But it might take a little while to get my thoughts unjumbled."

"Take your time," he said, slipping the chain around his neck and tucking his old pal into his shirt as before.

"Did he make it?" Gromyko asked eagerly, as he and Tselitel approached.

"He's fine," Hunt reassured them. "Just needs a few minutes to get his thinking straight."

"What happened to the room?" Tselitel asked groggily, trying to make sense of where she was.

"Come on," Hunt said, taking her from Gromyko and leading her toward the tunnel through which they'd entered. "I'll explain on the way back."

CHAPTER 19

"Young, blind, stupid–," Ugo growled, when they'd finished relating their tale inside Milo's bunker. "You destroyed the only chance we had to galvanize the fringe against the oppressive policies of the imperial government! Now things will proceed piecemeal. Worlds will break away one by one, instead of all at once. The government will crush them with ease, snuffing out any real chance for freedom in our lifetime. Once they make an example of the first few that try it, none of the others will have the courage to so much as whisper the word 'rebellion.'"

Hunt sat at the long dinner table next to Tselitel and Gromyko. His brother leaned against the wall, holding a plate in his hand and eagerly devouring what it held. Several others were in the room, among them Wanda.

"At least the room can't threaten anyone, anymore," Milo said without looking up from his meal. "There's no way they'll ever be able to put it back together again."

"It was just one way to enslave the population," Ugo replied sourly. "The worst imaginable, to be sure. But without it they'll just resort to more brutal methods. One way or another, it all leads to the same result."

"Too bad we didn't have the time to download the data from their experiments," Gromyko said casually, sopping up the rest of the soup in his bowl with a piece of bread. "But we had to get in and out of there quickly. Besides, what could we have downloaded it with?"

"The Order could have supplied you with the necessary devices!" snapped Ugo.

"Well, that's all over with now," replied the smuggler, glad to give the knife in Ugo's ribs a little twist. "And like Milo said, the room can no longer threaten anyone."

"They'll begin a crackdown," Ugo said ominously, more to himself than to the others. "They'll target anyone who could have been connected to the plot. They've got lists of suspects as long as my leg. If you had *just* given us a little advance warning we could have moved the higher risk agents out of danger. But we didn't find out about this until everyone else did, and by then it was too late. Any attempt to move our operatives after the fact would instantly put the finger on them. Now they'll have to stay in place and hope for the best. If you had only *cooperated* with us!"

"You put that beyond the realm of possibility," Hunt said seriously. "Not us."

Ugo scowled at the scavenger, his eyes narrowing into bitter slits.

"You think your trivial personal loyalties trump the interests of *billions!* An entire galaxy full of humans will never taste freedom because of your petty emotionality!"

Hunt, his face turning to stone, began slowly to rise from his seat. In an instant Tselitel's thin hand found its place upon his. Half erect, he looked down at her, and then retook his seat.

"Yes, yes," Ugo muttered contemptuously. "Listen to the soothing voice of your mistress. She's the one who guides you now. Neither reason, nor your own conscience can overcome her siren's song. You even killed Lavery for her, which is something we cannot tolerate."

"What are you talking about?" Gromyko cut in, incredulously. "He had us backed against the wall! What other choice was there?"

"He didn't have to be *killed*," Ugo snapped, as though lecturing a schoolboy. "He could have been paralyzed, stunned!

It would have been sufficient to fill him with so much fear that he couldn't pose a threat any longer! But loverboy here had to repay the insult to his girlfriend, and the only price that would suffice was the offender's blood!"

"Lavery was killing her!" Gromyko retorted. "You can't act with restraint in a situation like that! You just throw everything you've got at the target until it stops moving! I would have done the same. More, if it were possible!"

"I don't doubt it," Ugo sneered.

"Besides, Lavery was an evil man," the smuggler said. "Delta-13 is better off without him. I don't see why that's hard for you to swallow. After all, you recruited Rex because he can inflict his gift on others. That's all he did."

"He inflicted *death*!" replied the old man.

"We are a healing organization," Wanda said modestly, trying to inject some calm into the discussion, though her manner conveyed that she didn't quite believe her own words. "That is why we can't tolerate what Rex has done," she continued, trying to fill out her voice a little more as she heard her own doubt. "As long as he drew forth the fears latent in people he could act as a corrective. He could be used to drive back the evil intent of people like Lavery. But to kill." She shook her head side-to-side.

"You can't tell me that you *agree* with this?" Gromyko asked. "And what of the precious civil war your lot is so hot to ignite? That would have led to slaughter!"

"Yes, many would have died," Wanda said regretfully. "But they would not have died by our hand. We would have done all we could to lessen the loss of life throughout the struggle. A terrible, but necessary fever would have overtaken mankind, and we would have done all we could do to end it quickly."

"That's doubletalk," the smuggler replied with annoyance, sensing that it was merely an excuse to nix Hunt for proving unmanageable. "It just means that the Order is willing to load and aim the gun as long as someone else pulls the trigger. The result is the same. It's just a quibble over mere process."

"It's 'mere process' that separates a hangman from a common murderer," Ugo replied. "One serves himself, and another serves justice."

"A concept about which you know precious little," Gromyko shot back.

"I refuse to discuss this any longer," Ugo said, slamming his hand on the table. "Rex Hunt is hereby expelled from the Order for crimes against its very essence. And you, smuggler," he added, pointing his finger at Gromyko, "you had better watch yourself, or you'll be out as well! And without your precious 'Underground' to hide behind, the government will pick you up in days!"

"Don't bet on it," he replied with a sly grin. "Gromyko is a shadow dancing on the wall. And no matter how hard you try, you cannot catch a shadow!"

"Oh, spare me your propaganda!"

"I'll spare you a great deal more than that," Gromyko said, standing up and putting a hand on Hunt's shoulder. "If Rex is out of the Order, you can scratch me from your membership rolls as well."

"Antonin," Wanda cautioned. "If you do this we can't continue together."

"I'm sorry, Wanda," he replied grandly. "But the quality of a man is measured in his personal loyalties. And if the Order rejects a man like Rex, then it must reject me also, or I am no friend. And then I should be less than Gromyko, and that I cannot ever be."

"Then get out, all three of you!" Ugo growled. "And don't ever come looking for help from the Order, because you won't get it!"

"You seem to forget that this is *my* bunker," Milo said, pushing off the wall and joining the other three, standing just behind his brother. "If anyone is gonna get out, it's *you*."

"This bunker is useful to the Order," Ugo ground out

from between clenched teeth. "And it will remain in our possession. We shall not leave except under the threat of force."

"I think that could be arranged," Milo smiled, patting his brother on the back.

"If you so much as *wheeze* at us, you will gain an implacable enemy for life," Ugo warned them. "I know thinking isn't your strong suit. But try to reflect on that for a moment before doing anything rash. You already have a great deal going against you in the Order's eyes."

Slowly Hunt rose to his feet and moved out from between his friends. Crossing to Ugo, he leaned a hand on the table, his face mere inches from that of the aged mystic.

"We're going to let you keep this place," he said quietly, "out of the memory of past services that have been rendered. But if you *ever* try to doublecross us, either by informing on us or undermining us in any way, I'll come and find you. If I have to chase you across half the planet, I'll find you. And when I do, you will truly know fear."

Ugo's eyes smoldered with outrage, but he said nothing, watching mutely as the foursome left the room.

"What now?" Milo asked, as they gathered in the storeroom where their clothes and gear were stashed. "I've got hideouts all over the place we can go to until the crackdown ends. With just the four of us to support, my supplies can last for months at any one of them."

"Wherever it is, it should be close at hand," Tselitel said. "The storms have only gotten worse since they started. I don't want to risk a long journey."

"I have another place south of town. It's only eight or so hours away. Ten, in this weather."

"No, we need somewhere out in the wilderness," Hunt replied. "The government is going to beat the bushes for us for months. They'll turn over every rock and fallen log for miles around Midway. Don't forget that we just kicked over their only real shot at total control of the population. I wouldn't be surprised if they ship in troops from the inner worlds to help with the search. We've got to bury ourselves deep in the countryside where they'll never find us. It needs to be just as far as we can go."

"I've got a place like that," Milo grinned. "But it'll be the worst journey of your life in this weather. It's some kind of hideaway the aliens carved into a mountain, far beyond the great temple. An old scavenger told me about it a few years back on his deathbed. Otherwise I never would have found it. It's the kind of place you'd walk right past without suspecting a thing."

"Sounds perfect," Gromyko nodded. "How is it fixed for supplies?"

"Solid for months, provided we ration things a little. There's an underground spring that'll give us all the water we need. And once you get lower into the mountain the temperatures aren't bad. A little chilly. But that's Delta-13, even on the best of days."

"Gather up whatever supplies we'll need for the journey," Hunt told them. "We leave immediately."

Half an hour later they stepped out of the bunker for the last time, the powerful wind immediately forcing the breath down their throats, nearly choking them. Mutely Milo pointed in the direction they must travel, and as before he moved off into the lead, tied to the rest by a series of ropes.

For days they struggled through the snow and wind, barely able to see the next person in the human chain. A dense shroud of white concealed everything around them. Only the guidance of the 600G, or, had that failed, Wellesley, kept them from being fatally lost.

"I've...never been...so cold," Tselitel muttered in Hunt's ear through chattering teeth one night, as they closed in on the great temple. "How much...farther?"

"Just a little way," he assured her, doing his best to break the gale that beat against her with his own body. All feeling had long since left his extremities, and he walked numbly beside her on club-like feet. "Just a little longer," he said, awkwardly putting his arm around her shoulders.

Ahead of them Gromyko swayed side-to-side as he walked. Though he had bravely broken away from Wanda and the Order for the sake of his friend, the loss of both her and a group to call his own had hit him hard. The smuggler was inherently a social animal, and the sense of isolation that now crept in on him sapped much of his enthusiasm, and with it, his energy for withstanding hardship. Hunt viewed him with concern, wondering how much longer he could go on.

"At this rate we'll reach the temple in a little over ten minutes," Wellesley said, seemingly reading his thoughts. "Just keep it together a little longer."

Hunt bent his head down against the cold, trying to shield as much of his face as possible with his hood. Only the rope that was tied to his belt kept him and Tselitel from wandering hopelessly into the frigid darkness.

"We're here," Milo said through numb lips, the wind stealing his words and carrying them away from the ears of his companions. But words were unnecessary. They knew only one thing would cause him to stop, and they hurried their shuffling pace to catch up.

"Good job," Gromyko said, clapping him on the shoulder with a hand he could no longer feel. "Now, let's get inside before we become snowmen!"

Fumbling with dull hands, it took all of them to fight the door open. Once they were inside, and had shut it behind them, they each stumbled down the stairs, nearly tripping and falling into a massive, half-frozen heap at the bottom.

"I love these warm stones," Gromyko said, pulling his gloves off with his teeth and pressing his hands to the floor. The instant they regained a touch of feeling he was wrestling his boots off, followed by his jacket.

"I never want to leave here again," Tselitel said, her words muffled as she lay face down. "Never, ever again."

"We won't have to, not for a while," Hunt said, sliding

off his backpack and slowly lowering himself to the floor. Rolling onto his back, he was content to let the heat seep slowly into his body through his clothes.

"I can't understand why the storms are still raging," Gromyko said once he was warm enough to want to talk. "I figured Delta-13 was in an uproar over the experiments in the room. I thought it meant they were getting close to a breakthrough."

"So did I," replied Hunt. "But like Wellesley said, the planet takes corners slowly. Maybe it'll be a few more days before it can settle down. You can't just cancel planet-wide storms at the drop of a hat."

"I don't suppose so," the smuggler replied, unconvinced. "Still, I can't help but feel that something continues to agitate it.".

Shortly thereafter they all fell asleep, the delicious warmth of the temple carrying them away.

In his sleep Hunt saw himself standing in a wide expanse of darkness that was dotted with little points of light. One of these dots grew bigger until it was as large as Hunt himself.

"Delta-13," he said to himself, recognizing the icy world at once. He could see storms twisting about on its surface, and through this he knew that the vision was contemporary.

Several of the other dots drew near, revealing themselves to be planets as well. Soon dozens, and then hundreds of planets approached, working themselves into a ring around Hunt and Delta-13. Surveying them, he saw that most of them showed no signs of life, being barren and desolate. The few that did were inhospitable, much like Delta-13, but technically viable for human life.

Curiously he watched as the barren worlds moved away, permitting the few lively ones to form a new, tighter circle. It was then that Delta-13 arose, floating higher than the rest, seemingly taking a position of leadership among them. It slowly began to spin, and the other worlds followed its example. They did this for some time before finally fading away, leaving only Hunt and Delta-13 behind.

The planet grew larger. Hunt drew close, his instincts telling him that he was about to be shown something. Suddenly a rift was torn in space, and massive starships became visible. They were much larger than any Hunt had seen before, with enormous, evil looking tentacles reaching from their hulls into space. On closer examination they revealed themselves not to be ships as he knew them: they were living organisms, and they gave off the vile aura of a parasite. They formed a blockade around Delta-13, quickly destroying the much smaller human ships that happened to be in orbit. A fleet of imperial warships warped in from a neighboring system and closed in to attack. But the parasitic craft physically drew near and used their tentacles to tear them to pieces with startling ease.

"What is this?" Hunt asked himself, as the vision began to fade. Gradually he became aware of a shrill whistling sound that was calling him back to consciousness.

Opening his eyes, he saw *Selek-Pey* hovering over them, earnestly trying to rouse them with the noise he was making.

"What's going on?" Tselitel asked groggily, still face down on the floor. "What's that sound?"

"*Selek-Pey!*" Gromyko exclaimed, jumping to his feet. "How have you been?"

"*Thu falas, beyen pah, Groomeekah!*" the mist replied urgently.

"Wellesley?" the smuggler asked, looking towards Hunt and the medallion he carried.

"Put the speaker on me," the AI told him. "This doesn't sound good."

Quickly Hunt pulled Wellesley out of his shirt and attached the tiny speaker from the 600G.

"He says something terrible has happened, Gromyko," Wellesley translated.

"*Palak forsa holis. Palak forsa treekya holis!*" exclaimed

Selek-Pey.

"It has happened. It has finally happened."

"What?" asked Hunt, stepping toward *Selek-Pey*. "What has happened?"

"*Vailo teren sah. Quero youvar sec teren paralan sef loh.*"

"The ancient ones," Wellesley said ominously, "the Devourers of all life, have returned from their banishment."

Far above them the Devourers' vessels descended to Delta-13, their massive forms penetrating the thick clouds of the storm that raged all around the planet. Hovering in the sky just above its surface, enormous tentacles reached down from the ships and buried themselves in the ground. Burrowing deep, they began siphoning the planet's precious life force off for their own use. A thunderous rumble emanated from the depths of Delta-13 as the planet groaned in agony.

Innumerable *karrakpoi* clambered down the tentacles to the planet, spreading out across its surface towards the shantytown that stood just a short distance away. They broke into the dilapidated houses that stood in the center of the city, eager for warm flesh after spending countless generations without it. Once the town was reduced they made for the prison.

Watching this unfold hours later on the giant hologram in the labyrinth, the group stood huddled together despite the oppressive heat of the chamber.

"The equipment in this room is picking up radio chatter from across the empire," Wellesley said. "The Devourers have appeared all over the galaxy. They've brushed aside the imperial navy wherever they've appeared, and have set to work draining the other sentient worlds."

"You mean there are others besides Delta-13?" asked Tselitel.

"Yes, according to the computer," replied the AI, going over the data. "There used to be many of them. Apparently they drew together in a confederation over one hundred thousand years ago and used their vast psychic powers to banish the

Devourers to another dimension. It was the only thing they could do to stop their onslaught. But the effort cost them terribly and killed most of them."

"That's why most of the other planets in my vision were barren," Hunt said, having told them about it hours earlier. "They sacrificed themselves to stop the parasites."

"Just so," agreed the AI. "Delta-13 was the chief of these worlds, being the strongest. That's how it managed to survive, although only as a shadow of its formerly lush, vibrant self."

Just then another shudder went through the planet, and the *kral* powered lights flickered and grew dim.

"What's happening?" Tselitel asked anxiously.

"The planet is growing weak," Wellesley said. "It can't take much more."

"What can we do? asked Gromyko.

"There's nothing we can do," the ancient AI said. "This is the end of the world."

End of Book I

THANK YOU!

I hope you enjoyed A Son of the Shadows!
If you did, please leave a review so others can enjoy it too!

Printed in Great Britain
by Amazon